ALSO BY ADRIAN McKINTY

Orange Rhymes with Everything

DEAD I WELL MAY BE

A Novel

ADRIAN McKINTY

SCRIBNER

NEW YORK   LONDON   TORONTO   SYDNEY   SINGAPORE

SCRIBNER
1230 Avenue of the Americas
New York, NY 10020

SCRIBNER and design are trademarks of
Macmillan Library Reference USA, Inc., used under license
by Simon & Schuster, the publisher of this work.

For information about special discounts for bulk purchases,
please contact Simon & Schuster Special Sales:
1-800-456-6798 or business@simonandschuster.com

Designed by Colin Joh
Text set in New Caledonia

Manufactured in the United States of America

1   3   5   7   9   10   8   6   4   2

Library of Congress Cataloging-in-Publication Data
McKinty, Adrian.
Dead I well may be : a novel / Adrian McKinty.
p.   cm.
I. Title.
PS3563.C38322D43 2003
813'.54—dc21   2003042796

ISBN 0-7432-4699-3

DEAD I WELL MAY BE

And if you come, when all the flowers are dying
And I am dead, as dead I well may be . . .
—*F. E. Weatherly, "Danny Boy," 1910,*
adapted from "The Londonderry Air" (trad.)

PROLOGUE: BELFAST CONFETTI

No one was dead. For once they'd given a good, long warning and there'd been no fatalities. We arrived after it was all over, and when the forensics officers were done, the policemen raised the yellow tape to let us through. We carried the glass from vans, a sheet at a time, to foremen and builders' mates who forklifted it up to carpenters on cranes and cherry pickers.

We climbed the stairs, put on our gloves, unloaded the pallets. We caught our breaths and took in the view.

The gray certainty of a December sky. Cold fathoms of paralyzed lough. Sea rain and peat smoke drifting over the shipyards and the town.

We walked back to the huge spindle-sided vehicles and carried more sheets, all of them precut and lying there in sailcloth and plastic, well wrapped, and seemingly long ready for an event such as this.

Sore fingers, aching backs.

We worked hard and drank water and smoked and a man brought beer and chicken-salad sandwiches from Marks and Spencer.

Someone had bombed the Europa Hotel again, no casualties but every window within a half a mile was out. It was the stuff of glaziers' dreams and the cops were on overtime and the army on foot patrol and the journalists chasing copy for the morning papers. TV crews, radio reporters, still photographers, the gloaming dark, the broken glass like diamond on the leadened streets.

We labored, talked.

A fog had oozed down from Cave Hill and Black Mountain, bringing cold and damp to the tangle of runaway alleys off Sandy Row. We were underdressed and a foreman gave us knit caps and hard hats and that helped a little.

All of us had met only a few hours ago outside the bookie's when a man said he was looking for fit guys to move pallets of glass into and out of vans. The pay was fifty pounds the day and a bonus for a clean job.

And everyone, including those on disability, had of course said yes. Unemployment was at 35 percent and the man could have offered half the wages and still we all would have come. In any case the market rate was unimportant since the Europa's insurers were footing the bill and the insurers were indemnified by the British government and ultimately, if you traced it back, the burden was falling on the taxpayers of Surrey and Suffolk and Kent, and really, if you lived in one of those places your worries were small and undisordered and you could well afford it.

The fog encouraged levity and more than once we put our hands to our throats and pretended we'd been dragged off by Jack the Ripper.

The real tragedy, of course, wasn't the modern Europa Hotel but the Crown Bar opposite, whose stained glass windows and gaslight had been fixtures since the 1840s. The bar was a gem owned and operated by the National Trust—its crystal sea patterns and ship anchors and Celtic turns utterly destroyed and in pieces on the pavement.

The Europa, "the most bombed hotel in Europe," had been re-designed with crumple zones to absorb the impact of explosions. And now it had done well on its first field test: the whole building intact, except for the windows on the lower floors where the hijacked car had erupted with most effect.

But the Belfast glaziers couldn't complain about that, for with Christmas coming the payday from surrounding buildings would be enough to keep their own in Islay whisky and Belgian chocolate and Italian shoes. And we didn't care. It was a job, there was money at the end, and it was heavy lifting, which is a tricky thing if you don't look out.

We laid down a long sheet for a lobby door and an AP man snapped our pic and said it was a good one and walked back with us behind the police lines. We chatted and he said he was from Jacksonville, Florida, and couldn't believe how dark it was so soon, and I explained, having taken geography, that Belfast was on the same latitude as Moscow and the panhandle of Alaska and the nights were long in summer and in winter you paid the price.

The AP man jogged down to the offices of the *Belfast Telegraph*. The army boys got in their Land Rovers and drove to base. The coppers yawned and changed shifts, and the crowd, such as it was, was drifting away now and back to other occupations.

We laughed when our photograph appeared on the front page of the evening *Telegraph*. There we were rebuilding the proud city, the indomitable faces of Belfast. "Their Spirit Will Not Be Broken," a headline proclaimed.

Aye, just our bloody backs, a man called Spider said.

But we walked with swagger as the vans unloaded the last of the big plates and the side windows and the boards for the pub.

We worked, the rain eased, the wind changed, and papers, fragments, bits of the hijacked car, and pulverized brick and glass coated us as we moved. The dismal stuff of explosion so familiar now in many cities. A confusion of words and particles that the poet Ciaran Carson calls Belfast Confetti.

Putting in the windows would take weeks, but that was the purview of professionals. At the end of the day our work was done, the glass unloaded, and we were paid off with a wee bonus for no breakages and no thefts. A few of us saved the dough for Christmas presents but most went to the Mermaid Tavern for a pint or two.

We drank and bought rounds of the black stuff and ate pickled eggs and Irish stew.

I left to do some shopping before the late-night closing. I got myself a couple of books and the new Nirvana record. I bought Nan a winter coat. She's been a chocolate addict since wartime rationing, so I couldn't resist a giant bar of Toblerone. On the bus back I met Tommy Little, whom I'd known in the army, Tommy staying in and making sergeant and me getting kicked out and ending up in the brig, in, of all places, Saint Helena—a nasty, windswept shithole whose other famous military prisoner, Napoleon, died mysteriously. So you could say I got off lightly. We laughed and Tommy said that I was a wild man and I said he was on his way to general.

Another bus, the road, the long walk up the hill. The ever-present conspiracy of fog and rain.

Nan was watching *Coronation Street*. No problem to smuggle in a hidden coat. We had a late dinner of Ulster fry: potato bread and bacon, soda bread and egg.

She only ever watched the soaps, so she hadn't even heard about the morning bombing. I didn't enlighten her. She would have been upset. I produced the Toblerone and Nan practically laughed with delight.

Oh, you shouldn't have, she said.

I picked up a wee bit of work today, I explained, and she made the tea and we ate the chocolate and I helped her get the last clues in her crossword book.

The darkness filled, the fires went out. I showered and retired to bed. The late-night noises of the house and the street began around me. The pipes in the attic water tank. The dogs communing across the town.

Mrs. Clawson yelling with only half a heart: Were ye on the dander again, you drunken scut?

Below me the creaking of boards and beams as the chimney took away the last heat from the fire and the house chilled and the floor timbers shrank and cooled.

And I was gone, off in a deep, hard-work sleep . . .

Late next morning a man from the dole office was waiting for me. A big man with glasses, tweed jacket, blue shirt, red tie, and a clipboard, but who otherwise, in different circumstances entirely, could possibly have been an ok sort of bloke. He should really have been a skinny wee fella with greasy hair, but this was a tough part of town and he was here on business. He was sipping Nan's tea and eating the last piece of Toblerone. I sat down and the man had news.

It turned out that my picture in the *Belfast Telegraph* had been enough to convince the Department of Health and Social Security that I was not unemployed at all but was in fact engaged in active work while claiming unemployment benefit. It was impossibly unlucky that my first bit of doing the double in months had been exposed in Northern Ireland's most widely circulated newspaper. On page 1, too. But still, the boys in the DHSS are not that smart and I had the feeling that they would never have found it but for some sleekit nosy neighbor tipping them off.

What if I deny that's me? I suggested.

Are you denying it's you?

I don't know.

Well then, the man said, adjusting his glasses.

Nan offered us more tea. I said no but the man took a dish, as well as some of her drop scones.

How old are you again, Mr. Forsythe? he asked after a while.

Nineteen.

No longer a juvenile. Dear oh dear, he said ominously.

Look, what exactly are you saying I did wrong?

You were claiming unemployment benefit while working on a building site. I am afraid, Mr. Forsythe, you'll have to go to court.

Yeah, but what for?

For benefit fraud, mate, the man scoffed . . .

But I didn't go to court. I pleaded guilty the next week and signed off benefit forever. I was unemployed, had been so for over a year, and now I was never going to get any more money. I moped for another week. Nan couldn't support me on her pension so there was no choice but to do what my cousin Leslie said I should have done twelve months earlier, which was to work for her brother-in-law who worked for Darkey White in America. Darkey would pay for my ticket, and I'd pay him back in time served.

I didn't want to go to America, I didn't want to work for Darkey White. I had my reasons.

But I went.

1: WHITE BOY IN HARLEM

I open my eyes. The train tracks. The river. A wall of heat. Unbearable white sunlight smacking off the railings, the street and the god-awfulness of the buildings. Steam from the permanent Con Ed hole at the corner. Gum and graffiti tags on the sidewalk. People on the platform—Jesus Christ, are they really in sweaters and wool hats? Garbage everywhere: newspaper, bits of food, clothes, soda cans, beer cans. The traffic slow and angry. Diesel fumes from tubercular bus engines. Heat and poison from the exhausts on massive, bruised gypsy cabs.

I'm smoking. I'm standing here on the elevated subway platform looking down at all this enormous nightmare and I'm smoking. My skin can barely breathe. I'm panting. The back of my T-shirt is thick with sweat. 100 degrees, 90 percent relative humidity. I'm complaining about the pollution you can see in the sky above New Jersey and I'm smoking Camels. What an idiot.

Details. Dominican guys on the west side of Broadway. Black guys on the east. The Dominicans are in long cotton pants, sneakers, string T-shirts, gold chains. The black guys are in neat blue or yellow or red T-shirts with baggy denim shorts and better sneakers. The black guys are more comfortable, it's their turf for now, the Dominicans are newcomers. It's like *West Side* bloody *Story*.

In the deep pocket of my baggy shorts I start playing absently with the safety on my pistol. A very stupid thing to do. I stop myself. Besides, these guys aren't the enemy. No, the enemy, like the Lord, is subtle, and in our own image.

Some kids playing basketball without a hoop. Women shopping; heavy bags weighing them down, the older women pushing carts, the younger wearing hardly anything at all. Beautiful girls with long dark legs and dreamy voices that are here the only sounds of heaven.

Harlem has changed, of course. I mean, I'm not talking about the 125th Street of today or even of five years ago. There's a Starbucks there now. Multiplexes. HMV. An ex-president. This is before Giuliani saved the city. Twice. This is 1992. There are well over two thousand murders a year in New York. Gang wars. Crack killings. *The New York Times* publishes a murder map of Manhattan with a dot for every violent death. Once you get above Central Park the dots get thicker and east and north of Columbia University it becomes one big smudge. A killing took place yesterday at this very corner. A boy on a bicycle shot a woman in the chest when she didn't give up her pocketbook. Those guys down there are packing heat. Shit, we're all packing heat. The cops don't care. Besides, what cops? Who ever sees a peeler around here except in Floridita? Anyway, it's 1992. Bush the First is president, Dinkins is mayor, Major is PM, John Paul is the pope. According to the New York *Daily News,* it was 55 degrees yesterday and raining in Belfast. Which is par for the course in the summer there.

With a handkerchief I wipe away the sweat from the little Buddha fat gathering on my belly. The train is never coming. Never. I wipe under my arms, too. I stamp out the fag and resist the temptation to light another. Are people giving me looks? I'm the only white person at the station and I'm going north up to Washington Heights, which, when you think about it, is just plain silly.

The guys wearing the wool hats are West Africans. I've seen them before. They sit there serene and composed, chittering about this and that and sometimes scratching out a game of dominoes. They're going downtown. On that side there's no shade, it's boiling on them and they're as mellow as you please. They sell watches from suitcases to marks on Fifth Avenue and Herald Square. I know their crew chief. He's only been in North America four months and he has a twelve-man unit. I like him. He's suave and he's an operator and he never flies off the handle. I'd work for him but he only employs other boys from the Gambia. If you've ever checked, it's a funny-looking country and I mentioned that to him one time and he told me all about the Brits, colonialism, structural exploitation, the Frankfurt School, and all that shite and we got on fine and laughed and he took a Camel but still wouldn't give me a job selling knockoff watches from a briefcase. And it's not like they're kin to him either, it's just a question of trust. He won't even hire Ghanaians. I can understand it. Do the same myself, more than likely. Today no dominoes, they're just talking. English, actually, but you can't follow it. No.

I put the hanky away and try and breathe for a while. Look around, breathe. The cars. The city. The river again: vulgar, stinking, vast, and in this haze, it and Harlem dissolving and despairing together. There are no swimmers, of course. Even the foolish aren't that foolish.

I look away from the water. In this direction you wouldn't believe how many empty lots there are, how many buildings are shells, how many roofs are burnt away, and it gets worse as you go east towards the Apollo. You can see it all since there's a fine view from up here where the IRT becomes elevated for a while. 126th Street, for example, is behind the state's massive Adam Clayton Powell Jr. building, where I got my driver's license and you get social security cards and stuff and you'd think that that would be prime real estate. But it isn't. Nearly every building is derelict for about three whole blocks. And 123rd, where I live, well, we'll get to that.

Yawn. Stand on tiptoes. Roll my head. Lazy stretch.

Aye.

Sooner or later—minutes, hours—the train is going to come and it's going to take me to 173rd Street and I'm going to meet Scotchy coming down from the Bronx and Scotchy is going to be late and he'll spin me lies about some girl he has going and then Scotchy and I will impose our collective will on a barkeep up there and after that just maybe the tight wee bastard will spring for a cab to get us down to the other bar on 163rd where we have a bit more serious work to do with a young man called Dermot Finoukin. Because walking those ten blocks would just about kill me on a day like this. He won't though, he'll make us walk. Nice wee dander for you, Bruce, he'll slabber. Yeah, that will be the way of it. Crap from Scotchy. Crap from Dermot. Down by myself. Dinner at KFC and a six-pack of beer from C-Town Supermarket for four dollars. Shit.

A black girl is talking to the Dominican boys outside the bodega and it's more Leonard Bernstein than ever as the hackles rise between the blacks and the Dominicans on this side of the street. Jesus, gunplay is all I need. Just make the train come and when it comes make the air-con work. But it doesn't and I look away from the boys in case afterwards I'm asked to be a witness by the peels.

Lights appear in the tunnel at the City College stop. The downtown train comes and the Gambians and the other passengers get on and it's just me now and a few wee muckers at the far end spitting down the sixty feet to Broadway beneath us.

A homeless man comes up the steps having leapt the barrier. He's filthy and he smells and he's going to ask me for a quarter. He's coughing and then he says:

Sir, spa-carter.

His hands are swollen to twice what they should be and he could have anything from untreated winter frostbite to fucking leprosy.

Here, I say, and I don't want to touch him, so I put the quarter on the ground and then immediately repent of this. How unbelievably humiliating to make a sixty-year-old man bend down and pick up a quarter. He does bend down, picks it up, thanks me, and wanders off.

The pay phone rings. Who knew the phone even worked? It rings and rings. The kids, spitting, look over at me, and eventually I go and pick it up.

Yes? I say.

Michael? a voice says.

Yes, I say, trying not to sound amazed.

It's Sunshine, he says.

Sunshine. Sunshine, how in the name of bloody Jehovah do you know this pay-phone number? I ask, giving up any attempt to play it cool.

I'm paid to know these things, he says mysteriously.

Yeah but—

Listen, Michael, it's all off for today. Darkey's going to see the Boss and he's taking myself and Big Bob with him. The rest of you have the day off. Scotchy'll call you tomorrow.

All right, I say, and I'm going to ask him about money but he rings off. The prick. Sunshine is Darkey's right-hand man, and if ever there was a more weaselly-looking man-behind-the-man type of character, it's Sunshine. Thin, thinner than Scotchy even, with one of those skinny mustaches, and a bald head with a ridiculous comb-over that makes him look a bit like Hitler. I had him pegged for a child molester the minute I saw him but apparently that's not the case. Scotchy says not and Scotchy hates him. I don't. After you meet him a bit he's ok. Actually, I think he's a nice bloke, on the whole.

I hang up the phone and look foolishly at it for a second and one of the kids comes up and asks if it was for me. He's about ten, braver than the others, or more bored. Big hands that are restless behind him. Neat clothes, newish shoes.

I nod.

And who the fuck are you? he asks, squinting up at me and into the sunlight.

I-I'm the bogeyman, I say, and grin.

You ain't no boogy man, he says, his American pronunciation half accusing, half scared. After all, I can look intimidating on occasion.

You always do what your mother tells you? I ask.

Sometimes, he says, thrown by the question.

Well, listen. Next time you don't, don't be surprised if I'm under your bed or in your cupboard or out there on your fire escape. Waiting.

He turns and wanders off slowly, trying to appear unimpressed. Perhaps he is. Not easy alarming little kids around here. Christ, most of their goddamn grandmas scare the hell out of me.

Ok, home. No point lingering. I suppose it's impossible to get my token back since I didn't ride the train. I scope the clerk and she's a tough big lassie whose fucking shadow could kick my ass. She gives me the evil eye while I'm considering the options, so in the end I don't even bother. And then it's step, step, step down the broken escalator, which since I've been here has been unrepaired. Slime on the bottom step.

I turn and walk along 125th past the live chicken store and the discount liquor and the horrible doughnut shop and the thinly disguised All-Things-Catholic, but really All-Things-Santería store. Cross the street. A man in a makeshift stall is selling bananas, oranges, and some green fruit I don't know the name of. It's all well presented but with all this pollution and crap around here you wouldn't eat anything he's vending, you'd have to be fucking crazy. People are, of course, and there's a queue.

At the junction you stop and you take a long look. You have to. For it's all there. The traffic. The pedestrians. Bairns and dogs and men with limps outside under the overhang. The slick off the Jackie Robinson. Public Enemy blaring from the speakers, Chuck D and Flavor Flav out-snapping each other. The hotness and the sizzle and the crack and the *craic*. Dealers and buyers and everyone in between. It's rich and it's overwhelming but really, in Harlem, all is sweetness. No one bothers me. They take me in. It's a scene. It's like the beach. The moisture, the temperature, the people on the dunes of sidewalk and the great hulking seething city is, in this analogy, the dirty gray Atlantic Ocean.

Up the hill. It's only two blocks but by some freak of geography it's really the equivalent of about five.

I reach in my shorts for my keys and turn on 123rd. Vinny the Vet is ahead of me going in the building, having a full, angry conversation with no one at all. His shopping bag clinks. Danny the Drunk is on the corner in the sun propping himself up. That purple face is leaning down over his walking stick, dry retching. And me as the third repre-sentative of the Caucasian race on the street, what am I like?

Aye, what indeed.

Keys, pistol. Pistol, keys.

Nerves are bad.

Keys. But the lock is screwed up and I have to jiggle it. Must tell Ratko, not that he'll fix anything. But guilt-ridden by his laziness, he will invite me down for some foul Polish vodka and Serbian delicacies prepared last year or so by the missus. But at least in my warped brain it'll be home cooking.

Sounds like a plan.

It's 1992 and Serbs are beginning to get a bit of a bad reputation. But it's not so terrible yet. Ratko'll pour me a full tumbler of something clear and awful and we'll toast Gavrilo Princip or Tito or the memory of the bloody Knights of Kosovo and I'll have a cold sausage-and-lard sandwich and another glass and when the drink is sweating me close to a bloody heart attack I'll slink away and stumble up the three floors to the apartment.

Second thought, no.

Inside, Freddie's there doing the mail.

Freddie, I say, and we talk for a minute about sports. Freddie can see I'm beat, though, and lets me go. Nice chap, Freddie.

Go up the stairs. The door. Keys again. Inside. Hotter here than the street. I put on the telly for company. Free cable somehow. I look for something familiar and settle on Phil Spector and John Lennon and some irritated long-haired session musicians being lectured by Yoko Ono on chord progression.

Run the bath. Water comes out brown. Sit on the tub edge and have a brief premonition of the phone ringing and me picking it up and it's Sunshine, come over all ominous, saying that Darkey wants to see me.

I shiver, get up, and take the phone off the hook. Disrobe, climb into the bath. Light a fag. Convince myself that this phone call will never happen. Get out of the bath and actually disconnect the phone from the wall, think for a moment, lock the door, get my gun, check the mechanism, leave it where I can grab it. Climb into the bath again. Sink into nothingness. Sink.

❋   ❋   ❋

Murmurs, hymnals, and in the vestry quiet whole colonies of insects give me kisses and I'm too buggered to do anything about it. Vodka spills from my mouth. I'm sleeping and on the shores of some immense creature's back, a giant bovine eye and blue nerves and a labyrinth of tentacles. Jesus. I get up out of the water, which is by now cold, and grab a towel.

Later. The phone, the TV. The heat. Fag after fag until the ashtray is full. The fridge works and brings me vodka with ice. Small mercies but mercies nonetheless. I lean back on the sofa and contemplate my surroundings.

And let me describe the beautiful haven Scotchy and Darkey have picked out for me. Not that I'm ungrateful. Took me in, gave me a place. But it's not as if I haven't earned my keep. Only one with two brain cells to rub together. Anyway. They, of course, live in the nice part of the Bronx at the end of the 1 line. But it was full up there, see? Scotchy's claim, anyway. More fool me to believe him. This place apparently is five hundred a month, which comes out of my pay. As did the furniture, which Scotchy admitted later he got all for sweet FA in the street. It's a one bedroom. A toilet whose stink greets you when you come in. Next to it, a bath on little feet and under the bath there are more flora and fauna than David Attenborough could handle with the entire resources of the BBC behind him.

Corridor and kitchen. Forget about swinging a cat, a cat couldn't swing a mouse in here. Gas stove whose pilot light is perpetually going out. Years, perhaps decades, of grease everywhere. Holes in the walls and skirting.

Living room: TV, free cable, a big wooly yellow disgusting sofa.

Bedroom: futon on the floor, cupboard, table, chair.

There is no natural light anywhere. The living room's gray windows overlook a tiny courtyard, the bedroom peers onto the backs of the buildings on 122nd. If you go out onto the fire escape (which I often do) and you set up a chair and look up, now and again, through the skunk trees, you can see a plane or a bit of sky. The fire escape is rusted and rickety and will kill us all when the fire comes, but even so it's the nicest place in the apartment.

The roaches are the big problem. I've been here since last December and I've been fighting a guerrilla war with them ever since. I haven't grown used to their existence. I haven't reached Zenlike tranquillity that allows me and them to share the same territorial and metaphysical space. In Ireland there are no roaches. No creatures of any kind like this. Occasionally, a field mouse would come in the house. Or perhaps a bee or some benign beetle or ladybug. No, nothing like these things.

I respect them now, though. I hate them, but I respect them. I have beheaded them, poisoned them, scalded them, burned them, poisoned them again and somehow they seem to survive. I dropped a liter bottle of Coke once on one big water bug and it lived. I poured a half pound of boric acid on another and put a pot on it that I covered with a brick. I left it there for a week while we all went to Florida for a wake and a funeral for Mr. Duffy's brother. Got back, removed the brick, bastard cleans its antennae and crawls off into the wall. This was about kill two hundred and I had to go and scratch out the table and make it one kill less. The lesson was chastening. Like the RAF pilots in the

Battle of Britain, you only report your kill when you see the plane hit the ground.

Anyway, they're everywhere. They crawl on you at night. You hear them in walls. You feed them in the traps. Occasionally they fly. You tell Ratko and he laughs and he shows you his place in the basement. Which if anything is worse.

Still . . .

The fire escape.

Another fag. Sirens. Dogs barking. People yelling. Smoke, sit there and draw it in and hold it. Hold it. Let it go. Let it all go.

I live on 123rd and Amsterdam. A block away is the edge of the Columbia University security zone and there they call the neighborhood Morningside Heights so that concerned parents don't freak out, which they would if they had to send mail to bloody Harlem. But this is Harlem. There are projects one block to the north, not particularly bad projects but projects nonetheless, and to the east it's the real nightmare. The buildings are derelict and most of them seem to be inhabited by crack cocaine addicts. Morningside Park is pretty hairy after dark and all the way up to 125th Street is no picnic. I stick out, too. I have learned some Spanish and have told myself that thus equipped I can pass as a Dominican. However, my paper white Mick skin is not entirely convincing.

I have no air-conditioning and the fan only moves hot air around the room.

I toss the fag and climb back in through the window. I go to the kitchen and get a beer. Milwaukee Great Gold. It's the worst beer I've ever had—they brew it with corn, if you can believe it. But it's cheap, and if you put the fridge up enough and it gets freezing cold you don't really taste it anyway.

I go back out on the fire escape and watch a few squirrels and way up in the blue the odd ascending vapor trail. The beer goes down and it's almost nice now. The day seems to be getting a little cooler.

The phone rings.

I hardly remember reconnecting it but I must have. Duty, responsibility, that's me.

I let it bleat. It goes on and on and it wears me down. I finish the last of my drink and hurl the can off the side of the rail trying to hit Ratko's pit bull, but I don't and the dog looks up at me and starts barking. I climb in through the fire-escape window and tramp across the bedroom and into the hall. I turn off *Nevermind* on the cassette player. I pick up the phone.

It's Scotchy. I can tell by that nasally intake of breath before he speaks. He's excited.

Hey, Bruce, something's come up.

Name's not Bruce, I say wearily. Scotchy's perpetual little joke.

Bruce, gotta get uptown. Andy got a hiding. You know Darkey's away, right?

I don't answer him.

Bruce, are you there?

Must have the wrong number mate, no Bruce here. No Bruce, no spider, no cave, no salvation for Bonnie Scotland.

Stop fucking around, Bruce, you dickless wonder, this is serious.

I choose again the path of silent resistance. There is a good fifteen seconds of dead air on the phone. Scotchy starts mumbling and then in a bit of an exponential panic he says:

Hello, hello, hello, oh Jesus, Mike, are you still there?

I'm here, I say with just enough lassitude to irritate the hell out of him.

Well, what the fuck? Christ. Jesus man, I'm holding the fucking ship, you know. Look, Andy got a hiding and Sunshine and Darkey are out of the picture, so I'm the boss, right?

You're the boss? I say, hoping to convey as skeptical a tone as if he's just told me that he is, in fact, Anastasia, lost daughter of Tsar Nicholas the Second.

Aye, he says, my clever intonation going over his head.

Is that how the chain of command goes? I ask in a more neutral voice.

Aye, it does.

Fergal's been with Darkey a wee bit longer than you, hasn't he? I ask mischievously.

Fergal's an idiot, Scotchy says.

Pot calling the kettle black? I suggest.

Bruce, I swear to God, I'll fucking come down there, he says, right on the verge.

Line of succession bumps you up is what you're claiming, I say.

Yes. De factso, I'm in charge, he says, a bit hesitant with the Latin.

De facto, surely, Scotchy, I say condescendingly, to really take the piss.

He's angry now.

Look, I'm in charge and I'm giving the fucking orders, so get the fuck up here, you bastard, he says.

Keep going, Scotchy. I have to admit you've almost convinced me with your earthy machismo.

Jesus Christ, were you put on this planet to fucking give me a stroke? Fuck me. Will you stop acting the fucking eejit, stop wanking off down there and get up here, Scotchy barks out in frustration.

Is he all right, is he in the hospital? I ask with belated concern about our Andy.

No, he isn't, he's over here. Bridget's looking after him. We're maybe taking him to the hospital. He'll be ok, though. Shovel, you know. That lamebrain Fergal thought it was the fucking Mopes but it was fucking Shovel. I know it. I mean big Andy. Shovel must have been half tore. Andy was unconscious, in the street, in the street, Bruce, hasn't come round yet, I mean he . . .

I'm not listening because I don't care. I don't care what Shovel has done or what has happened to Andy or what Scotchy is going to do about it. I don't giving a flying fuck but of course he tells me everything anyway. The boss has gone and he, Scotchy, is going to take the initiative. Lesser men than me could foresee trouble in the tea leaves. Scotchy's always been an ill-starred unlucky lout and chances are we'll go over to Shovel's house, me and him, and then Shovel or Shovel's girlfriend will end up throwing hot fat on us or shooting us or calling the bloody peelers or sticking our fingers in the toaster or something worse. That would be typical of Scotchy. 'Course, whatever happened he would live and in the incident I'd be blinded in one eye or lamed or scarred for life. That would just be the way of it.

Suddenly a thought occurs to me.

If he hasn't spoken, how do you know it was Shovel? I ask.

Stands to reason, doesn't it? He was over at Shovel's asking for cash; Shovel had already told me he wasn't paying nothing. Bastard must have got Andy in the street, from behind.

Oh yeah, stands to reason, Sherlock. Clearly that's the only fucking explanation, I mutter sarcastically.

Fucksake, Bruce, you fucker. Fucking fucker. Listen to me, you insubordinate wanker, just get the fuck up here, Scotchy yells furiously.

Oh Scotchy, keep your hair on. Look, I'm on my way, ok? I say with just a hint of deference now.

Scotchy hangs up. I take the phone and kill a water bug on the wall with it. I hang up and go back into the bedroom and close the window.

I'm going to have to take the train after all. This also is typical and it'll cost me another token. I sigh and splash water on my face. I get my jacket, and in case it's going to be an all-nighter I put cigs, reading material, matches, and cash in the pockets. I pull on my Doc Martens, brush my hair, shove in extra ammo, the wee .22, and go out.

✤   ✤   ✤

I know at least five Scotchys. Scotchy Dunlow, who beat the shit out of me every Friday night at Boy's Brigade for seven years. Scotchy McGurk, who was a player and whom I personally saw drop half a cinder block on some guy's chest for a tremendously minor reason and who got shot in a typically botched robbery on a bookie's. Scotchy McMaw, who lost a hand in a train-dodge accident in Carrickfergus and who was quite the weird one after that but who ended up saving a boy's life when they were out fishing in a boat, swimming to shore with one arm and later getting some bravery award from Princess Diana. Scotchy Colhoun, who also was a bad lad and got himself nicked for racketeering and murder and went in the Kesh (though he must be out by now because of the Peace Process). Finally, of course, is our Scotchy, Scotchy Finn. None of them needless to say has or ever had any connection whatsoever with Scotland. How they all became Scotchy is a matter of mystery to me and probably them as well.

Scotchy Finn himself does not know. He grew up in Crossmaglen and then Dundalk, which, if you know Ireland at all, could only mean one thing. And sure enough, it turns out his da, ma, three brothers, two uncles, and an aunt were all at one point in the Lads. They started

Scotchy early and he did time at some kind of juvenile prison for something. He says it grew too hot for him across the *sheugh,* which is why he ended up first in Boston and then the Bronx. To be honest, I'm a bit skeptical about all his stories of "ops" and "encounters" with the Brits, the Proddies, the Intelligence Corps, the SAS, and the cops. He says it was the Irish peelers, the Garda Síochána, that gave him his limp for petrol smuggling (a limp that only ever appears when he wants sympathy for something), but I heard from Sunshine he fell off the roof of a parked car after he'd had eleven pints at Revere Beach. This was before he started working for Darkey, and you can't really imagine Scotchy at the beach because his skin is as thin and pale as fag paper and he looks like yon boy that gets beat up at the beginning of the Charles Atlas ads. Red hair, white skin, bad teeth, bad smell disguised by bad musk and that's our Scotchy. I don't know how long he's been here. Ten years, fifteen? He still has a Mick accent (funny one too, touch of the jassboys Crasssmaglayn) but he has Yank clothes and Yank sensibility to money and girls. He doesn't whine on about the Old Country like some wanks ya run into, which I suppose at least singles him out from your average Paddy bastard. That's not to say that he's likable. Not at all. Sleekiter wee shite you'd be hard pressed to meet, but he's ok if you don't mind that kind of thing, which personally I sort of do. He's a bloody thief, too, and he robs me blind behind my back, and if I wasn't the new boy on the block I'd say something but I am and I'm not going to.

Our man, our fearless leader for one night only, thank God. Typical that it would be this night Scotchy was running the show. For, of course, I wasn't to know, but tonight was going to be a night that helped set off a whole wonderful series of violent and unpleasant events. Indeed, the only caveat you'll get is right now when I say that if someone grows up in the civil war of Belfast in the seventies and eighties, perhaps violence is his only form of meaningful expression. Perhaps.

The train ride was uneventful. I brought a book with me about a Russian who never gets out of bed. Everyone was upset with him, but you could see his point of view. I got off at the end of the line and walked up the steps. It was this walk every day that was the only thing at all keeping me in shape. These steps that separated Riverdale from the rest of the Bronx. Hundreds of the buggers. When the Bronx rises up to kill us, at least we'll have the high ground, Darkey says.

I was nearly up, hyperventilating, almost at the Four P., when one of the old stagers grabbed me. It was dark and he scared the shite out of me. Mr. Berenson was in his seventies, very frail, and was hard pressed to frighten anyone, but I suppose I was feeling jumpy. I didn't really know Mr. Berenson and only found out his name later. Much later, when it had all started to go pear-shaped and I felt bad and he was topped and I did some research and discovered he wasn't really called Berenson at all, but was actually some East German geezer who'd changed his name because probably he worked for Himmler in Poland or something. Anyway, he's not at all important in the big picture, so I'll just say that he was stooped, with one of those vague East European accents that you think only exist in the movies. His fingers were stained with nicotine; he was waving them in my face and he was in a mood.

You wor for Scoshy? he said.

No, I work with him. I work for Mr. White, I said.

I tell him, mons ago someone bray in house, prow around.

Someone broke in your house? I said.

Yes, I'm telling you, I get up, I frighten him, he go.

When was this?

December.

Maybe it was Santa Claus.

He was a bit pissed off at that.

Now you lissen to me, young man. Some nigger bray in house, steal nothing, no come back. I thin to myself, why? Why do this? Time passes, I forget. Two neiss ago, he comes back. I am out. But I know he has been.

He take anything?

No.

What's your problem?

He bray in.

Go to the peelers.

What?

Cops, go to the cops. Or get a locksmith. Aye, a locksmith.

He wasn't too happy at what I considered to be a sensible solution.

But I wasn't too happy either. You're a sort of social worker when you come up here, especially with the old timers. There's never really anything wrong or anything they want. They just want to peg you down and chat away their loneliness for a while. Scotchy's better at deflecting them than me. I'm too new, look too understanding.

I was going to say something comforting and bland but just then Fergal saw me at the top of the steps and shouted down:

Hey, Michael, get your arse up here pronto.

I excused myself and went up the stairs. It's diverting to think that if Fergal hadn't picked that particular moment to see if I was off the train yet I might have investigated Mr. Berenson's claim a little more carefully and maybe he wouldn't have gotten killed by some character looking for a hidden stash a week or two later. But Fergal did so intervene and I went up. (The final burglar, incidentally, was one of Ramón's lieutenants, and if you think this is a coincidence you don't know Ramón, for even back then, clearly, he was making stealthy incursions into Darkey's territory, testing its limits, finding its boundaries, plundering its goodies.)

What's the *craic*, Fergal boy? I asked him, using the Gaelic word for fun or happening, which is pronounced the same as "crack," so you could see how it could lead to confusion in some circles.

The *craic*, Michael, is all bad, he said sadly.

Fergal shook his big head at me. Fergal was tall and brown-haired, with a disastrous russet beard covering cadaverous cheeks. He wore tweed jackets in an attempt to appear sophisticated. It was a look that he just might have carried off at, say, a Swiss tuberculosis clinic circa 1912, but it was hardly appropriate for a hot summer in New York eight decades later.

I said it was a shame about young Andy, and Fergal nodded glumly and we went across to the Four Provinces. Clearly, he wasn't in the mood to speak tonight, which was good because when he did it only annoyed people.

The Four P. is such a prominent place in all our lives that it deserves description. Alas, though, if you've seen one faux Irish theme bar you've seen them all. The original Four Provinces burned down in a mysterious fire a few years back and the reconceived version lost the snugs and the back bar and sawdust floor and instead took on an open-plan *Cheers* look with vintage Bushmills whiskey posters, Guinness mirrors, pictures of aged Galway men on bicycles, a "leprechaun in a jar" next to the dartboard, and above the bar, in a glass display case, a large stringed harp that undoubtedly was made in China. It was normally unobservant Andy who noticed that the shamrock carvings on the wood paneling had four leaves, which made them four-leafed clovers and not shamrocks at all—Saint Patrick having used the three-leafed shamrock to explain the Trinity. The best you could say about the place was that at least Pat and Mrs. Callaghan kept it clean.

I nodded to Pat tending bar and followed Fergal up the stairs. Scotchy was there waiting for me, eating a bun, cream all over his nose. Andy was lying in the bed. He looked all right. Bridget was bathing his forehead with water like I suppose she'd seen Florence Nightingale do in some picture. She looked at me and I tried to make it seem as if it was just a casual look, which of course made everything much more suspicious.

There's cream all over your big nose, I said, under my breath, to Scotchy.

He wiped it on his sleeve and looked at me, irritated.

How is he? I asked Bridget kindly.

A little better, she said, and her breast heaved after she stopped speaking. She was wearing a tight T-shirt that said on it a bit confusingly: Cheerleader Leader '89. It was very distracting and I would have asked her what the T-shirt meant to cover the fact that I was staring at her breasts, but in the circumstances of Andy being at death's door and all, it seemed inappropriate.

Fucking finally arrived. Right, we're going right now, Scotchy said.

Here I should point out that every time you hear Scotchy speak you must remember that each time I put in the word *fuck* there are at least three or four that I've left out. You'll have to take my word for it that it would begin to get very tedious hearing Scotchy the way he actually speaks; for instance, a sentence such as the one above in reality was much like:

Fucking finally arrived, fuck. Fucksake. Right, we're fucking going, right fucking now.

Shouldn't I pay my respects or something? I asked.

Bugger can't hear you, can he? Scotchy said, tense, and tight all around the edges. He had that wee-man syndrome though he was only a couple of inches shorter than me and I'm nearly six foot.

Shouldn't we get a doctor at least? I suggested.

Fucksake, Michael, would you shut the fuck up and come on, we're taking care of it, Scotchy said.

I looked at Bridget but the wee girl was lost in the high drama of it all. She was clueless about anything medical. I knew that for a fact from when she tried to take a tiny wood skelf out of my finger with a hot knitting needle. I still have the fantastically large scar. Poor oul Andy could have a goddamn hemorrhage or anything, she wouldn't know. Still, it was Scotchy's call.

Ok, I said, and went downstairs with Fergal and Scotchy.

Scotchy began: So the plan is—

I interrupted him with a hand.

Scotchy, listen, before we go and do anything stupid, shouldn't we talk to Darkey? I asked gently.

Aye, Scotchy, really we should talk to Darkey, Fergal said, for once erring on the side of sensible.

Scotchy was angry.

Jesus Christ, youse boys would ask Darkey if it's ok to take a shite and ok afterwards to wipe your fucking arse. Didn't you see Andy up there?

As a matter of fact, both Fergal and I probably *would* have asked permission to take a shite if Darkey were around. Darkey White didn't get to be Darkey White by putting up with kids thinking they could run the show when he was off the stage. Don't think of Darkey as Brando in *The Godfather*, think of him as Brando slumming it as Jor-el in *Superman*, all full of himself, overacting, clever, pretentious, and clearly a bit fucking bonkers. But still a heavy presence, distorting the well of gravity around him. Even when, like now, he was off the screen.

Scotchy, look, I began, I just don't want us to get in trouble. Sunshine told me everything was off for today and—

Fucking Sunshine, are you afeared of him, too, 'fraid of your own shadow, Bruce? Now come on.

Fergal looked at me and shrugged. I sighed and followed them outside.

We piled into Scotchy's brand-new brown Oldsmobile Something-shite, which was very uncomfortable and extremely uncool besides. The window wipers would come on every time you put on the left turn signal, but this was never a problem for Scotchy because he never used the turn signals. We drove for about ten minutes, up into some winding streets in Riverdale, into not a bad area but not a great one either. None of us said anything except for Scotchy, who was busy muttering to himself.

We were nearly there. Like I say, if it were me I wouldn't have done anything until I'd talked to Darkey or at least Sunshine, but Scotchy wasn't built that way. He wanted to show that he could handle things. He couldn't but he wanted to show that he could. That was why we were the lowest members of the totem pole. That was how we ended up with the rubbish jobs and Bob's crew ended up with the money jobs.

We stopped outside Shovel's apartment building. This was the point for me to make a final plea for a quick wee phone call to Darkey, a minute, that's all it would take. One of us had to be the grown-up and if it meant me, the youngest, taking on that role then so be it. I was going to do it too, but Scotchy got out of the car too fast and by the time I'd caught up to him, the moment was gone and I'd lost my nerve.

Got your pieces? Scotchy asked us. I nodded.

Ach, shite, I left it at home, Fergal said.

Dumb-ass fucker, Scotchy said, furious. See if there's one in the glove compartment.

We all went back to the car. Fergal looked in the glove compartment, but there wasn't anything useful there.

Hey, your lights are on, I said to Scotchy, but he made as if he didn't hear me.

Your lights are on, I said again.

They're on on purpose, he said angrily.

Oh yeah, what purpose is that? I persisted.

Jesus, Bruce. Look, it's just a fucking purpose, ok? I don't have to fill you in on every fucking detail, do I? Scotchy said, really boiling.

No, you don't have to fill me in on every fucking detail, but you would inspire my confidence better, and Fergal's too, no doubt, if you admitted that you made a mistake by leaving the fucking lights on rather than trying to bullshit me with some line about having them on on fucking purpose. A good leader, Scotchy, admits his bloody mistakes.

All right, all fucking right, I fucking left them on by fucking accident, ok. Fucking, you fucking bastard, I'm not fucking Alexander the fucking Great but I would like you to do what I fucking tell you for once in your miserable fucking life.

Scotchy screamed all this at me, pretty near apoplexy.

Well, there goes the bloody element of surprise, I thought but didn't mention.

Ok, fine, Scotchy, fine, I said.

Scotchy composed himself and looked daggers at me.

Do your deep breathing, Fergal suggested.

Shut up, Fergal, Scotchy said.

Aye, shut up, Fergal. You don't know the burdens of command like Rommel over here, I said.

Scotchy untucked his black rayon shirt, seethed, scratched his arse, and said nothing. I grinned at Fergal.

Ok, Michael, Scotchy said, pulling me close. Let's just get on with this, you and me first, Fergal behind us.

Fergal shook his head.

I don't want to go if you two are fighting, he said.

Jesus, we're not fighting, Fergal, I said.

Scotchy was rolling his eyes, but even he saw that he had to placate him.

It's all over, Fergal, ok? he said.

Fergal was unconvinced. I put my arm around Scotchy.

Look, Fergal, we're mates, me and Scotch, I said.

Fergal nodded.

I nodded.

W-what if he has a dog? Fergal asked me.

Fergal, I remembered, had a phobia about dogs. He probably got bitten as a kid or something.

Fergal, relax. Shovel doesn't have a dog, I said.

He smiled, contented, and walked ahead of us into the building.

You think we can rely on Fergal? Seems a bit off, Scotchy whispered to me.

Ach, he's ok, I whispered back.

The building door was locked, so Scotchy pressed several apartment buttons until someone buzzed us in.

Third floor, Scotchy said. He was tense. He was giving off a ton of sweat and a stink of fear. I was feeling fine. I had a .22, Scotchy had a .38, and lanky Fergal was not, despite appearances, a complete idiot. We'd be ok. Probably. We went up the stairs and stopped outside the apartment. Number 34.

Ring the bell or break it down? Fergal asked.

Scotchy was thinking.

Make a lot of noise breaking it down, I said.

Aye, you're right there, Bruce, Scotchy said, fumbling for his pack of Tareyton. We all waited while he lit one.

Ok, you ring it, Fergal, we'll keep out of sight, Scotchy said finally.

Fergal rang the bell.

Who is it? a woman's voice asked.

Fergal Dorey, Fergal said.

What was that?

Friend of Shovel's.

He's not here. He went out, the woman said.

Fergal hesitated and looked back at us.

You've got one of those new microwaves for him, Scotchy whispered.

Aye, I have his microwave for him, Fergal said.

His microwave? the woman asked.

Yes.

There was a long pause and we could hear footsteps down the hall. There was a pause and footsteps coming back.

The door opened and Shovel was standing there grinning.

Fergal, you bastard, you finally brought— Shovel started to say, but Scotchy was yelling at Fergal now:

Grab the fucker, grab him.

Fergal charged through the doorway and rugby-tackled Shovel to the ground. I bundled in behind Scotchy and closed the door.

❖   ❖   ❖

Later that evening on the ride back on the IRT, when I thought, wrongly, that the night was all over and done with, I replayed everything that happened. The whole house of horrors. Bridget cleaning the blood out of my shirt, the food stop, the car ride, and most of all the feathers over Shovel. I wasn't a sadist, I wasn't enjoying it. But I wanted to remember. It was a lot to take in at once and I wanted to be sure I had it all. I needed to know that I was certain of what I was doing. I wasn't just being carried away by youth and emotion. Things were happening and I was part of them. But also occasionally I was stopping, analyzing events and saying to myself that it was all ok by me. And it *was* ok, too. Why? I don't know. That's another question entirely.

Mrs. Shovel, or whatever her real name was, had appeared in the hall. All four of us stood in the apartment's corridor. It was wallpapered in flowers, narrow. It was hard to move. She had to be in her early thirties, tough-looking, suntanned, surprisingly pretty. She had a black wig on, flip-flops, a nightie. She was yelling. Scotchy smacked her across the face with his gun. She went down like a doll, thumping into a picture frame, breaking it. Shovel screamed and tried to get up. but I had the .22 in his face.

One move, big guy, and I'll have to shoot you, I said, trying to bring an air of calm to the proceedings.

Scotchy had the opposite agenda. He bent down and started beating Shovel with the butt of his pistol. He was roaring. It wasn't entirely coherent. Spitting the words out:

Fucker, why did you do it, why, you fucking idiot? Are you stupid? Did you think we wouldn't know? Did you think we were such fucking pussies that we wouldn't do nothing? Huh? Is that what you thought?

Blood was pouring from Shovel's face. He was protesting. He was innocent. He had no idea what Scotchy was talking about. Fergal was still sitting on him. Scotchy took the pistol butt and smashed it into Shovel's mouth. He started to struggle wildly. I sat down on his legs and Fergal wedged himself on the torso. Scotchy stood up and started kicking him in the back and head. He exhausted himself after a few seconds. Blood was everywhere now. It was on our clothes and pooling dark and awful on the wood floor. Shovel had lost consciousness.

Get a pillow, get two, Scotchy barked at Fergal.

Fergal went off to find the bedroom.

Are you going to shoot him? I asked dispassionately.

Aye, I'm going to shoot him, Scotchy said.

I felt myself go a bit weak. This I hadn't signed on for. The teen rackets seldom came to this in the Cool or Greenisland or Carricktown. A chill went through me. I'd never seen a real murder before and I didn't want to now.

Fortunately, I was not to break my duck that night, for even Scotchy was not that big of an eejit.

Belfast six-pack, he said after a pause.

Harsh, I said.

With fucking Andy dying on us, probably brain-damaged for life, Scotchy yelled in my face, spittle landing on my cheeks.

I said nothing. He glared at me.

Fergal came back with the pillows.

Fergal, turn the TV on, loud, Scotchy said.

Fergal went off again. I looked at Scotchy and then at Shovel.

I'll do it, I said. Better the .22 for the noise.

Scotchy nodded. I was thinking more of Shovel than the noise. Me with a .22 was going to be a lot easier to get over than Scotchy with the .38. I put one pillow over his ankle and pushed the gun in deep. I waited until the TV got loud. I pulled the trigger. Feathers, blood. I did the other ankle. Same again. Cordite, the pillow caught fire. I put it out. I did the left knee and Shovel convulsed and woke and vomited. Scotchy knocked him out with a surprisingly deft kick to the temple. I did the other knee and gave the gun to Fergal to do the elbows. I couldn't hack it anymore. I stood and took a breath. Scotchy thought I was just giving Fergal the weapon because he was in a better position. He didn't realize I was on the verge of fainting or puking. Fergal shot him in an elbow, messily. I should have done it myself. Not that I was any expert, but I'd more sense than him. I took a breath and grabbed the gun back.

More like this, Fergal, I said and shot him in the other elbow, aiming for the fleshy parts. His body convulsed and there was just the bleeding and the feathers and a low moan from the wife.

I remembered to breathe again.

It was a terrible thing. It had been ugly. Kicking someone, punching them, is one thing but shooting an unconscious man six times is something else. A mate, too.

All three of us got up. We stood there, stunned.

Six shots, Belfast six-pack, Scotchy said in a whisper, and a gurgle that apparently was laughter came into his mouth. Fergal nodded and broke into a smile.

Always wondered what that meant. Is that really how they do it, Michael? he asked, quietly awed.

That, Fergal, is how they do it, I said clinically, as if it was all second nature to me now, as if I'd maybe seen it dozens of times. Perhaps it was even a little tedious. Of course I'd never done it, seen it once and had been sick for a week. Fergal looked at me in a new light. I was quite the cold motherfucker. He would spread it around too. Even Scotchy, I could see, was a bit appalled by what we had accomplished. Last time in the Four P. Shovel had bought us all a round.

Their discomfort was an opportunity and I took it.

Let's go, I said and opened the door. The others followed. Scotchy was going to kick him on the way out but he felt bad now and didn't. We were spattered with blood, but it was night and the car was just outside. Scotchy was shaking and trying not to show it. He handed me the keys.

You drive, he said.

I wasn't used to driving on the right, but I took the keys and started her up. I headed back. There was a McDonald's drive-through and I saw this as another opportunity. I turned the wheel.

You boys want anything? I asked. I'm narving.

Scotchy was pale in the front seat. Fergal dry-heaving now in the back. Both shook their heads. I pulled in and ordered a Big Mac meal and ate it as I drove. Fergal would spread this around too. It would reach Sunshine. It would reach Darkey. It might even reach Mr. Duffy. We stopped outside the Four Provinces and went in to get cleaned up. Bridget took my clothes. Andy was no better.

I seriously think you should take him to the hospital, I said.

Scotchy was in no mood to argue now and Mrs. Callaghan dialed the number. I showered and waited until the paramedics came.

When we were alone, I found Bridget and kissed her.

I absolutely have to see you, I said.

She didn't say anything.

Tomorrow, I said.

I don't know, Michael, she said.

For God's sake, Bridget, we've both been through the mill. Tomorrow, please. Come on, we'll do something fun.

She nodded her head ambiguously and went downstairs.

I stood there for a moment. Was she tiring of me? Would she come? Who knew? I shook my head wearily and followed her down.

I had a free pint off Pat and drank it and chatted about the upcoming English football season, ate some Tayto crisps, and went down the steps and caught the train. . . .

All over.

Done.

You got through.

You got through. Ugly, but it was Scotchy's fault, not yours. No.

You look for that paperback about the Russian guy but it's gone. You sit in the subway car and you think. Not your fault. Not your fault. The train rattles and it nearly rocks you off to sleep. It stops at the stop and doesn't move again. After a while a man comes with information. There's a problem on the line and you have to get off at 137th. You get out and they give you a useless transfer.

It's dark now in Harlem.

You walk down the hill from City College and St. Nicholas Park. The streets are empty. No junkies, no hookers, no undercover cops, no delivery boys, no workers, no nothing. Bodegas are shut and barricaded. The moon. The deserted avenue. The tremendous sleeping buildings and the rusted octopi of fire escapes. It is still warm and Harlem is all around and comforting. It's straight here. Simple. You know how things stand. You know who you are and who they are. You know your place. You know how things will be. You know everything. You can exist here without pressure, without history. You can be anonymous.

It's a pleasant walk down Amsterdam. A gypsy cab comes by and honks. You look at it and nod. It stops. You get in. Three bucks to 123rd and Amsterdam, you say.

The man nods, smiles.

Some day, huh, he says.

You don't reply. But in the silence you agree and look out of the window.

2: DOWNTOWN

That should have been it. The night should have ended there—but it didn't. Instead it got dragged out into a jazz of drink and *craic* and bars and cars. I was asleep and abed only about forty minutes when they came calling in their transport. A big yellow van that they must have borrowed. Guy called Marley driving, whom I'd never previously encountered and after that evening did not meet again until the night, several months later in real time and an epoch in psychological time, when I put a screwdriver through his throat and he went down into the embrace of the soft Westchester snow without even a whimper.

Even though I was knackered it was deemed necessary that I be got up and forced to join in the jollity, for Darkey, when he was on a bender or even a mild celebration, was like a Jack ashore, everyone possible was to be brought within the compass of his merriment. And I, after all, was the star of the evening or so they all kept saying. Sunshine, Big Bob, and Darkey had arrived at the Four Provinces—after their important chin wag—not too long after I'd buggered off home following our own little escapade. Darkey and Big Bob had been drinking, so Sunshine was driving them back (though Marley was doing the actual driving). They'd all ended up in the lounge bar of the Four P. intercepting Scotchy and Fergal just as they were belting one for the road. They were both the worse for drink, but somehow Sunshine got the story out of them and with indignation Darkey had asked how they could have let me go back home on the subway when clearly I was the hero of the hour for my coolness in dealing with Shovel.

Darkey is, if anything, a man of the whim and he decided that all of them were going to the hospital right that minute to see poor Andy; and then that done, they were all going to go down to Harlem and call on and subsequently fete me.

Jesus. Poor me.

Like I say, I was only asleep forty minutes but I was away, already reasonably untroubled by conscience or anything else. Yeah, I was off somewhere, but resistance was useless.

They didn't get in to see Andy but they came on down to 123rd Street anyway. They rang my buzzer, but I had the fan on and cotton wool stuffed in my ears to keep out the racket from east of here.

Come on you fucking lazy wee hoor's spawn bastard. It's us. We're fucking doing a Petula, Scotchy was no doubt screaming through the intercom. They buzzed for about ten seconds and then Darkey's patience must have got the better of him for he told Big Bob to jemmy the lock, which Big Bob did. They probably would have broken my door down had I not finally heard their cackling and yelling and banging. For some reason I thought it was a bunch of drunk Serbians up from Ratko's pad to raise hell and I went to the door with a metal baseball bat in my hand and a revolver in my boxer shorts.

They laughed when I opened up the door. Boxers, Zoso T-shirt, gun, baseball bat, hair askew, snarl on face.

Darkey leaned forward and punched me on the arm.

Well done, you wee fucker, he said.

Darkey, who had never been to Ireland in his life but who took on a bit of the accent and manner when he was around Scotchy and myself. It was terrifying.

They dressed me in jeans and boots and leather jacket and hauled me out into the night, dragging me downstairs violently. For just a second or two I thought that perhaps all this bonhomie was a cover and really they were going to drive me down to the Hudson and shoot me in the back of the neck. No, worse. First, Darkey kicks my face in and then when it's a bloody mess and I'm blinded and brains are coming out my ears, Scotchy says: I'm very disappointed in you, son. And then he fucking tops me.

But instead of turning left at Amsterdam we turned right and it seemed that we really were going downtown after all. The boys didn't see, but my heart stopped beating like a steam engine and the tension eased out of me. It'll be a bad night: drink, smoke, and some terrible restaurant at the break of dawn, but at least I'm going to live, which is something.

Darkey poured a half pint of some single malt down my throat and fell asleep in the backseat. With him practically out of it, Big Bob and Scotchy got to arguing about where we were going to go and, of course, with Scotchy and Big Bob trying to get things done it all ended farcically with us being pulled over by a cop. It was left to Sunshine in the front seat to deal with the peeler and take us to the first den of I., which was a strip joint in the vicinity of Madison Square Garden.

Darkey was revived and led us in. He was well received. The place was standard fare: dark booths, a gangway, stripper poles, main act, side acts, filthy glasses, spaced-out clientele.

I found a quiet corner to try and kip and I really must have nodded off, for Fergal's droning voice woke me with talk about a redheaded girl he'd fallen in love with. Fergal was maybe traumatized by the whole Shovel business or maybe he was just being Fergal. He was a gangly bloke and always a bit of a high-strung character. He'd been a thief back in the O.C. Fingers, he tried to get everyone to call him, but no one did. He had a good five years on me, but I was the older brother.

There she is. Tell me, Michael, tell me isn't she amazing. Jesus, look at her, Michael, come on, look.

I took a look and I thought he was pulling my leg, but he was serious. Aside from the fact that she was a working girl and coked out of her mind, she was four inches taller than him and with the heels it was nearly a foot. She was dancing at a side booth, not even the main show, and added to that she was skin and bones, she hadn't eaten or seen sunlight in a good few moons, and the hair was a wig. Fergal is six foot two, so there was at least a possibility that the girl was in fact an emaciated, coked-out bloke.

I see what you're saying, Fergal. She might be the one for you, right enough. Fair skin, red hair—man, you're made, and you a big-time player and all.

You really think so? Really, Mike? Mike, I'm dead serious. I just looked at her and I had this feeling come over me. No, not what you think. It's like this feeling of love or something, you know. Love at first sight. I mean, you can't help it. It just happens. Jesus, out of the blue. You could be riding the bus and see somebody and they'd be gone forever. Could be anybody. . . .

During this neat dissection of love, which wasn't exactly Ovid, I was scanning the ill-lit club for a sign of the others. I didn't see any of them and assumed that they'd either left us or retired to a private room somewhere. Either way, it was a sly move to leave me with love-drunk Fergal, and I thought I was supposed to be the man of the hour.

Bastards.

What?

Not you, Fergal. I was wondering where the others were.

I don't know, Mike. Have you been listening to what I've been saying?

Of course, Fergal, your words are pearls.

Well, look, what do you think I should do? I have this warm feeling in my stomach.

I have that too, Darkey's so-called single malt, I think—

Michael, for fucksake, be serious. What do you think I should do? I mean, she's a dancer, maybe even a—he lowered his voice—hoor or something. Jesus, that would be bad. And anyway, I mean, do you think it would be right if I went over, and if I did go over, what would I say?

I beckoned him close.

Listen, Fergal, she seems like a perfectly charming girl. She might, for all you know, be a divinity student who dances to pay off her school fees. You simply go over to her and say politely: Madam, I wonder if it might be possible to see you sometime when you finish working in this establishment, not for any untoward purpose but rather merely to have a coffee or something similar, a meeting of minds, ideas and cultures, that would, I believe, be mutually rewarding.

You think that would work?

Undoubtedly, Fergal, my son of the sod, with your native wit and good looks she will be bowled over.

Fergal finished his Dutch and did go over. I slapped him on the back and watched him begin his little speech. He didn't get terribly far into it before she said something to him. He immediately clammed up and came back broken and reasonably distraught. You wouldn't have thought he was the same boy shooting people earlier.

She says they can't go out with customers. It's a rule.

I took Fergal by the scruff of the neck and pulled him over beside me.

Fergal, do you love this woman? Do you want her? Do you?

He nodded.

Then tell her that you are a Celt of noble race and you care nothing for rules, that if she will be yours, you will remove her from this place and give her a pad of her own and pay her divinity school fees and library fines and you will work tooth and nail twenty hours a day if necessary to keep her in the lap of luxury, anything to see her happy. Now, go. Say as I have told you and do not come back until victory lights your drunken Paddy cheeks.

I shoved him and he went over, and I closed my eyes again and leaned back in the chair. Sleep came like a welcome assassin and kept me away from all the crap for a while.

I was back in the gorse and heather for a brief but delightful moment. Slemish at my left and it was all fields and white flowers, bog grass and the loughs over the water to the low hills on Galloway. All of the highlands before me, blue and mysterious, and it must have been dawn or dusk or some other part of the Golden Hour because I could see lighthouses and counted six of them before being summoned back to the more prosaic world.

The next time it was Scotchy who woke me, kicking the chair leg from under me and laughing as I sprawled onto the dubiously stained floor. Darkey, Big Bob, and Marley were all laughing too, everyone in fact except Sunshine, who nearly always contained his emotions splendidly.

Ahh, you idle wee fucker, missed out, so you did, lap dances for all of us, Scotchy was saying.

Aye, there was this Thai girl, gorgeous she was, and I says, Where are you from? and she says, I'm Thai, and I says, I'll tie you with this, love, Big Bob declared. I could see that he was attempting to be funny, but not feeling particularly generous at this moment, I said that I doubted that she would find anything but fat in the ample area of Bob's lap.

Bob was too drunk to get it, but he knew it was an insult and called me a wetback bastard.

I was about to get into a long thing about *his* ancestry, but Scotchy shook his head at me.

Where's Fergal? Sunshine asked.

And true enough, Fergal had vanished.

He went off with some ginger tart, I said.

For a quickie or the night? Darkey asked.

I think the night, I said.

Well, in that case, we've lost a man, because we, my friend, are moving on to pastures new, Darkey said and helped pull me up off the floor.

You should have seen your face, Scotchy said as we walked back out to the car.

Aye, you're lucky you can still see yours, Scotchy, I said.

Is that supposed to be a threat? Scotchy mocked.

It is a threat, I said, getting angry now.

Aye, you talk the talk, big man, but I don't see you doing anything about it, Scotchy said with a toty wee bit more than his usual sneer.

I stopped. I measured the distance from his head. I clenched my right fist and socked him one in the face. It was a good one too, an uppercut catching him square on the nose and staggering him back into a streetlight.

You wee fuck, Scotchy spat and came at me like a box of wild cats, clawing, biting, and spitting so furiously that I had to drop-kick him and even then when both of us were on the ground he was on me, pulling out my hair in big chunks and sinking his skanky teeth into my hand.

You vile bastard, I screamed and attempted to nut him in the face but before further damage could be done we were separated by the others. Both of us were bleeding and I was furious.

Darkey was yelling at the pair of us, but I couldn't hear him and even when my ears stopped ringing I couldn't make head nor tail of it. Sunshine was holding out my hand and Darkey was holding out Scotchy's and I could see that we were supposed to shake. I shook my head and backed away.

That wee shite can keep his handshake, Sunshine. He's a no-good wee turd, from a skitter family full of them, and he's the fucking runt, I said.

I heard that, Bruce, you bastard, Scotchy yelled at me.

Aye, there's more where that came from, I shouted.

Aye, well bring it on, cuntface, Scotchy screamed, almost hoarse now.

That's enough, the pair of you, Darkey said.

Darkey was holding back Scotchy, Big Bob was holding me. All this, somewhere near to Madison Square Garden, though not on a game night, so not too many prying eyes or peelers.

Sunshine grabbed me by the shoulders.

Listen, Michael, you will shake Scotchy's hand. You'll be sorry about all this tomorrow and you'll call me up and apologize and say that you couldn't believe that anyone could have acted in such an infantile manner and if anyone could take a joke it was you. Everyone knew it.

Not touching him, I muttered, pride rather than the booze backing me up.

Sunshine, though, knew he had to end it right here if he wasn't to start losing face. He smiled and spoke calmly, but loud enough for all to hear.

If I have to put a gun to your head, Michael, you will shake his hand, Sunshine said.

I looked at him. Sunshine, five foot eight, skinny, that insane comb-over hairdo and mustache, almost no eyebrows. Really, he looked a bit like an egghead from a 1950s science-fiction movie. You could very easily see him explaining to Steve McQueen that the Blob was coming. The thought of this made me lighten up. I grinned at him.

Is that an order? I asked.

He nodded and his eyes tightened in what for him wasn't a cold expression but rather one of empathy.

I relaxed. Sunshine had given me a way out. It was usual for him. You could trust him. Sunshine looked out for us, and lived not in the moment but in the tomorrow and in the next week too. I went over to Scotchy and stuck out my hand. To my surprise, Scotchy pulled me in and hugged me.

You really are a fucking cunt, he whispered in my ear, his voice cracking with emotion. I thought he was going to cry actually, so I grinned at him and pushed him off.

Jesus, now he wants to fuck me, I said to the audience and Scotchy took a swipe at and managed to connect with the top of my head. But we were old pals now and inseparable until two bottles of Dewar's later Scotchy collapsed in the outside bog of the Mat Bar, an old speakeasy in the West Village that still had sawdust on the floor and pictures of famous prewar writers and several bar dogs to slurp your beer.

Leaving Scotchy off was now a priority, so we had to make a long detour up to the Bronx, and as we were going past 123rd I mentioned that it was getting late and might I also be excused, but Darkey was having none of it.

We stopped outside Scotchy's place and Bob and myself lugged the wee shite up the stairs. We threw him on his bed, and while Bob helped himself to stuff from the fridge, I adjusted Scotchy into the recovery position so he wouldn't choke on his own vomit. We left him and drove back to the Village, this time the East Village, where Darkey knew a good place for a stout. The bar, unfortunately, was closed, as it was late, and so we made do with somewhere close in Alphabet City, a trendy place that was loud and full of pretty girls going to NYU.

On my shout, I met at the bar an amazingly cute Israeli girl, with the cropped black hair, beautiful dark eyes, and large gravity-defying breasts wonderfully typical of the type. I'm not a bad-looking chap myself and I figured the gloominess of the surroundings would no doubt conceal the sleep rings around my eyes and any residual trace of the earlier murderous violence in my countenance.

I told her she looked Irish and asked if there was any Irish in her and when she said no, I said, all ironic and postmodern, Well would you like some? What worked for Bono worked for me, and she said, The chutzpah of you, and I said, Bless you. I spun her some yarn about being an exchange student from Queen's University, Belfast, up at Columbia for a year. I was studying tensile loss in large mechanical apparatae (which I guessed was the plural of apparatus). It turned out to be an unfortunate choice of major because she, apparently, was a sapper in the Israeli Defense Forces and knew quite a bit about such things. She said she was a lieutenant, and I was disinclined to believe her and told her so, but she convinced me by her officerlike offer to get me a drink. I sent back my round to the lads via the barkeep and retired to a shady corner with Lieutenant Rachel Narkiss. I was not keen to mention my own undistinguished army career, which had lasted less than a year and ended up ignominiously in the brig on Saint Helena.

Lieutenant Narkiss had grown up on a kibbutz near the Lebanon and had had a wry old time of it up there dodging Katyushas and running through the mountains of northern Galilee. She was studying history at NYU and aside from Hebrew, she spoke English, Arabic, Yiddish, and French and a smattering of other tongues. She was clever and she was funny and for some reason my drunken Paddy chatter wasn't wearing thin.

We talked about the pictures and travel and she pretended to be absurdly fascinated by a holiday I'd taken in Spain once. A riot had started between British and German football hooligans on the Canary Island of Tenerife. I'd been kept out of it by older friends, but in this new version of the story I got swept up in the trouble, and it ended with me saving the life of a lost shepherd boy and getting a minor bravery award from the Spanish government. She bought not a word of it, but she was curious about the landscape (being a photography buff), wondering if it was at all similar to the Negev. I said I'd no idea, although I did mention that *The Good, the Bad and the Ugly* was filmed around there, so all she had to do was to rent the flick.

So you see, the bank at El Paso wasn't really at El Paso, I added helpfully. She said that the bank at El Paso was in a different film completely. *For a Few Dollars More,* she thought.

That killed that subject, but there were many more and we talked about Belfast and Jerusalem and the kibbutz, where she had worked in the machine shop. Of course, we also drew parallels between the situation in Israel and Northern Ireland, and by dint of common sense and hasty maps drawn on the back of a drip mat, we solved both problems to the satisfaction of all parties. She wasn't a name-dropper, but she did let slip that her brother worked for Rabin. I wasn't a name-dropper either, and most of the names I could drop, although famous in Ireland, were a little less savory: Johnny "Mad Dog" McDuff, "Chopper"

Clonfert, "Bloody Boy" Halrahan. I sensibly chose to leave them undropped and instead waxed eloquent on the delights of university life. She asked me about the Columbia Core Curriculum, and I had no idea what it was but said that I wondered about its relevance in these changing times, which seemed to work well.

We chatted for a long time and finally she asked if I'd like to come back to her room at NYU. It wasn't a dorm, and so we wouldn't have to sneak in, but apart from that, it would still be quite fun. She had just bought a brand-new device for making tea. It was a little wire-mesh ball into which the tea leaves were put, mesh small enough to keep the leaves in but big enough to allow water to pass through, hence allowing for improved infusion. . . . I'd stopped listening to the tea explanation and was lost completely in her eyes, which, as I've previously said, were dark and bewitching.

Do you have a picture of yourself in your army fatigues? I thought, but realized, to my horror, had also said.

She said that she did not. Oh, wait. She had a small one on her ID. She laughed and brought it out and this clinched the whole deal. I would go back to her place and experience with her the miracle of the tea-infusion ball. It was then that I did something extremely stupid. Something so stupid that it would ultimately lead to the death of our poor driver David Marley with a screwdriver in the throat on that snowy Westchester Christmas Eve. It would also unfortunately mean the end of everyone else sitting at Marley's table. What I did was this: I said to her, I just better go tell Sunshine that I'm away.

If I hadn't done that, things sure would have turned out differently. I would have spent the night with her. What happened the next morning wouldn't have happened. There would have been no Mexico, there would have been no death. There would have been just me and this beautiful girl and a different narrative, a better one.

Ok, she said, not knowing that she'd sealed my fate.

I went over to Sunshine.

Listen, mate. Met this girl, have to go, if you know what I mean.

You can't, Sunshine said. Darkey wants to take you to this restaurant in Brooklyn, treat you, a big meal. We're going when he gets back from the bathroom. You know, because we're impressed with ya. Vendetta. You did well, teaching Shovel a lesson. It's easy doing your enemies. But it's hard doing your friends. You showed real moral courage.

Listen, Sunshine, if it's all the same to you, I've met this girl and Jesus, she is absolutely the cat's pajamas, I kid you not, my old china, she is the business and—

End of conversation, Michael. We're going to Brooklyn, Darkey's wish. Wants to treat you and he will, Sunshine said firmly.

Christ, it must be near four in the morning. Will it even be open at—

Michael, come on, I won't tell you again. Get the girl's number and call her tomorrow.

I could see that there was to be no discussion, so, shamefaced, I went back to her.

Listen, what's your first name again? It is burned in my heart but temporarily my memory is failing to reach my pulmonary system.

Rachel.

Listen, Rachel, my boss, uh, my supervisor, university supervisor, is over there and he's taken it into his head to take us out to dinner and I have to go. But please, please, give me your number and I'll call you tomorrow. Ok?

She looked disappointed, but she gave me the number. She bit her lip. It was too much. I leaned over and kissed her. She kissed me back, wet and delicious, for a half a minute.

You really can't come tonight? she asked.

It's agonizing, but I really can't.

Well, I'm going to Miami for ten days the day after tomorrow, so you will have to call soon, she said.

Are you kidding me? I'll definitely call.

No, really.

I will. Listen, I'm really awfully sorry about the tea. I will call. I promise.

I kissed her on the cheek and put the number in my jacket pocket.

Are you ok for getting home? I asked.

Yes. It's just across the street.

She went off, leaving me tealess and heartbroken. Needless to say, I didn't call the next day. The next day a different girl came back into my life. And the next day Rachel was gone (though I did phone up to check just in case) and when she came back I wasn't in the country anymore, and then when I came back, finally, I didn't want her to see what had become of me.

❖   ❖   ❖

The restaurant in Brooklyn turned out to be some awful Italian shithole with a night view over stinking mudflats and an abandoned container dock. I don't know Brooklyn well, but it was in the neighborhood of Williamsburg and the L train. The food was bad, but at least I didn't get the fate of Big Bob, who ordered lobster in some kind of white sauce and for his many sins was puking most of the next day. But that was in the rosy future, for now he was sitting next to me bullshitting his way through a biography that even Scotchy wouldn't have had the cheek to make up. I was in a foul temper, mainly over the girl, but I suppose also a combination of factors. It hadn't been the most successful of days for my self-image as a lovable Artful Dodger type. First, I had to shoot poor old Shovel; then they woke me up after no sleep and dragged me downtown; then Scotchy and I went at it hell's bells; and then they deprived me of Lieutenant Narkiss—a woman deadly out of, and I'm sure in, the sack.

We were alone in the place and there was only one waiter and the cook and the manager, a man called Quinn. None of the three looked or sounded very Italian. I closed my eyes and drifted for a time. Bob was lecturing Sunshine on the benefits of central air-conditioning. Marley was smoking. Darkey was standing at the window. And then to my absolute horror, Darkey called me over.

He had a cigar, he was half-toasted. I hoped more than me.

Michael, my boy, come here, he said.

I came.

We haven't really talked, have we, Michael?

I shook my head.

Sunshine does all of that, Darkey said sadly.

Yes.

It's a pity, though. I like to get to know people. I like to know who's working for me, but the higher you go the less you can stay involved in the nitty-gritty. You have to let go, Michael. You have to trust your sub-ordinates. More like Reagan, less like Carter. You get me?

I didn't at all, but I nodded.

Darkey put his head on my shoulders. He was smaller than me, and I'd already slumped over into an uncomfortable stoop to be eye level with him. His hand felt heavy.

Listen to me, you did a fine job and don't think there won't be something extra in your pay packet. Shovel disrespecting me like that. Who does he think he is? Man's a lunatic. A fucking lunatic. What price loyalty? Look at you. You came from Ireland. From Belfast. I gave you a job and you've done a good job. Sometimes it's lifting people. Some-times it's lifting furniture, ha, ha. You have to start at the bottom. Earn our trust. Sunshine gives me reports.

I see, I said.

But you see, the thing is, I like you. You and Scotchy. Andy, I liked him. He went out with Bridget, you know. But he wasn't her type. Not at all. You, I see you, Michael. You are the lad, the original Wild Colo-nial, but listen. I know you're good. Scotchy tells me, Sunshine tells me. Listen, Michael, I know you. You're young, and young is as young does, that's just the way of it. But I won't have any trouble. I think I'm a fair man. I think I am. But I won't have trouble. I come down like the son of Solomon. My father chastised you with whips and I will do it with scorpions. Iron fist only way. Cut out the cancer. If it's there. Have you seen that film about John Wayne where he's the boxer?

No, I don't think—

Very good, very good. I've never been, but I will one day. Quiet life. You want to settle after a time. You want to settle. How I began is not important. It's how I'll finish that's the key. Construction brings in three times what Sunshine does. You understand?

Not really, I admitted.

His hand pushed down on my shoulder. It was actually hurting a little.

How old are you, Michael?

Nineteen. I'll be twenty in—

See, you boys might have the youth, but I have the persistence, Darkey said and pointed his finger at me. I can outlast all of you. Mr. Duffy, me, we grew up with this. You realize that, don't you? You, Bob,

Scotchy, even Sunshine, you don't know the half of it. You're too young. You see that? Intelligence is no substitute for wisdom. Live long enough to get wise, eh?

Yes, I suppose so, I said, completely baffled and now increasingly afraid. Was this all some kind of horrible joke? Was this the whole point of the evening? Get me to Brooklyn to Darkey's place, everyone feigns to be wasted, and then Darkey deals his hand. Bob comes over with a knuckleduster. Darkey starts to scream: You think I'm a fucking moron. You think you, some potato-stuffing fucker just off the boat, can pull a fast one on me. Me, Darkey fucking White. You think you can fool me?

I was pale and sober now. Trying not to shake. Oh, Christ. Was that why they'd ditched Scotchy? 'Cause he might stick up for me?

I turned round, Bob *was* walking over.

I started to feel blind panic. Was there any way I could make a run for it at all? What the fuck was going on?

I have to make use of the facilities, Bob grunted.

I'll join ya, Darkey said, cheerfully. And then I suppose it's time we should all head on. It's getting late.

He gave me a grin and a wink.

Youth does have some advantages. I can't stay up all night no more, he said.

Me neither, actual— I began, but Darkey interrupted me with a shout back to the table.

Hey, Marley, off your ass. We're heading. Go and get the van started.

Marley heard and said: Ok (his only speech in this whole narrative, as it turns out). Darkey went off to the bathroom. I sat down at the table, panting, relieved. I could see now that nothing was going to happen. Paranoia, that's all. That's all. I took a drink of someone's wine.

You ok? Sunshine asked.

Aye. Darkey's in a bit of a mood, though.

Sunshine regarded me.

I haven't noticed anything, he said.

Sunshine was not to be drawn into any criticisms of Darkey whatsoever. He was loyal. You could grant him that. He'd be the Goebbels poisoning his weans for Darkey, you could see it. I'd be more of a von

Stauffenberg character, I was thinking, but wisely I kept these observations to myself.

How did you get that pay-phone number, Sunshine? I asked him for
something to say.

It's not important, Sunshine said.

He wanted to keep it secret. He was clever, I liked that.

You went to university, didn't you, Sunshine?

Yes.

Where, what?

NYU, French, Sunshine said.

Hey, I did French in school. *Tu es une salope:* I said that to the Haitian woman in C-Town. It was funny, she wouldn't give me a refund
for . . . but I didn't finish. I could see Sunshine was not impressed. I
went on on a different tack:

Point is, Sunshine, you're smart. I mean, what exactly are you doing
with us lot?

Darkey and I go back, Sunshine said, simply.

Like he saved your life or something. You were drowning in the
YMCA pool, he dragged you out, forever loyal, or better. You were the
smart kid with the glasses, he protected you from the school bully. . . .

I was trying to be funny, but Sunshine was not amused.

What if I said it was something like that, would you believe me?
Sunshine said.

Uh, yeah, I suppose I would, I said, a little embarrassed.

Let me give you a piece of advice, Michael. Never underestimate
Darkey or me, ok?

Jesus, Sunshine. Don't get all heavy on me, I was just joking, I said.

Sunshine smiled.

Me too, he said.

To change the subject, we talked movies for a while and I said I
liked Orson Welles in *The Third Man* and Sunshine said I should really
rent *The Lady from Shanghai.*

Darkey and Big Bob came back. Bob was looking peaky. Darkey
came over and slapped me on the back. No harder than was strictly
necessary, which was a relief after all his slabbering. He put me in a
headlock and made me cry mercy. Again, there was no malice in it, and
he didn't hurt me. But even so, I was still filled with a sudden and dan-

gerous resentment against him. Darkey, all things considered, was a bit of a prick, and I wouldn't work with him for all the pay in hell, except that most of the time it was Sunshine, not Darkey, who had his steady hand on the tiller. I looked at Sunshine and he looked at me with what I took to be sympathy. Bob did the bongos on my head for a minute, and Darkey laughed.

He's a bodh ran, a human bodh ran, Bob said, until Darkey told him to quit it. He let me go.

It's pronounced "boran," you ignorant shite, I said to Bob.

Sunshine, always eager for a new word, asked me what that meant, and I told him (with a nasty look at Bob) that a bodhran was an Irish side drum, not a bongo drum.

Darkey paid and left a miserly tip, and we were all about to leave when suddenly a joke occurred to him. Normally, his jokes were of the practical kind, such as telling Scotchy to kick my chair from under me, but occasionally he came up with a good one. Darkey wasn't an unintelligent man, and often I think he tried to appear heartier and dumber than he actually was.

Ok, lads, joke. Everybody sit.

We sat. Darkey began:

Old monastery in the west of Ireland. Galway. Two parrots in a cage, and all day long they pray and recite the rosary and twirl the rosary beads in their little claws. Visiting priest is amazed, sees the birds and tells the abbot that they have precisely the opposite situation at the nearby convent, where they rescued two female parrots from a brothel after the police closed it down. Unfortunately for the nuns the parrots say all day long, "Fuck me, please, I'm a filthy whore." The abbot suggests that they move the parrots from the convent and put them in with the good-living parrots in the monastery. The priest thinks that this is an excellent idea. The foul-mouthed birds will learn by example. Anyway, the two monastery parrots are in their cage one day when the two female parrots are brought in beside them. Both female parrots immediately say, "Fuck me, I'm a filthy whore," whereupon one male parrot looks at the other and says, "Seamus, you can put the beads away now, our prayers have been answered."

We all laughed. Sunshine louder than most, and that, believe me, was a scary thing to behold. Again, Goebbels came to mind.

They dropped me at 123rd. Darkey got out of the car and shook my hand.

I can count on you, can't I, Michael? he said, his heavy-lidded eyes boring into me.

Without blinking I said, Of course. (I almost added "Sir.")

Sunshine was also out of the car. I was bleary from drink, cigarette smoke, too much food, and exhaustion, but Sunshine wanted to tell me well done too.

I preempted him.

You know, Sunshine, Shovel didn't do a damn thing. Not one thing, I said.

Sunshine nodded. I couldn't be sure that he could see what I meant, but I didn't want to go into it now. Maybe Sunshine knew all along, maybe it didn't matter.

I walked up the steps to the apartment building. I checked that Rachel's phone number was in my pocket. It was. I could smell dawn in the air. What a long, weird, awful night. I opened the jemmied door. The hall was full of steam from a broken radiator. Typical and insane that the steam heat would even be on in summer. Of course, in winter . . . I spat and ignored it and went upstairs. I hoped that I wouldn't be so hopped up and overtired that I wouldn't be able to sleep.

I was to be disappointed.

3 : THE NICE PART OF THE BRONX

Ssshhhh, ssshhhh, listen. Blot out everything else. The dark whispering. Can you hear it? Can you hear? Singing truths like apples. In a language that is universal and easy to understand. It's singing for you. Big man, player, dealer in bruises. Its breath condenses on the mirror and its trace is visible. Curling from the sewers and the gutters and the storm drains, and speaking with the voice of graveyard stone.

I *can* hear it. I can feel its breath. Rank and awful. It makes things up: lies, half-lies, stories. It's hushed but the building's alert and attends and passes them on. Up the skunk trees, up the brick, through the window.

You're a thief, you're a bully. You hurt people. You're nothing, a shadow. You're a fool. A nasty wee piece of work.

Accusations. From the world out there. Go away. Please. Please.

But the world out there. It isn't quiet. It never is. . . .

My eyes fill, flutter. I wake.

It is impossible to sleep. I generate white noise from a fan which on level three does its best to erase the sirens, the crying, the yelling, the music, the nightmares, and—melodramatic but nevertheless true—the gunshots.

It's around dawn. I've been in bed at most an hour.

The clunk is the arrival of the *Times.*

Jesus. Bad dreams. Not what you'd think, but bad dreams nonetheless. I throw back the cotton sheet and yawn and go to the front door and bring the paper in. I throw the paper at a roach in the hall. I take a bagel from the freezer and put it in the microwave. Something about microwaves, I remember. Oh yes, Scotchy, last night. Where did he come up with that? Wait a minute. Last night. Suddenly I feel the need to sit down in the middle of the kitchen floor.

I sit.

Exhausted and nauseated.

Alone.

Relax, be calm. Try to breathe. Breathe. I lean on the window and cough so hard my lungs hurt. It goes on for about a minute.

I'm going to stop smoking, I say.

The microwave dings. I get up and eat the bagel. You can get six for a dollar, so this one is sixteen cents. And the paper is free for some reason, like the cable. It just keeps getting delivered.

I tie my dressing gown, make some coffee, and retire to the fire escape. There's no news. I read the sports section. Things are not going well for the local baseball teams. The leader writer is explaining why the Yankees will never win another championship with George Steinbrenner as the owner.

Sun is coming up. The day banishing the thoughts of yesterday. I stretch and go back inside and decide to shave and shower. I turn on the water for the pipes to get going and look in the mirror. I was in a fight, so it's worth doing an inspection. Really, is this the face of a monster? My hair is sandier than it's ever gotten in Ireland and my stubble is blond too. I study myself. No bruises. Ok-looking, green eyes, good jaw, a wee bit more filled out than I used to be, which is good, because I was always too thin, nice eyebrows, reasonably symmetrical face, bit of a broken nose, though, which fucks things up a bit, but still a decent, dependable-looking chap. Probably, but for the green card problem, I could get a real job, in a real company, for real money. I can do better. I'm not thick.

I'm not thick, I say aloud.

I sigh and take out a new safety razor.

Shave. Stop. I cough and spit. I'm bloody famished. A bagel is just not going to cut it this morning. I take the headlines and quickly dress and turn off the water and open the door, go down the steps, and head for Broadway and the McDonald's on 125th. . . .

It's definitely early. On the far side of the street there are still homeless men sleeping on filthy mattresses on the sidewalk. I wonder for a moment how they manage to get through a night without being stabbed or beaten. Shit, maybe they *have* been stabbed and beaten. The homeless camp from here all the way up to Riverside Park and some sleep in the Amtrak tunnel beneath the park. Generally, only the hardiest ones sleep east of here on Amsterdam, and there a few mad souls who make Morningside Park their home.

If it were me and I was cut off from Darkey and the boys and I couldn't get home and I had to be on the streets (a recurring fantasy/nightmare of mine, incidentally), my plan is to buy a hammock and attach it to a rope and throw it up over a tree limb, hoist myself up, and sleep up there in the canopy. In the summer you could probably get away with it. In the winter you'd freeze to death. North Central Park is where I'd go, big and anonymous and reasonably safe. For some reason, every time I think of this plan it gives me a great sense of comfort. If all else fails, I can live in the trees of Central Park. It's a bit silly, but that's the best I can come up with.

Down to 125th.

Past the bodega and the impressively armored Chinky with its steel walls and buzzer to get in and thicker-than-thick Plexiglas counter and vandalproof reinforced iron chairs. When Klaatu and the other aliens finally show up and nuke the world, Mr. Han's Chinky will, I'm sure, be the only thing left standing amidst the rubble. His food is probably nukeproof too, for it leaves your body about three hours after it enters virtually unchanged by digestive juices. I wave to Simon, who, of course, is up already, but out here in the early light and through that five-inch glass he fails to recognize me.

McDonald's is just opening, and there's me and a line of homeless guys. I order the pancake breakfast and a nasty cup of coffee and sit at the window.

My "hotcakes" come and they forget the syrup and there's a whole ta-do while they find it, and suddenly I'm the pushy white guy making a fuss. I'm not the only one, though. Danny the Drunk is here and he's already plastered. I don't know how he does it. The man has dedication. He's getting a milk shake for breakfast and paying in pennies and nickels. There's word in the building that there's more to Danny than meets the eye, but frankly I don't much care. I don't believe in the homeless sage who has attained wisdom by years of hard knocks and brutal experience. Danny has nothing to teach me. He's a hopeless purple-faced alcoholic, of which I've seen plenty in Ireland, and I'm really not bothered if he was the president of some company or one of the Apollo astronauts or a bigwig at MIT. He wasn't, in any case. He worked for the subways in a ticket booth, but that's a fact getting in the way of the myth and Ratko, in particular, is always ready to emphasize the mysterious nature of his fall.

Since we live in the same building, I suppose he feels a kinship. I can smell him getting closer, and then he comes and sits down opposite, the bastard.

Morning? he says, as if unsure of his bearings.

Aye, I say, head down, shoveling in pancakes with whipped butter and corn syrup.

Cold, he says. Whether this is about the air temperature, his milkshake, or my demeanor, I'm not sure, but I say again:

Aye.

They have the story about the body on 135th?

What?

Your newspaper, do they have that story?

Uhhh, yes, they do, I mumble reluctantly.

It was the story I was reading. They found a body on the campus of City College. Black guy, he'd been shot, and maybe that would have gotten it onto page 23 or something because of the college connection but for the fact that his heart had been removed and straw placed in the cavity where the heart had been. It would grip the city for about a day until the next grisly murder came along, which it would—tomorrow. The police spokesman in the *Daily News* said that in the Jamaican gangs this is what they did with a stool pigeon. It shows that the man had no heart, no loyalty, that he wasn't a real man at all. A dummy.

Stuffed him with straw, Danny said and took a bit of his shake. I suppose liquids are the only thing he can stomach now. I suddenly felt a bit more charitable to the poor bastard, there but for the grace of God, et cetera.

I'm surprised they don't call it the *Wizard of Oz* killing, you know, because the straw man wanted a heart, I said.

That was the tin man, Danny said.

Oh, I said.

More like the Emperor Valerian, Danny said. Heard of him?

Rings a bell, I said, truthfully.

They stuffed him.

Who?

The Persians.

Why?

To mock Rome.

What?

He was taken prisoner and they used him as a footstool and stuffed him when he died.

I was annoyed. You see, this is the sort of thing that gets Danny a reputation for having sense. He really doesn't, but Ratko or someone else in the building will hear him come off with this sort of shite and think that he's on to something. It pissed me off. And I knew that I was going to be forced to tell Ratko this little story and it was going to reinforce all his prejudices.

Have to head, I said and got up.

You want the rest of your coffee? Danny said.

No.

I passed it over; our eyes met for a second.

Did you go to university? I asked him for some random reason.

I did. Rutgers.

Huh, well, look at you now, I wanted to say, but of course didn't.

I dumped my plastic utensils and plate in the garbage and went out. I was dying for a fag now, but I tried unsuccessfully to kill the thought. Danny waved at me and grabbed the paper that I'd left.

Outside it was getting a wee bit hotter, but it was still ok. From 125th you can see up to the City College campus, and I shook my head. It was all a bit awful, that killing; I thought about it while I looked in my pockets for my cigarettes before remembering I'd left them in the house.

Shite.

Later, when I'd come back from the Yucatán and was thirty pounds lighter and shell-shocked and was in a bar with Ramón Hernández, I found out all about that murder and, believe me, it had nothing whatsoever to do with Jamaicans or stool pigeons. The cops couldn't have been more wrong, in fact, unless they'd been deliberately misleading the press. Ramón told me that it was all a Santería thing. The heart gets burned and the straw that would have been burned goes where the heart was. As long as the heart stays in your hearth or fireplace no harm can come to your house; the bigger the villain whose organ it was, the more evil is warded off. Santería is really crazy, but Ramón believes it and a lot of other Dominicans do as well; it's what comes of sharing an island with Haitians, I suppose. But also, you have to ask yourself, how many people in New York actually have a fireplace in their apartment? Not too many I would imagine.

Anyway, at this time, I didn't know Ramón, and after about five minutes that killing went out of my head completely. I was too annoyed with Danny showing off to care about another dead black guy in the long, vague list of horrible violence which was engulfing Upper Manhattan this year.

To walk off my urge for cigarettes, and perhaps for some other reasons, I decided to dander down to the river. It wasn't too far, and there wouldn't be anyone about to hassle me.

Not the nicest walk in the city. Chop shops and tough little bodegas and empty lots. On the left-hand side of the street, the relocated Cotton Club, which seems a sad reflection of the original. Next, the West Side Highway, whose elevated steel girders form themselves into a beautiful series of diminishing arches. A Columbia building, parking spaces, another chop shop, a few guys fishing, but that's about it.

To see people fishing in the Hudson always made me unhappy. They weren't just fishing for sport, they were eating those things or selling them. Little black ones and green ones and big ones that in another universe entirely could perhaps be trout.

Morning, I said to the boys, and I got some grunts back in reply. Didn't want to upset their casting, so I went up about half a block and sat down on some tires. I was sweating now, some kind of hypoglycemic reaction to all that sugar at breakfast, no doubt. Probably kill me.

On the water an enormous garbage barge going up to the 135th Street depot. Farther up, coming under the George Washington Bridge, there was a yacht with its sails tied up and motor on. I sat on the railing for a while, looking at the water, thinking about cigarettes. I decided to head home. Shower, disconnect the phone, go back to bed.

I'll set the alarm for twelve so I don't destroy my sleep cycle too severely. Maybe call that girl later.

I looked at my watch; it was around seven. I wasn't as tired as I should be.

Riverside Park was relatively empty, a few dog walkers, a few joggers, homeless guys, and the Columbia University women's volleyball team, which cheered me up immensely. At the top of the many steps, I had to catch my breath for a moment or two. I went by the dreadful wreck of Grant's Tomb and down 122nd past the music school. I got my keys and did that gun-keys-keys-gun thing I'd been doing recently and went in the building.

I made some more coffee. Showered, shaved again by mistake, brushed my teeth, put on the fan, and climbed into bed. Only about another hour and the doorbell went and it rang and rang and I almost cried out in frustration: Dear God, will no one let me sleep in this world? I got up, and when I opened the door Bridget came in without a word.

*　*　*

Bridget. She is almost too beautiful. Ethereal, poised, elegant. Some days, it's as if she's just stepped out of a poem by W. B. Yeats. Aye, you can imagine her haloed against a dewy wood, singing of Tír na nÓg, summoning you to a barrow in the earth. You would know all this and still you would bloody follow her.

Yes.

Bridget. Heart-attack red hair. A dancer's grace, but with curves and long, long legs and a bum Rubens could have spilled a few pots of paint depicting.

She dresses well, too. Today she's in jeans and a white T-shirt that has a daisy in the middle of it, between her breasts. She's wearing Converse high-tops, which make her look goofy, a counterbalance to the haircut that makes her look a little older. None of this, though, is important. She could be two hundred pounds heavier and wearing a potato sack and it wouldn't make a difference. It's her face. The expressions that move across it like a storm on the lough. The thin nose that gives her an aristocratic bearing. The pale skin. And those eyes. I can't describe them. Lieutenant Narkiss and all other women are put out of your head in a second. Blue and green on different days, but those are just the names of colors. When they flash dark you want to crawl into a hole somewhere, and when they're lit up you feel the universe is too small to contain your happiness.

Bullshit, I know, but once you've seen her, you'll get it.

She was going out with Andy for a while, but Andy has enormous, complex, and ongoing problems with the INS, and apparently the buggers hassled the poor kid so much that he couldn't really give her the time that she deserved. He had to work and he had to get down to the INS office at four in the morning (they only let in the first thousand applicants every day), so Bridget eventually dumped him. Bridget was seventeen then and Andy, who was nearly two years older, was her first boyfriend, I think. It was a very tricky situation, and I, for one, suspected that Andy was relieved not to be going out with Bridget anymore. I'm not a huge conspiracy theorist but if one was of a conspiratorial nature, one might have gotten the impression that Andy was somehow not really into Bridget at all, and in fact he was perhaps the stalking horse for another party entirely. Sure enough, Darkey started going out with her about a month later. Darkey is mid-forties, and her parents might have been more disturbed about the age gap had she not shown that she could handle men by dumping that inconsiderate eejit Andy, who was always arranging to go places with her and then pulling out at the last minute because of his difficulties with the authorities. Though now, with Andy apparently skulking around death's door and in a coma, I'm sure all is forgiven.

Anyway, the upshot of all this is that Bridget is Darkey's girl. Whether she's the only girl, I don't know, but he plays it like she is. They've been going out over a year and there is some old-fashioned talk from Mrs. Callaghan of an engagement. Bridget is the youngest of five and the rest are scattered to the winds at university or in California or wherever, so it wouldn't be such a huge loss for cute wee Bridget to end up with less-than-cute Darkey White. She could do worse, in fact, for although twice divorced, Darkey is sitting pretty with his building business, his glass company, and his shares in Mr. Duffy's various coys. Both Pat and Mrs. Callaghan like Darkey too, and it's not that they're afraid of him; they're not, they really like him. They're afraid of Sunshine (and who isn't?), but Darkey they like and trust.

So poor Bridget, it's all mapped out, and the only alternative would be to fly the coop, but she isn't the type. Besides, the coop suits her fine, and if nothing dramatic happens she will, I suppose, settle down and marry him. I doubt she's in love with him. It's possible that she's in love with me, but who can know their heart at that age. At my age. I am crazy about her, though, and it's not because she's a looker. I don't know what it is, actually, but it's more than that.

Within a minute of coming into the apartment the high-tops were off and the button-down blue jeans were being buttoned down.

This place is disgusting, is her opening line.

I know. I do clean it, Mouse, is my romantic response.

Mouse is the cute pet name I've been attempting to impose on her, with some success. Her name for me was Rat, but I was never very keen on this and it has petered out recently.

Fucking bugs everywhere, she says.

Not literally everywhere.

There's a dead one beside the phone, on the wall, disgusting.

I'm sorry, Mouse.

I mean to say, Michael, can't you get DDT or Raid or anything?

I've tried boric acid.

What about the exterminator?

Been and gone.

So far it's hardly Abelard and Héloïse, but she is naked, which is something. I pull off my jeans and T-shirt and carry her into the bedroom.

Have you got a beer? she asks.

It's hardly my place to lecture her about the hour, so I go get one from the fridge. I take one myself and it hits the spot.

On the bed her back is arched and tense like a long bow, her lips are red, and that's all it takes. She's so pale, you could lose her in the sheets. I kiss her white belly and she lies there and grins at me, that hair curling down onto her shoulder. Looking at her, I sometimes forget to breathe. It's all worth it, the risk, the fear. I mean, Jesus. I slip beside her and we make love, very slow and intricate for a half hour, and when we're done we take a drink and lie there and then we do it all again. Fast this time, frantic. I climb on top of her and she wraps those long legs around my back; she moans and digs her nails into my shoulder. She's intoxicating. Heady. I close my eyes and drink in her smell and feel her touch. I kiss her breasts and her neck and I lick under her arms, and she bites me on the shoulder.

More, she says.

More what?

Shut up, she says.

We screw like I've just been released from prison, and we come together and lie there panting in each other's sweat.

When we're both recovered we have another beer, stick on the radio, and I wander into the kitchen to make her breakfast.

I'm taking up riding again, she says from the living room.

Horses?

No, pigs, what do you think? Darkey's getting it for me.

Nice of him.

He's a nice guy, you know.

Yeah, that's the rumor.

It's when I've made scrambled eggs and tea and a toasted bagel that I remember to ask:

How's the big guy?

Andy?

Aye, Andy.

A little better; he's breathing well. Darkey phoned this morning with info, and he says he's good, he'll be ok. They've moved him to some new place.

What sort of a place?

Different part of the hospital, not the morgue or anything.

Good.

It was terrible. What do you think about it?

I don't want to tell her what I think about it, so I just say:

That's good about Andy. How did you get down here, anyway? The bar must have been crazy still with people.

No, no one's there. Just Mom and Dad and me.

Yeah, well anyway, shouldn't you be in bed? You were up with him half the night.

I was, and me and Mom actually went to visit him first thing this morning. We didn't get in again, of course. Mom says she was always very fond of Andy, which isn't true at all. Anyway, you're right. I am tired. Mouse is tired. I want to sleep here, with you.

I'm suddenly very thoughtful. I wouldn't put it past Darkey to have had her followed. Could be a goon outside right now. It's by no means impossible. Andy getting beaten up and all Darkey's talk about Bridget being his and the young don't have his stamina or whatever. A chill goes through me.

No, seriously, though, how did you get down here? I ask.

I took the train. Where's my eggs?

Eggs are coming.

You know, Bridget, I think in the future we have to be a lot more careful about—

Where are my eggs? she screams, pretending to be a diva.

We eat and go to bed, but I can't sleep. I find myself obsessed by the idea of Darkey tailing her. In my first week in America, Scotchy sold me a pair of binoculars he'd stolen from some guy's car. He said I'd need them all the time in this line of work and, of course, I've never used them. While she snoozes by the fan, I pull on some clothes, grab the binocs, and take the stairs up to the roof. It's a hot day and the light up here is blinding off the water tower and the roof and it takes me a minute or two to adjust to it. I go over to the side of the building and look down. Most of the cars are familiar, but there are four I don't recognize. It's hard to tell if anyone is inside them. If you walk on this roof and over to the next building you can get a better look at the plates and the make of vehicle. I stare through the binocs and memorize all four numbers to write down later. I wait for a long time for something to happen but nothing does.

I go back downstairs to Bridget.

I meet Ratko outside the apartment, and he's coming in to see me. He has a bottle and three glasses. Three. Christ, she must have been pretty damn loud and obvious.

I open the door and shout through:

Mouse, make yourself decent. We've got company.

I hear her wake groggily and go off to the bedroom to pull on some clothes.

Her panties are in the hall, and I crack open the bedroom door and pass them through to her.

Your whips, I say.

My what?

Underpants.

That's so Irish of you, she says and kisses my hand.

Ratko sees me smile and laughs his Santa laugh.

He loves to see me and Bridget together. I sit next to him. She comes out in my jeans and my Undertones T-shirt. Of course, she looks devastating.

Ratko Yalovic pours us a drink from a clear bottle. When he's in a good mood, he pours me from the bottle that has the gold leaf in it, but it's hot and his wife has been on to him about the mice and the roaches, so today it's the rotgut.

He tells us about his problems, which are all domestic, involving wife and child, and are not really problems at all. I solve them with platitudes and clichés and he seems satisfied and genuinely grateful.

We talk about the weather, and he asks Bridget about her life. She gives him answers that are neutral and noncommittal, designed for my ears too.

I ask Bridget if she wants to nap while we talk, but she doesn't. She likes the different company. She kisses me on the cheek as a thank-you for my concern.

Handsome couple, you two should just go off together, Ratko says, maybe getting a little buzzed and weepy from the booze but eerily echoing what I've been thinking for the last couple of hours. For my heart is suddenly filled with warm feelings towards Bridget: a little difficult she may be, but she's good and sweet-natured and you'd be lucky ever to come across such a one again.

Strong childbearing hips, I say.

Bridget laughs, and it pleases all of us.

No, you should go, leave the city, go to country, Ratko persists.

We'd go to California, she says. Or Hawaii or someplace where there's sun and a big ocean.

Sounds good to me, I say and look at her, and she takes my hand.

What's Yugoslavia like? she asks Ratko, knowing that he would love to tell her.

Beautiful country, coast, mountains, rivers, my parents from close to Nis, where Constantine the Great is born.

We could go there, she says.

No, you could go Ireland, Ratko says firmly.

He leans over, clinks my glass, to emphasize his point.

Yeah, we could go to Ireland, she says, liking the idea.

I thought you wanted sun, I say.

It must be sunny sometimes, she says.

I shake my head.

She laughs again.

Sometimes? she asks.

Not a time, especially not in summer, Mouse. Hell no, why do you think they're always killing each other over there? It's the bloody weather. Depressing.

She's not listening.

I really would love to go to Ireland. It's my roots, she says.

She wrinkles up her nose and looks wistful for a second or two. It makes her so unbearably beautiful that I get a little mad at her.

Get Darkey to take you, he can afford it, I say, with a hint of a sneer. She doesn't pick up on it, though.

Oh, he is, next year. We're going for three weeks. Darkey knows someone that owns a castle in Donegal. Maybe it doesn't rain so much there.

Listen, in Yugoslavia, Ratko says, and he's off on some story about the Old Country. This one involves Tito and the National Science Institute's attempt to control the weather for a crucial World Cup match in the middle 1970s. The whole story reeks of bullshit, but Ratko's fat face is choking with laughter, and whether it's true or not all three of us are in stitches by the end of it:

The snow comes—Ratko concludes—and Yugoslavia beats West Germany, two to nil, and Marshal Tito promotes the colonel to general after game and everybody in the whole country but Tito knows truth but we like him, and no one wants to spoil it by telling, and poor Tito go to his grave thinking Yugoslavia leads world in controlling atmosphere. . . .

Ratko laughs, and his face goes pink and he is barely able to contain himself.

Tears are in my eyes, too, and Bridget looks over at me and kisses me. And I'm thinking we *should* run away together. Ratko, of course, is right.

We have another shout, and Ratko must have knocked a few back already this morning because he starts to sing a depressing little Serbian number about the Field of Blackbirds.

Michael, you sing something, Bridget says, and it's not the time and it's not the place and I'm not in the mood, but how could you say no?

Oh Danny Boy, the pipes, the pipes are calling, from glen to glen, and down the mountainside, the summer's gone . . .

I give her the first couple of verses, but I can't finish the song. I'm all choked up and a little disappointed in her. Why doesn't she ever listen to me? I was serious about us going away together. I mean, really, what is there for us here?

Bridget lies down on the couch with a grin on her face, but Ratko senses my mood and a cloud of gloom passes over him, and I know I'm going to have to cheer him up now with the one topic that will please him.

Listen, Ratko, you know the way you're always saying that Danny the Drunk is some kind of genius, well, this morning, I'm in McDonald's and he comes off with some remark about the emperor V—

Why is this place always so dirty? Bridget asks Ratko, sitting up, interrupting me. It annoys me and my mood flips. Maybe we're not so bloody compatible.

Ratko stands, sighs.

I better go, my friend, he says, terribly slowly and tragically, like bloody Topol or some East European dissident being carted off to Siberia. I can see he really has to go, so I don't press him.

Aye, well, see ya, mate, I say, closing the door after him.

I turn to Bridget.

Well, that was nice, wasn't it? I say.

But she's been quiet, and now she lifts her head and stares at me. It's the look. I can tell. She's about to say something that will frighten the bejesus out of me. Please, God, make her not be pregnant. Darkey would insist they get married, and then if it came out looking like me? Please make it not be that.

Let's go away this weekend, both of us together, she says.

Where would we go? I ask, relieved.

She shrugs, tugs at a knot in her hair. She looks like the mouse I always call her.

What happened last night, Michael? she asks.

I can't tell if she's avoiding the question, or bored with the subject, or suddenly remembering that she likes to live only in the world of the possible, or maybe she's just now recalling the horror of less than a dozen hours ago.

With Andy?

No, afterwards. What did you do? she asks.

What did I do or what did we do? I ask.

What did you all do afterwards? To get back for Andy. You had that blood on your shirt, and, and I heard something, she says and does not finish.

I look at her. This baby talk has irritated me, irritated me more than it should irritate me, but it still has.

Ok, Bridget, if that's the game, let me ask you a question. What exactly is it that you think this nice guy Darkey does?

He works, he has a business, she says nonchalantly.

And what is it we do, me and Andy and Scotchy and Big Bob and his boys? We have our union cards, but I'm no brickie or spark or anything like that. I wish I was, I'd get more.

I know what you do. I think I do. Darkey pays Mr. Duffy and Mr. Duffy gives Darkey building contracts and Darkey employs you to make sure that all the regulations are right.

She doesn't fool me. She's being coy. She knows it all. All the ugly little details, which makes me wonder even more what game it is exactly that she's playing. Does she want the details so it strengthens me over Darkey, or do the details strengthen him over me?

Well, that's mostly it, I suppose, I say, confused.

What happened last night? she asks again.

No one died, if that's what you want to know, I say.

Breath escapes from her body and her face loses its rigidity. So that is what she wanted to know. That's the line. Murder is the line. As long as it stops at that. But that's ok. There are worse places to draw it than that.

You should head up. You should head up home, and I'll come on a different train, I say after a moment.

She looks at me. Her eyes are green. Emerald, in fact.

Michael, what do you want to do with your life?

What do you want to do with *your* life? I say straight back.

You first, she says, twisting her hair with a finger.

I don't know. You know, I, I read a lot of books on the train and stuff, I begin, embarrassed.

You read books?

Yes, Jesus, of course. Anyway, I might try to get to college or something. I don't have any O or A levels, but I don't think that matters over here.

She yawns inadvertently.

What does Darkey want to do with his life? I ask, sarcastically.

She smiles in a dreamy way. Jesus, they've discussed it—their future—and it's one she likes. Christ on a bike.

He has all these silly romantic notions, she says.

Darkey, romantic? The thought makes me sick, but I don't say anything. I stare at her but she doesn't see. She's getting ready to go.

I'll take a cab up, she says.

Lucky for some, I say, but it doesn't touch her.

She gets dressed and kisses me with real fondness. I walk her to the front door. She looks at me and kisses me again on the cheek.

Say goodbye to me in Irish, she says.

I don't know it, I say.

Say goodbye, she insists.

Slán leat, I mutter.

Slán leat, she says.

The person leaving says *slán agat*, I say, wearily.

Slán agat, she says happily, kisses me, turns, goes down the stairs. When I hear the front door wheeze open I run up the three floors to the roof and check to see if any of the cars I'd singled out earlier follow her. She's in the street and she's walking down to Amsterdam to get a cab. A blue Ford, which was one of my four plates, turns on its engine and does a U-turn and heads down to Amsterdam. Could be complete coincidence, I tell myself. A cab comes and she gets in, and the Ford accelerates past the cab, just making the light, which the taxi doesn't, and, on balance, you have to think that this is a wee bit of a good sign.

❖   ❖   ❖

The train again. This time it was full of commuters and slightly more cosmopolitan. Harder getting a seat, but I managed in the corner. I got out my paperback. Rich people, Long Island, days gone by. A death.

The crowd thinned as we edged out of Manhattan. I put the book-shop bookmark in and as I did so I noticed that a note had been written on the back of it. "Too much reading, not enough fucking." Bridget's ornamental handwriting. It ticked me off. Bloody dangerous. What if someone in the Four P. says, "What's that you're reading there, Mike?" grabs the book, bookmark falls out, sees the scrawl, recognizes it? Jesus. I ripped up the bookmark and dropped it on the floor.

I got off at the last stop and went up the steps.

Early, Pat said.

Aye, train wasn't as bloody useless as it usually is, I said.

Time for me to pour you a pint, Pat said.

Cheers, I said.

He poured me a pint of Guinness, but Pat, bless his heart, was sec-ond-generation Irish and, in any case, something happens to the black stuff when it leaves the Pale. It takes a real professional schooled in Leinster and within a stone's throw of the Liffey to pour a stout cor-rectly. Pat hadn't got the gift or the patience or indeed the right mate-rials to work with. It wasn't a bad jar for the Bronx or indeed New York, but still . . .

I thanked him anyway and took a big gulp and ate some Tayto Cheese & Onion.

The others arrived and I bought a round, and at seven we went upstairs to the meeting. Darkey must have come in the back way, because I didn't see him till we were up there.

The room was full of cigarette smoke, which was particularly annoying since I was, as of this morning, trying to give up. Darkey was sitting at his usual spot at the head of the table and Sunshine was to his immediate left. Darkey liked to run this side of his operations the way he ran the other aspects of his business. This was a meeting, he was the CEO, we were executives.

We were in the function room above the front bar of the Four Provinces. The room was seldom used for anything else but Darkey's weekly meetings, which usually took less than an hour. Darkey had a lot on his plate, and this side of things he left to Sunshine.

Under Darkey and Sunshine there were two small crews. Me, Andy, Fergal, and Scotchy in one; Big Bob, Mikey Price, and Sean McKenna in the other. Various people floated in and out, David Marley being a good example. Of course, we were one short tonight because Andy was in Columbia-Presbyterian down on 168th recovering from his pretty nasty hiding. When I say crew, it was less formal than that. We didn't really work all the time. Sunshine more or less took care of everything, and it was only in extreme cases that we had to be sent charging in. Pay was a bit erratic too, because Sunshine doled it out in terms of hours worked. If he could have made us punch in and out, I'm sure he would. We hardly ever saw Big Bob and his two boys, because it was the rare day that all seven of us were needed for something. Most of the time Big Bob, Sean, and Mikey did the collections. These were monthly or fortnightly, and it was usually pretty easy work, and I think they got regular pay for it. Certainly they dressed nice (Bob wore suits), and they hardly ever had to do any of the seedier stuff. (They were the ones, too, who got to go to the meetings at Mr. Duffy's in Nassau County, and this made Scotchy madder than anything because that was supposed to be some place. I'd been once to Mr. Duffy's Tribeca pad, and it was spectacular enough.) Under Scotchy the three of us did all the shit jobs: anything that needed doing, heavying, guarding, collecting, a lot of times manual fucking labor.

The arrangements couldn't have been more different from back in the Old Country, where there's a rigid command structure and a cell structure, and everything gets talked to death before anything gets done. Here it was laid-back and informal and looked a lot as if Darkey kind of made things up on the hoof. But Sunshine kept people in line. Basically, my job was as a bruiser. I'd been reluctant to come to America, because from the ages of fourteen to sixteen I'd been part of a gang running rackets in North Belfast. I'd seen some pretty unpleasant things, and when my cousin Les suggested I go to work for Darkey White in New York, I didn't really want to be part of it. I was sick of all that. At sixteen I'd quit the life and run off and joined the army, but that hadn't worked out either. And then I'd been on the dole forever and when my check went up the old fiasco spout I'd really had no choice. Les promised she could get me a job as a brickie like her brother-in-law (and we'd all done a bit of that when on the double), but Sunshine didn't need brickies. So it was the other side of the law. The operation wasn't as big as I'd been expecting, though. Darkey basically ran two rackets, Union and Protection, and with only mild intimidation they pretty much ran themselves. There was some loan-sharking too, but only to the very latest immigrant Micks, and this business was not so important. In fact, I supposed that none of this was that important to Darkey now that he had successfully diversified his portfolio into other areas.

I was dreaming. Darkey was speaking:

So it seems that Scotchy took the initiative and settled things in a way that made clear our position. Shovel is in the same hospital as poor Andy, but from what the doctors tell us Andy will probably be up and around in a couple of days. Shovel will be lucky to be out before Christmas. A job well done, Scotchy.

There were nods and murmurs of contentment. Darkey continued:

And if anyone thought about visiting young Andrew, I'm sure all of his friends would consider this as a nice gesture. I have been to see him already and he's a brave one.

Darkey smiled.

He was a middle-aged man with lots of worries, but I had to admit he looked well. He was pudgy, but he worked out and dyed his hair, and he had a slightly corrupt state senator sort of cast about him. He had blue, almost black eyes. He was lightly tanned, and you couldn't tell him, but he didn't look Irish at all. Arabic, I would have guessed. Scotchy, extremely drunk, sells a story that Darkey's father was in fact some Portuguese boy and not Darkey's father at all, which is just typical Scotchy talk, but you can see where he's coming from. The nickname was inevitable since his last name was White. Hs real name is Terence, but everyone in his presence calls him either Darkey or Mr. White. For a minute, as I was sitting there, I wondered what Bridget called him at home.

He was still speaking. Loved the sound of his own voice:

But once again to that fucker who did him. Excellent job. I heard you in particular performed wonders, Michael. When you want the cream, Sunshine, you have to look to where the pasture is greenest, and Michael, you and Scotchy are two of my very best, Darkey said warmly.

I was, despite myself, glowing with pride, and Scotchy up at the other end of the table turned and winked at me.

Thank you very much, Mr. White, we both said.

Sunshine gave us an appreciative nod too, and Big Bob muttered something like "Well done." It was true that Scotchy, Fergal, and myself were the only real Irish at the table, all of us from the North too, and despite our lowly positions in the hierarchy, being from Northern Ireland did give us a certain cachet. Scotchy typically played his up to the hilt, of course, talking about his teenage scrapes and how to make nail bombs, booby traps, and other crap, but I liked to keep quiet about it, and I think that worked even more effectively.

Darkey's spiel was done and Sunshine took over, telling us about a few wee boring things. Darkey then began again with a bit of talk about some local union election, but I'd long since stopped paying attention. There was some further housekeeping after that, but Sunshine didn't like to burden us with details. The only thing that really stuck in my head was the meeting with Dermot we'd had to postpone from yesterday, Sunshine saying that he would go with us in a few days to impress the serious nature of the situation on the young scallywag.

There was nothing much left, and after a while Fergal, myself, Sean, and Mikey Price were dismissed downstairs. Bob came with us to use the bathroom, gave us a pissed-off look, and went back up.

The bar was pretty full, and Pat had to find us a poky table in the corner. It was Mikey's shout, but I went since Fergal was well into the story of the first part of last night's adventures. When I got back carrying—rather precariously—four pints, Fergal was finishing up the story at McDonald's, except in this version we all got Big Mac meals to show what hard bastards we were.

Mikey was lapping it up, but Sean McKenna had been to federal prison in Texas and had done four years upstate at Ossining or Attica or one of those places and therefore wasn't that impressed by our little tale. You could tell he had something better on the back burner. In his narrative someone was going to be beheaded by a jigsaw or disembow-eled with pliers or crucified to a ceiling or tortured with arc-welding gear. I went to the bathroom before it got started.

I chatted to Pat and Mrs. Callaghan and asked around for Bridget, but apparently she was out with some girlfriends.

When Scotchy came down, he said that Darkey and Sunshine wanted to see me.

This is the moment when I really should run for the bloody door, I told myself, but I didn't have the bottle for it and went upstairs.

Darkey, Sunshine, and Big Bob looking at some papers.

Uh, wanted to see me? I said.

Darkey, not looking up, Sunshine smiling.

Yes, Michael, come over here, Darkey said.

I sat. Darkey turned and looked at me. Bob stood up. To free his weapon hand?

Michael, we talked last night and Sunshine and I were discussing you earlier. I just want you to know that if you continue to be loyal and work hard you will go far with us, Darkey said and handed me an enve-lope containing five twenty-dollar bills.

Thank you, Darkey, I said.

Sunshine grinned. Now be off with you, he said.

I tried not to appear like I was running out of there.

Try to see Andrew, Darkey said as I was just at the door.

I'd had my regulation four rounds anyway and so I said goodbye to the lads. It was a long ride back and, following Darkey's hint (despite my exhaustion), I wanted to stop at 168th to drop in and see how Andy was doing. Not to visit—visiting hours were probably only daytime anyway—just to look in and see how the big wean was.

Try to see Andy, he'd said. As an example of what might happen to those intimate with Bridget? Hmmm.

The hospital was spread out all over the shop, and I had to ask four different security guards before finding the right place, and even then I walked into a huge homeless shelter by mistake.

'Course, no visiting in the ER, and once the nurse found out that I wasn't family, she sent me on my way with instructions to come back at a presumably more Presbyterian hour.

I tried to exit after that but instead found myself in a different part of the hospital entirely. I discovered a bog and went and relieved myself and was just trying to figure out how in the hell I was supposed to get out of there when who should I see but Mrs. fucking Shovel. She was standing there, staring right at me with murder in her eyes and a shaking cup of coffee in her hands. I'm sure Scotchy would have turned and legged it. I should have bolted too. It would have been the sensible thing, but instead I went over to her and said:

Look, I'm not here because of Shovel. I was seeing someone else and I got lost and I'm just heading out. I didn't mean to upset you. Sorry.

She stared at me for a long time, and I thought she was going to lash out or throw the coffee at me, but instead she started to cry. She was sobbing and the coffee was spilling out over the sides of the cup, burning her fingers. I took it out of her hands and led her over to the plastic seats. She cried and pulled out a hanky and blew her nose and cried some more. After a while, she stopped and looked at me again. It was unsettling, and I felt I had to say something.

How is he?

He's awake. Four hours of surgery. Four hours under the knife, pumped full of anesthetic and painkillers and he's fucking awake. Typical of him. The nurses were impressed.

He's a tough guy, I said.

Not against three, she said.

No.

We sat there and didn't say anything for a while. I looked at her.

It doesn't help, but I hope he gets better, I said.

Why did Scotchy have to shoot him? He would have paid. He always pays, she said.

She thought Scotchy had done the whole thing. That I was just help. Well, I didn't enlighten her.

Scotchy thinks he beat up big Andy, cold-clocked him, really gave him a hiding, I said, letting Scotchy take the guilt.

He didn't do that, she said sadly.

Yeah, I know, I said.

There was a bruise turning blue on the side of her face where Scotchy had pistol-whipped her. Her hair was short and blond and it suited her, and it made me wonder why she'd had the wig on yesterday. The wig didn't become her at all. The thought became word.

Are you Jewish? I asked her.

No, why?

You were wearing a wig.

His idea, she said and jerked a finger behind her towards the ward.

Shovel's? I asked stupidly.

She nodded, then shook her head.

I cut my hair short and he hated it, and he said he would make me wear that thing until it grew, she explained.

I wasn't sure if she was serious or not. It was certainly an odd occasion for levity. She was younger than Shovel by a good ten years. She seemed to come from a more elevated social sphere. It made me wonder how they'd met, how they'd got together. It seemed an unlikely pairing now, big boozy Shovel and his demure, soft-spoken wife, but then again, love's a wild card.

Why a brunette wig? I asked.

She laughed. Ask him, she said.

He went out and bought it? I asked.

I don't know, she said and laughed again.

Jesus, he's a bit of a bloody nutter, that Shovel. You look so much better without it.

You think so?

Without a doubt.

She bit her lip and sighed.

I'm surprised at you and Fergal, following that monster Scotchy. He's a mental case. You two must be born stupid.

I hadn't thought that she knew us that well. Certainly I don't recall speaking to her before. But probably she'd seen us in the Four P. or somewhere. I said nothing, and we sat there for a minute or two.

Let's get out of here, she said.

That's what I was trying to do. It's bloody impossible. I've been here since this morning, and I only came to get a prescription, I said.

She gave me a thin smile.

Get me a cab, she said.

She stood, and I got up with her. She led me to the exit.

So I hear he's not going to be out until Christmas? I said.

Who said that?

What I heard.

Be out in a couple of weeks. He's a strong motherfucker.

Aye.

We waited on the street for a while, and she pulled out a gold-covered pack of cigarettes. She offered me one.

I'm trying to quit, I said.

How long? she asked, conversationally.

Since last night, I muttered.

That's when I started, she said.

I saw a cab and hailed it. She got in.

See me home? she said.

I go downtown, I said.

See me home, she insisted.

And that was that. We rode up together, and I paid the cabbie since I was flush.

She walked me up the stairs of yesterday. You hear stories of female Provos who lure Brits into their houses where they or an Active Service Unit kills them. Classic honey trap. And all that time it wasn't completely out of the back of my mind that at some point a pistol was going to be shoved in my face, followed by furious yelling and recrimination and then a muzzle flash, and that would be the end of it. Even as she took off my T-shirt and jeans and took off her blouse and pants and led me into a pink bedroom and a big bed, I wasn't entirely sure that everything was as I thought it was.

You're beautiful, she said.

I asked her her name but she wouldn't tell me. She put her finger over my lips, she didn't want to say anything now. Words were dangerous, they were reminders and could ruin everything.

I held her and touched her. Her breasts were small and her body was thin and supple and that hardness I'd seen in her yesterday was a reaction to us and was not reflected in her kisses and her touch and her warmth. She was so pale, and where Bridget was passionate and businesslike and pretty, she was all need. That was everything about her, and it was almost overwhelming. She was hungry for a body. No, not just a body, I could see that: it was me. It was me, and it almost hurt to be with her.

And this was me punishing Bridget for being with Darkey. Punishing Darkey for loving Bridget.

She could see that I was afraid that she was broken, fragile, but she showed me. She was tender and composed and urgent. She was all need. I kissed her bruises and her eyes and her mouth, and she kissed me and we spent the night giving and being given unto, and sleeping into the new day.

4: ACROSS 110TH STREET

Vignettes: shopping in C-Town; crazy men yelling in the two-dollar cinema; drinks in the Four Provinces; evening collections with Scotchy; Fergal dinging a gypsy cab and having a go at the cabbie; a black girl's body in Marcus Garvey Park; two lads going at it with a knife on 191st Street; Bridget leaning over and kissing me for the first time as we changed the kegs; an empty lot bursting with trees and life on MLK Boulevard, and opposite, a hurt guy on a bike splayed in front of the Manhattanville post office; rows of fresh fruit in West Side Market; flattened rats; pepper trees; whole plazas of urine; me and the boys extorting some guy in Fordham into giving us a ton a week for doing precisely nothing; the bakery on Lenox; soul food at M&G; delivering a sofa set for Darkey to some cousin in Yonkers, up two flights and past a goddamn corner; the Nation of Islam screaming at me at the A train stop on 125th; the doe-eyed girl with her boyfriend in the hall; Sunday service all along the hot street in the morning, Christ's children in a merry wee conspiracy of happiness; choirs; the tiny, forgotten synagogue on 126th; the Ethiopian lady wandering half-naked in the lobby; Ratko's Santa laugh as another bottle opens; rice and beans on 112th; KFC; McDonald's; rice and beans at Floridita; M&G again; the Four P.; Bridget; Bridget again . . .

The whole summer's events compressed into a single point. Eight weeks in one second. The colors, smells, humidity, tastes, all of it condensed into a moment, folded and pushed together like an old-fashioned brass collapsing telescope.

An instant. Held. So much brighter than Belfast. Faster and richer, too, and not in the sense of money.

Life flashed, and I was momentarily stunned. I got down.

Hit the deck.

Hit the deck.

Yelled.

Holy fuck.

Noise.

Breathed.

Breathing . . .

I was breathing hard, sweating, and then, to my horror, I realized that I'd been shot in the left hand, a ricochet. A chunk of flesh had been ripped away behind the knuckles, leaving an angry gash that was just figuring out that with this level of injury it really should be starting to bleed.

They must've got me when I'd stuck my hands up over my face and it had taken me and the hand some time to realize what was happening. What was happening, of course, was a cock-up of tremendous proportions, a cock-up perhaps just as big and scary as the multifarious and diverse fifteen-year-old-boy cock-ups I'd gotten myself into in North Belfast and Rathcoole. It didn't, however, necessarily have to be a fatal cock-up, because we were all very close to the door and Dermot had blown the gaff by not having a man cover behind us to cut off an exit.

It was five days after the Shovel incident, and I was in a shoot-out at the long-postponed meeting at Dermot's place. When I came on board, Scotchy had promised that there would be the occasional shoot-out. The way he said it was the way kids would tell you about a game of Cowboys and Indians. Scotchy said he'd been in Bandit Country and I'd been in North Belfast, so neither of us should be strangers to gunplay, but in America there was a glamour that attached to things. He and Fergal could talk up a storm about some shindig they'd gotten into in Inwood Park a year or two back: bullets whizzing, Fergal taking one in the foot, two black guys running for the hills by the end of it. The details were vague and unconvincing and informed, seemingly, by years of TV and the movies.

But this, unfortunately, was the real deal. Eight months working for Darkey, and the worst I'd seen was Scotchy and Andy giving some boy a powerful, coma-inducing hiding. No, be honest. The worse I'd seen was actually me and Shovel. I mean, I'd hit a couple of recalcitrant types myself, but mostly our actions could be implied with menaces. But now in the space of a few days I'd delivered Old World violence into a New World setting, and now I was in a real honest-to-Jesus fire-fight, one that conceivably I might get killed in. It was some kind of apotheosis, some kind of tear in the fabric of things, and if I was of a suspicious nature I might have been suspicious.

I was behind the bar with Sunshine, and on the other side in a more exposed position were Fergal and Scotchy. Andy, of course, was out in the car, and if he'd any sense at all in that thick head of his, that's where he'd stay. Andy was only out of hospital that morning, and Scotchy, instead of letting him rest, had brought him down with us to a potentially hazardous assignment.

I really should have known to stay in bed, because today already had been atypical. The trains had all come promptly, the weather had taken a cooler turn, and although not a big believer in omens, I'd won twenty bucks on a scratch card in the fake bodega on 123rd. Unpleasantness was sure to follow.

Our original plan was to have Andy's coming-off-the-sick party all day today but Sunshine had put flies in that ointment with his patience suddenly collapsing in the face of Dermot's singular insistence that he was fucking "quits with you, Sunshine, and if you and Darkey know what's good for you, you'll be keeping out of my fucking way."

Now Dermot's men were shooting at us with automatic weapons, big ones, too, and they were carving up the bar above us and making a hell of a lot of noise, enough noise to grab the attention of the neighborhood and lure it away from the Yankees game. Sunshine was shaking like a Jell-O-molded pudding that has somehow attained sentience and is being shot at with machine guns. He was staring at me in abject terror. I was breathing.

What the fuck are you doing? Sunshine asked.

I was in no mood to give him an answer. Sunshine's fabled brilliance with intelligence had let us all down here. There were at least two shooters and Dermot himself and maybe a bloody barman, and Sunshine had failed to warn us about any of this.

I'm centering my *chi*, I said.

What?

Centering my *chi*.

You're centering your fucking *chi*? Sunshine asked, frightened.

Aye.

How long will that take?

Not too long. My life was flashing before my eyes earlier, I said, a little less angry with him now and hoping to calm his nerves.

It was?

Yeah.

And now you're centering your *chi*?

Aye.

The big Kalashnikovs, or whatever they were, were shooting at us from semidarkness in the lounge bar a good fifty feet away from our position. What Dermot's plan had been was none too clear, because it didn't seem to be the ideal place at all for an ambush. More than likely Dermot had told his boys to let us come completely into the pub and then open up on us from oblique angles; but the boys must have been inexperienced or jumpy or cracked up because they'd started as soon as we'd walked in. Sunshine and I had dived for the bar. Fergal and Scotchy had ended up near the tables. About a minute and a half had gone by, and I'd spent all of it flashing my recent life before my eyes and lying on the floor with Sunshine trying to figure what was going to happen next. It seemed to boil down to three possibilities: they'd get us, we'd get them, or maybe we'd all get nicked.

I mean, although shooting was not uncommon after dark in this part of town, even if it was just guys firing off .9mm clips into the air, it would really be expecting too much for the average lazy, frightened copper to ignore this palaver. Although this was Washington Heights, it was midmorning and these were machine guns. The nonincarceration window of opportunity couldn't be more than about five to ten minutes.

Scotchy was signaling at me from across the room. The shooters almost had a sight line onto him and Fergal, and he was making some kind of gesture for me to stand up behind the bar and let them have it to draw their fire, enabling the two of them to get in a better position, maybe scramble over to us.

I had a .22 revolver, and there was no way I was standing up anywhere and firing at anyone with that. The .22 was there to intimidate a little bit and wasn't really a gun you'd shoot. Not that I'd have a semiautomatic anyway, because the only time you'd ever need it, the thing would be sure to jam on you. Your revolver, your serious Yankee revolver, a .38, will shoot clean, dirty, waterlogged, and arse-deep in a blanket. Sunshine had a .38, and I suppose it was conceivable that I could have carried out Scotchy's dubious plan with Sunshine's gun, but really the smarter play was to pretend not to understand what Scotchy was talking about and just to nod and do nothing.

I did this and Scotchy started miming again, more furiously. I looked at Sunshine, but he had his eyes closed and was muttering what I took to be the Rosary. It surprised me. He'd always seemed the scientific, agnostic type, but I suppose atheists, foxholes, all that.

I could see through the door that there were people outside now, the usual eejits who show up and get killed by a stray bullet, but I knew that at least none of them were calling the authorities. It was a mental couple of blocks, but it knew when to keep its mouth shut. Malcolm X had been assassinated just around the corner, and there had been a six-person homicide just last month, so we weren't Halley's comet or anything, but if things went on like this for much longer, you knew that an annoyed new mother trying to kip would call it in, and some wanker would eventually turn up to lecture us through loudspeakers and then teargas us out and lift us. It was all fucking inevitable—well, unless Dermot's boys got their shit together and killed us first. Either prospect was less than pleasant, and I knew that perhaps I really would have to do something. What, exactly, I wasn't sure, but something, a withdrawal by sections or a mad dash for the door or a truce, something. Sunshine's mutterings got louder, and Dermot's boys stopped shooting and shifted a wee bit and started getting an even better angle on Scotchy behind the overturned table, churning up the floor with huge slugs that sent burning splinters all the way over here. I thought for a moment or two, and cleared my throat.

Dermot, Dermot, you Fenian wee cultchie, motherfucker, parley, fucking parley, I shouted. There was no reply, so I shouted it all again with increased vehemence. But still nothing.

Dermot Finoukin was a new boy in town from Toome in County Antrim. He was something of a smoothie—NEXT suits, holidays in Ibiza, charm, a midnight blue MG midget—but he'd done the wrong boy's daughter and upped and left for the New World under sentence from a top player. He'd opened a bar in the tiny Irish neighborhood around the 160s and Broadway. It was a disastrous and foolish scheme, because the Micks were leaving for better places in the Bronx or Jersey or Queens and Dermot didn't encourage patronage from Dominicans or Puerto Ricans. The bar, when we went, was always empty. Sunshine had loaned Dermot a bucket of money at 50 percent a month on the collateral of Dermot's knowledge of and access to a cache of weapons compiled for the Provos somewhere upstate in 1988 and then abandoned because of the arrests of the principals in the case. Sunshine was no fool and expected the bar to fail in about three months and then we'd get our hands on the guns and move them on to people who needed them most, people who, coincidentally, generally lived in Dermot's neighborhood. But as it turned out, Dermot's strategy wasn't as stupid as it looked because he made his payments every month and even gave us a good bit of the capital back; in fact, sleekit wee Dermot didn't give a shite about the bar, and the whole time he'd been manufacturing crack cocaine in the basement under license from a local boy known only as Magic Man. Magic Man, it turned out, was really a fellow called Ramón, and Ramón would, much later, be a helpful little bee to me, too.

Anyway, Dermot's was a nice setup and perplexed young Sunshine for quite a while until somehow someone ratted and Sunshine had insisted on accompanying us on a visit to Dermot's to investigate these claims for himself. What was even better was that the rat was probably Dermot himself and this wee operation was a move to bring us down there and wipe us out with a minimum of fuss and then move his crack factory to new premises in a whole building on St. Nicholas. It was supposed to go something like this: kill us, dispose of us, set fire to the bar, disappear, and then when Darkey investigated, there wouldn't be a trace. Dermot would be debt-free, well established as a cool customer, and he could sit and make his fortune, giving the odd handsome donation to the Provos in the Bay State who would thereafter provide him additional insurance cover. It wasn't a bad plan as harebrained, unworkable, ill-thought-out schemes go, and the killing-of-us bit was the most doable part of the operation and at this point, I'd say, had about a fifty-fifty chance of coming off, unless one of us could think of a way out.

Dermot, you cultchie cow-fucking bastard, parley, are you fucking deaf? Parley, I yelled again.

The shooting went on for another few seconds and then abruptly stopped.

There was a pause, and then Dermot yelled out from somewhere: What?

Dermot, listen, it's Michael, listen, bloody listen. Peelers are gonna be here in a minute. Your boys fucked up, fucked up big-time, can't get us from where you are.

See about that, Dermot said, menacingly.

Wait, you fucking wanker, wait. You're not getting us and we're not getting you, and the peels are gonna show up sooner or later, and then what? Slammer, five years, and then deportation. Is that what you want?

One of Dermot's boys yelled something in Spanish and the shooting started again. Sunshine grabbed my arm and was having some kind of asthma attack. I looked over at Scotchy sarcastically, asking him to get a load of this, but Scotchy's face was contorted with rage, either at me or his predicament, you couldn't tell. The shooting stopped.

What do you suggest? Dermot shouted.

Cease-fire and withdrawal. You let us go and we'll give you twenty-four hours to get to pastures new, I said, and looked at Sunshine to see if that was ok with him. Sunshine seemed to understand and nodded.

Who says I want to go anywhere? Dermot yelled.

Listen, Dermot. What was the idea, were you going to kill all of Darkey's boys? You must be heading somewhere. You can't sit it out here, you're not that powerful.

There was a long silence and in it we could hear sirens.

All right, Michael, your word. You'll give me twenty-four hours if I let youse out? Dermot said.

My word and Sunshine's too, I yelled.

I turned to Sunshine.

Tell him, I whispered, tell him.

My word too, Sunshine yelled, somewhat shrilly.

Ok, Dermot said.

Ok, I said.

What now? Dermot asked, uncertain.

Uhhh, we get up and you don't shoot us, I said.

Scotchy was shaking his head at me and mouthing "Fuck no," but he didn't say anything. He had that much sense, at least.

Ok, that's all right, Dermot announced.

So we get up and you don't shoot us and we back out to the car and get away before the peelers come, ok, all slow and simple like, ok?

That's ok. I agree, Dermot said.

Sunshine was tugging at my sleeve. I crouched beside him.

What? I asked.

Are you sure this is going to work? he asked.

I think so.

How do you know he won't shoot us as soon as we get up? Sunshine said nervously.

He *will* shoot us as soon as we get up. That's the whole plan, I said and took his .38.

Sunshine paled.

I looked over at Scotchy and did a little pantomime of my own now. I leveled the .38 and showed that I was going to keep it by my side and then bring it up fast to full extension and shoot. Scotchy looked at me quizzically, and then he seemed to understand. He whispered to Fergal, and Fergal shook his head before Scotchy pulled some sense into him by the hair. It was really just a copy of Scotchy's dim-witted plan that I'd dismissed earlier as completely ridiculous, but there didn't seem to be anything else. It wouldn't be the first time I'd been shot at; as it turned out, it wouldn't be the last, either. I had the bottle to do it. If Scotchy had it too, we might just be ok.

Ok, Dermot, we're getting up, no shooting now, I said, and then in a whisper to Sunshine: You better stay down.

I looked over at Scotchy. He was psyched. Say what you like about Scotchy being a dick and all, but he comes through for you when you need it.

I nodded.

He nodded.

Scotchy was ready and, shit, was that boy a fast one. Fergal you could discount, but Scotchy might do something.

The problem as I saw it was that with our handguns there was no way we could get in a decent shot at the opposition without exposing ourselves. With a machine gun you can spray at random, but a handgun needs a target. I'd figured—and Scotchy had telepathically agreed—that the boys with the heavy equipment would open up as soon as they saw us. The muzzle flash would show us where they were, and we could try to take them out with our pistols. Scotchy was a shot and I wasn't bad myself, but the whole plan depended upon Dermot's boys being an awkward squad and not really able to control a big gun like a Kalashnikov, which was hard enough to aim for a pro.

It was risky.

This won't work, Sunshine said.

It'll work, I said.

I nodded at Scotchy; he nodded back. We started getting up, and it all took place in an instant. Sunshine, of course, was right. It didn't work.

Sure enough, we stood and the boys opened up, and they were so excited the weapons rose and tore big holes in the ceiling above our heads. I took the fire on the right-hand side and let go three rounds. Scotchy took the left and got off his whole clip. I wasn't sure about him, but I might have hit something. It wasn't enough, though, and both of us had to hit the deck again as the gunfire starting getting our measure.

You didn't get them, Sunshine said.

I shook my head.

And it is true we didn't kill them, but Fortune, however, had not completely neglected us. We had hit someone, and after a moment we could hear him yell. An argument began in Spanish.

The sirens now were even closer.

Dermot, can't you see we're all fucked? Completely fucked. You have to let us go. You go out the back way and we go out the front, I yelled.

Kill them, Dermot was screaming.

Fucking come on, Dermot, you fucking brainless cunt, Scotchy contributed.

I waited for the reply, but the argument was still going on, and then there was more gunfire. Scotchy leaned his gun over the top of the table and shot back blind. The shooting from their side lasted only another second, and then it stopped.

Jesus, Dermot, can't you see we'll all be in the shite? I yelled again.

I listened for any response, but this time there was complete silence. I looked at Scotchy and he shrugged his shoulders.

We heard the back door bang, and immediately Scotchy stood up.

They've fucking scarpered, he said.

It was all very fast now.

I pulled up Sunshine. Scotchy, suddenly all business, made a break for the back office to get cash and any papers relating to Darkey before the boys in blue got there. I followed, but before we got back there we saw Dermot lying sprawled on his side, bloody and quite dead on the floor. There were several big holes from the AKs.

Accident? Friendly fire? I asked him.

Scotchy shook his head, either to say he doubted it or didn't know. I stood and looked at the body for a moment or two, paralyzed. It was the first corpse I'd seen since working for Darkey. Fergal snapped his fingers in front of my face.

Come on, he said.

To be told off by Fergal was just too much. I followed him to the back office. There was a blood trail that led to the back door. It began to fit into place. We'd hit one of the boys, the boys had wanted to go, Dermot had been against this proposition, and you don't get into an argument with a couple of lads with Kalashnikovs. At least not at point-blank range.

The sound of sirens was close, a few streets off. There was a mini-safe in a false cupboard by the wall. Scotchy, whose talents I some-times underrated, had already searched the drawers, found the safe, and was shoving it out.

You're going to have to help me carry it, no time to open it, Bruce, he said.

Fuck it, I said.

Bruce, listen. Can't leave anything for the cops. Give me a hand.

Thing must be twenty stone, I protested, but I was already putting away the .38 and crouching down.

Knees bent, keep your back straight, Scotchy was saying, calmly, as the sirens got still closer.

Do you want a hand? Fergal asked.

Get Sunshine out to the car and come back and then give us a hand, Scotchy ordered Fergal.

Fergal went off and we lifted up the safe. It was a complete bastard, and we got about ten feet before dropping it.

Fucker, come on, Scotchy yelled.

We picked it up and got it as far as the door before Fergal showed up to help.

Crowd, he said.

We carried the safe outside, and there was a bit of a crowd. About twenty, all men, some yelling in Spanish, most mute.

Get the boot open, Fergal, I yelled, and he went and opened it. Andy was revving the engine, nervous, shitting himself, no doubt. We dumped the safe and got in the car, Scotchy in front, all the rest of us in the back.

Is everybody here? Andy asked.

Drive, you fucking fuck, Scotchy yelled at him.

Some people clapped, and a man from the crowd told us to do a U-turn, 'cause the cops were coming from the other direction. He cleared the people and directed us down towards the river. I knew when the peelers did show up, he'd point them in exactly the opposite direction. Helpful bastard.

Andy was panicked and got us on the West Side Highway and then almost over onto the George Washington Bridge, but he got himself together and took us east and up into Inwood. We stopped the car and adjusted the safe so that the trunk closed properly and then Scotchy, Fergal, and Sunshine got out and took the train up in case they were looking for five people. I had to stay with Andy because I was still bleeding. Indeed, after all that, I was the only one hurt (not counting Dermot or his boy).

Andy was still close to hysterics and almost got us into three or four accidents.

You know, we drive on the right in America, I told him as he turned left into the left lane of an intersection.

Been here longer than you, he said huffily and got us on the correct side of the road.

Yeah, but I didn't lose half my brain cells in a coma, Andy, I said.

Neither did I, Andy said, angrily.

True, half of nothing is still nothing, I said.

You're a very negative presence, Andy said, fuming.

But it had worked. I'd distracted him, and for the rest of the trip he huffed and calmed down.

We went over the bridge onto the mainland of North America and up Broadway and out of that weird cut-off bit of Manhattan, and we were safely back at the Four Provinces before Pat even heard the first of the reports on the police radio.

❊   ❊   ❊

My hand hurt, and it woke me. Mrs. Callaghan had bandaged it because bloody Bridget Nightingale had been off with dickhead Darkey at some poxy place in Long Island. I hadn't seen her in a few days, and it made me wonder if the ardor was fading or whether Darkey was getting more protective.

It was a pisser. Andy's party had had to be postponed. Everyone getting shot at had spoiled the mood a bit. It was rescheduled for tonight.

I'd got the 1 train back, gone to the apartment, slunk to the sofa, slept. I felt awake now and in pain and dirty. Fucking shooting people for a living. What kind of a life was that? Bloody ridiculous. Jesus, I wasn't fourteen anymore. I was practically twenty. In a couple of weeks, in point of fact. Maybe it was time to turn over a new leaf. I wondered if I'd paid off my plane ticket yet. Jesus, but what would I be going back to? Nothing. Bloody nothing. Fucking rain.

It was late afternoon now, so I dialed the number, put on an accent that I hoped was Jersey Shore.

Is Bridget there?

Hold on, Mrs. Pat said.

A long pause and then that voice:

Yes?

I haven't seen you in forever, I said.

It's been impossible. Our schedule has been so busy, but, uh, don't think I haven't been thinking about you, Bridget said.

I want to believe you.

It's true. Listen, M—, listen, I can't really talk here. I'll call you, ok?

Ok.

She hung up.

I looked at the phone for a half a minute.

I stripped and went into the shower.

I felt filthy. I scrubbed and soaped myself and scrubbed again. I sat down on the floor and let the water come over me. I banged the floor and cursed for a minute or two. I remembered what I'd said to Sunshine about my *chi* and laughed. I washed my hair and got out. I was absolutely bloody famished, so I decided to go down into Harlem to get some Chinese. It was hot now, so I dressed in shorts and a cotton T-shirt and desert boots. I still had the .38 and there were slugs out of it, probably in some crime lab right now being looked at by some bespectacled fuckwit. Somehow, I'd have to get rid of it. I wiped it and washed it and put it in a plastic bag. I got my backpack and put the gun inside with a book and a water bottle. I went downstairs. In the hall, steam was again escaping from the heating. I dodged the jets, put on my sunglasses and Yankees hat, and turned right towards Amsterdam.

There was a building Dumpster on the corner. The street was empty, so I took out the bag with the gun and threw it in. It was as dumb a place as any, but whoever found it around here would probably keep it.

I went by the projects, crossed 125th, buzzed the Chinky door, and Simon let me in.

I told him I'd waved to him last week but he hadn't seen me. He apologized. The place was clean, and there was a new calendar with views of Hong Kong Harbour. Simon looked well. He stared at me from behind the bulletproof glass.

Wha happ your han? he asked.

I cut it, banged into something, hurts like a bastard, I said.

You gey stiches?

No, I didn't. I bandaged it up myself.

Go to emergence room Sin Luke, no quessions. They do it, quick, no quessions.

I thought you had to fill in lots of forms and stuff.

Do, fill in fake name, Simon said, as if he knew all about it, but really, someone must have told him and he was just passing it on.

I'll think about it, I said, knowing full well I would never be so stupid as to go to the emergency room with a heavy-caliber gunshot wound the same bloody day as a major shooting involving heavy-caliber weapons. Besides, it would be a cool scar.

When, much later, I had been betrayed twice, lamed, severely traumatized, and had a .22 slug in the gut, and I thought I was fucking dying, my scruples, however, somewhat lessened and I actually did take myself to trusty old Saint Luke, painter, Greek, bit of a fabulist, and, of course, doc.

But that was still to come, and for now I could afford bravado.

Fuck it, Simon. Useless quacks will take your bloody hand off by accident or something, I said.

Simon laughed, and I could sense his brain filing away the word *quack* for later use.

I ordered curried pork with fried rice and sat in the corner with the three tabloids I'd bought. I'd already read the *Times*, so these would do for lunch. I ate some pork and rice and drank some of my Coke. It was another hot one.

The air-con above the door was hardly making a difference.

Hey, Simon, you wouldn't put the air up a wee notch, would ya? I asked, but he wasn't coming out from behind that bulletproof glass if it was World Peace Day and it was the pope and the Dalai Lama asking him. He nodded and went back to watching a Bob Ross painting show on his black-and-white TV. Bob's stoner voice relaxed me.

Before I could open the papers, the door opened and Freddie, our mailman, came in. I knew him quite well, because we'd talked about getting me into the postal service as a casual when I'd first arrived. Bureaucratically, it was impossible, but we'd talked and he'd helped get me a bar job. He was a huge black man in his forties, three hundred pounds at least, stereotypically jolly, and seemingly happy with his lot. Even on a day like today when the heat must be murder for him.

Michael, he said, shaking my hand, I haven't seen you around.

No, I've been working, Freddie.

Shit, man, where you working? At Carl's?

No, Freddie. Don't you pay any attention? I was only there for a week, just until they fixed me up, up in the Bronx.

Freddie grinned and ordered an egg fried rice and a sweet-and-sour chicken and spring rolls and sat down beside me. His mail cart was outside, and on 125th Street you'd think that someone would have wheeled it off, but no one did.

That was some funny shit, you working in Carl's, you know, the only white dude in the whole joint. You musta taken some.

I did, I agreed, but I still go in there sometimes, Freddie, not regular, but I go.

Carl's was a bar a few blocks east of here. I'd worked there while Scotchy checked me out and passed me up to Sunshine for final approval. It wasn't called Carl's anymore, and I didn't go in there ever, but I wanted Freddie to think I was a cool customer.

Freddie, though, didn't give a shit whether I was a cool customer or not. His grub was up. He ate his food with gusto and we chitchatted about this and that, mainly sports. We ate and talked, and Freddie finally had to leave. I was sorry to see him go. He was a good presence in people's lives. A horrible, lazy mail carrier, but a good man and about the only black guy I knew in the city. He was a steady bloke and knew a bit, and I would have liked to get his perspective on one or two things, but daylight wasn't the time and we were both sober and it was too soon after recent events to be levelheaded about them.

Listen, if I'm at Carl's this Friday, will you be around? I asked him as he was going out.

No man. Apollo. Monday, Tuesday maybe, he said.

Really, Tuesday? I don't want to go down there and stick out like a sore thumb and you not show up.

Michael, what's on your mind? Women, huh? Freddie asked with a huge grin.

I nodded and said I'd see him, but of course by Tuesday I was in fucking Mexico and not destined to be back in Harlem for quite some time.

I finished my food, which was so loaded with MSG I was starting to see visions.

I said a pleasant cheerio and went outside and fixed my shades and my hat. Freddie was chin-wagging with some Costa Rican guy, and he introduced us and then he disturbed the hell out of me by asking if I was still seeing that big-chested, redheaded girl, which could only be Bridget, and here I was thinking that I was Mr. Secret Agent Man with her, but if the goddamned postie knew then half the fucking city knew.

I told him no, I'd never been seeing her and that he was mistaken.

I went down to the 125th IRT stop. I thought about calling Mrs. Shovel (her name was Rebecca); she wanted me to call, she would be waiting. But no. In New York, at least, Bridget was my girl. She was mine. It was all her. Darkey would fuck up. He'd hit her or get drunk; she'd come to me, we'd fly away together, over the ocean. Safe. Aye, oh aye . . .

The train came, and I took it to the Bronx.

*   *   *

It troubled me that now I was mixed up in a killing. We were implicated in the death of Dermot and surely this would amount to something. Surely the cops would be on my trail, pounding doors, relentless. That's how it was on TV. But, in fact, Dermot's death barely even registered. It made no difference whatsoever. A drop in the bucket. No one stuffed him with straw, so it didn't even make the evening news.

I was still concerned, though, for if you look at the newspapers of the early nineties, they're absolutely full of stuff about organized crime in New York. There were over three hundred FBI agents working on breaking the Mob's power in New York City, and to your average reader it seemed that every bloody cannoli shop was bugged or video-taped and every second dough tosser in your local pizzeria was a bloody federal agent. You saw rat after rat and trial upon trial on TV, U.S. Attorney and later Mayor Giuliani grinning in the Sunday papers and boasting about how he was sticking it to the Families. It wasn't him alone, by any means. I mean, there were the cops, the FBI, treasury men, state police, tax guys, even the fucking Royal Canadian Mounted Police. So you'd think with all this that it would be impossible around then to run an operation like Mr. Duffy's or like Darkey's, but it wasn't.

It wasn't at all.

For as exciting as the Mob story was in New York in the early nineties, the grander narrative wasn't their decline, their collapse, their self-immolation. No, the big story was the drug-addled slaughter taking place nightly in Harlem and the South Bronx and Bed-Stuy. The big story was who was moving into the vacuum created by the decline and fall of the Mafia.

And the truth was that above 110th Street the rules were different. No one seemed to care about what happened up there; certainly, in all the time that I was in Harlem and Washington Heights, I never came across a single agent, a single narc, a single goon.

Not that it would have made much difference even if the Feds had ventured north of 110th, because Darkey was very smart. Very goddamned smart. Darkey concerned himself only with recent Irish immigrants, the poor wee illegal weans fleeing 30 percent unemployment and a civil war and of whom there were tens of thousands in Riverdale, Washington Heights, and the odd wee pocket in the Bronx. Those boys and girls weren't going near the cops, never mind the United States government. It wasn't Boston and it wasn't San Francisco, but look at the INS figures for Irish immigrants to the United States in the late '80s and multiply that by about a dozen and you'll have some idea of the scale of what I'm talking about.

Of course, the Micks weren't just going uptown. Woodside was a big draw in Queens, and there was Hell's Kitchen and the Upper East Side around Second and Third. But that was someone else's space. Not Darkey's, but probably still under Mr. Duffy. The point of all this is, I suppose, that despite the FBI and despite Mayor Dinkins and despite the cops, Mr. Duffy and Darkey weren't having any bother at all. I shouldn't have worried about the peelers looking for me. Jesus, I was nothing. I was protected, and Darkey had them confused and bent. I was safe as houses. Sunshine would look out for us all, and our

Darkey was charmed and on to a sweet thing. He had no legal concerns; potential enemies were destroying themselves; the Micks kept coming. He had his girl, his crew, his skinny guardian angel, and but for that flabby and slightly pockmarked face of his you could say he was sitting pretty. So, as I sat there later that night in the public bar of the Four Provinces getting hot and drinking vile Harp Lager and feeling a wee bit sorry for myself and a wee bit anxious about the morning's events, I had to admit to myself that I really shouldn't be that concerned. We were fine. And I told myself that things were going to be ok and go on that way for the old foreseeable. Darkey was raking it in and it would trickle down to us and we'd get fatter and richer and maybe we'd retire in a year or two and get to a university or have a bar ourselves somewhere.

And sure enough, events might just have gone that way but for a process already in motion that three of our little crew knew about, but crucially not me and not Scotchy.

But again, that's the future and this is now, and at the minute I was getting a bit eggy about the death of some wee shite called Dermot and getting all existential about organized crime and the racial nature of policing policy in NYC.

You look troubled, Andy said.

Do I?

Yes.

Oh.

What were you thinking about?

I was thinking that we're bloody lucky we're uptown, otherwise the peelers would be down our fucking necks.

Yeah.

You ever see that film *Across 110th Street*? I asked him.

No.

No, me neither, but I bet it makes some pretty good points about organized crime and the racial nature of policing policy in New York. Peels don't care what goes on up here, fucking don't care, I said.

Andy cocked his head.

What's the matter with you today? he asked. Do you want to be fucking caught?

No.

Well, Jesus.

All right, forget it, excuse me for thinking, Andy. Big mistake around here. Forgot who I was talking to, I said.

Andy looked hurt.

Joking mate, joking. Sorry. Tell me, big fella, how ya feeling? I asked him.

Andy started telling me how he was feeling, and I sat there. Keeping it in, nodding my head, making him think I was interested in the bollocks he was spieling me. Sighing, scratching my arse, Andy jabbering, me drinking, listening, and neither of us had a clue that Scotchy was going to come down the stairs in ten minutes and blow all of my concerns about the cops, the city, and every other aspect of my present life not just out of the water but out of the universe in which water can even exist as a molecule of bonded hydrogen and oxygen.

Yeah, it's coming. And I should have been up there at that fucking meeting to register my protest and see Darkey in the face, but I wasn't because I'd gotten there late.

The meeting was still going on, but Andy was down here now because all the smoke had been making him a bit sick. He was telling me about the stuff I'd missed, and apparently it had been exciting.

Fireworks, Andy said, and went on to explain that Darkey (a bit unreasonably, I thought) considered the whole Dermot thing a complete cock-up because Dermot was dead and the peels were involved. Darkey had exploded at Sunshine and given him a really big seeing-to. He must have been really furious or else this was the standard Andy exaggeration. I looked at old And. He was big and blond and dopey-looking. He wasn't a complete idiot, but he wasn't going to be invited to the Institute for Advanced Studies anytime soon. He was really sweet, though, and he didn't deserve that beating the other day. Scotchy needed a beating, Fergal did, but Andy didn't.

Turn your head, I said.

He turned his head. He had a few bruises on him but he looked ok. You don't look too bad, you big eejit. Want a pint?

Aye.

I went up and bought him a Guinness. I got myself a bottle of Newcastle Brown and came back.

Have you seen Bridget? I asked him.

Aye. She told me this joke.

Was it about parrots? I asked.

Yeah, it was funny.

Where is she now? I asked.

Think she left with Darkey, going to the opera or something, Andy said.

They've both gone already?

Andy nodded.

Says she's thinking of changing her name.

What?

Yeah, to Brigid. Pronounced the same, but it's the Irish spelling, apparently. She's the patron saint of Ireland, along with Patrick. Bridget says that she was the earth goddess, mother Eire, that the early Christians co-opted to—

I never heard anything about this, I interrupted him.

Oh aye, you're out of the loop, Mikey, Andy said, and his mind jumped to other things: Tell you it was wild, boy. This morning, I mean. I mean, Jesus, I was keeking it. Really, keeking my bloody whips. I had no clue. No clue at all what was going on. Just sitting there revving. And waiting for the peels. All those bloody people. You'd think it was a parade or a free show or something. Me just sitting there. All in Spanish. I have it, you know. The lingo. Too fast, though. Christ, Michael. Look at you, all calm. You're cold, man. You and Scotch standing up and shooting, cool plan.

Didn't work.

Sure it did. You must have got him.

His own boys shot him, I said.

Not the way Sunshine sold it. Said you were aces. You and Scotch. Jesus. Cold. Super cool. Why didn't you think they'd shoot you? You boys. I didn't know, though. I was just sitting there. They say that's the worst. The waiting. At least you were doing something. Ha, I'm sure you boys were thinking up excuses for the meeting with your Maker. Is this Guinness? Tastes funny. Hey, and you know I heard what you did to Shovel, thanks for that. Thanks for getting him.

It was nothing, I said. I tried to think of something to change the subject, but nothing came, and on he went about his driving.

And on my first morning out of the hospital, too. I mean, you have to admit it was impressive.

It was impressive.

It was, wasn't it? he said, his eyes wide and excited.

Aye. And you're feeling ok, big lad?

I'm ok. I could have been out yesterday, but they were covering themselves, Andy said.

Nice nurses?

Not really, although there was this one girl from, like, Jamaica or something. I thought I was hitting it off but she was just being nice, I think.

You get her number or anything? I asked him.

Nah, nothing like that. Here, you want some chocolates? he asked.

I wouldn't say no to chocolates. These wouldn't be a present by any chance, would they? I asked.

Aye, behind the bar for safekeeping, Andy said, grinning.

I let him get another round and the chocolates, which I had contributed five bucks towards, so they better be pretty fucking special. He came back. I was drinking lager now, because of the heat. It was extraordinarily bad stuff, but easier going down than the Guinness.

What you do after? he asked, giving me my pint.

I picked out a hazel log and a couple of caramels and a nice nougat one. I shoveled a couple in at once.

What? I asked him.

What did you do after this morning?

Uh, nothing. Slept.

I couldn't have slept, could you? he asked.

I just told you I slept.

Tell you, you're cold, man.

Thanks.

I was pumped. Pumped. Suppose for you it was all automatic, but I had to sit there, just sit, you know. Then drive afterwards. How's your hand, by the way? Scotchy says you were the only one stupid enough to get himself hurt.

Scotchy said that?

Aye, when he was telling Mr. White and before the fireworks. He was dead calm at first, you know, Mr. White, I mean, he just listened, and then goes all ape and starts yelling at Sunshine—

What exactly did Scotchy say about me? I interrupted.

Nothing. Just said typical Bruce got himself a nick to show the girls. It was jokey, like.

That bastard Scotchy. He was lying on the floor keeking *his* whips, and I was the only one doing anything, I muttered.

Sunshine appeared at the top of the stairs. I nodded a hello and he came straight over. He was smiling. He'd had what was left of his hair cut, shampooed, and plastered on his scalp. Must have needed the attention after this morning's debacle. He didn't seem perturbed in the least by Darkey's firestorm, and I wondered if Andy was completely yanking me.

Michael, I want to talk to you, he said.

Sure, go ahead, Sunshine.

Over here, Sunshine said, and led me over to the bar.

This is for you, he said and gave me an envelope. I wanted to be cool and not look, but I couldn't help it. I opened it and there were ten fifty-dollar bills inside. More than twice (after Darkey's taxes) what I got in a week.

What's this for? I asked.

For this morning. If you hadn't talked with him, we all would have been arrested. Or worse. You convinced his employees, not him. But that was enough. You saved my bacon, Michael.

Our bacon.

Yeah.

Well, look, thanks for this, I said.

It's not much.

No, thanks, anyway.

Scotchy made the report, but I told Darkey what you'd done, Sunshine said, significantly.

Aye, I know. Andy was just after telling me, I replied, sounding pissed off.

Listen, I made sure Darkey knew what happened, Sunshine whispered.

He looked at me; he seemed odd and off-kilter. Still shook up from the morning. He wouldn't go on a job again in a hurry, I thought. Conditioner wafted at me from his strands of hair.

Uh, again, thanks for putting in a word, I said, finally.

Michael, we're very much alike, you and me. I think you're a bit underappreciated around here, but don't worry, I know what you did. Anyway, enjoy yourself with that.

Ta, I will, I said.

Don't mention it. Literally, don't mention it, he said.

Ok.

He wanted to say something else, I thought, but instead he just nodded and went back upstairs. I had to run after him.

Listen, Sunshine, I got rid of your piece, but I'll need mine back.

He looked at me and grinned as if this level of competence was unheard of.

Well done, Michael, always thinking. That hadn't even occurred to me. Of course I'll get your .22 back or anything else you want.

The .22 will be fine. I don't think we'll get in anything like that again.

We won't, he said, firmly.

Ok.

He padded up the stairs and then stopped halfway. He came back down again.

Michael, look, whatever else happens, I just want you to know that, that . . . I'm really grateful and sorry. Thanks.

He turned and went back up again.

How fucking weird, I thought.

I stuffed the envelope inside my jacket and dandered back to Andy.

What was that all about? Andy asked.

Uhh, nothing, um, gave me a bit of roasting for being late, nothing major, but he didn't want to do it in front of you, didn't want to embarrass me. Considerate, I suppose, I said.

Aye, he's like that sometimes, Andy agreed.

Yeah.

See the state of him, though. He got a manicure, you know, like a fucking poofter, Andy said.

I must say, Andrew, I disapprove of your homophobia, I said.

My what-a-phobia? Andy said, having never heard the term before.

Most of the great generals have been gay or at least bi. Alexander, Caesar, Octavian, Marlborough, the list is long, I said with an air of world-weariness.

I don't know what you're talking about. Are you saying Sunshine's gay? Andy asked.

No, I don't think so. There was some talk of a girl, but anyway you're missing my point, Andy, my point is—

Jesus, you don't think I'm fucking queer? Andy interrupted, but before I could reply Scotchy and Fergal appeared on the stairs, both of them grinning like a couple of banshees. They went to the bar and came back with four pints and chasers.

Pick up your Bushmills, Scotchy said, sitting down and giving us one each.

We picked up our shorts dutifully. Scotchy took a breath for what promised to be a long-winded toast:

Gentlemen, raise your glasses and listen up. Because of our recent good works and our years of dedicated service (in your case, Bruce, nearly a year of dedicated service) and our recent near brushes with death and the forces of law and order, we have been given the fucking plum of fucking plums. Drink.

We drank, and Scotchy sat there grinning at us. He filled our glasses again and winked at us. I wasn't going to give him the satisfaction, but Andy cracked.

Well, what is it? Andy whinged, desperately.

Andy, my boy, you are lucky you are off the sick because, my young friend, you and me and young Fergal here and even Bruce (and unfortunately Big Bob too) are all off to the climes south of the border to the sunny Republic of fucking Mexico.

Mexico? Andy said.

Ayeup, Mex-eee-co. Girls, tequila, beaches, music, more girls, you name it, we are there, boys. Sun, sand, and fucking R&R. Glasses up and down the hatch, Scotchy yelled.

I brought the glass up, but I couldn't drink.

Sometimes, occasionally, now and again, a hint of the future will leak into the present. Not often, but it happens once in a while. You feel it in the back of your neck or your toes or fingertips. At that institute in Princeton that Andy's not getting invited to, they'll tell you that events take place at the quantum level and the light cone from these events extends backwards as well as forwards along time's arrow. And sometimes, if you're attuned, sensitive, you get a hint. This was one of those times. As soon as Scotchy finished his toast, a shiver like Baikal ice went down my spine, as if in premonition.

Scotchy shoved me.

Drink up.

I looked at him, ignored the message from the future, and drank up.

Somebody walked on my grave, I muttered.

Aye, well.

What's the job? I asked him, to cover any embarrassment.

Job, nothing. The job is the smallest part of it. The job, Bruce dear, is your proverbial slice of pie, forget talk of the job. Think rather of long walks on the golden sandy beaches of the Caribbean Sea with charming señoritas and a room of your own in a luxury villa to take her back to. Think of booze and pot and swimming and lasses by the score. Uncle Scotchy has fixed us up.

When do we go? Andy asked.

We leave Saturday, Fergal said, excitedly.

What if your passport's not in order? Andy moaned.

Then you can't fucking go, Scotchy snapped.

Andy looked at us gloomily.

I'm not sure I'm allowed to leave the country while my INS status is being investigated, he muttered.

Andy, of course, had been silly enough to enter the system while all the rest of us had let Sunshine get us passable work permits and visas.

Don't go, Andy. More girls and booze for the rest of us, Fergal crowed.

Andy looked on the verge of tears. Last week and this morning and now this.

Don't worry, you'll go, Andy. Sunshine'll sort it, won't he, Scotchy, I said, giving Scotchy a look.

Oh, oh aye, aye, don't worry, Andy, only joking. 'Course you'll go, can't do it without big And, Scotchy said, hurriedly.

Really, we'll fix it? Andy asked me.

We'll fix it, And, I said, and he smiled.

We all looked at one another and grinned, and then we started to laugh. We were getting out of town. Getting away from the daily grind. Going to bloody Mexico. We were laughing, and the tears were running down our faces. It would be such a relief. The timing couldn't have been better. All the tensions evaporated and we drank and talked, and even when Bob showed up, he couldn't dampen things, and we bought the bastard a round and stayed so late Pat had to throw us out so he could get his weary arse bones to bed.

5: WE GO TO MEXICO

New York City. The abiding blue of the Atlantic. The sweeping curve of coast. Woods, fields, cities, great spits of land given up by rivers. Swamps. Islands. Keys. The Caribbean Sea. Jungle. Down.

Our place was a villa on the lagoon side of the Cancún strip. Large and white, ringed with palm trees. It had a veranda and a swimming pool under an overhang. The pool had leaves floating in it, but not that many. I guessed that the last occupants had left a week earlier. The bedrooms sprawled over the top floor, big and airy with watercolors of local girls. The beds themselves were huge wooden affairs with eiderdowns.

I picked a room, lay down on the big bed, and closed my eyes. There were birds and the sound of a bell, and if you imagined just a little you could hear the ocean. I slept for an hour or two and got up and showered. The boys were down at the pool, passing around a bottle of rum. Scotchy was dressed and ready to go out and was urging them to hurry the fuck up.

I read Bernal Díaz's book about the conquest of Mexico until they were all ready, a cheap Penguin edition but a great plane book. Cortez had just appeared and the Spanish were getting their shit together. They came close to Cancún and stopped at an island nearby. Isla Mujeres. I went out to the balcony on the east side of the house to see if I could get a glimpse over to the ocean and spot any islands, but you couldn't see through the trees. In any case, the boys were all set. I got changed and splashed some water on my face.

After some confusion we got through to a taxi service on the phone and went to a restaurant that Sunshine had recommended, though how he knew we'd no idea.

The restaurant was near the bullring and served Mayan food and Mexican food and all of it with lime and all of it hot. Excellent stuff. We all enjoyed it except for Fergal, who loaded up with tons of chili sauce and could barely eat it. We had about a six-pack of Corona each and tequilas afterwards.

It was a nightclub next. We took a bus to the resort area. Scotchy paid the cover for us, and we went in.

I was too beat to dance or drink, so I just found a quiet cushioned place in the corner. The music was ten years behind the times and consisted of New Romantics and disco. They kept playing some Bowie song from 1981 over and over as if it was the latest thing. If it hadn't been too loud, I might have slept again over my cocktail.

I lay on a couch and drank and watched the boys make eejits of themselves. Scotchy joined me and I raked him about the aftershave he had poured on himself, stuff that, were it released into the wild, would make Rachel Carson weep. Scotchy had no idea who Rachel Carson was and called me a pretentious wanker. We both got margaritas, but before the conversation got maudlin, big And came over. He'd got himself a girl and wanted advice. She was a skinny-looking lass of perhaps dubious virtue, which Scotchy and I agreed was a good thing.

I told him to say nothing, but to hint at great depth. Scotchy told him to ask her if she had any Irish in her. Whatever tactic he took seemed to work because soon he was snogging her in a corner.

I tried to ask Scotchy what we were going to be doing down here, but he explained it had to stay secret until tomorrow. And with Scotchy such a big blabbermouth, it really must have been a secret, so I didn't press him.

Around midnight the place started to fill and the tempo picked up a little. More Yanks came in. Bob cried off home, saying his belly hurt, and we were all glad to see the back of him. Scotchy was having a spastic attack next to a group of girls, but he didn't seem in much distress, so I assumed that this was him dancing. I was doing my own low-key moves near the bog in case Montezuma got me as well as Bob. But I was ok. Fergal had been bringing me things with umbrellas in them, and they'd given me a second wind. Everything was in a haze and speeded up, and before I quite knew what was happening I was in a bus with a blond girl wearing cutoffs and a University of Kansas T-shirt. We were kissing. She looked like she could be Bridget's pudgier, blonder, slightly younger sister. She talked a lot about nutrition.

She said her hotel room overlooked the water, and when you got up to it, seven floors, you could believe her because it was as black as pitch out there. She took the blankets off her bed—one of three beds in the room—and went out onto the balcony and laid them down. It seemed a very foolish thing to do, because the place was crawling with ants, but she explained that it was so we'd be private when the other girls got in.

The thought of two other girls showing up conjured interesting visions in my brain for a while, and my focus was elsewhere. She went back inside and brought us beers, and we sat and looked at the party boats cruising past in the darkness. I kissed her and pulled her down onto the blankets, but I had a very hard time getting hard. I hadn't seen Mrs. Shovel or Bridget or any girls, for that matter, for four days, and you'd think a healthy young man, on only his second ever holiday abroad, would have no problems getting into the swing of things. But the booze, the girl, the flight, the anxiety, all played their malicious little parts, and it took an incredible amount of concentration just to stay in the game. Finally, and heroically, I managed to get it together just long enough for her—but not actually long enough for me—and the girl yelled loud enough to let most of peninsular Mexico know that she was adequately fucked. My head was spinning and, but for my innate Irish politeness, I would have thrown up over the balcony. I breathed in the sea air and asked her where she was from. I'd never heard of it, so I said that that was nice and she asked me where I was from. I told her, and it came to pass that she had a whole host of relations from County Cork. We talked about the multifarious delights of the southwest of Ireland and a little about *The Wizard of Oz*, the only thing I could think of that involved Kansas. My gaffe with Danny the Drunk had already demonstrated my shaky knowledge of the film and, unfortunately, she had seen it and had strong opinions about it; she explained that she, you know, despite appearances and everything, had been brought up right and her folks hadn't held with making light of devilry and witches and such. I said that from what I remembered the whole thing was a dream, and she told me that that was besides the point and that she was good folks and her grandpappy from Tennessee had been a juror in the famous Monkey Trial. Neither of us quite knew what the Monkey Trial was, but I imagined it was some antivivisection thing and praised her grandfather for his civic duty.

We sat up and drank some more beer, and there was a lighthouse. I counted the flashes, and I lay down on the blankets while she talked about some famous University of Kansas football team and then some more about nutrition. My diet, apparently, was completely wrong; indeed, everything I ate came from the top of the food pyramid rather than the bottom.

At four in the morning it began to rain, and we moved into the bedroom, where I was introduced to two other girls who, in fits of giggles, demanded to know my name and what college I was from and whether I had used protection.

She whispered to them that for most of the time I had been unable to perform; at this stage I pretended to be asleep.

The pretense transformed mercifully into reality. I slept on the floor and woke with the dawn.

I dressed and slipped out. I had no idea where I was, and I was still a little drunk and looking ragged. I pissed against a wall, and a copper slowed down; he would have booked me if I'd been a local. He saw that I didn't have the lingo and was some kind of Yankee bastard. It could have been the luckiest fucking break of my life if he had lifted me. But he didn't. Instead, he swore and spat and drove off muttering. Under a huge Mexican flag, a nasty little boy threw a stone at me, and it hit me on the back of my head. I chased after him and ended up even more lost than before. A Mexican man and woman out for a walk saw that I was in some distress and tried to help, but we couldn't communicate. They insisted on walking me at least part of the way to the shoreside hotel strip and then gave me change for the bus. The bus didn't come, however, and from there I wandered around Cancún for another two hours before eventually finding the airport road and, by a process of reverse geography, the villa. The front door was open. Scotchy was fully dressed and on the phone with someone.

There you fucking are, you fucking get. I thought you'd bloody fallen under a bus or something, he yelled at me.

Morning to you, too, I said.

I suppose it was some wee tart, lucky bastard. Find yourself a coffee and a bun and get your shit together, we have to go pronto, he said, remembering this time to cover up the receiver on the phone.

She was a very nice girl, actually, I muttered.

Fergal and Big Bob were in the kitchen making eggs. Andy was upstairs having a shower. When he came down, I could see from the glow off him that his night hadn't been unsuccessful.

Tell you, Michael, I'm quitting this thieving game and getting into higher education. All these girls at college. Don't know what we're doing with ourselves, he said to me over coffee.

She was all right then, was she? I asked him.

Andy was insulted. This wasn't some piece of stuff, this was a real girl with whom he had bonded and joined souls and reached dizzy plateaus of intellect, all of it in her hotel room for almost forty-five minutes.

All right? My God, she was wonderful, wonderful, Andy said, protesting a wee bit too much, I thought. Andy must still have been freaked out by my observations on sexual preference, and I considered for a moment messing with his head but decided against it.

That's great, Andy, I said.

Yeah, Michael, it really was.

So you pulled. Well done. Took my advice, kept your mouth shut, then, eh? I asked him.

I didn't say much, but I didn't need to. She was so interesting, Michael. She was studying history. There's so much history, you know, there's a whole stack of it, all this stuff out there, Andy explained.

I looked at him to see if he was being funny, but his face was expressionless.

So you want to pack in the life of the highwayman and turn to academe. Andy, my lad, it's funny you should say that. Actually, I was having the same thoughts just—

You want some eggs? Big Bob asked from the kitchen.

Aye, what type?

Scrambled with stuff in them.

What sort of stuff?

Onions.

Aye.

Fergal came over. He was grinning with jealousy at me and And.

Aren't you the boy too, Michael. Jesus, Scotchy says she was a real looker, Fergal complained.

Did he? Was she? I said, and we all laughed.

The eggs came, and they were fine. Andy pontificated about possible majors he could undertake, and I assured him that with his large frame and youthful exuberance he would be sure to get an American football scholarship at some university. I told him that Kansas had a good program.

He slapped me on the back and started telling me further about his new philosophy of existence and the delights to be had in the life of the mind, and he kept on about it even though he could see I was in no fit state to listen to his bollocks. Scotchy came in to save me, telling me to shower and get changed. I went upstairs. The back of my neck was all bloody from something. I remembered the stone. Wee bastard. I showered and pulled on my boxers, button jeans, and an old brown T-shirt. I grabbed some sandals. Everyone else was wearing shorts, and I would have gone back upstairs and changed had we had the time.

The rental car came, and Scotchy tipped the delivery driver. He asked for a lift back with us, but Bob told him to fuck off. Scotchy got in the front with Big Bob; the rest of us got in the back. Big Bob had a map and for the next forty-five minutes they argued about directions before figuring out the place to go. I only noticed then that Bob was carrying a large shopping bag from Zabar's. It was odd, you couldn't imagine a less likely person to shop in Zabar's. I thought for a minute and then I got it. Sunshine went to Zabar's. It was Sunshine's bag. It contained money. We were swapping the money for something. Either drugs or guns. Drugs. What drugs? I was never to find out.

I started to giggle and couldn't stop.

Andy poked me in the ribs.

What's so fucking funny? he whispered.

We're smuggling knishes, I said, pointing at the Zabar's bag. Andy laughed because I was laughing, but I don't think he got the joke.

Would youse shut up back there and act your ages, Scotchy said angrily.

We drove on for a bit and when we were close, they stopped the car.

Here, boys, Scotchy said, and reached round and gave us each a pistol. They were huge, old-fashioned things from World War I.

Where did these come from? Fergal asked.

Need-to-know basis, boys, Bob said, annoyingly.

Scotchy, what's the job? I asked, pretending that Bob didn't exist.

The job, Bruce, for you is just to stand there and look menacing. Me and Bob are taking care of everything, Scotchy said, soothingly.

How are we going to get drugs back into the States? Smuggling is like ten years, you know, I said.

Ten years? Fergal sputtered.

Who said anything about drugs? Scotchy growled and looked angrily at Big Bob.

I never said a word, Big Bob whispered, unsure of himself.

Don't you worry, Bruce, it's all been thought of. This is going to go smooth as silk, Scotchy said, looking at Andy and Fergal in the mirror the whole time.

Bob was sweating but Scotchy looked calm, so maybe it would go ok.

They drove for another five minutes and stopped again.

We're here, Big Bob muttered up from his map.

We'd halted in a poor neighborhood in the north end of town, right on the edge of a marsh. The road was a track and the houses were finished only on one side. They were two stories and seemed as if they'd been built in the last few months. Maybe they would look ok when they were painted and the marsh was drained and the road was better and Cancún got a planning board and Mexico got sustainable growth, improved infrastructure, and an end to one-party rule.

Are you sure this is it? Scotchy asked.

Aye, he's drawn a wee bit in pen where the map ends. This is it, Bob said.

We all got out of the car. There was no one around. The houses didn't even look occupied. They had no electricity or phone lines.

It's a fucking slum, Fergal moaned.

It's not, it's a new development. Expansion, that's what it is. They all start like that, Scotchy insisted.

It's the wrong place, there's nobody here, Andy said.

I think it's the wrong place too, Fergal agreed.

Let me see the map, Scotchy said and grabbed it out of Bob's hands.

It's the fucking place, Bob said, sure wasn't I in—

Whatever Bob was in was not to be discovered, because the aluminum house door opened and a voice said:

Señores.

Scotchy looked in triumph at Fergal and Andy and marched down the dirt path to the house. Bob turned to us.

Ok, boys, weapons in your trousers. You won't need them; don't do anything stupid. Be super cool. These boys don't want any fuss. You hear me?

We nodded, and Andy said: I hear you.

We walked down the path to the house. There were tire tracks from several vehicles in the clay soil, and at the time I thought this was a bit odd. Tire tracks but no sign of a car. I didn't think about it too much, though. We went inside the house. Dust was everywhere, and it smelled of resin, wood sealant, and tobacco smoke. Scotchy was in the front room with three Mexican guys in jeans and T-shirts. They were talking in English. Scotchy presented Big Bob, and they shook hands with him. We weren't introduced. I leaned up against the wall. My throat ached from last night and all the dust in here wasn't helping. Big Bob opened the shopping bag and brought out bundles of twenty-dollar bills. One of the Mexicans opened a satchel and gave it to Scotchy. He looked inside. There was white powder inside plastic bags. He gave it to Big Bob to check, but before Bob could do anything the side door burst open and two men in ski masks appeared with pump-action shotguns. They were yelling:

You are under arrest, you are arrested.

The Mexicans all produced guns and screamed at us to lie down on the floor.

A man appeared behind me and I tried to shove past him and make a break for it, but there was no chance. With infinite patience he blocked me and hit me on the head with his rifle butt.

❖   ❖   ❖

The cell was very nice: new and concrete, and if you stood up and held on to the bars you could see out over Cancún and towards the sea. It contained an iron bed, a plastic-covered mattress, thin black woollen blankets, and a stainless steel toilet without a seat that lurked in the corner but worked well when I flushed it. It was all a bit dark, but clean. I paced twelve feet by eight feet, which wasn't too bad at all.

When I woke it was night outside, and I was very disoriented, but soon I climbed up to the bars and stared out over the town. There didn't seem anything else to do but go back to sleep, so I did. I lay down on the bed and kipped quite well, considering.

In the morning, the door opened and a very old guard came in with toilet paper and a stainless steel cup of water and tortillas with bean paste on them.

Buenos días, I said.

Buenos días, he said and laughed.

His teeth were terrible, but his grin was infectious and I found myself mirroring it.

Eat fast, I take away, quick, he said in heavily accented English.

I ate the tortillas, which were warm and spongy. The water was ice-cold and hit the spot.

He took the water cup and the tray and ripped me off about four sheets of toilet paper and went for the door. Another guard stood in the corridor with what I took to be a stun gun in case I tried anything silly.

Where are the others? I'm an *Americano,* I want a lawyer, I said anxiously.

The guard shrugged, didn't reply, and closed the metal door behind him.

I sat down on the bed.

Jesus fuck, I muttered, and put my head in my hands. I sat for a long time and I think I might have gotten weepy a little. I cursed Scotchy for the eejit born of an eejit that he undoubtedly was. I yelled out Scotchy's name, Andy's name, all of their names. I yelled and yelled and banged the walls. I listened for answers, but I heard nothing. A few hours after the guard had gone I heard some tapping and I thought it might be a *Darkness at Noon* type of message or something, but I realized after ten minutes of eager listening that it was the plumbing in the ceiling above me.

I seemed to be alone in the whole cell block. Had the others escaped somehow? Or maybe they'd tried to shoot their way out and they were dead. I paced the cell and tried to stay calm. Panic was mounting inside me and I wasn't sure if it was a good thing to let it out or not. Maybe I should.

I banged the floor and thumped the mattress and tried to lift the bed, but it was bolted down. I kicked at the toilet, but it was pretty indestructible too.

I want a fucking lawyer. I'll have you all on fucking *60 Minutes,* I screamed through the door.

I groaned. Every time I go abroad I end up in the bloody slammer. Saint Helena, here. I must be bloody jinxed. No, just an idiot. Trusting Scotchy with something as important as my entire future. I deserved it. Really.

I sat down on the floor and found myself laughing.

That glipe Scotchy. That dick Sunshine. Ten years we'd get for this. Fucking drug smuggling. I could protest ignorance. I mean, I really didn't know anything about it all until that morning. I could volunteer to take a lie detector. I didn't know anything. It was just bad luck.

Night came, and even after all my anxiety I slept well. The bed was extremely comfortable and the cell was cool. In fact, it was a lot nicer than my apartment in New York.

In the morning the guard brought more tortillas, bean paste, water, and a lime. I ate and drank and he left more toilet paper, even though I hadn't shat in a couple of days.

I did some push-ups after breakfast and stretched a little. I lay down on the bed and waited. Something would happen, eventually. And, of course, it did. Late in the afternoon, two guards appeared and asked me to get up. They didn't handcuff me or prod me or anything, they just asked that I follow them. Once I was outside the cell, one of them offered me a smoke and I took it. They led me down a corridor and they opened up a metal door with a set of keys. On the other side of the door, a guard was waiting with a machine pistol. He smiled at us, and we went along another corridor and stopped outside an office. One of the guards turned to me and said, confidentially:

Clean, clean.

He tucked my T-shirt into my jeans and the other one signaled that I should brush down my hair. When they thought I looked ok, the first guard knocked on the door.

Enter, a voice said in English.

I went inside. The office was large, with books and box files on the wall. Seated behind a teak desk was a thin, elegantly dressed man in a dark suit. Behind him an enormous window overlooked the lagoon. There were family pictures and prints of Mayan ruins. I sat down on a leather chair opposite him.

Mr. Forsythe, let me show you something, he said in perfect American English.

He reached into a drawer and set three sheets of paper in front of me. They were confessions in English and had been signed by Scotchy, Fergal, and Andy. As I read through them, the man spoke:

Possession of an illegal weapon, possession of controlled substances, conspiracy to smuggle narcotics, attempt to smuggle narcotics. Mr. Forsythe, you are looking at over twenty years in prison.

Who are you? I asked him.

The question upset him. He had forgotten to introduce himself. His whole rehearsed little speech had gotten off on the wrong tack. He tried to recover.

I am Captain Martínez, he said.

Captain of what? I was thinking. He was in civvies, but maybe that's what they did down here. I read the confessions. They were all the same, detailed, sensible, predictable. I could see Andy and Fergal signing but Scotchy never would. Never. They were shite. I knew this game. It was an oldie but a goldie.

So what do I get if I sign? I asked.

Three years.

Three years?

Three years.

Guaranteed?

Guaranteed.

Aye, but three Mexican years is like nine Irish years. Prisons are like dogs: America, you double; France, time and a half; in Sweden nicks are so nice, you actually divide.

Like dear old Queen Vic, he was not amused.

I picked up the paper and looked at the signatures. They'd copied Scotchy's off his passport; the other two might be genuine, but I doubted it.

Where's Bob's? Robert's?

Mr. O'Neill is being dealt with separately. He is an American citizen; you and your friends are not.

I had to concede that this was true. We were all in on Eire or UK passports. But there was no ring of truth at all about what he'd said. Had they killed Bob in a shoot-out? What was he covering up?

How about getting me a visit from a consular official or something? I asked.

Everything will be taken care of, Captain Martínez said.

No, really. I want to see the British consul, like, today.

Let me show you something, he said, giving me a little grin I didn't like one bit.

He stood stiffly and went over to a cupboard. He opened it with a key and wheeled out a new television set. He turned it on and pressed a button on a VCR that was underneath it. Black-and-white video began to play, of us doing the deal at the rendezvous. Scotchy was opening the money bag and taking possession of the drugs. The rest of us were standing around waiting. Martínez froze the frame when there was a good shot of me.

Making a big mistake, mate. I was hitching. Them boys give me a lift, told me to wait in the car but I came in anyway, I said and smiled at him.

He glared at me and turned the TV off.

You always hitchhike with a firearm?

Dangerous country, but I'll cop to that if you like. What's that these days, big fine, couple of months?

Here, he said, and reached under his desk. He passed across the same form that the others had supposedly signed.

Go easy on yourself, Mr. Forsythe. It is only a token. You will be released in perhaps a year or a little more. Please go easy on yourself, he said.

Like I was saying, Mr. Martínez, sorry, Captain Martínez, when exactly do I get to see my consular representative? I'm a British citizen, and I want to see someone from the fucking embassy. If I don't, I'll make sure your name gets bandied about, I said, calmly.

You are in no position to make threats, he replied, equally at ease.

We sat in silence for a moment, and then he stood and motioned for the guards to take me away. I got up and walked down to the cell again. At the door I asked for another smoke. I was giving up, but surely these were extreme circumstances. I wanted to save it for later, but they wouldn't give me a match, so I had to light it now.

They locked me in.

That night the old guard came with water and tortillas. He sat with me until I'd eaten and then surreptitiously he produced a piece of lemon cake from his pocket. It was soggy and a bit tart, but clearly his missus had made it or something, and the gesture was so unbelievably nice I got a little teary. I talked to him in English, and he said a thing or two in Spanish and left.

At dawn the next morning, instead of breakfast, the guards came and cuffed me behind my back. They were gentle about it, and I appreciated it.

Where to now? I asked, but they didn't understand.

They led me along a different corridor to an elevator.

I felt a wave of despair and terror. If I didn't get in the elevator, nothing too bad could happen. I struggled for a bit, but they saw it was halfhearted. They shoved me and I went in, meek and head bowed. They pressed the button for the basement, and when it stopped they took me out to a van. Inside were Scotchy, Andy, and Fergal. I was pleased to see them, but before I could say anything a guard held my head and put some duct tape over my mouth. The boys had been similarly gagged.

The guards helped me up and into the van. There were two benches opposite one another and an iron bar running along each side wall. The guards undid one of my cuffs and hooked it behind the bar at my back so that I could sit but not move forwards, and barely to the side. Two of the guards got in the front, and I could see another car waiting behind us with a couple of peelers inside. They would presumably follow us in case one of us was Houdini and could get out of cuffs and the bloody iron bar. I made eye contact with Scotchy, and he gave me a nod and then a wink. That boy was a hard case. It reassured me. A fuck-up, yeah, but a tough nut to crack. We sat while one guard filled out something on a clipboard. This reassured me too. Paperwork. We were in the system somewhere. They couldn't pretend we never existed. The other guard took the paper, folded it twice, and put it in his front pocket. That, by contrast, didn't look so good. Somebody out of sight closed the van's back doors and in another minute we were off.

❖   ❖   ❖

The van drove quickly out of town and onto a straight road. There were no windows, so you couldn't see anything except for a little scrape in the blacked-out glass partition between us and the drivers. Through that, there were tiny glimpses of what I took to be a two-lane highway through what looked like jungle. It must have been a pretty good road, since we weren't bounced about and the vehicle managed to go quite fast.

The boys seemed in ok shape. No bruises and no cuts. We looked each other up and down to reassure ourselves, and Fergal tried to say something, but we couldn't understand him and he eventually gave up. Scotchy closed his eyes and somehow managed to doze. The rest of us laughed behind our gags when he started to snore.

After a couple of hours, the van turned, and this time the road wasn't so good. The going was slower, and we followed this trail for about another hour.

Finally, the van stopped, and we heard voices outside and then, very slowly, we heard it move again as if we were pulling in somewhere. Scotchy woke and the boys tensed up.

The back doors opened.

The sunlight blinding. A huge trail of dust that you couldn't see through. A smell of piss and shit.

I blinked a few times. The dust cleared. We were in a prison.

Four guard towers hung over a central courtyard, and around the courtyard, almost like a cloister, there were cells, each with a big metal door slotted with a Judas hole. I looked around me. The walls at the front gate stretched about thirty feet high, rolls of razor wire on top. Also at the gate sat a three-story building that I took to be the guardhouse. Through the gate, surrounding the complex, I could see another fence with razor wire on top. The guard towers had spotlights, and the guards themselves were men in faded blue uniforms who carried double-barreled shotguns. There were no other prisoners about, but you could sense their presence behind the cell doors. It seemed to me that if you could get through the cell wall, all you had to do was make it over the fence and you were out of there. It didn't appear very secure, and that reassured me. It made me think that this must be a remand prison for nondangerous felons.

There was some discussion between our driver and the prison guards. We stood around and waited. Heat, an azure sky, the gray prison walls, the dusty white courtyard.

After a time the van drove off, the big metal gates opening to let it through. Half a dozen guards came and led us over to one of the cells. They opened it up and shoved us inside. They took our handcuffs off but produced manacles, which they then bolted to our wrists in front of us. Between the manacles, they locked an eighteen-inch-long piece of chain: heavy iron, old, but still strong. Then they made us all sit down. The cell was stifling and the floor stank. The only ventilation came through a tiny barred hole on the wall near the ceiling. Cobwebs hung on the ceiling and the floor was alive with insects. When we were sitting, the guards put a manacle on our left ankle, which was connected to another heavy chain. There were six ring bolts embedded in the concrete floor, and they positioned us so that we were all near at least one of them. The guards produced huge padlocks and attached each ankle chain to a ring bolt. A guard pointed to a black bucket in the corner, and they all went out and locked the door behind them.

We ripped off our gags and all started speaking at once. Everyone had suffered more or less the same treatment. The sham with the confessions, no access to a lawyer or anyone from the outside. No one had talked. No one. Not even Andy. I was so proud of the boys. I couldn't believe it. Jesus, even Andy. He was pleased with himself. We were all excited. I mean, we were in a hell of a spot, but we were pumped to at least be with each other. Scotchy was the first to come out with an important question:

Where's Big Bob? he asked.

They said because he had an American passport he was being dealt with differently, I answered.

Oh, Scotchy said, skeptically.

Why, what do you think? I asked.

I don't think anything, Bruce, Scotchy said.

Fergal stood and stretched. You could do that and maybe walk about three feet before your ankle chain stopped you.

How long do you think we're going to be here? Fergal asked.

We all shook our heads. I was thinking that this would be it until the trial. Why bother to move us at all unless it was a reasonably permanent change? And letting us all be in the same cell together wasn't too bright, unless they were completely confident about winning their case, which with the video they probably were.

They said we were looking at twenty years, Andy said, quietly.

No way, Scotchy said, reassuringly. No way, Andy. For a start, Darkey will pull some strings. That's how these countries work. We'll sit tight, Andy boy, and sooner or later they'll have to give us a lawyer. This isn't Africa, this is Mexico. They need to keep tight with America, do things right.

Yeah, they'll give us lawyers, Fergal said hopefully, sitting down again.

That's right, eventually we'll get a lawyer, and you'll see how Darkey comes through for us, Scotchy said, and I could see he really believed it, he wasn't just saying it for us.

When will Darkey get us out? Andy asked.

Well now, Andy, don't for one thing get your hopes up. I mean, he can't just get us out. He'll send a boy, and he'll probably make us plead guilty to something, so he will. Darkey White is Darkey White, but he's not God. We'll do time, but it won't be much, Scotchy said sagely.

How much is much, do you think? Fergal asked.

I don't know, but not hard time, nothing like that. Just enough to make you tough and give you a story for the girls back home, Scotchy said and winked at him.

I didn't say anything. I was thinking of Big Bob. I was thinking of the map he had. I was wondering where the hell he was now, and I had a terrible suspicion that I knew exactly where that might be.

We talked some more. Our morale was pretty good, Scotchy had done a job cheering us. Night came, and we lay down on the concrete floor. The temperature dipped, and it got a little cold. I was thankful that I'd been wearing my jeans the day we'd left; the boys, of course, were all still in their shorts. The insects were tiny bugs that you got used to. The spiders up there had eaten all the bigger ones, but still, with them and the hard floor, it was difficult getting over to sleep. . . .

In the morning we'd half-filled the slop bucket. It had been a bugger passing it around all chained up. We waited for the guards to come and open up the door to let us pour it out. The smell was bad and flies were hovering around it. The heat was no worse than my place in Manhattan but, like I say, the stench was terrible.

There are rats, you know, Fergal said while we waited.

I didn't see any, I said.

There's rats and lizards and they come onto you when you're sleeping, Andy said.

Andy had woken loudly a few times in the night, terrified. I wondered if he was imagining it, but then I did see a couple of rats skulking near the door. The gap under the door was only about half an inch, but rats can do an impressive limbo when they want to. They didn't bother me, though, they've never bothered me, and wee lizards I could handle as well. And the boys, I knew, would get used to them.

You'll get used to them, you'll see, I said, but Andy looked doubtful.

We waited all morning but no guards came, and it wasn't until evening that the cell door opened and a guard put down a jug of water and four bowls of rice.

Veinte minutos, he said and closed the door behind him.

We ate greedily and drank the water, and he came half an hour later for the empty bowls and the carafe. We hadn't finished the water, so we all desperately took a final swig before he grabbed it back.

Here, we want to empty the bucket, Scotchy said, but the guard didn't understand.

Bucketo uh, Andy tried, but the door was already closed.

In the night, something big bit me—a spider, I think—and I was concerned that it was poisonous, but in the morning I was fine. Scotchy kept us all talking, and that night our morale wasn't too bad either.

The black bucket was close to overflowing with piss now, and most of us had succumbed to a drizzly diarrhea. We hoped that today was the day they let us empty it. But we were wrong. We eventually learned that you slopped out every third day. The prison was on a quadrangle, but one of the cell blocks was empty, so there were three walls of prisoners. Every third day, a cell block was allowed to slop out and spend the morning exercising in the yard. We had heard them come every morning and knew that sooner or later our turn would arrive, or at least we hoped so.

There was no prison work and no canteen and no medical facilities. Prisoners stayed in their cells all the time except for that one morning every three days. We guessed that the prison held three or four hundred prisoners, with maybe thirty or forty guards, though it was impossible to tell for sure.

When the prisoners were let out we heard a lot of talk, and once a voice outside our cell said:

Gringos. Hello, America.

On that first third morning the guards came and undid the padlocks on the ring bolts at our ankles. They put the padlocks in a sack and went out, leaving the door open. We were still shackled at the wrists, but we all immediately got up. The guards yelled at us to sit down. They jabbered something important in Spanish that I hoped Andy was getting since he had the language.

What's he saying? I asked Andy.

He's saying we have to wait until, a word I don't know, I think the whistle, I think, Andy said.

Andy had done O-level Spanish. He'd only gotten a C, but it was better than nothing. I thought I'd heard a whistle the two previous mornings, so maybe Andy was just guessing.

We waited and, sure enough, there was a whistle, and we heard the other prisoners start to come out into the yard.

Have to empty that fucking bucket, Scotchy said. Fergal, you grab it.

Why me?

Because I say so, Scotchy said. And when we get out we all stick together, is that clear?

We nodded.

Complaining, Fergal lifted the bucket gingerly, urine slopping over the sides and onto his hands. None of us had been capable of a big shit, though, so at least that was something. When we got outside, the sunlight was intense, and it took us all a minute to adjust. The other prisoners on our block came out of their cells and the guards watched warily from the towers. I imagined this was the most dangerous time for the guards, for if we'd chosen, we could have all run out and overpowered the four guys who'd been going from cell to cell unlocking us. Probably there was some kind of rule that if anyone came out of his cell before the whistle went (at which point presumably the guards were clear), he got shot.

Prisoners emptied their slop buckets at a latrine near what we discovered later was the disused cell block. The rest walked around the yard. They were a skinny, badly dressed crew, Indian looking. About a hundred of them. The majority barefooted, bareheaded. None of them looked at us. They talked in low tones, most walking, a few immediately setting up to play dice games on the dusty ground.

We walked over to the latrine with Fergal.

Again the big sky and the dust from the prisoners' feet rising in spirals like djinns over the cell wells. The smell of openness and air and jungle and a great mass of human beings that weren't the boys or me.

Swarms of flies over the latrine and a streaking bird, whose plumage reflected back light in wavelengths I had missed: red and emerald green and gold.

Four guard towers, two guards a tower, shotguns, searchlights, I said to Scotchy.

He was looking at me and grinning.

Bruce, dear, it isn't the fucking *Great Escape*. We're sitting tight and not doing anything stupid, is that clear? he said, cheerfully.

Is that what you did in the Kesh? I asked him.

Aye, it is, as a matter of fact, he said.

I'd tried to catch him out because he had said that he had been in the Kesh, but Scotchy never remembered anything and I was hoping he'd confound me by saying No, actually, I was in the Big Bad Magab or something.

How long exactly were you in? I asked him, conversationally, but before he could answer I interrupted and pointed to where some of the prisoners were making for a big pile of straw that had been left near the front gates. I elbowed him.

It's bedding, look, that's what it is, I said.

Ok, we all go, he said.

He called Fergal and Andy over and we stuck together. We went over to the pile of straw and grabbed a bunch each. We wanted to take it back immediately, but we got the impression you had to wait for the whistle before going back to your cell.

Let's just shove it in, Fergal said, but when he edged over to the cell a guard walking along the cell-block roof pointed his shotgun and yelled something at us.

What's he saying, And?

But Andy couldn't make head or tail of it.

See, sorry, lads, but uh, I learned Castilian, not Mexican Spanish, he explained.

So we stood there near our cell block and waited for the whistle. We were pretty conspicuous, not just as the new boys but also as the only non-Mexicans there.

Straw'll make things easier, Fergal said, and sat down on the dust. Scotchy pulled him up, and he almost tripped over the chain still dragging behind his ankle.

Let's just keep our eyes peeled, Scotchy scowled.

And he was right, because before we knew what was happening a gang of about a dozen or more guys had come up to us. They'd just walked over, taking a detour from their circuit, but it was so quick and confusing that suddenly they were on us from four sides. They started saying things in Spanish and pointing at us. Aye, where's the guards now? I was thinking.

What are they saying, Andy? Scotchy asked, but Andy couldn't get it. The head guy was a small man in a string T-shirt and baggy blue jeans. He was pointing at Scotchy's red hair and grabbing his own and making a joke. They had surrounded us completely now and had done it so incredibly fast we hadn't even been able to get to a wall. They were all smaller than us, but some of them had leather belts and were wrapping them around their fists. Others brandished their manacle chains. The yelling was so loud now I was sure the guards were going to intervene. I looked up at the watchtowers to see what was going on, but no one paid any attention.

Here they come, Scotchy said simply, and they rushed us. I took a swipe at some boy, but before I could do anything I'd been kicked in the back and I was on the ground. I got a kick in the head and the legs. I felt my sandals getting pulled off. Someone was trying to get my T-shirt. I curled into the fetal position and waited. The guards would come. The kicks came in again and again. There was no pain at all. Nothing. I bundled myself tighter and moved my arms down to protect my ribs. Someone started pulling my hair. Dust was in my throat. A foot came onto my neck and I grabbed the ankle and bit into it until I got bone. A belt buckle thumped me in the ear, but still I bit into the ankle. I could taste the blood now. A bare foot kicked me on the forehead and I went backwards over my head and scrambled up and found that I was standing. I hit the guy next to me with my elbow and I felt his nose break. There was a whistle and through the dust I could see the men run back to their cells.

Now I started to hurt.

I'd been scraped all over my back, and despite the head kicks, that was the worst. I'd bitten my tongue and I spat blood. I felt an arm underneath mine and Scotchy yelling at me. I couldn't understand a word. He yelled, and then he saw that I wasn't getting it and he showed me. Andy and Fergal lay flat out on the ground and he wanted me to help get them up. The guards were yelling at us to get back in the cells. It was a fucking joke. I bent down and lifted Fergal under the arms, but it was impossible. I slipped, went on my arse. Before I could try again, the guards were there screaming at us and hitting us with billy clubs. They shoved us back towards our cell. I was shouting, but they cut me off with a dig in the mouth. They pushed us inside and beat us down and locked our ankles into the ring bolts.

A minute later, two guards dragged in first Fergal and then Andy and locked them in too. They were both unconscious. All of us had been robbed of our shoes. Andy had been in nice new high-tops that Scotchy and I had bought for him at the airport. He'd put up a real fight to keep them. He was covered in dust and blood. They seemed to have got his T-shirt, too, but I couldn't tell, because my eyes were stinging. Fergal lay beside me, though, his polo shirt torn off him. Scotchy was bent over and hacking now.

Jesus, I said.

I closed my eyes, and when I opened them it was night. My sides were on fire and my back felt like I'd been flailed. There'd been a noise all this time, and I realized it had been Scotchy, as close as he could get to the door, yelling for medical attention. The guards came in and beat him quiet, and it stayed that way until morning. I shivered through the night, and when I woke I dry-heaved for fifteen minutes.

Bruce, Bruce, Scotchy was whispering.

Name's not Bruce, I managed.

Bruce, Scotchy said.

What?

Are you ok?

Aye, no. Aye, I suppose, I said.

Scotchy crawled over to me. He was right at the limit of his foot chain and his whole body was stretched out so he could talk to me.

Bruce, are you hurt bad?

Not bad, I said.

Fergal's in and out of sleep, Scotchy said. He's ok. But Andy's in a bad way. I think his ribs are broken. Do you know anything about first aid?

I shook my head, but we both crawled over to Andy anyway. Fergal was moaning on his side. He was in terrible pain, but at least he knew he was in pain.

Andy had been stripped to his boxer shorts. He breathed erratically in shallow, desperate little breaths, blood in his spittle. His face gaunt, horribly pale. He wasn't conscious, but he wasn't out, either. His lips formed words, but there was no sound. I looked at his chest. His ribs didn't seem right, and I could see blood beneath the skin, pooling there at his lungs.

Jesus Christ, Scotchy, I think he's dying, I said.

Scotchy looked at me, one eye closed over, his face puffy and blue.

When they come in to give us dinner, you pull the guard down and I'll wrap my chain around his neck. We'll say we'll kill him unless they get a doctor for Andy, Scotchy said, cold and deliberate.

I nodded. I really didn't see how it could work, but what choice did we have?

I heard you yelling, I said.

Aye, they just come in and shut you up, Scotchy murmured.

We waited and girded our strength, and the light started to come in the little cell window. We heard the whistle blow and the prisoners get let out. The afternoon became very hot and the day dragged by.

Andy's lips were parched, and he was paler than before. Each breath was a tremendous effort. We crawled over to him.

Andy, if you can hear me, it's going to be ok. We're going to get you some help, I said.

Aye, we are, big lad, we're not going to let you down, Scotchy agreed.

The afternoon ended and finally the door opened. I rugby-tackled the guard, but he kicked me off easily and I sprawled against the back wall, my chain going taut and almost dislocating my ankle.

Doctor, doctor, doctor, doctor, Scotchy was pleading and pointing at Andy.

The guards ignored him, left the food and water, and went out. We tried to give Andy some water, but he choked when we brought it to his lips.

The guards came back for the wooden bowls, and we grabbed some handfuls of rice.

Dying, morto, morto, I yelled, hoping they would understand. The guards looked at Andy for a moment, then closed the door. They went away, talking, and we held out hope that they would send someone. We waited and waited, but no one came.

In the evening, Fergal was fully awake and doing a little better, and we took turns cradling Andy's head in our laps. We didn't know what to do. None of us had any medical experience. All I knew was the recovery position thing. I held Andy and told him it was going to be ok. His breathing was even shorter. Fergal relieved me after a while, and I lay down. Night came, and sometime after midnight Scotchy shook me awake. Fergal was beside him, his eyes vacant in the moonlight.

What is it? I asked.

Andy died, Scotchy said, simply.

I sat up. I looked at Fergal, who nodded.

Are you sure? I asked. It was a stupid question. Scotchy didn't answer it.

I suppose he wasn't fully recovered from that first hiding, Fergal said.

No, they murdered him, they murdered him, Scotchy whispered. They killed him.

I crawled over to Andy and touched his hand. It was cold. They'd closed his eyes.

Jesus, Andy, oh Christ, I am so sorry, I said. Fergal patted me on the back. Scotchy spat and then, turning to the pair of us, he said:

If I don't get back I want youse to promise me you'll see to Big Bob. You'll see to him, promise it.

We both nodded.

Scotchy lay down on the floor. I wiped a mantis off my arm. I put both arms under my head and curled my knees almost up to my chin.

I closed my eyes, and, after a time, I slept.

6: THE LOST WORLD

Yes. It's true. We're lost. We're in a boat on the wild ocean. The seas are high, and there is no compass. We're fucked. Blind. Ignorant. The night bewildering and there is no dawn. We are outside latitude or longitude or maps. No land, no dead reckoning, no horizon. Fucked in spades. In this cabin of stale air, with asthmatics, fellow fools before the mast, who know no shanties but who cough nocturnes for me. But they're more doomed than me. I'm ok, really, for I'm not with them. I am not a boy or a man, rather I am a cow, or a black buffalo, or a bird, or a tiny caterpillar crawling under the door. I am, that is, until one of the others wheezes or says something and I'm back again, a haunted passenger, seasick, lost, fucked.

I close my eyes and lean back and open them.

Days go by.

And it's not that bad, for I have, as contingency, made myself another world. I've been staring at the ceiling, lying on my back, head on the straw, arms on my chest. There are above me valleys, ridges, craters, lines. Funnel cobwebs in the corner. The color is a washed-out gray. Often I imagine they're cities, rivers, an aerial map of a country. The topography is surprisingly uneven; it's a mountain kingdom. We haven't been talking much, so I've been building a story of an imaginary civilization. The big crack down the middle separates two continents that are at war. They're always at war. There are canals, too, like the ones Percival Lowell used to see on Mars. The continent nearest the door is drying up, dying, so the inhabitants want to conquer their neighbors. The continent near the tiny barred window hole has plenty of water; those people live an agricultural, tractable existence, though occasionally death comes to Arcadia, for there are damp and flood marks. The window continent also has the spiderwebs, and I imagine these are desperate, impenetrable morasses where only fools go, of which in a pastoral idyll there are many.

There are wars and negotiations and sometimes individual narratives within the grander themes. There are factions and religions, and perhaps down here we are gods.

My story gets interrupted in the morning for a feature. The window lets in the sunlight and every day there's a black-and-white movie: shadows marching across the canyoned ceiling surface, slowly, for about three hours and then they disappear. It's not much of a show, but the plotting is at least linear and unconflicted.

It's been a fortnight, and we are lousy, scabrous, and covered in bites. Our wounds have not healed well. Fergal sits towards the corner nearest the light. He's filing part of my belt buckle into a lock pick. He thinks the locks on the leg irons could be reasonably straightforward to pick since they're all standard bolt jobs from the seventies. Fergal was a jemmy for a while, so maybe he would know, but Scotchy and I, unfortunately, know Fergal too well to hold out much hope. In any case, the lock on the door needs a big thick key and we don't have the metal, so Scotchy doesn't see the point of getting us out of the leg irons if we could never open the door. But he's only saying that. He needs it as much as both of us.

It's been ten days since they took out Andy. He's buried by now, or cremated, or whatever it is they do around here. Eaten in some Mayan ceremony, for all I know. No one has said anything to us about him. No one's said anything to us about anything, but I imagine now we're pretty much screwed sideways. A dead gringo—that can't be something you'd want the world outside to know about. They'll bury the case, do nothing about us, let us rot. I mean, they couldn't hush this up if we ever got out to tell the papers. I really don't see how they can bail us now, of course. It's the word of a drug smuggler, but the whole thing would still stink. I haven't said anything about this to the others. Scotchy probably has his outside hopes still pinned to his friendship with Darkey, and Fergal's energy is concentrated on his silly little pick.

We've been out to the yard several times and no one has bothered us. I think Andy got killed because they were after our clothes. It sounds stupid, but now that they have our shoes they're leaving us alone. We got some straw for bedding, and for a while Scotchy had us making an attempt to clean the cell out a bit. He's stopped in the last couple of days. It's not the futility of the thing; rather, I think, he just doesn't have the energy to boss us and keep himself together.

So there's Scotchy sleeping, Fergal filing the belt buckle against the concrete. The flies, caterpillars, roaches, the sweat on my skin, and of course the ceiling.

The movie's over, and it's only four hours until dinner. The narrative kicks in without me. Agriculture, herds of animals. The dust rising from pilgrims coming to wash in the sacred river. Millions of them. The primary cult of the two kingdoms is shared by the majority of the population, but like the Endians, they hector one another over trivialities. One says you bathe only up to the waist, the other that the head must sink beneath the water. Scholars at universities debate it. Everyone wears turbans, incidentally, but some tie at the front and others at the back. They argue over that, too, it's crazy. It's like that Frank Gorshin episode of *Star Trek*.

There are hunting parties, dare raids over the divide, and occasionally kids are captured like Gary Powers, and there's a whole ta-do. It's tense, and everyone's bored with their life and this is bringing on war fever. People grumble, and there's hysteria mounting in the press. A prime minister of the left continent is debating with his cabinet the consequences of mobilization. They're at a country house in an island group near the continental divide. The peace party thinks there will be universal slaughter if war breaks out; they're right, of course. The peace party recalls to memory the events of the last border war. He's talking and they're listening, jaws agape. It's not my story now, it's Granpa Sam's, the mudbath shambles of July 1916, shit and skulls. The Ulster Division slaughtered by companies and then by battalions and then by week's end there is no one left at all. From the picture on the piano Granpa Sam loses forty-five friends, forty-five out of fifty, in the first twenty minutes. The piano and the brown photographs and a sword and a violin. How rigid everyone is, how formal. Were they like that, were they not profane like the rest of us?

And now where have these thoughts come from? Home. War. It's a universe away. An ocean. But the *sheugh* is wide. Aren't we still in the New World? Possibilities.

I leave them there in the mud, poison gas drifting back into their own trenches. I'm back with the farmers of the window continent. Mechanization has not yet hit. Neither has enclosure. There is proper crop rotation and the fields are left fallow in winter and every seventh year. The crops are hardy and adaptable and disease in this kingdom is rare. They have malaria in the swamps, but they have discovered quinine. There's a light rain, a sun shower; people are tilling soft drumlins and in the background there's a blue lough. They're wearing woolen trousers and cotton shirts, flat tweed caps. They have butter and buttermilk and potato bread and veda. Yes, that's better. For breakfast there is a toasted slice of soda with Dromona and Lyle's Golden Syrup. And then, bejesus, you're out in the crisp morning and into the fields. The sun's out over the lough and it's a wee bit like County Down. There's a church and a tractor, and you're baling hay. I don't mind being back here. A big ganch with a blue face is driving the tractor and we're on the ground with forks shoveling it up onto the back of the truck. Sweating and cursing and spinning yarns. It's lunch and we're only thirteen, but the oul boy's wife has brewed us cider and we're half tore from just the smell of it. Big jam pieces on batch bread with butter and homemade blackcurrant. Yeah, that'll do. I close my eyes and drift.

Later.

Sitting up. Both boys are sleeping now. Scotchy: a scrawny red beard, hollow eyes, lank, slablike skin. Fergal: bloody fingers from his pick and a wild untrimmed beard like that of an insane man. Hair sticking out everywhere—I think the Indians are frightened of him. Fuck knows how I look. Never had a beard before. Got one now with no mirror to see how it becomes me.

In a wee while, Scotchy will wake and scratch himself, crotch first and then feet and then hair and then the rest of him. He'll do that for half an hour and talk to himself for a minute or two and then, if he's got the energy, he'll talk to me. He'll pare down his fingernails and scratch himself some more. Fergal will wake and lie still; you won't be able to tell when he's conscious or not. He'll lie there, off in some private place. He'll speak even less than Scotchy, and if he has his energy he'll work on his pick. Of course, our hair will start to fall out soon. Scotchy informs us that vitamin C is stored in the body only for about six weeks. After that, it's scurvy.

I'm thinking logically, trying to get a grip. Blacker thoughts. Things do not stand well. We've lost weight and we're weaker, and I know for a certainty that I'm starting to get bedsores. My nails are brittle and my throat's cracked and I'm crippled by lethargy. If they would only give us some limes it would make a huge difference.

Mealtime. We eat rice and drink water. I keep waiting for variation, but it's not coming. Scotchy mumbles something about eating the crickets for protein, but I'm not there yet.

A day or two later, he orders us to do it. It's a joke to think that Scotchy is in a position to give orders, but he has a point. The crickets are easy to catch, and it's diverting. You crunch them and pretend they're potato chips. You crunch them well, otherwise they writhe about on the way down your throat. The mantises, if anything, are worse for that behavior. Fergal refuses to eat the insects, and Scotchy laughs and says that that's more for the rest of us.

Fergal goes back to his filing, Scotchy to his rage and mumbling. I go back to nothing. Nothing and then thoughts, regrets, fear.

Night.

Morning, we pick the lice out of each other's hair. My story, the farmers, the war, the movie. Mealtime again. Evening coming so fast, and then the night again. And every night and day it's louder out there. All the noises of the forest that go on forever, stopping only to pause and tease us, for an hour or two, in the hottest part of the day.

The morning comes, and there are no cockcrows or songbirds, just the end of that nighttime roar and the beginning of the daytime one. Back to my other place. Late summer and the harvest is coming in and the window people are fat and happy and unprepared and the door continent is envious as its people tug and pull at the dry earth.

Light comes in. We know a few of the guards: Squinty, Poxy, Bandit (because of his one arm), Pacino (his scarred face), Chunnel (his big nostrils), FDR (he can barely walk). Except for Squinty, they don't speak any English or, if they do, they won't. Squinty only has about five words and it's pointless asking him anything. We know none of the other prisoners. If there's a leader, it's an Indian in jeans and Andy's shoes. Some of the others seem to defer to him. But really, that's not important. They don't give a shit about us; they don't even see us anymore.

Dreams of food. Cadbury's chocolate, cream doughnuts, golden glistening fish and chips. Beer, a real pint of Guinness, viscous, bitter, smooth.

And her, always her. Those eyes and that smile. Those long legs that invite you to touch her, to hold her, to take her on the bed, to remove her green skirt and white panties. To feel her breath on yours, to ease yourself inside of her, to screw her and hold her and lick her sweat. And then to lie next to her on the cool sheets.

Sit there, bored, scratch myself, throw Scotchy a cricket, but he doesn't stir. Sit there.

I pick one fly out of the hundreds and try to follow it. It lands in the slop bucket, takes off, lands on Fergal, takes off again, back to the slop bucket, over to me, lays something on my arm (got to keep still, so it can), and off again. It's a nice symmetry, Scotchy, Fergal, me—the flies keeping us moored together through a bucket of our own liquid shit.

Eat your crickets, Bruce, harder to catch now, Scotchy says, and throws his back. I grab the fucker and I do eat it, and he smiles at me.

It's another third day and we get unlocked. The whistle goes, and we walk around the yard, keeping to ourselves, frightened. No one speaks to us; we stay away from everyone else. For a minute, I stare angrily at the man wearing my sandals and then I catch myself at it and stop. The whistle blows, and we take our bucket and our straw and go back in.

Guards come and produce padlocks from a bag. Lock us down. Close the door.

I sit there wondering if the others will bother to speak. Fergal's agitated and he does:

Boys, listen, wee old bloke with the limp was giving me the eye. Think I might be on ta something. He's got information for us, I can tell, maybe about Big Bob, Fergal says, excitedly.

Maybe he wanted your arse, I suggest, slowly.

Scotchy grins at me.

No, no, he knows something, Fergal persists. Doesn't trust you two, but he does me.

Aye, maybe he's the head boy on the fucking escape committee, wants your help with the glider they're making in block C, Scotchy says, with heavy sarcasm.

I wink at him.

No reason to get all eggy, Fergal says.

All the reason in the world, I think, Scotchy retorts.

Fergal grunts and goes back to the belt buckle.

Scotchy nods at me and I nod back. I try to think of something funny that will cheer us up, but I can't. My brain is slow and won't move.

I lie back and pick things out of my beard. I huddle down into the straw. Food comes, and we gobble it down. Dark, and we get afeared, but the noise at least keeps us company.

Another day and another. The weather breaks, and one day it rains and the whole floor oozes with damp, as if things weren't bad enough. Scotchy develops a cough and his hacking keeps us awake at all hours. Fergal and I are probably thinking the same thing: that he's going to be next. In the morning, we're expecting him to be coughing blood, but he isn't, and he actually looks a little better. He saves his voice, and when night comes he's coughing less.

Gave us a scare there, mate, I whisper in the dark. Thought you were getting cholera or, more likely, AIDS or the clap or something.

Scotchy doesn't say anything, but I can feel him smiling. I go back to sleep. Night, bad dreams. Another day of the same shite. Scotchy recovers from his cough, and we don't get anything worse than we have. We are getting weaker, though, malnutrition and diarrhea, and I know that this cannot go on indefinitely.

But what else can we do but conserve our strength and hope for better times? Micawberism, but my brain is too addled for anything else.

On one day I decide that it's my birthday. I don't tell the others. I just sit there with the knowledge that my teenage years are done. And it's that night that I go back, way back to where it all began.

Does the memory work like a journal or a logbook? Can you record words and faces and read them back years from now? Most professionals say no. You either use it or lose it. The mind isn't a video camera or a computer or a big book. Oh aye? Well, how do you account for the smells and the details and the dialogue?

It's all there.

Really.

And big brother, where are you? And Ma and Da, are you still in this world? You exist somewhere, even if only for a time in that place of dreams. Oh, I see it all.

My eyes close. It's set. All those moments, together in one moment. Future, present, past.

And it comes back. PJ hiding. Davey Quinn. Mrs. Miller. The hair falling in tiny helicopter blades.

All those moments, together in one. Weird that many of them come together around the solstice, Saturnalia, Nativity, the mass of Christ; no, not weird, it's a hard time. The Christmas of last year at the Europa, the Christmas of long ago in the lean, black tenement streets, the Christmas yet to be . . .

*   *   *

The rain ghostwriting itself on the windowsill. The smell of turf from the kitchen grate. Belfast there, in winter memory, oozed up from the mudflats of the lough.

PJ under the shed. Hiding. Toys with him. What toys? Fluorescent patches on soldiers moving about in the darkness. He's playing antipersonnel mines and hurling the plastic bodies away from imaginary explosions. He's three years older, but I'm more mature, preferring Lego to Action Men, which (oh, yes) is a moot point because I've lost all my Action Men to him on a bet as to whether I can make an effective parachute out of bedsheets that would take me without injury from the washhouse roof to the back garden. . . .

Yes, I remember.

I want to hide too, and I think about either running away up into the fields or sneaking under the bunk in our bedroom, but that would mean going upstairs, which is out of the question since Granpa is wandering around up there in his pajamas, looking for his teeth and muttering things about the pope, the prime minister, and sometimes the kaiser.

Granpa.

I can run over to Davey's house and try and wangle an extra dinner from his parents. They would hide me all evening if they could. They like me better than Davey himself because, despite being a Protestant, I always say "please" and "thank you" and call Shirley "Mrs. Quinn," even though all of us know she isn't really married to Davey's da.

I'm mulling over the possibilities in front of the *Flintstones* on TV when the living room door opens.

Ma comes in with a pound note. She's so pretty, young.

Here, she says.

What's that for? I ask, affecting an unconvincing air of ignorance.

You know full well. Now get your brother.

I don't know where he is, I attempt.

You don't?

No.

Not even if there was ten pence in it for you?

You want me to squeal on PJ for a miserly ten p.?

Take it or leave it.

The coin sitting in her hand. Heads up. It's one of those that has been defaced by the Provos. A big cross over the face of the queen.

Sometimes they don't take those vandalized ones in the sweetie shop.

Ma looks at the ten pence and shrugs. She reaches in the pocket of her slacks. Blue ones, the ones with the permanent jam stain on the buttocks.

She brings out a Free State ten p. with a fish as the head side and a harp as the tails.

He's under the hut, I say, taking my piece of silver and putting it in my shorts.

She opens the window.

PJ, get in here. I can see you.

He does not come.

PJ, you're under the shed. I can see you from here.

A minute later he appears in the living room, shooting me a dirty look.

You grassed me up, ya bastard, he whispers as Ma goes to get him a new T-shirt to wear.

I never did.

Oh, you liar.

Are you calling me a liar?

Yes.

I'll kick your bake in.

Like to see you try.

Like to see you stop me.

Like to see you try to stop me.

Oh, I'll try.

Try is right.

Try and succeed.

Aye, you will?

Think I won't?

Uh-huh.

Well, we'll see, so we will.

Aye, we will?

Aye, we will.

I shoot him a confused expression.

What were we talking about again? I ask.

He grins at me and we both crack up laughing.

Wee bugger, he whispers to me as Ma comes back with a yellow T-shirt.

Put this on, she says. I can't believe you were crawling under the shed with all those worms and things. Son, I tell you, I think your head's cut sometimes. Good job your da's not here.

Aye, when's he ever? PJ whispers. I don't answer, and we walk outside into the road.

Is there any way out of this at all? he asks me.

Not if you want any presents this year, I say.

We walk sullenly along the street. It's dusk and there are a lot of kids out playing kerby and tag and football. For a December night, the weather isn't bad. A group of girls playing hopscotch and jumping with a big rope. A mild evening and everyone excited about tomorrow.

A big tawny hound sitting right in the middle of the road, cars driving around it and honking at it, the dog paying no attention to them or to anything.

Mr. McClusky is trying to get his pigeons to fly into the coop, but they're way up on the telephone wires.

Come down, you wee fucks, he's saying to them over and over. Sooner or later his wife will come and reprimand him for his language in front of the kids. The pigeons will go into the coop anyway as soon as it gets cold.

Davey sees me farther up the road.

Hey, Mikey, what's the *craic*? he shouts.

Nothing.

You wanna do nets?

I shake my head.

Can't, I shout back.

What did you call me? he jokes.

We walk on, and a few doors down come to the house with a big hole in the fence. All the houses on the terrace are identical. They're all redbricked and joined to one another in rows of six or seven. To get to the back garden, you have to go through the house itself or through a narrow entryway that two houses share. The only thing that distinguishes one house from another is how the gardens are kept. Some people grow flowers, others vegetables, some people have it all grass, and others—for some reason that neither PJ nor I understands—have the whole garden concreted over.

The Millers have gone for the uncared-for look. Their garden has three-foot-high grass and weird mechanical objects lurking in the undergrowth. We know they have a dog because of the amount of dog shite everywhere. The animal itself we have never seen. PJ speculates that it got lost in the grass and never made it back home and was now surviving on crickets and bits of postmen.

Or bits of little boys.

The only obvious concession to the season is a handwritten sticker in the window that says Double Milk Christmas Eve. *Christmas* they have spelled with no "h."

We walk up the cracked path and bang on the knocker. At first no answer, and then a lot of swearing from the living room. We shrink back a little as footsteps come closer to the door.

It opens and Mr. Miller looks at us, very confused and angry for a second.

The bloody carols, is it? he says. Why aren't you singing, ya wee fucks?

Er, it's not, er . . .

If you think I'm going to give you a bloody penny without youse even opening your bakes to sing, you've another thing coming. Jesus, today youse weans want everything on a plate. That's what's the trouble. Fenians have the right idea. You always see them on the TV, working away, singing and doing that Irish dancing. They're outbreeding us, so they are. Look at the Quinns down the road. They have ten weans, so they do, and she's still up for more. You'd think they'd come to the door and not sing? Not that I'd give them anything. Bucket of water, maybe. Heh-heh . . .

Uh, we're here for a haircut, Mr. Miller, PJ says, nervously.

Mr. Miller looks at the pair of us askance, cocking his head and thinking.

Oh aye, he says at last. Come on in. I'll tell Mary.

PJ nudges me ahead of him into the house.

Go straight through to the kitchen, Mr. Miller says.

We walk along the hall, past the familiar pictures of war scenes and paintings of the Battle of the Boyne, all done by the head of the house himself with an uncanny and unfailing lack of talent. Mr. Miller has unorthodox views on perspective and characterization. In his paintings, King William looks much more a shipwrecked Ringo Starr than the commonplace image of a bewigged and magnificent King Billy that you can find on almost every Protestant street corner. Mr. Miller always paints Catholic King James to appear devilish and evil, although it's hard to say which of the two kings looks the most like an actual human being.

PJ is always careful not to comment on the paintings, since the one time he did, Mr. Miller spent the next forty minutes explaining his motives and inspiration.

PJ pushes me in through the kitchen door and we sit down on the stools that are next to the table.

She'll be down in a wee minute, Mr. Miller says and turns the lights on. He steps out of the kitchen, back into the living room, leaving us alone.

Through the open window all the smells of the street are coming in, teasing us with the promise of the world outdoors. Someone is cooking a fry and you can smell the bacon and the crisping of the potato bread.

There are big swarms of midges out doing maneuvers in the air and a few wasps that have survived the early frosts are buzzing from weed to weed in the Millers' garden.

Maybe we could still make a break for it, PJ says. Nip out the back and over the fence.

I look at him with disdain.

Are you out of your tree, wee fella? Oul man Miller would shoot us.

How could he do that?

How do you think? With a gun.

He doesn't have a gun.

He's in the paramilitaries, I say, my voice dropping to a whisper.

You don't know that, PJ mocks.

Ask Da when he gets in.

I will, and then you'll feel wick.

No, you'll feel wick.

No, you'll—

PJ stops speaking as Mrs. Miller appears in the doorway.

She must have just gotten out of bed, because she's still wearing her nightie and slippers. Over the top of them she has pulled a big red dressing gown that's tied round the waist with a leather belt that has an Elvis buckle in the middle of it. It suddenly occurs to me that she was on the night shift down at the mill and that we had woken her up in the middle of her sleep.

Hello, boys, she says and runs her fingers through her long reddish blond hair a couple of times to take out the knots. I give her over the pound note and she smiles.

Who's first? she asks.

I point at PJ before he can point at me.

Ok, up you come, PJ, she says, and moves his stool into the center of the floor. She danders to the sink and lights herself a cigarette and puts it in her mouth. She ties a tea towel round PJ's neck and then pulls a pair of scissors and a comb from her dressing gown pocket.

The comb looks none too clean and I'm glad that PJ is getting his haircut first.

I tilt my stool back against the work surface and look around the room. The Millers have wallpaper which says "Du Pont" all over it. Mr. Miller had worked at the Du Pont plant up in Derry before he had gone to jail for whatever he had gone to jail for. All the parents in the street know his criminal past but no one will tell the kids, which only makes it seem much worse. Of course, there are rumors—the one that I believed had Miller as a getaway driver for the paramilitaries in a robbery that had gone wrong. Because (another rumor said) Mr. Miller had been too drunk to drive . . .

The rest of the kitchen is uninteresting, except for the two calendars on opposite sides of the wall. One is from a Chinese takeaway and has a picture of Hong Kong on it. The other is a calendar from the *Sun* newspaper and has a woman holding a football with her breasts out over the top of it. It's always a new woman each month, unlike the picture of Hong Kong, which stays the same. I look at the *Sun* calendar and instantly color and feel sure that Mrs. Miller knows that I've been looking at the woman's chest.

I stare at the floor and watch PJ's brown snips of hair start to gather there on the tiles.

Mrs. Miller's toenails are painted pink and you can see them through the holes in her slippers. You can see her leg, too, when she moves. I wonder how old she is and steal a look at her.

Around thirty is my guess. She has no lines on her face and the bags under her eyes are probably from tiredness more than anything else. She's certainly an attractive woman—at least to me; and it makes no sense that she's married to an eejit like Mr. Miller.

I look up at the calendar again and see that the girl's name is Stacy. Her breasts are like enormous honeydew melons, shiny and plastic-looking. They're amazing and repulsive at the same time, like a particularly gruesome monster from *Doctor Who* that you both want and don't want to look at simultaneously. To end the confusion they're causing, I look at the floor again.

I find that I'm sweating. I gaze over at PJ and see that he's only half done. I'm breathing rapidly and my hands are all clammy. I try looking out of the window, but the Millers' backyard is just as grown over as their front and you can see nothing.

Suddenly the door opens and Mr. Miller comes in.

PJ says Ow as Mrs. Miller nicks him on the ear with the scissors.

Look at what you made me do, Mrs. Miller says to her husband, ash pouring out of her cigarette all over PJ's head.

I made you do? Jesus. Can't even get a drink of water in me own house, Mr. Miller says, angrily.

Jesus Christ, can you just wait five minutes, for God's sake, Mrs. Miller says, spitting the words out.

Aye. Fucking shite, Mr. Miller says and stomps out, banging the door behind him. We hear him storm up the stairs, cursing all the way.

PJ and I are both bright red by this stage.

Mrs. Miller looks at me and smiles a sort of half smile.

Hold on, she says to PJ, and slides out the kitchen door after her husband. We hear her go up the stairs too. PJ turns round and looks at me. His face is a study in anguish.

I wish I was already bloody bald, he says quietly.

Aye, like Simon Baskin.

Who?

Yon boy from P4, cancer boy.

Oh, aye, PJ says, but I can see he's too afeared for conversation.

We sit for a minute, PJ picking the bits of ash out of his hair and me biting my nails. The door opens and Mrs. Miller comes back in.

Ok, she says cheerfully and lights herself another cigarette. In two more minutes she declares that PJ is done. He takes the tea towel from round his neck and thanks her.

And, uh, now I have to go home to go to do some homework, PJ says.

Oh, you do? Mrs. Miller says.

Yes, PJ says, ignoring my telepathic protests and a desperate grab at his sleeve.

I'll see you out, she says, and leads him to the front door. I can hardly believe it. He is supposed to wait for me. I don't want to be alone in this house. I watch him go down the hall and Mrs. Miller open the front door. Light comes pouring in and PJ runs into it and then he's suddenly gone. Spirited away, like the wee fella from *Close Encounters*.

Your turn, Mrs. Miller says.

I sit on the stool while she ties the tea towel round my neck to collect the hair.

Same as usual, Mikey boy? she asks.

Uh, yeah.

It's hard to breathe over the cigarette smoke and the odor of her perfume. I struggle not to cough.

Mrs. Miller starts cutting my hair. Her hands combing a bit and then cutting it. Her fingers are cold and smooth. She works a little at the side and then comes forward to do my fringe.

As she leans in I can see through the fold in her dressing gown, right through to her nightie. I blink for a second and look away. She tilts my head until I'm looking into her hands. Keep still now, she says.

The scissors make their way across my forehead, snipping little cusps of black hair onto the tea towel and down onto the floor.

There, she says, blowing smoke towards the window. That's better, isn't it?

Uh, I think so, I say, barely able to get the words out.

She takes another puff on the cigarette. Her fingers are almost as white as the paper around the tobacco.

I'll touch up the back, she says.

She slips behind me and begins trimming the hair round the back of my ears. I can feel her breath on my neck as she struggles with the difficult bits. She had been a hairdresser for five years before she got the job at the mill. She was quick and she was half the price of the hairdresser down at the shopping center, or the barber in town. She was a friend of Ma's, anyway, and Da let Mr. Miller in to use the phone all the time. Ma says she could cut our hair herself, but with him unemployed, it was all she could do to help.

There's a noise from the living room like something falling. Mrs. Miller stops cutting. I turn round to look at her.

Just then Mr. Miller shouts, Mary (so loud you could probably hear it at our house).

Oh, I forgot completely, Mrs. Miller says in a panic. She puts down the scissors, dashes to a cupboard, and grabs a glass. She goes to the sink, runs the tap for a second, and fills it with water before practically sprinting out into the hall.

There's more swearing from the living room. The only words I can make out—from Mr. Miller, of course—are: On bloody Christmas bloody Eve.

There's the sound of something that might be a slap.

Mrs. Miller comes into the hall, staggering. Mr. Miller is right behind her. His fist clenched, he pulls it back and turns and stops. He stares at me sitting there under the kitchen light with the tea towel around my neck.

What the fuck are you looking at? he says.

Nothing, I'm going to say, should have said. Definitely should have said. But instead, these words come out:

A real hard man.

Mr. Miller is flabbergasted. He knows I'm being sarcastic. A ten-year-old taking the bloody piss. His face goes white, and then red. He storms into the kitchen and stands beside me.

What did you say? he whispers, leaning close.

N-nothing, I stammer.

He hesitates, unsure of whether to brain me then and there or tell my da, or get me in some more devious way.

Damn fucking right, you wee fucking bastard, he yells and brings his fist right up to my face and shakes it. He turns to his wife.

Gimme your money. I'm going to the fucking Rangers Club. Fucking bitch. Fucking weans.

He grabs the pound note and storms out, slamming the door. She picks up the scissors and starts cutting my hair again. She does a few combs and then cuts the back line and then that appears to be it.

Well, she says. That's all, folks.

Thanks, I say.

She comes round to face me. She's smiling, but there are tears welling up in her. She sniffs a little and dabs her eye with the hem of her dressing gown.

Are you ok, Mrs. Miller? I ask, anxiously.

She looks at me and smiles again, her lips parting a little and becoming moist and crimson under the strip light. Slowly, she reaches out her hand and touches me on the cheek with fingers so cold you would have thought she was a long time dead.

You're a good boy, Michael, she says, and then her hand comes down to my neck and undoes the tea towel. She shakes the hairs out onto the floor, the loose curls floating down like tiny rotor blades.

Thank you very much, I say.

See you next month, she says, and puts her hand on my arm and sees me to the front door.

She runs her fingers through my hair, and I stand there on the porch for a moment.

She touches my face again and smiles, turns, and closes the door.

I run down the path into the street.

There's light outside from the aurora. It's white and gold and so strong you can almost see the outline of Knockagh Mountain.

Who's the skinhead? Davey Quinn asks me, and I chase him all the way up to the graveyard.

Later, we both come down to the street and take opposite sides in the football game. Davey's team wins, but I score a goal, so everything works out ok in the end.

When it's late and chilly, I find PJ out in the shed and we sit by the paraffin lamp and tell each other scary stories. Many about Mr. Miller. We're happy. The haircut's over and tomorrow is Christmas and we'll go to Nan's house and there will be presents that Nan has bought for us out of her pension. She'll have made dinner, too. Turkey, potatoes, pavlova, trifle.

We sit there and just think for a while. Ma should be calling us in to bed but Ma's next door smoking and chatting with Mrs. Parkinson.

You know the way I asked Nan for the cardboard Death Star? PJ says after a time.

Aye.

I don't think I want it now. I think I'm sick of all that *Star Wars* shite.

Really?

Yeah.

And your Action Men, too?

Aye, sick of all that. You can have them back.

I can?

Aye.

What's got into you?

I don't know.

Later, under the cool sheets of the upper bunk, I ponder this and other things, but eventually they all vape and there's only one topic on my mind. Someday I would rescue her. In just a few years. When I was older. I would go in and punch him out and take her and we'd disappear across the water to England or America or somewhere where the sun shone and the sky was blue and we were far from soldiers and paramilitaries and bombs and violence. But, of course . . .

And yes, that was the night.

Later that evening Da came in singing and blitzed to high heaven. There were voices. Things flew. Things crashed.

Ma said, Over my dead body you will.

And he said, You'll fucking do as you're told. This is man's business, and you'll keep your fucking neb out of it.

And Ma's one to overegg the custard when she gets the chance and said that if it was man's business what was it to do with him.

He said that she was to shut the fuck up if she knew what was good for her.

And she said something that I'm sure was sarcastic and funny and he couldn't think of a reply, and there was an almighty smash of something and she screamed that that was a wedding gift. A slap. A sob.

I knew that PJ would have the pillow over his ears, but I could hear. I could hear.

It was 1982 and the year after the hunger strikes, and tension was as high as I ever remembered it. In Belfast, riots were as general as Joyce's snow. Every night, petrol bombs and blast bombs, the peelers keeping apart Protestant and Catholic and sometimes nobody would get killed. Here in the northern suburbs, though, it was less of a problem; things were calmer, but it was like your pan of milk on the cusp, a slight notch up on the heat . . . Anything or anyone could make it overboil and scald.

And Mr. Miller believed that he was the boy who could make the magic. Really, he wasn't much of a player, big to us, but small time in the larger scheme of things. But still. He was the boy. And later, when it went to shit, I couldn't help but feel that I was partly responsible. You do that as a wean, you think the world revolves around you. Sometimes I used to think that when I left a room all the people in it froze like with the pause button on a video and only started up when I came back in again.

Epiphany came thirteen days early for PJ and me and Ma and Da. Oh aye.

Seething with fury and looking for trouble, Mr. Miller went down to the Rangers Club. Mr. Miller talked a great game and said that they were all yellow bastards down there, and if they really meant what they said about helping the police and the forces of law and order, they'd do something about it. He persuaded about half a dozen eejits that the best way of assuring the future of Northern Ireland as a political entity was to do a firebomb attack on a Catholic housing estate. In the brilliance of their plan they were all to go home and make Molotovs, and he and Arthur Durant would drive them over in Arthur's van. Mr. Miller made especially sure that our da came along. Oh yes, that was how he'd get me. Maybe he would have had Dad fire the first Molotov or maybe he'd have got Dad's prints on a bottle. In any case, he was arranging it so that ever after he would have something over him. The best laid plans . . .

They never got anywhere near the estate.

They were stopped by the army for driving too fast, the Molotovs were discovered in half a minute, and everyone was arrested. Marty Bains turned rat, and Da and Mr. Miller and all the rest got five years for conspiracy to cause explosions.

There followed an inevitable, clichéd, and speedy progression: Ma divorced Da, turned to drink, started smoking again, turfed out Granpa, starting going with Mrs. Miller to the Central Bar, took up with Mr. Henry, who owned the butcher's, and since Mr. Henry and us didn't get along, sent us to live with Nan in East Belfast.

Mrs. Miller stayed with her husband and somehow conceived a bairn, who is, I'm sure, a credit to his people.

Like his grandfather and great-grandfather before him, PJ went to sea, leaving at the age of fifteen, and is now . . . where?

Me? I lived with Nan, and God bless her, she's a wonderful woman, but no disciplinarian, and things fell such that I went to the world of violence: the rackets and the army and America. From there to here.

And that was then and this is now.

Events, trapped by them, by history.

Trapped, and in this cell forever? I don't think so. For like I say, Another Christmas coming. Another Christmas Eve . . .

7: VALLADOLID

Night and half-light and then the dawn. The days come and sometimes they wake us, other times we are up already. Scratching, squirming, moaning, dreaming.

All the agonies of memory and the present. Pain and guilt and recrimination.

Of course, I can never tell the boys what I suspect, that they're here because of me. And that makes me think about her. Hair, eyes, but distant, fading, and I try for them, all the long day.

The same old view. Fergal, Scotchy, flies. Change position, lean back, look up.

The story, the movie, food. Exercise and slop on the third day. A scramble for dry straw. Lockdown. Water and then a squat above the bucket as only liquid comes out. Dry yourself with straw and try not to rub too hard. Last thing you need is a bleeding arse.

Sometimes Fergal mutters a Hail Mary. It irritates Scotchy, but he doesn't say anything.

Watch Fergal at his pick. Watch Scotchy scratch himself.

Stare at the ceiling when light comes in.

My story continues.

Above me the big war has begun and it progresses in a terrible, infantile bloodbath. The door continent has committed half its resources on a broad attack on many fronts. But its initial success has led to a crisis of supply and logistics, and both armies are bogged down into a static line of trenches. Wave upon wave beating against one another. It's Shiloh or Ypres or, again, the Somme. A slaughter of innocents. With the resources of continents this could go on for decades. The press is becoming discontented and the governments introduce censorship at source; victories are proclaimed. It's always victories.

More night. More days.

We take out our wet straw and replace it with dry stuff. Our hair is long and our beards are shaggy. We stand out even more from the Indian prisoners, who somehow manage to groom themselves. Occasionally, we hear a truck in the yard and prisoners are moved in and out. There are some new inmates, you can tell by their clothes rather than faces. For everyone else, this might be a transit prison, but I know that we're here for the long haul. Maybe the longest haul.

At night and sometimes in late afternoon, now on a regular basis, giant rumbling thunderstorms shake the prison. The rains drip down on us from the ceiling and the floor floods. We move our bodies pathetically onto little hills of unevenness on the concrete and thus on any convex mound we try and sleep.

The floors dry but never for very long. It's a little cooler, but we're heading into what must be the wet season. I try to remember from my geography whether we're in the tropics and I believe we are.

Thunderstorms, dry patches. More night. More days . . .

And then, wonderfully, amazingly, incredibly, finally, something fucking different:

A hand on my shoulder.

Fergal wakes me before daybreak, holding something in his hand. I look up. It's an object, I can't make it out. Everything is a bit out of focus still. It's curved and round. I stare at it for a while and then sit.

What is it?

Fergal cannot fully contain his excitement. He punches me on the shoulder.

It's my fucking leg iron, you stupid wanker, he says.

I sit bolt upright.

Jesus, your fucking pick worked?

'Course it worked.

Does it just work on yours? I ask anxiously.

No, man, it'll work on them all; all the locks are interchangeable. They just put 'em in a bag, you know. They're old, twenty years old, I'd say. They test them for brittleness, but that's all. Old, easy. Tell ya, it was piss easy.

It took you four fucking weeks, Fergal, I say.

Yeah, but with the tools I had, he says.

I'm grinning at him, and he's practically laughing.

Do mine, Fergal, do mine, I say, excitedly.

Ok.

He sits down in front of me and grabs the lock attaching my ankle chain to the ring bolt. He works on it for about ten minutes and incredibly the lock clicks. He lifts it up in slo-mo and dangles it in front of my face.

You're a fucking genius. All this time, you've been a fucking genius, I say, biting back something like a breakdown.

I am, too.

We gotta wake Scotchy.

We walk over to Scotchy. We fucking walk over. Delight in it, and stand behind him, something we haven't been able to do since we've been locked in.

Scotchy, I whisper, and he wakes instantly and turns to us, gobsmacked.

How in the name of fuck, he says, far too loud.

That wee shite did it, I say, gleefully.

Fergal is beaming. Scotchy thumps him in the leg.

You bastard, you tricky wee sleekit wee bastard. Wee fucking sneaky wee fucking shite, Scotchy says.

Fergal bends down and undoes Scotchy's lock. This time it takes him only about five minutes.

Every time it's easier, he says.

Scotchy is momentarily thunderstruck and silent.

What now? I say, excitedly.

Can you do the door at all? Scotchy asks.

Fergal shakes his head.

You need a big key. We don't have the metal, and even if we did, it would be a tough job. Loud, too.

Scotchy's spirits are up, though, and I'm thinking even if we can't get out, at least we've got one over on the bastards.

Scotchy tenses and turns on us.

Hands, he says.

Our wrists are manacled together by a foot and a half of chain: one end of the chain is welded to the left manacle, the other attached to the right by a lock. These locks are never undone, and I think that they might be rusted or harder, but Fergal says that they're all standard issue. He goes at mine for a few minutes and that lock clicks too. Scotchy insists he's next, and Fergal does himself last. We have complete freedom of movement for the first time in weeks. I do jumping jacks and touch my toes, and the two boys stretch and laugh at me.

Scotchy huddles us close.

Ok, boys, got to get our shit together. All right, let me think, ok, something I've wanted to do since I got in here. See what's out that fucking window. Bruce, you get Fergal on your shoulders there, hoist him up.

I nod. I'm still the strongest; Fergal is the lightest. It makes sense. We go over to the barred window. I cup my hand and he stands on it. I lift him up, and he clambers onto my shoulders.

What do you see? Scotchy asks almost frantically.

Ok, there's the towers at the corners and guys on them, two, I think. There's a fence beyond our cell wall here. It's, um, I suppose twenty feet high and there's razor wire in two loops at the top of it.

How far between the wall and the fence? Scotchy asks.

I don't know. Thirty yards, twenty, I can't really judge.

And what's beyond it?

Beyond the fence?

Of course, beyond the fence, Scotchy snaps.

About another thirty or forty yards of grass and then there's trees.

All right, get down. You're fucking killing me, I groan.

Scotchy is pumped, and I am too. But Fergal still on my shoulders is all business:

Even if we get through the door and into the courtyard and up over the cell-block wall and we do get out, there's still the fence. I mean, it's a big fence, and they probably have guard dogs all along it at night, Fergal says.

Would you just get down, ya eejit, I say.

No, wait, tell us everything again, height of the fence, how far, how far to the trees. Are there spotlights on the towers? Scotchy demands.

Scotchy, we can look again later, I say, and Fergal climbs down my back just as I'm about to collapse on the floor.

Scotchy comes over to Fergal and sits down beside him. He looks serious.

Fergal, tell me again, slowly, why you can't pick the lock on the cell door, he says. He doesn't want his hope to vanish so quickly after it just appeared. None of us does.

Fergal shakes his head.

The locks I just opened are easy, standard, from years ago. Once I had his belt buckle filed, it was pretty straightforward. The lock on the door is different: it's big and needs a big key and there's no way I could pick it with this, it's impossible. I'd need the key itself, or a big wad of metal to mold, and even then it would take me months, maybe years, to file it into the right shape.

Fergal has said all this with great patience. Scotchy is quietly appalled. There really isn't a way out, even with our leg irons off. We could never tunnel through the wall. They'd notice that, and the floor's solid concrete. It has to be the door or nothing.

So what's the fucking point then? What difference does it make if we're fucking free in here if we can't get out of the fucking cell? Scotchy says, antagonistically.

I didn't say it makes any fucking difference, Scotchy, so why come on with the attitude to me? Fergal says.

I'll come on with the attitude with whoever I fucking well like, Fergal, Scotchy says.

Aye, well, save it for the tough guys of Crossmaglen, Scotchy. You're not impressing anyone here, Fergal says.

Aye, well, when you did ever impress anyone, ever?

I got us out of the fucking lock.

Aye, and what good is it?

What have you done apart from fuck us up in Mexico with your bollocks? Fergal says, at breaking point.

Now you listen, boy, Scotchy says with menace.

No, you listen.

Let me fucking tell you one or two things.

They start pushing one another. I close my eyes to escape it. I put my hands over my ears.

You fucking can't tell me anything, Scotchy, you have to know something first.

You wee fuck, I was fucking fucks like fucking you before you were born.

Aye, Scotchy, so you say, and you can . . .

I drift out. I can't hear anymore. It's morning and the show'll come on soon. I lean back and look at the rivers and the towns and the canals. There's a railway I haven't noticed before. It connects two of the larger provincial cities on the left continent. Even with its water shortage and irrigation problems it still seems the most technologically advanced of the two kingdoms. There's a new invasion plan that will break the war wide open. The war minister looks at his minutes and notes that this scheme is coming along nicely; that railway line will help. A feint to the south and then a rapid movement of troops to the north and across the Great Ravine. The window continent's forces will still be stuck down in the south. They won't be able to deploy fast enough. They'll be out-flanked. The whole northern side of the window continent will be captured before they can do anything about it. Unless they can retreat, draw the army back to the funnel cobwebs, aye, into the Pripet Marshes, into Siberia. Draw them in, bleed them. I smile. The show's starting. The shadows of the bars are progressing from right to left. I stare at the ceiling. Hmmmm. I-stare-at-the-ceiling. At the ceiling. At the bloody ceiling, and then I have it.

Eu-fucking-reka, I whisper to myself.

*　*　*

It had taken a week, but finally we had made a hole big enough for a man to fit through in the ceiling. We had worked with our bare hands and the manacles on our wrists. (Fergal had refused to let us use his delicate pick. After all, he had to lock us up with it every day when our guards came and he didn't want to damage the thing.) We'd scraped the underlayer of concrete almost the whole way through to the bitumen roof covering.

The prison roof was made of reinforced concrete that had been prepoured into long slabs, craned up, and placed on thick ledges that ran the length of the cell block. The roof was basically a series of simple bridges. The walls were supporting structures, so the whole thing was pretty rigid. It was a cheap job and I wouldn't like to be underneath it if an earthquake hit, but it was good for our purposes.

The concrete was about six inches thick, but the years of weathering had not been kind to its components. It crumbled easily, and the only thing you had to watch was tearing too big a hole in case a chunk of it caved in or the ceiling collapsed on top of you.

As additional protection against rain, over the flat reinforced concrete roof, a layer of tar had been laid down, a sort of bitumenlike substance, that allowed water to run off. That had obviously been years ago and it had warped, torn, and buckled since then. Over the bigger holes they had placed aluminum siding. Still, it was no obstacle at all.

We'd all been builders at some point and knew what we were doing. The cell-block roof was flat, and we checked from the exercise yard that we could get onto it without being seen. At night it would be very dark, and from our observations it seemed that the searchlights only scanned every once in a while. Fergal had done most of the scraping, working on my shoulders and then Scotchy's, but we'd all done our bit. Like I say, the concrete was flaky, pathetic stuff and we'd have got through sooner had we not been careful about not puncturing the bitumen, and that stuff we could rip with our hands the night we decided to go. No point doing it too soon.

We'd made the smallest possible hole in the cell corner and we'd used the *Great Escape* tactic of concrete down our trousers to get rid of the evidence in the yard. Our only problem would be if they decided to do an inspection on the flat roof. Someone walking along might notice, or worse, might fall through it.

If you were in the cell itself and you looked straight up, you might see it or you might not, depending on the light and shade. But none of the guards ever did that anyway.

Our moods had changed. Fergal upbeat. Me, a second wind. Scotchy recalled to life. When we weren't scraping the ceiling, Scotchy had Fergal up on my shoulders checking ambient temperature, the phases of the moon, the regularity of the searchlights, the weather, the terrain beyond the wire, and, seemingly satisfied, he said that we were ready to go in the next few days.

The plan was simple: I'd hoist Fergal up, he'd break through the tar and get on the roof. I'd hoist Scotchy up onto my shoulders and then Scotchy would pull himself up to his waist and I'd grab hold of his ankles and then both of them would pull me up. Once on the roof, we'd drop down onto the grass on the other side of the cell block and make a break for the wire. If there really were dogs (and Fergal in many, many observations hadn't seen one), we'd just have to kill them, and then we'd climb over the wire and make for the forest. Scotchy would head us north to the sea, using (he claimed) the Pole Star, and then we'd steal a boat for the U.S.

Objectively, the plan seemed a bit dodgy, but none of us was or could be in the objective universe quite at the moment.

I think it'll work, Scotchy, I said one day, but if we don't go soon, I'm a little concerned that the guards will discover the hole. I mean, a heavy rain could mess with that film and crack it.

It'll be ok, Bruce. Dark of the moon we go, couple of days, Scotchy reassured me.

Two things we haven't totally thought through, Fergal said.

I smiled at him.

What?

Well, one is food when we get out, and the second is the whole dog thing again, Fergal said.

I looked at him.

We live off the land for food, and really, Fergal, you've got to stop worrying about the dogs. It's something we'll just have to deal with if it happens, I said, doing my absolute best to sound reassuring.

No probs, Fergie boy, Scotchy said.

And Fergal: sure, they'd be Chihuahuas. You know, those wee small ones with yon ears, I said. No probs for the likes of us.

Oh aye, those wee, wee ones, Fergal said, taking what I suggested seriously. It clearly comforted him, so I didn't press it.

I gave Scotchy a look that he didn't see.

Your man Jimmy Deacon had one of them dogs, used to carry it round in his sea jacket, Scotchy said, getting all ruminative with us.

God, Jimmy Deacon, I haven't heard of that name for a while, Fergal said.

I hadn't heard it at all, but I was saying nothing since we seemed to be well off the subject of attack dogs now.

Aye, you remember him, Bruce, don't ya? He was the boy with the one arm that saved yon boy from drowning.

That was Scotchy McMaw, Scotchy, who you don't know before you pretend you do, I said.

I do know him, Scotchy said.

Fergal was speaking, but I was tuning out. It was good to hear the boys talk about home. Talking about anything. I snoozed and I smelled chimneys and peat fires and there were chips in the chippie and hot whiskeys in the pub and the *craic* was good. . . .

Later the same night, and Fergal was looking at us skeptically. He had just climbed down off my shoulders, counting the seconds for the scanning searchlights again. There really was no time period as it turned out. The guards just shone the light haphazardly wherever they liked, but it was rare that they would come back to the same place quickly after they'd swept it.

Soon, Scotchy said. In forty-eight hours no more moon, and we're out of here.

Fergal shook his head. Fergal, even with his optimism, sometimes had a bit of a knack for seeing the black cloud.

What is it, Fergal? I asked him.

He said nothing for a while, but then sure enough it came to pass:

Ach, this fucking plan's full of fucking holes, he said, clearly the culmination of a mounting concern that had grown within him.

Hopefully one big hole, anyway, Scotchy said, giving me a wink.

I laughed, but Fergal wasn't to be diverted.

Well, look, if it's so fucking simple, why haven't they tried it? Fergal asked, jerking his thumb towards the other cells.

'Cause they're remand prisoners; they're awaiting trial, be stupid to escape, Scotchy said.

I was now a bit peeved. This was typical Scotchy.

How do you know that, Scotchy? How could you possibly know a thing like that? I asked.

They are, he insisted.

Aye, Scotchy. How can you fucking know anything? What if there still is dogs, wee or not, between the wall and the fence? What if the fence is electrified? Fergal asked.

Electrified. We're in bloody Mexico, Scotchy snorted.

So what if we are? It could be mined. They have mines, don't they, Fergal insisted.

Come on, Fergal, be realistic, Scotchy said, soothingly.

We all wanted to believe. But we were terrified. Why hadn't the other prisoners made escapes? What did they know? Maybe they didn't have the gumption. Shit, maybe they had made escapes, maybe there'd been lots of escapes. How would we know?

I think it's because they don't have a lock picker as good as Fergal, I said.

'Course they do, must have, this is the criminal element of Mexico. I betcha they make us look like bairns. No, they know something we don't, Fergal said, gloomily.

Well, we can't ask them, we don't have the lingo. And none of them will have anything to do with us, I said.

Aye, and they killed Andy, are you forgetting that? Scotchy said.

Shouldn't we try, at least, have one chat, they're not all killers, just get the lie of the land, Fergal said.

I shook my head.

That oul boy who wanted to talk to me before. One chat. Look, in one minute we could clear everything up. Are there dogs? Is the fence electric? Two quick questions.

Everyone will know we're doing an escape, you buck eejit, I said.

Aye, you'll give the plan away. I forbid it, Scotchy said.

You forbid it? Fergal asked.

Aye, I do.

And who the fuck are you to be giving orders now? Fergal said.

They both stood and stared at one another, each waiting for the first move. I thought for a moment that Scotchy was going to take a swing. I got up and put myself between them.

Sit down the pair of youse, acting like weans, I said.

We all sat down warily.

Fergal, I know it seems silly. I mean, intelligence is important and all, but Scotchy's right, we can't trust those bastards, can't ask them anything, I said.

Aye, you just remember Andy, remember, Scotchy said.

Fergal said nothing. I patted him on the shoulder. Scotchy continued:

Look, it's simple, they just don't have the initiative. Look at us and look at them. You're a star, Fergal, they don't have people like you.

Fergal cracked a smile, but we could tell he was uneasy. I wasn't sure how much of it was genuine concern about the effectiveness of our plan or just plain old-fashioned cold feet. Fergal was no chicken, at least no more than the rest of us, but none of us had been in a situation like this before. Me and Scotchy, though, had both been in the clink, him in Belfast and me in a wee barracks on Saint Helena. But we'd neither of us even bothered with thoughts about escape. Scotchy had been in short term and I was being dishonorably discharged in a matter of weeks. I don't know what it was like for him, but for me it had been a holiday. Fergal, though, was a different kettle: he was a craftsman and a thief and he'd never done time. He'd come to America, and I suppose he'd ended up in the wrong crew working for Darkey and Mr. Duffy. He should really have been pulling scams somewhere or been part of a soft-glove outfit. I mean, he'd handled his gun ok in that shoot-out at Dermot's, but mainly that was because of the hours Darkey made us all spend on the range. He wasn't a heavy, he wasn't cut out for this.

I looked at Scotchy and he looked at me. I wondered if we were both thinking the same thing. We had to calm him down. Andy's death had been terrible for him. We needed to be easy on him. And after all, we owed him everything.

Look it's going to be ok, ya big wean, I said, and patted him on the back.

Aye, it is, Scotchy agreed, smiling too. Sure, isn't it all for you that we can do anything? Like I say, you are a star, Fergal, and when we get back I'm going to see to it that you get a fucking medal.

Fergal smiled at us.

Boys, look, I know it's going to be ok, he said after a time.

We chatted a while and cleared the air. Scotchy said that tomorrow night or at the latest the next night would be the night, depending upon the weather. If there was no lightning storm, we'd go. We agreed and talked some more. Fergal locked us back in the ring bolts and the guard came with rice and water. We ate and drank, and they came for our bowls. I pissed in the bucket and solid shat for the second time since coming to Mexico and wiped my arse with straw. We spent the evening talking, something we rarely did. Scotchy spun us some tales about his childhood, and I told them a made-up story about the girl who used to baby-sit for me.

We slept and it rained and the morning crept up on us. The story in the ceiling was all about the floods and recent devastation in the window continent—flooding, which had postponed all possibility of a quick invasion.

That day was a third day and they came and unlocked us. Every time they did this it made me extremely nervous. I was sure they would notice something about the locks, but they never did. My other fear was that since they just grabbed locks from the big bag when they locked us up again, Fergal wouldn't be able to open the ones they stuck on our ankles. But he was right, they were all more or less the same and none of them took him over two minutes to break.

We walked into the yard.

It all seemed normal, but I wasn't to know that it was going to be a hell of a day.

I dumped the slop bucket in the latrine at the old cell-block end and on the way back grabbed some straw. Fergal and Scotchy walked close behind me, just in case. It was a hot one and the guards were paying less attention than usual. We were all feeling pretty good, though.

Everyone walked clockwise, I'm not sure how, or why, but that's what always happened even if it started out randomly.

In front of us was the little oul boy that Fergal had noticed before. He was maybe in his middle sixties, flat face, Indian. Seemed like an old lag, in and out. I never paid him any mind. Always when we weren't talking the only thing I was thinking about was the bugger who was wearing my sandals. But the old geezer must have been on Fergal's mind, because Scotchy told me later that Fergal had said that last time out he'd heard him singing what he thought was "My Darling Clementine." Scotchy had said to Fergal, Well, so the fuck what? But for Fergal, it was proof that the oul boy knew at least some English. I mean, Jesus fucking Christ.

We dandered round the courtyard and the whistle went, and Scotchy and I broke formation with everyone else, heading quickly back towards our cells. (Sometimes they thumped people who were slow off the courtyard.) We assumed Fergal was behind us, but when we turned to check he wasn't there.

Ach, Jesus, I said, and looked for him in all the melee of people and dust. I thought he'd fallen over. I didn't think it was anything serious, because, like I said, once they had our shoes (or maybe once they knew that Andy had died) the other prisoners weren't interested in intimidating us or giving us a hard time.

Eejit's tripped himself up, I said to Scotchy. But when we looked through the dust we saw that, sure enough, the dumb-ass wanker had gone over to the wee Indian fella and was asking him something.

Trouble, Scotchy predicted in a whisper.

Fergal's voice was ridiculously loud and oddly alien:

Excuse me, mate, I was wondering if you could do me a wee solid and— but before he could continue, the man had turned and started yelling at him, harsh and guttural. He was pushing Fergal, screaming in his face. He was frightened of gawky, harmless Fergal. Any fool, including Fergal, should have seen that.

Fergal grabbed the man by the shoulders.

Calm down, mate, making a whole fuss. We don't want everybody over, Fergal said.

The man shoved Fergal's arms off him and caught Fergal a glancing blow on the face.

That's it, come on, I said to Scotchy, but before we could make it over, Fergal had punched the little man on the jaw. He went down like a collapsing stack of cards, crumpling there in the dust. Fergal backed off and looked about him, but it was too late. Another man had been running over, all the time, from the lower end of the cell block. Our age. He had something in his hand. It was glinting.

He's got a fucking knife, I yelled, and we both ran.

Fergal heard me and turned his head, but the man had jumped him from behind. There was a yell and a lot of dust and when we got over,

158 / ADRIAN MCKINTY

Fergal was lying on his back with a piece of glass embedded in his chest. In his heart. Scotchy and I both wailed for the guards. The whistle blew again and they fired a shotgun in the air. They yelled at us to move. We sat there.

Everywhere dust, in vortices, ascending like prayers.

I tried doing mouth to mouth, but there was no breath in him. Guards came and beat us away and dragged us back to our cells. They locked us in the leg irons and howled at us and shook their heads in amazement and disgust. They spat and left, banging the door behind them.

Scotchy crawled over to me.

Do you think he'll make it? he asked.

I shook my head.

No chance.

Scotchy scrambled back to his side of the cell and we sat there saying nothing, staring wide-eyed at one another.

❖ ❖ ❖

Our condition worsened. Scotchy began to get his cough again, and both of us were weak as kittens. We hardly had the energy to catch the crickets anymore, and Scotchy concealed from me the fact that his hair was falling out in clumps.

Our luckiest break was that Fergal had left the pick in the cell near a wall. I'd found it after a panicky half-day search. I suppose he'd had the gumption to realize that he could have lost the pick out in the yard, could have dropped it. He had that much bloody sense, at least. I thought about him. Fergal was an only child. His folks were still alive. They'd take it hard. What a complete fucking eejit.

It took Scotchy about a week to figure out the way to pick the locks on our wrist and ankle chains. He'd done a wee bit of that line of work before with cars and bike locks, but Fergal had really made it seem simple.

Scotchy didn't care anything about the moon now, he just wanted us out of here. It was getting colder at nights and the cell was damp. We were exponentially weaker every day and we could both see that we couldn't wait much longer.

He got himself out in five days and in the early morning, a day later, he got me out. It wasn't a third day, so we wouldn't have to go into the yard, thank God. Indeed, the very minute he got both of us out of the leg irons, we were ready to go. He spent the rest of the day working on the locks on our wrist manacles, but these weren't so important. We both thought that somehow we'd bloody manage it even if our wrists were chained. Which, as it turned out, would have been disastrously wrong.

It was academic, anyway, for Scotchy got himself out of his wrist manacle at noon and he literally had just gotten me out of mine a few hours later when the door opened and the guard came in with food.

I'd been leaning over next to Scotchy and I leaned back and tried my best to rearrange the chains. He started to fake-cough to give the guard something to look at. The guard was Squinty, who had a bad eye and a jowly face. He was the nicest of the bunch, though, and sometimes, rarely, made a remark.

Today of all days he decided to stop and speak to us while we finished our food.

Scotchy was tense. Our legs and wrists were obviously unlocked. I knew he would be formulating a plan which would be a suicide mission. Squinty would notice that we weren't locked in our irons and Scotchy would leap up and kill him immediately with his manacle. The only thing then would be to make a break for it across the yard, somehow overpower another guard, get a gun, get over the gate, get a car . . . Certain death.

Squinty was practicing his terrible English:

Is baseball is no good, *fútbol, sí, fútbol,* everyone play *fútbol,* he said.

Normally I liked to encourage Squinty, to get more rice out of him. Today, though, I just wanted to get him the fuck out before Scotchy did something stupid. But even so, I didn't want to act out of the ordinary, either.

In Ireland, where we're from, remember, we play football, we don't play baseball, we're Irish, not Americans, Irish, we play football, I said slowly.

Squinty grinned and looked up at the ceiling.

He pointed. Of course, he doesn't notice our leg irons, but today he sees the big hole in the concrete roof.

Oh, Jesus fuck, I whispered.

Scotchy began to get up.

Squinty lowered his arm and made a mock shiver.

Huracán, hurricane, big wind, he said.

There's a hurricane coming? I asked, and made eye contact with Scotchy, pleading with him to sit the fuck down.

Big wind, he said, grinning.

Maybe big wind blows away prison and we all go free, I said, and forced a laugh.

Squinty didn't understand but laughed anyway, took away our plates, and locked the door.

Scotchy came over and patted me on the shoulder.

Did well, Bruce, he said.

For the rest of the day I tried to keep my food down, and I mostly succeeded.

We waited until nightfall. As soon as it was good dark, we were leaving.

Getting up through the high ceiling with three people would have been relatively easy—with two it was going to be difficult. But we had a plan.

You all set? I asked him.

He nodded.

I hoisted him up onto my shoulders and he scraped away at the bitumen until there was a hole in the roof that let in the stars. Yeah, with two of us it would be harder to get out but what we were going to do would probably work. Instead of Scotchy going first, Scotchy jumped down and I got on his shoulders. He was pretty unsteady, so as soon I was up there I started pulling myself up through the hole. The light was incredible, there was a huge sky filled with stars. The spotlights on the three occupied towers were playing randomly over the yard and the roof and the fence. I pulled myself up, and when I had my elbows over the edge of the hole, Scotchy jumped from the cell below and grabbed onto my ankles. He was heavier than I'd thought and it took a painful effort not to fall back down into the cell again.

I gritted my teeth and, drawing some reserve of anger, I attempted to pull myself and Scotchy up through the hole. It was almost impossible, but I managed it. When my thighs were through, I lay almost flat on the roof and crawled with straight legs towards the edge of the cell block, Scotchy hanging on the whole time. It was difficult, but gradually I was making it, using the roof as a lever and going slow. I felt Scotchy's hands let go of my ankles and grab the sides of the hole. I turned round and grabbed him by the remains of his shirt and tugged the bastard, and he was up.

We were through the roof and hadn't been seen. We crouched there for a moment, elated. Breathing hard. The searchlight beams were tracking lazily and indiscriminately on the far side of the cell block. Only two out of the three were working and they weren't particularly powerful.

That was easy, Scotchy said.

I grinned at him. Aye, easy for you, I whispered.

We looked down the other side of the cell block. We weren't going the way of the courtyard and the front gate; it was the fence or nothing.

The only thing for it now would be to get down. I could see that the drop was about fifteen feet. Higher than the ceiling, much higher. The concrete floor of our cell was clearly raised above the ground, probably because of thick foundations. It was a good job we hadn't decided to tunnel.

We had to jump, but if we went for it, there was no way we could climb back into the prison again. If we jumped, we were committed. We couldn't scout the fence and go another night. It was tonight or nothing.

Scotchy, look, I whispered, it's a big drop. If we go now we're not getting back in.

Why the fuck would we want back in?

I don't know.

Just go, you big girl.

I turned and crawled away from the hole towards the edge of the cell block. I looked over and then turned round and began lowering myself down as far as I could by the arms. When I was holding on only by my fingers, I tensed and dropped. I hit the ground and rolled to the side and I was ok. I'd stuffed straw down my trousers and T-shirt to help with the razor wire, and as I rolled, it helped cushion the blow a little. Nothing was broken, and I got up. I started walking backwards to give Scotchy space to jump. After about three yards I discovered perhaps why the other prisoners hadn't availed themselves of our brilliant method of escape. My feet went suddenly into sucking marsh up to my knees. I looked and it all became obvious: nearly the entire prison was surrounded by a swamp. In an instant, I could see the whole thing clearly. The prison was built on a peninsula of hard rock, with layers of concrete on top. The area at the gatehouse and the road were also on good land, but within ten feet of the east, west, and north walls it became a bog. It could be that they designed it that way as an extra precaution against escape, but I doubted it. The whole countryside seemed swampy, and more than likely they'd built the prison on the best bit of hard ground they could find and the swamp was an added bonus. Once you put a wire up, it would be impossible to get through. The only way in and out of the prison was along the road and through the gate. The only bit of solid ground was at the gate and, of course, the gate was crawling with guards. For a third-world country it was all pretty ingenious, and I would have been impressed had I not been so completely gutted as I stood there, horrified and amazed.

As far as I could tell, the only way out would be to make your way round to the gatehouse and climb back over into the courtyard and then try and get out over the front gate where there was solid ground. I couldn't believe Fergal, in all his long observations, hadn't realized this was a bog, an impassable, quicksandy fucking swamp. He thought it was fucking grass. The idiot. The bloody stupid no-brained bastard.

Scotchy landed awkwardly in front of me. He grunted and came to his feet.

Are you ok? I asked.

Aye.

Scotchy, bad news, I said.

What?

It's a bog. All this over here isn't grass, it's bog all the way to the wire. The fence is on pile drives. None of it's solid ground at all.

I'd tried to keep the panic out of my voice. Scotchy, similarly, was not to be perturbed.

We'll just wade through it, Brucey boy, he said, breezily.

It'll take a long time, if we don't get stuck or drowned. They'll pick us up on the lights, I said. Can't do it.

What fucking choice do we have? We can't go back, can we? Scotchy said, furiously.

I shook my head, but of course he was right. We couldn't get back in. If we walked round to the gatehouse they'd see us for sure. We had no other options. Scotchy went first. The swamp was thick with mossy grass on top, but your weight immediately broke the surface. Scotchy sank to his waist and for a second I thought he was going to be sucked all the way down. He was a country boy, though, and maybe he knew a bit about bog walking. At first, however, it seemed not. His arms flailed, and he fell back and sank up to his elbows. Then he flung himself forward and he began to float a little, but as soon as he tried to move, he went under. Farther out from the prison, it seemed that it became more watery and less boggy. Scotchy scrambled onto the floating grasses and tried to swim, but still it was too thick. His head kept ducking under, and now he looked as if he was going to drown.

The whole thing was a fiasco, but I went in after him anyway. I waded up to my waist to see how deep it got and when it was neck height I tried to swim too. It wasn't quite quicksand, but it was still pretty thick stuff. Swimming was utterly impossible: your legs were so buoyant, your body buckled up and your head kept sinking. Your arms were too weak and coated to help you anyway. Everywhere in suspension were grains of sand and silt and thick muck. The only thing like it I'd experienced was when I'd swum in a quarry sinkhole as a kid, garbage and cars and mud and reeds making it all a potential death trap. But this was worse. Even dog-paddling was impossible; you kept going underneath the surface and bobbing up under the grass, swallowing the thick, grainy water. I tried the crawl and breaststroke, but always the same problem, I would sink rather than swim, my legs coming out of the water and my shoulders and head going underneath it. Again and again, water went into my lungs, and I scrambled for the surface. Finally, I turned round and started clawing my way back to the cell block. There was no way I could get through twenty or thirty yards of this to the wire. I turned slowly and pointed myself towards the prison, but Scotchy saw and stopped me and whispered loudly:

On your back, on your back, Bruce, on your back.

I looked over to discover that he was doing a sort of backstroke through the swamp and he was actually making good progress. His head and arms were cutting the mossy surface like an icebreaker and his legs were kicking and giving him momentum. He was evenly buoyant and he wasn't sinking. I couldn't quite figure out why this worked and not the breaststroke or the crawl, but it did. I rolled over on my back and began gently moving backwards, following in the trail that Good King Scotchylass was making. The surface was thick and closed in behind us when we got through it, but we were getting through it, slowly, but we were doing it. The spotlight beam was tracking along the swamp, but this time it was going so sluggishly, it was easy for us to duck under when it was a few feet away and then come up again. It probably wouldn't be back now for a while.

We swam and pushed our way through and then waded a little backwards until we got to the fence. Thank God, Scotchy had had the patience to get our wrists unchained too; we would have failed otherwise.

We were utterly exhausted, and we both could hardly believe that we'd made it.

Scotchy was saying something, but he was so excited it was incoherent.

Get our breath, I was saying, and Scotchy nodded. We hung there for a long time on the bottom of the fence. We were breathing hard, and our arms and legs ached.

Can we go under it? I asked.

Scotchy dived down to see if we could get underneath the fence, but according to him it went a good bit down.

It can't go all the way down, do you think they had fucking divers? I said.

Listen, Bruce, the swamp is probably seasonal, rainy season and all that. I'm telling you it goes all the way down to the mud.

Aye, well, I'm checking, I said.

I tried pulling myself down to the very bottom of the wire, and after about four or five feet I did find the bottom. You could maybe squeeze underneath it, under the wire; it was tight, but you could maybe do it.

I came up gasping for air and told Scotchy what I'd found.

Look, we're not going to fucking drown under that thing. We'll never make it, we're going over.

I saw his point. We probably would get stuck under there and die a horrible suffocating death. I nodded. I didn't want to go over, but under was too hard. When we were rested, there was nothing else for it but to climb.

We started out, and climbing was a lot easier than the swamp. The fence had big holes that feet could fit into and it was fairly rigid so it didn't wobble everywhere. We climbed steadily, not wanting to slip or make any noises. Scotchy was to my right. We'd decided to go up together, though it probably would have made more sense to go one at a time.

When we were near the top of the fence, we took a breather. We were now at the razor wire, and we were both beat.

What now? Scotchy asked, as we hung there panting.

We just got to go over it, Scotchy, that's all. We just got to.

I grabbed a piece of wire and hauled myself up. There was a sharp, stabbing, terrible pain in my palm; I'd cut myself already, a gash right under my thumb.

Fuck, I whispered. Jesus, Mary, and Joseph.

I pulled myself up halfway onto the first roll of wire. Most of the straw had fallen out of my T-shirt and I was scraped and cut all over my chest and arms. I pulled myself up farther, my right hand and my legs getting a slashing. I knew it would be worse for Scotchy, because at least I had jeans to protect my legs a little and he had only his shorts.

I tugged, and the razor wire dug into my chest.

Christ.

I was in a complete panic now. The pain was awful and the thought of going on was worse. I was in the middle of the front roll of wire and here the coil wasn't tight or thick, so I was leaning way out backwards over the swamp.

My bare feet shivered on the edge of the fence and I knew it would be a new horror when I pulled them up onto the first coil of wire. I had to find a spot on the coil at the top of the fence where there were no razors. I stood there for a long while, raised my foot, and placed it on the coil. I took a breath and pulled myself up, placing all my weight on the wire. I'd missed the razors but the whole coil of wire trembled and leaned back, and for a second I thought I was going to fall off backwards into the swamp.

Shit.

It was moving like a great writhing serpent. It was impossible to get a steady grip.

What's going on? Scotchy whispered.

I couldn't reply. I took another breath. Whatever happened, I couldn't stay in this position, I'd fall in a second or two. I was leaning way back, my hands digging into the wire just to hold on.

Scotchy was whispering something again, but I couldn't hear him. I froze for a second, unsure of what exactly I was going to do. I rocked back a little and then pushed forward with all my strength. The coils of wire returned to the vertical.

I took my foot off the razor wire and put it back on the top of the fence.

I pushed the razor wire hard and the big curl of wire moved forward to a position where it seemed more rigid.

Scotchy was still there on the fence. He hadn't gone near the wire yet. I was glad, for if both of us had been on it when it went backwards we would have gone off for sure. But even so, he couldn't linger there all night.

Scotchy, for fucksake, come on, I said.

Ok, I'm coming, just getting my breath, wanker, he said. It was the last thing I ever heard him say.

I lifted my leg and planted my foot on the first roll of wire again. I was trying to be delicate, and I did get lucky, my toes finding a safe area. I heaved my body up and leaned forward on the first roll. I put the other foot on and pushed. My hands were cut to shite, but I was nearly halfway over the first roll. If the wire had been put on better, tighter, it would have been easier, but it was so loose it was practically hugging you, slicing at you. Pain and the fear of the pain between breaths.

I scrambled up another inch. The wire embraced me again, tearing me, ripping me. I convulsed and threw up.

The wire vibrated horribly, and I could feel Scotchy on it to my right.

Everything happened at once now.

The searchlight, which had been scanning to our left in the swamp, suddenly raised itself and went along the wire. There was nothing we could do, we couldn't drop off now, we just had to hope that it lowered itself at the last moment.

It didn't.

The beam swept straight past us and then came back and stayed there.

Voices began yelling in Spanish. I scrambled up the second roll, falling up it. The razors cut horribly into my feet and fingers and I hooked one along my face. I heard a shotgun pop and misfire and then another one spray a barrel of shot into the fence to our left. The prison was a big old guard dog, shaking itself and coming to life. I heard more yelling and then a high-powered automatic rifle, an M16 without a doubt, and I saw Scotchy get hit in the back.

Scotchy, I yelled, but his body went limp and tumbled downwards almost all the way through the first coil of razor wire. The razors nearly decapitated him, slicing into his neck and hanging him there. His arms shook and, as blood poured grotesquely from his mouth, his jaw moved up and down, as if he was trying to speak.

Jesus Christ.

I stared and cried out and then desperately climbed on and reached the top of the second coil through a threshold of screaming nerve endings. The wire swayed and wrapped itself about and in me. It went effortlessly into my flesh and I used the purchase to pull myself on.

At the top of the second coil, I balanced on my stomach and all the while there were shotguns firing and the whirr of a couple of Armalites. I forward-rolled over the crest of the second coil of wire, my hair and shoulders getting caught and pulled and torn, and then I fell thirty feet into the swamp on the other side. I stayed under the water and swam and briefly surfaced for air and swam again. I did this for two minutes, and I realized I'd gone way to the left but hardly any farther from the fence.

The whole prison was awake. They were ringing a bell and shining the two big searchlights at the swamp where I'd originally fallen in. Everyone taking potshots at the water. I ducked out of the spotlight beam and moved with my backstroke towards the trees. The shooting was deafening and continuous, but they didn't shift the spotlight beam at all. Perhaps they think I've broken my neck and drowned, I was saying, comforting myself.

I waded to the trees. The forest was waterlogged and thick with vines that tripped me every few yards. It gave way to solid ground and I ran, my feet shrieking with the hurt, my eyes full of blood. My hands were burning, my thighs, my feet. I'd sliced off two or three toes, gashed a hole under my eye.

I ran the whole of the night, and when day came I slept under the giant roots of a jungle tree, and when night came I got up and ran again.

8: *SUR DE LA FRONTERA*

Out of the waste and in the prodigal rain nothing animate breathes or moves or lives above the height of man . . .

The abyss, emptiness, a scorched and sunken earth. An abandoned quarter. A place out of a nightmare. A slough over a hard ground and an impenetrable sky. Night and day are indistinguishable and become one long dread universe outside of time. The rain is cold and falling with such force and mettle that it makes divots in the clay. The wind with it whips and buries itself into every groove and crevice on the ground. It veers and backs and brings the rain horizontal and slantwise and sometimes, in mock of physical laws, upwards.

Nature has cast itself as the destroyer, as the scourge, Shiva wiping the slate clean. And here, out here in the wild land, it is being born again of water.

It's the hurricane and everything has a burrow.

Well, nearly everything . . .

Above is a vast black cloud out of which comes terrible light and the downpour, which leaches out loam and color and washes everything away. An awful wind that carries seawater, stones, bicycle parts, branches.

The topography is frozen into fragile inclines and declines and a horizonless perspective. A vast steppe devoid of beings and every living thing. Underneath there are sharp stones and lava rocks and here and there are ghosts of trees and a ruined house, as if from the days of the famine.

Another Ireland, the far northwest, the Sperrins, the bogland around Slemish Mount.

A pulverized sheet of ground and a landscape so familiar and yet unfamiliar that there can be naught but an epidemic of memory. Coffins of wet glassy stones and withered alphabets and celestial tracks in the red clay.

And everything punctuated by wind and rain. Rain, especially that.

Another mile, another ten, and over this hill ancient pylons are clambering on the terrain like a virus, following a line of steel and wire, clumping together perhaps in the direction of a settlement. In the country that is and can be. Civil and uncivil and metallic. But you're on the run and that way is barred, if it is the way of people.

West, then. A green land of slabber, an invisible mesa on the world's edge. A rise and a valley, hours of movement and a lake that did not exist a week before. There are scrubby bushes and reeds and suffo-cated trees. The world postdiluvian with water everywhere. No lizard or insect or belly crawler remains above the ground. Their homes are inundated and battle-scarred, gone into the book of insurance agents and loss adjusters. Mars has used his influence and braised the globe closer to the fastness underneath.

It's the hurricane and rain is unceasing. Aye, it's obvious now. Apparent in the signs and portents. The rain is a baptism and a cleans-ing agent. There is transparency in its coldness. The wind, too, speaks. It casts up euphonies of the dead. They have promises and they make you swear. Their talk is easy and reposed, but such are the words of phantoms, for they have time on their hands and are removed from the pressures of the Earth. They haunt you and urge you on. Pressure you, hint. It isn't the banshee, there's no death, at least not yet. Just voices. Their talk is Spanish and Mayan and Olmec and languages that have died here long ago but whose parallel exists somewhere in Kamchatka or Mongolia or the Aleutians. They murmur softly and tug your beard and trip your feet.

Paddy fields, a river valley, a collapsed stone wall for shelter. A cough and an adjourned heartbeat. Your eyes close and reopen again slowly, with sleep in them. The grass makes a hole for you.

The rivers rise and the rain and wind come so loud you lose yourself. The trees are less (or more) than dead now, they are stone: fossils, and around them the smell of sage becomes overwhelming. It's almost enough to make you long for the jungle. But it'll come again. You'll see.

One foot in front of another. Pain that is no longer there. It has ceased to exist, for how can there be pain when there cannot be that intensity of feeling. It is possible to move to a plane beyond pain and beyond hunger. It is possible to exist just barely above the level of the realm about us. To coast on a slender splinter of consciousness. That's how a shadow moves. A ghost.

How many days?

Half a week?

A skeleton, a specter, sliding across the land.

A hill, a river, and now a place where humans have been—evidence in the dead wood of telegraph poles. Ancient pines that have been blackened and grooved by weathering and that have numbers on them and strange symbols and the cracks of heat and cold.

But no birds on the wire or the uprights, for the animal realm entire is disappeared; indeed, only the simpler forms of plants survive: sage and small grasses and shrubs and blue lichen and black mosses that coat themselves thinly over a hard, dark soil and bare rock.

Where are compassionate stars, where the sequences of people, the friendly cows and horses? It's the hurricane, and they have all abandoned ship, deserted and left behind only their music and their trace.

Inclines, rolling valleys.

Scrub that eventually gives way to high grasses.

Fields flooded and everywhere the tracks of creatures making for higher ground. A corn crop ruined. Maize. A commonplace field of potatoes. You dig them up, those livid white tubers.

It's still night, it's always night. You can't see the moon, or Orion, you can't see where anything is. At least is this still the Earth? Or is it some new place conceived and brought forth by the ocean? These are answers to impossible questions.

A day of this and the contour lines are narrowing and there are palms, and before it is even announced, the forest is there again like a wall. Dense and vine-covered and resistant a little to the gale and rain. The trees whisper to themselves in a vocabulary that no human will understand. They are talking about water and the brown volcanic earth between their toes and the wind that tears through the upper branches and kills the young and very old.

You can't follow it but you are enough now of a jungle creature to get the gist. The trepidation. The excitement. The waxy creatures with a thousand eyes and ears. The forest thickens and darkens and there is some cover from the weather. Unlit, and there are demons here. Black, coiled snakes. Jaguars, panthers, monkeys, and the beasts of childhood dreams. Great *el tigre* above you and fantastic beings: griffin and hawkman and things from the last book of Gulliver.

Run-off golden water, wild fruits, bananas. Half of them are poison. Crouch down on one knee and vomit them up, vomit them and drink off a leaf and get up and go on.

You're walking through the submerged and almost disappeared crater, two hundred miles wide, from a cometary impact sixty-five million years ago, a comet that struck the Yucatán with many times the force of every nuclear weapon currently on the planet, a comet that threw millions of tons of dirt and rock into the atmosphere and blackened the sun for months and changed the climate forever. That wiped out the dinosaurs and two thirds of all other living things on the planet. That made space for a little lemurlike creature that evolved through sixty-five million years into you.

You walk through the crater and you are weak and your wounds are not healing and animals inhabit spaces beneath your pale skin. You limp and the nails have fallen off your toes. You walk and you hallucinate and it occurs to you that perhaps you are already dead. That you are dead and this is hell. That this and all that follows is a rite of passage and a fantasy and you are dead on the wire or mad and in your cell.

You try and penetrate the veil to a higher form of existence, but at present you cannot. This reality appears to be the only one given to you. So it will have to serve.

Your skin is hanging from you and your hair is falling out, you are in rags caked with blood and filth. But you are a holy fool. Enthused. The Lord is in you. You are St. Anthony in the demon-filled desert. You are Diogenes mired in grime. You are the Buddha at Bodhgaya. You are a Jain priest, naked, with a broom before you to sweep away any living being that you might inadvertently step upon. You are holy because you are possessed by a vision of a future time. It is a bright vision and a tight one, compact. Simple. The truth of it has made you pure. It is you. You are healed and strong and patient. You have bided your time and you have slept alone in the city. No one knows you are there, you have been waiting. Watching. And now you are ready. You have acquired a firearm and you are taking the subway train. You are in a house and you have silenced bodyguards and opposition. You are in a study with a man explaining, pleading, he didn't know there would be deaths. You don't want explanations, you just want to pull the trigger and turn and leave. Which you do. You leave and that is all. What happens next, if anything, is irrelevant. The circle is complete, the future event comes back to the now. It is the clarity of this vision that makes your legs move and your lungs breathe. That drives every tendon and nerve within you. Yes, you are beyond pain and beyond hunger. Your mind is cast and your will is subservient to this pact with tomorrow.

What kind of an emotion is revenge? Oh, it is much derided. And observers to an execution will often say that they feel repulsed and unsatiated. That it made no difference. The Hebrew God knows this and reserves the right to vengeance for Himself. It's an eejit's game. The cycle of violence that spreads itself out from West Belfast and the Bogside and South Armagh. Tit for tat and eye for eye; didn't someone say that these rules leave us all blind? And yet what if it's all you have? There are other motivations for a narrative of your life. Love, ambition, greed. But you have erased them all and there is only one thing left. It's either that or absorb yourself further into the wraith's world, disappear completely. No. It isn't noble, but it'll do. It is good, good enough.

Not that your thoughts have coalesced into a plan, or even that they make sense at all. It's rather more that in the cold and the unfeeling extremities of your mind there is one glowing coal that helps you to move, put one foot in front of another.

The vines trip you and the trees talk, but they let you pass. The jaguar sleeps and does not stir. The snake rests. You are a fellow being. You cannot see any of them, but they are there and they recognize you. You are part of this now. The forest. Deep into the bush. The swamp comes up to your knees and the hurricane pauses while the eye crosses.

It is only a respite, but in fact, as you'll see, the worst is done. The peninsula has broken it. The wind and the rain come again, but they are halfhearted. They have exhausted themselves. It's a harsh autumn in Rathlin for a day and you sleep in a forest clearing that in County Antrim they would say had been enchanted by the wee people. And when you wake, the sky is gray and the rain is less and the dream within you is fast and clear.

❋   ❋   ❋

The hurricane had moved northeast and died to a warm drizzle. I slept under a highway bridge, and as the river rose, tiny crabs came out of the water and sidled up the bank. I killed one with a rock and tried to eat the flesh, but it was rancid and not fit for human consumption. The river continued to flood, and it became dangerous under there. I saw that I could be swept away or trapped under the overhang and drowned; but even so, I needed a break from the downpour. The crabs were coming out of the little holes in the mud and soon the concrete slopes were full of them. They crawled over one another and came up to investigate if I was still alive or not. I wondered where we were and tasted the river water and saw that it was fresh. I hadn't known then that there were such things as freshwater crabs, and for a while I'd assumed I was near the sea. I'd been walking directionless for a long time and, for all I knew, I might have circled back and been close to where I'd started, wherever that was.

I scooted the wee shites away, but they kept coming back and eventually the crabs were too much and I climbed up out of the overhang and went along the road. A road that in good times must be an impressive two-lane affair, cutting through the jungle and the plains, but now, quite frankly, was a fucking mess. Mud and branches and landslides had made it impassable. There was no hitching here, and it was actually easier to walk at a steadier pace going through the jungle.

I was feeling better. I hadn't eaten and I was sick with fever and I was concerned that the gash on my foot from the razor wire was turning gangrenous, but for some reason I was feeling better.

As the rain eased, the jungle soundtrack picked up again and I began to see the creatures. The ants were the first out, clearing up the

mess like the global janitors they are. Then there were flies and mos-
quitoes and lizards and then from nowhere came the birds. Blue ones
and a crimson one and a parrot or two. It cheered me. I ate some fruit
off the trees. By trial and error I'd found which ones didn't make me
throw up. The green prickly ones were ok and the red ones that looked
like oranges weren't bad either. I chewed bark, too, as I walked, and all
this time I wasn't really ever very hungry, which I took as a bit of a bad
sign.

Night came, and I climbed a few feet off the ground onto a wide,
splayed-out branch and tried to sleep a little. Songs were a great comfort; I didn't sing but just played them in my head.

Girls. Bridget. Rachel. Cousin Leslie, whose brother-in-law was
big-time in the building trade. A foreman. Yeah, don't worry, Michael,
Mr. White doesn't need muscle. He's looking for lads from the Old
Country who'll work hard and come on time and take minimum wage.
Yeah. Sure. And that's why I'm here. The jungle.

Noisy. My mind drifted and would not sleep.

What did you say? Revenge. Is that what you said? Is that enough to
get you through, can that drive an engine like you? Shouldn't it be hot,
won't it dampen? No. It'll do. It isn't much, but it's enough and I promise you, it'll do.

That's what I was saying. Foolish maybe, but that was it. Thinking
too much. Too much. My heart, a snare drum in my ears. And there
was a dullness beneath my left knee.

I managed to get off to sleep and woke in the morning, stiff and
shivering.

The rain was gone for now. I attempted to climb a tree and get a
perspective, but I wasn't made for climbing yet; walking was hard
enough.

I licked dew off a leaf and ate some of the things that looked like
pears. During the night, ants had come and made me part of their fra-
ternity, cleaning bits of scabs and exploring unwholesome aspects of
my skin. They hadn't woken me, so I chose to see them as benign
beings.

I walked along the springy forest floor, mulch and dead leaves making it an easy path for the weary. The vines were the enemy, though,
getting everywhere and trying to trip you. It wasn't hot, and this at least

was a relief. I walked directionless all day and lay down in the afternoon. My leg was almost numb, and this concerned me more than anything else. I sat down and sniffed it, but I didn't smell anything. I wasn't sure if that was a good thing or not. I tried to get up but sitting had been a mistake and I was too knackered now. I found another likely-looking branch and curled into the fetal position and slept.

The next day I realized I was having hallucinations. I might have been having them all along, but it took me until then to see that my mind wasn't completely clear. I woke with vultures tearing at my left leg, tearing huge chunks out of it. I sat up and tried to shoo them away, but they were massive, ugly, bold creatures that paused merely to look at me with contempt and continue their abominable activity. I screamed and thrashed wildly and still the birds hung on. I swung at them with my fists, and I overbalanced and fell off the low branch and onto the forest floor. I stared about and, of course, there were no vultures at all. I cracked up then, sobbed, and sat there for a long time. To have got out of the prison, clean away, and then to have made it through a hurricane only to die of fever in the jungle. It hardly seemed fair.

How was I going to get to America, to carry out my plan?

How indeed? I was lost. I was sick. My leg ached. And most important, my mind was not clear. I tried to think, but everything inside my head was sluggish. Christ, was I really going mad?

I drove away the panic and breathed and tried to get some thoughts together. I could either stay here and hope someone came by, or I could go on and try to find help. If it meant giving myself up to the authorities, so be it. Surely that would be better than dying insane out here in the tropical rain forest.

I tried to get up, but it was impossible.

I found a stick. I heaved myself up and started walking, going a third the speed of previous days and looking always at the ground to make my way easier. I went half a day like this and collapsed, exhausted, drenched with sweat and bleeding from scrapes on my arms and feet. It rained that night and woke me, and I lay with my mouth open trying to drink a little.

In the morning, I couldn't get up and I decided I would have to crawl. Crawling was a bit easier than walking, and I actually made better progress. On my hands and knees I could negotiate better the fallen trees and vines. I went like this that day and into the next. To my surprise, the jungle began to thin a little and I could see huge patches of sky through the canopy.

That night I had terrible hallucinations about snakes biting at my ankles and trying to eat my leg whole. They were wrapped around me and suffocating me. I screamed the whole of the night and begged them to stop, but they only fled with the dawn.

In appalling fear, I crawled away from the place I'd slept. I moved blind now, for my eyes didn't open. I crawled for hours, and I fell on my face and slept that way. During the night, I crawled again and I thought the end must be coming soon. I'm not overly defeatist, but I am a realist, and I could see that I was in trouble. I could see that I was in mortal shape. I crawled on, expecting, soon, paroxysm and death.

I was wrong, though. Old Atropos wasn't hovering overhead that evening and wouldn't be for some time to come. But it was night and the daughters of Nyx must have been guiding me, because if I'd turned a slightly different way to the left or right I would never have made it to the pig pen. I would have veered off into the jungle and died sometime in the next few days. But as I say, the Gods or the Fates or involved beings who'd heard about my story, about my narrative, about my plan, realized that to continue the show, they had to preserve me and so, out of the jungle, they made a pig pen with small, black, friendly pigs, and they allowed me to crawl up to it and stop and collapse and wait.

It wasn't long. The pigs snuffed my face and licked it. There were children's voices first, distracted, singing, and then silence for a while and whispers and then the sound of running. Not long after that, the voice of an older woman whispering at first too, and then barking instructions. And then arms, a dozen arms lifting me up. I was thinking that if this was another hallucination it was one I liked. Tiny arms lifting me, half-dragging me, not very far into darkness.

Water on my lips and questions in Spanish, many questions.

¿Quién es usted? ¿De dónde ha venido usted? ¿Qué sucedió a su pie?

More water, and then voices raised. A man arguing with two women, clearly about me. He was opposed to my presence, but I could tell that his heart wasn't in it. Someone began washing me and taking off my clothes and tiny fingers were picking the lice out of my hair. At the same time, a soothing voice fed me water and in the water there was ground maize. They cleaned me and put a blanket over me, and I shivered still and slept.

During the night I cried, and first the man and then the two women sat up with me, holding my hand, dripping water onto my lips.

Estamos consiguiendo a un buen hombre, él es médico, the woman said. The word *médico* stuck in my head.

I need Bridget, I said, she'll help me.

The woman talked to me in Spanish and sang to me a little, and I think I slept. In the morning there was another voice, stern and almost angry. He was talking to the women and the man. He asked me questions, but I could say nothing. Then suddenly, violently, he poked at my foot and I cried out. It seemed to confirm everything that he'd been saying, and he sighed and went outside.

Later, they fed me beans and water and milk and they bathed me again, wiping me down with wet rags and then wrapping me in a blanket. The woman spoke to me for hours, soothing me and comforting me, and then the angry man came back. He had brought other men with him. I was falling in and out of consciousness. I couldn't see. The word *médico* came up again.

I want Bridget, she's a good nurse, I want her. She'll look after me. She looked after Andy. He's in good shape. Get Bridget, please, please, I really want to see her. I want to see her.

The angry man came over, his voice mellow now, kind.

It is ok, he said in English.

I tried to open my eyes, and I did for a second or two, but everything was out of focus. I felt strong arms hold me down on the cot and then the blanket was removed. I was naked under the blanket and I was self-conscious. I tried to cover myself, but the arms held me by my side. Someone was pouring brandy into my mouth. I recognized it. How in the name of God had they gotten brandy? They forced a stick between my teeth and then I realized what it was they were about. I yelled and thrashed my arms, but they held me fast. I struggled for only about a minute and then I calmed my mind and resigned myself. The man holding my shoulders was the very first man. He kissed me on the forehead and whispered things in my ear in Spanish: it would be ok, it would be ok. I would be brave and it would be ok. The angry man, too, soothed me in broken English.

Please not worry, it is fast.

Then in a soft voice the older woman explained in slow and simple Spanish how everything would go. I got none of it, but her demeanor helped quiet me further.

Sí, sí, I said and nodded to show that I understood now. There were murmurs of approval. I was in a small hut and their breaths were close to mine. I bit down on the stick, and I was ready.

It was a hacksaw, but it had been sharpened. I felt it go in above my ankle and I was relieved, because I thought they might do it below my knee. The whole thing must have taken less than twenty minutes. The actual sawing under two. What he did down there, I don't know, but he stopped the flow of blood and mended the wounds and halted the screaming of the nerve endings. They gave me a sweet drink and told me to sleep, and after a while I did.

The next day I could open my eyes, and I saw that I was in a hut with a thatched roof and a hard dirt floor. It was swept and clean but hardly hygienic and not the place I would have chosen to recover from major surgery. I had the will to survive but will can't do everything, will can't do the job of antibiotics; just ask any of those prematurely dead Christian Scientists.

Still, if kindness counted for anything, I was way ahead.

The old woman was very ugly and the young woman was her daughter and the apple hadn't fallen far from the tree. They were so caring that I loved them both and the man too. They told me things about themselves and the place I was in and they asked me questions, so many questions, but I couldn't understand. I told them my name and they told me theirs, Pedro and María and then the old woman's name, which was Jacinta.

When the children came to see me, they taught me to count, first to twenty and then to a hundred. We played a game in which I taught them the English word for things and they taught me the Spanish and we argued over which was right. Every day, when the pain started to get bad, the woman knocked me out with a milky white juice that first numbed me and then drifted me off to sleep.

I had been a week in the hut when out of the blue one morning, Pedro helped me dress and got me out of bed. He was explaining something very important and serious. I nodded and tried to get it, but I couldn't follow him. María wrapped my stump in cotton bandages and then pinned my trouser leg up over it. Both María and her mother had skillfully repaired my jeans. They had patched them with heavy cotton that they had dyed light blue. When I arrived, they had been cut to shreds and more hole than fabric. I told them that now some hippie chick from NYU would have coughed up a hundred bucks for them. Pedro had made me a beautifully worked crutch that fitted well under my arm. It was carved with leaves and simple patterns and there were three little figures at the top, which were obviously him and his family. I choked up when I saw it. He helped me walk out of the hut into the village square: half a dozen huts, children, women, goats, and little brown dogs with long tails. The jungle on three sides and a clearing and a dirt path on the other.

Pedro had watched me walk and wasn't happy with his crutch and took it off me to shorten. He ran back inside while I leaned on María and her mother. It was to be a departure, as waiting out there in the clearing for me was a Volkswagen Beetle, a red one in reasonable condition. The driver came and tried to help me over to the car, but I shook my head. I wanted to say something first. I turned to the little assembled crowd and cleared my throat.

I just want to say thank you very much for looking after me. You have been so kind, *muchas gracias, muchas gracias*.

There was a smattering of quiet, sincere talk and some applause and María kissed me on the cheek. Pedro came back with the crutch and it worked even better now. Before I got in the car, I saw a man jogging through the jungle towards us, a huge, fat man with a beard, blue shirt, white cotton slacks. He didn't look at all as Indian as the people in the clearing. He was puffing, and his face was red. I knew he was the angry man who had been my surgeon.

He came over to me.

I want to see you before you go, he said.

Yes, I said, I remember you.

My English, I cannot talk.

No, your English is good, I said.

No, very badly, he said, and his eyes met mine.

The children have taught me to count to one hundred in Spanish, I said.

He smiled.

I do not want to miss you, he said.

Look, I want to thank— I began, but he interrupted.

Listen, please. I know who you are. You are American. Not safe anymore for here. We take to you somewhere else. The border. There you are safe. They are good men, but not everyone keeps, uh, keeps quiet when he is. Tell no one about where you are from, say that you are in trouble over girl if you say anything.

It seemed a bit hokey, but he was serious and his face was grave. I looked at him; his eyes were old and very blue.

All of you, and you in particular, you saved my life. I don't know your name.

He offered his hand and I shook it.

Príncipe, he said. You know that there is no choice, we know we cannot take you to hospital, you are famous gringo escape. Murderer. Famous.

They said I was a murderer?

Rapist, murderer, such things we hear.

It's lies.

Príncipe shook his head, as if I didn't even need to say it. The cops wanted me and that was good enough for them. For all of them.

Thank you, Príncipe, I said.

You are welcome. Thank also *la Virgen nuestra, nuestra madre, que se echa la culpa de nuestros pecados*. Now, my friend, you will go.

Ok.

He helped me into the car. I wound the window down and thanked Pedro, María, and the mother. I got in the VW and we headed off. I turned to wave, and they were all waving back. I was crying. I wiped away the tears and looked out after them for a long time.

❖   ❖   ❖

The driver of the VW didn't speak to me but was friendly enough and offered me cigarettes. We smoked and listened to godawful mariachi and Mexican rock music on the radio. The little Beetle was not in as great shape as I had thought and the exhaust seeped into the car from the backseat. The engine was loud and throaty and it seemed impossible that so great a rupture of sound could be coming from so wee a vehicle. The road was good for a long time, but then he turned off it and the new road was immediately terrible, and the car shook and made dreadful crashing noises over every pothole. I was feeling extremely sick from the fumes, and we had to stop every half hour or so for me to get a breath. When we got going again, I tried to focus on the horizon. I stared at the fields and occasional plantations, but my attention always wandered down to my left ankle. The horror of it got me every time. Jesus Christ. María had given me roots to chew on for the pain, and they'd dug up some white pills from somewhere. The root really helped, but whether through placebo or some natural emollient, I don't know.

When it was getting dark and we had climbed a little and it was colder, we stopped at a village and the driver helped me out. He led me to a hut and told me to use the roll mat on the ground. I lay down and he went back to the car and drove off. I couldn't sleep at all that night, and it wasn't from the vermin everywhere. My heart was pounding again in my ears, not from fever this time, but from something else. Nerves, panic. Was this the start of it? My breakdown? I calmed myself very deliberately and lay awake until just before dawn, when men came for me in a jeep. They laughed and slapped my back and said things in Spanish. We drove through a town called Tenosique de Pino Suárez, and then up into mountains. When it got cold, one of the men gave me a parka and I wrapped myself in it.

We came to the camp in the evening. For camp it was. Tents and outdoor fires in a clearing by a river. About twenty men standing about, and at first I assumed they were miners or prospectors or something; but it soon became clear that they were fugitives and absconders and the like. They weren't bandits, they didn't raid anyone, they just lived up here, gathered for mutual protection. A tall, thin man with a preposterous Zapata mustache came up to me grinning with a mouth of yellow teeth and said something in Spanish. He shook my hand and gave me tobacco to chew and introduced me to a couple of other men. He was the boss, and I said I was happy to meet him.

I suppose that he explained the situation up here and who everyone was.

Ok, mate, but I haven't understood a fucking word, I said, and smiled, and hobbled to a place near the fire.

The men were kind and saw me under a canvas overhang next to a rocky little patch which was to be my spot. There were blankets, and you could stuff saw grass into sacking if you wanted a pillow. They helped me clear away the stones and, when the ground was flat, I laid a blanket down and slept.

In the morning we ate beans and in the evening we ate rice and beans, sometimes with a tortilla. Where the food came from was a mystery; indeed, how the men supported themselves at all was a mystery, for it seemed that they did nothing at all. A few of them spoke to me in broken English, but it was so bad and their accents so heavy I could understand very little.

Príncipe must have spun them some yarn, because they were good to me. We were all in the shit together and that was what mattered. Someone was bankrolling us, though, and later when I looked at a map and saw that I must have been in Chiapas, I came up with a few ideas. It was 1992 and within a year the American papers were filled with stories about that most southerly, poorest, and heavily Indian of Mexican states.

In the evenings two of the old guys pulled out guitars and sang long, mournful songs about sweethearts. I didn't recognize them, but I picked them up, and when I tried a few later on Spanish-speaking friends, they knew them. One night one of the guys strummed "There's Only One Northern Ireland," the old football anthem from the Kop at Windsor Park, but it turned out that this was a very well-known song called "Guantanamera," which everyone on earth had heard of except me. Seeing I was excited by it, they sang it over and over and, in what seemed like no time at all, I had learned all seven verses. The days were all the same. The sky was blue, save for a few breaths of cloud. It was cold until noon and then hot for a few hours, then cold again at night. The landscape was high desert, cacti, a few scrubby trees, boulders. Once when I went for a walk, I saw a fox.

I had been there about a week when I started to get itchy feet (itchy foot, if you want to be literal). The guys sang songs and played checkers and eked out their scant tobacco in the evenings and slept most of the day. Like I say, they did bugger-all and there was no one for me to talk to. I ate their supplies and contributed nothing, not even a decent story or two to the conversation. Things had probably cooled down sufficiently, and it was ok to move on. And I wanted to go. I had to get north, I had to get back to New York.

On a Sunday morning (half a dozen of the men had rigged up church), I rolled up my clothes and got my stick and tried to make myself understood about heading north. The headman got the picture and told me to wait till tomorrow, since a car was coming and could take me to a road—this explained in bad English and more helpfully by drawings on the dirt.

I did wait and a car did come, a green Toyota Camry with a door missing. The driver left off a sack of rice and a tiny bag of coffee. The boss explained a few things and the driver nodded. I got in and the driver didn't ask me anything at all. He drove me down into the plains. At a road junction he stopped the car and gave me some Mexican banknotes, which I refused but he insisted upon, and told me which way to hitch.

Guatemala, he said, pointing in one direction.

United States? I asked.

El norte, he said, and pointed along a line of blue mountains. He started the car and asked with gestures if I was sure I didn't want to head back east with him. I shook my head. He shook his and off he drove.

I stood for a while, and then I sat. Just before nightfall a dust storm in the distance showed that there was a vehicle, the only one going in any direction that day. I hobbled up on my crutch and stuck my thumb out. It was a truck with an open back and no cargo. The driver saw me from a long way off and slowed down and stopped. He opened the cab door and said something in Spanish.

Can I come up? I asked.

He nodded, and I got up beside him.

¿Habla español? he asked.

I shook my head.

Bueno, he said, and started her up.

He drove the whole of the night and shook me awake in the late morning as we arrived at a small town. I could see it was the end of the line. I asked him where north was and he showed me. I got out and thanked him, and he seemed to say that it was nothing.

The town was so full, it must have been a market day. I bought water, dates, oranges, and tortillas with one of the banknotes and got a lot of change back. I sat in the market square in the shade of a church and ate everything I had. I asked around with sign language and found a standpipe at the back of the church where it was permissible to wash. I stripped down to my boxers and cleaned myself off, much to the amusement of some small children playing nearby with a ball. If the kids hadn't been around, I would have given my bollocks a good washing too. I air-dried and pulled on my mended jeans and a cotton smock that I'd been given in the village. I had a sandal on my good foot and a now filthy bandage on my stump. I safety-pinned the jeans back over and it was ok. I went back to the village square and found a bus stand and with much confusion explained that I was heading for the United States. This was tricky, I was told. I apparently could not get a bus straight there and should either go to Mexico City or take a bus up the coast, which would get me close but take much longer. In case of the peelers I chose not to go to Mexico City.

I got on the local bus, and we waited about three hours until it filled with passengers. It headed off, and a large woman in the seat next to me opened a black bin liner full of all her stuff and offered me a kind of sherbet to drink. She had one herself and then she produced a Madeira cake and a pot of jam. She cut me off a piece of cake and spread the jam for me too. She offered everyone on the bus a piece of her cake, and there was barely enough left for herself at the end. She told me stuff about her life and her kids and didn't seem to mind that I couldn't follow any of it.

The bus ride was very pleasant (especially since I wasn't on the sun side), and we went through a scrubby desert and a few towns and, once, a pine forest. I didn't see any coast at all and wondered if I'd gotten the wrong end of the stick somehow. In any case, we traveled for about seven or eight hours, almost everyone, including my neighbor, getting off at intervening places. We eventually stopped for good at another place similar to the one we'd left. It was a small coastal town called Puerto Arrajo on a large, curved natural harbor.

I must have screwed up, because it was the end of the line as far as the bus routes north were concerned. Exasperated, I explained to the bus station attendant that I was trying to go north and, equally exasperated, he explained that I had to go back south to Veracruz and get off and then go north from there. The bus south didn't leave until the next day. It was evening, so I got dinner in a filthy little restaurant which served a greasy pork stew with tortillas and which became the greatest meal I had ever tasted in my life. That night I slept on the second floor of a half-built house. I woke early and got scrambled eggs for breakfast at a sort of tavern. The bus station didn't open till eleven, so I walked around all morning (I was getting pretty handy with the crutch), took a shit in the public squat shithouse, and strolled down to the shore. I tried to take a swim but the salt water was bloody murder on my stump, so I got out and dried off.

At eleven I hit the bus station. More confusion. Apparently I had misunderstood the man yesterday, for the bus back was not coming today but tomorrow.

I began to fly into a rage, and then I stopped myself. It wouldn't help. I wandered to the outskirts of town and stuck out my thumb again.

A truck came, and the driver picked me up. I didn't even ask where we were going. He talked all day and into the night, and I was a good listener.

I thought the sun was coming up, but it was the wrong direction, west, and the man explained that we were in the outskirts of Mexico City. When the dawn did come, I wanted the night back. Soot, diesel fumes, a locust-colored sky. We were up high, and through the smog you could make out slums and shanties and housing estates that were conceived in the design institutes of hell.

When you read Bernal Díaz's book about the conquest, you get the impression that Mexico City is built upon a lake, with little barges plying between temples and wooden houses; it sounds beautiful, like

Venice. I don't know what happened to the lake, but when I was there, it was a nightmare of roads and concrete, insane traffic, poisoned air,

The driver was only passing through, but it took hours. At one point, in a nicer part I saw Americans at a café near a big church.

A man and a woman in shorts reading the *International Herald Tribune*. Americans, English words in a newspaper. I wanted to wind the window down and say something. Connect. But I did not. The light changed and we went on.

At a place called El Oro, the trucker stopped at a clothing factory. He asked around and we found a driver heading north.

Tall guy, chain-smoker, spoke a little English, wanted company. Said his name was Gabriel.

I told him mine was Michael, and he said that we were two of the archangels and that was good luck.

I shared his food and his little back sleeping cabin for two days. We talked *fútbol* and women and ate stale bread, and he told me long and complicated jokes that I couldn't get but cracked him up.

María's medicine was gone and the pain in my stump had become incredible. To help, Gabriel let me have some of his homemade moonshine, evil stuff that would have put hairs on the chest of the Lancôme girl.

In Chihuahua City, Gabriel said that we were at the parting of the ways. He was delivering shirts to California and had to turn west. I was going to New York City, and from here the Texas border was only about two hundred kilometers. Texas to New York was a much shorter journey than California to New York.

I could see what he was saying, but I wasn't quite ready to leave him. It was safe here in this cab, with grain whiskey and old bread and my chatty fellow seraph. I wanted to get back, I had to get back. There was a scene to be played out, the handgun flaring, a knee jerking, the pain to be extracted, the terror to be inflicted, but not yet, not yet.

I'll go with you all the way to the California border, I said.

He didn't mind at all, and we drove west to Tijuana.

❊   ❊   ❊

Tijuana, as most everyone knows, is a miserable place, and it was worse back then, but you only have to go to the nearest bar and be a little discreet before you can get hooked up with someone who can help you cross.

I was discreet, but I had no cash and I had to sponge off two American college guys in a VW bus. They'd been exploring Baja and surfing the Pacific side and had a lot of questions, and they bought me a beer, and I invented a story about myself that I'd been hitching around the Americas for the last few years, working and drifting and seeing things. They thought this very cool for a disabled guy and bought the whole shebang. My invention ran away with me a little, and I mentioned Colombia and Ecuador and the heights of Machu Picchu.

I explained to them I was going to have to cross illegally into the U.S. because I'd lost my passport months ago. They thought this was cool too, and offered to hide me in the bus, but I declined and said that that wasn't the way things were done, and what I really needed was money.

They gave me fifty bucks and I thanked them and watched them drive off towards the massive customs station that led back into the United States.

With dough in hand and a grilling in a back kitchen that convinced two teenagers that I was not in the employ of the U.S. government, I was told that we were going that night.

A dozen of us met outside a bar off the strip and away from prying eyes. We waited for a long time and I thought I'd been ripped off, but eventually a van pulled up and we drove off into the desert for a while.

I had to climb a barbed-wire fence, which was tricky in my condition, but not impossible, and then there was a solid metal fence, which was a piece of cake and had handy grooves, as if designed for aiding wetbacks with dodgy legs.

I crossed somewhere east and south of San Diego with a score of other guys of all ages. We walked into no-man's-land for some time and then a flashlight beam appeared which was either the agents of the Immigration and Naturalization Service or the boy we were supposed to meet.

Our boy. Young, short, black jeans, black denim jacket, and a black Stetson. He yelled at us as if we didn't see him and we went over, me muttering that half the bloody state of California must have heard the eejit. A van idled nearby and everyone gave the driver money. I didn't have any cash left now but they let me come along. They were good guys, and most of them were agricultural laborers who did this thing every year. Fruit-picking season was over, but in Las Vegas, building season was just beginning. We drove all night and into the next day and the final stop was an industrial complex just south of Las Vegas itself. Everyone was there to demolish and build hotels and with my experience I knew I could have been on to a good thing, and but for my leg I might have made a fortune. But as it was, no one was ever going to hire me, save to make the coffee, so I thanked the guys for the ride and started hitching again east.

I was on the road an hour and a half when a sheriff's officer picked me up and told me that hitching here was against the law. I said I wasn't aware of that and he recognized the accent and asked me what part of Ireland I was from. I said Belfast and Deputy Flinn said that his grandmother on his father's side was from Belfast. I'm not the biggest fan of peelers or other agents of the law, but Flinn was a big, ginger-bapped, pale-skinned, nice bloke who almost wept over my story, which was that I'd come to Vegas to work as a builder but a hod-dropping accident had cost me my foot and since I was an illegal I couldn't very well go to the authorities to get work comp. I was hitching my way back to New York, where I had an address of a distant relative in Brooklyn who might sport me the cash to carry me back broken and dispirited to the Old Country.

Well, Seamus, Flinn began (for I was called Seamus McBride in this little universe), that's about the worst thing I ever heard, and I want to lend you some cash to get the Greyhound. No, don't object. I know you guys are full of pride but I absolutely insist.

I did object and explained that I had got myself into this mess and would get myself out of it without having to rely on the well-meaning charity of strangers.

Flinn was not to be daunted and explained that this money was only to be a loan and I would pay him back. Surely it was foolishness not to accept a loan from a friend and wasn't that what I was going to do in Brooklyn anyway? Since he put it that way, it was hard for me to refuse, so I took his name and address and I did pay the bugger back about a month or so later, when, incredibly, I was on Ramón's payroll, wearing a thousand-dollar suit and carrying a bloody Uzi.

He gave me two hundred-dollar bills and left me with handshakes at the bus station in Las Vegas. I bought a ticket to New York and stayed on all the way to Denver, where I had to get out and stretch and get my wits together after a very long and unpleasant over-air-conditioned journey through Utah and the Rockies.

I found a motel, got a bottle of Jack Daniel's, stripped, and had a shower that lasted about an hour and a half. I watched TV like it was a new invention. A presidential campaign had been taking place all the time I'd been away and it was getting close to its climax. The governor of Arkansas was being tipped to edge out President Bush. It was boring, so instead I watched *Wheel of Fortune* and *Jeopardy* and flipped between endless daytime soaps.

I stayed in the motel for two nights. I spent all my money and cashed in my Greyhound ticket and ordered pizzas and drank beer. I rebandaged my foot and stood, agape, staring at my stump for a while, though fortunately I was pissed senseless at the time, otherwise I might have had a bit of a header. In any case, like I say, in two days I'd spent all my hard-earned cash. It was an idiotic and silly waste of resources, considering how Nyx's weans had escaped me from the prison and the jungle and given me dough.

But that was it, of course. I wanted to get back, I wanted to see blood on walls and pooling under the bodies of gray men. I wanted to see widows' tears. To hear screams and pleas for mercy. But I didn't want to go back for precisely the same reasons.

I tried finding Hibernians organizations in Denver, but there was only one in the phone book. I called up and explained my case, but the guy practically laughed when I said I'd like to borrow some money. After that, I packed my shit and walked down Broadway and tried hitching at the on-ramp to the I-70. No one gave me a lift and coppers waved me off and had no time to listen to the adventures of Seamus McBride. I slept rough that night under a bridge near Cherry Creek. I drank the creek water and washed in it before I started hitching again. I went back up to the I-70 ramp and this time I again got lucky.

An hour later, a man in a camper van was pulling up to the on-ramp and saw me and our eyes locked for a second and he jerked his thumb back for me to get in.

It was a huge white-and-yellow Winnebago of the very latest fashion. I climbed up. The man was in his fifties, white hair, the sunken gray face of an actuary or undertaker. He told me his name was Peter Jenning, though not like the anchor, he said, because of the *s* (but I had never heard of the anchor and immediately, from all this nautical terminology, assumed that he was ex-navy).

I spun him Seamus's sad story and he swallowed it, and I asked him about life on the ocean wave.

Well, Seamus, I was never in the armed services. Ear problems. But my son was in the Gulf War, not in the actual fighting, but he was a radar operator behind the lines. Reservist, got his medal, and don't think it wasn't dangerous, because it was.

I believe it. They kept firing those things. Those missiles, I said.

Scuds, he said, seething with the memory of it.

Yeah, very risky. I was in the British Army myself then, actually, but I wasn't sent to the Gulf. Pity, really, I told him. Not mentioning, as I've already said, that at that time I was finishing out a minor prison sentence on Saint Helena, and that in itself was a class-A double fuckup too, because after I got back, my regiment was merged with another regiment and a lot of the new recruits were offered semigenerous packages to get out of the army, though not, of course, the fucking dishonorable dischargees.

You seem upset about it, he said.

I nodded absently.

But, son, that war screwed up. Listen to me. The ground war. Gulf War was all based on the Battle of Cannae, you know, flanking maneuver. Cannae was a big victory and so was the ground war, but did Hannibal win the war? Did we beat Saddam? No, we did not. Let me tell you: *Vinse Hannibal, et non seppe,* um, *usar* uh, *poi. Ben la vittoriosa sua ventura.* Read that, memorized it.

I nodded sagely and said, Ah yes, good point, excellent point. He smiled at me, clearly well pleased with himself.

You must have learned Latin in school in Ireland, huh, Seamus? Jesuits, right, thumped it into you, he suggested in a leer that seemed to convey his distaste for popery but approval of the beating.

We did, but, you know, I was never very g—

Hannibal was victorious and knew not how to use victory given him. That's what that means. See my point? Bush and Powell, none of them used the victory to boot Saddam out of the country. Hannibal didn't march on Rome, see what I'm saying?

I had no idea what he was saying, actually, but there are certain very strict duties imposed on a hitchhiker and one of those is to agree with whatever the driver says. I agreed and he proceeded to break down other errors in the president's strategy.

They're going to have to go in again, you mark my words, son. You remember Cato?

Yeah, he was always attacking Inspector Clouseau in the Pink Panther mov—

Carthago delenda est, that's what Cato proclaimed, Cathage must be destroyed. You'll see, we'll go after Iraq again, Mr. Jenning said, and he outlined how we would win the war and further explained how every engagement in every war since 1860 could have been prosecuted more successfully. It didn't come as much of a surprise when Mr. Jenning told me that he was a bit of a history buff. He had been in sales for forty years and that wasn't a shock either, considering that he could talk the arse off an octopus. He had ended up, before retirement, as a regional marketing VP with the Kentucky Fried people. I had assumed that all the restaurants were franchises and wondered what they needed a regional marketing VP for, but Mr. Jenning had laughed at my naive appreciation of the ways of the world and further explained his role in the great corporate machine with endless and excruciating detail.

It was, however, my luck that Mr. Jenning was driving all the way to Vermont to see the fall colors, and he said he would swing by New York City and leave me off if I wanted. I did so want, and a few days listening to his yammering seemed a small price to pay. He explained Livy, Clausewitz, and Bismarck and, given encouragement, expanded further upon his theories of the universe. He was a widower but didn't seem to miss his wife that much, and once in his sleep in the big bunk of the Winnebago he said, Serves you right, you old hag, which elicited a few theories of my own.

He asked a couple of times if I could pay for the gas but I emptied out my pockets and I suppose it convinced him. He didn't let me do any of the driving, but I entertained him with made-up stories of Ireland. He especially enjoyed salty tales that involved women of loose virtue, and I had a few of those that weren't so far from the truth.

When we arrived at the George Washington Bridge, it was raining and cold and night. I thanked him much and he let me off and headed up the Palisades to cross the Hudson at some other point.

I walked over the GWB in the drizzly dark. There's no toll for pedestrians, thank Christ, for I had only a dollar and fifty-seven cents that I had husbanded carefully, and with that I took the A train to 125th Street. I came out in familiar old Harlem again. It was two A.M. and sleeting and such people as there were around gave me the cold shoulder. I walked with my crutch along 125th and turned up the hill on Amsterdam.

I found our building. The front door had been conveniently jemmied again. I walked down into the basement and rang Ratko's bell. I rang for a long time and eventually there was much swearing in Serbo-Croat and he opened the door holding a lead pipe.

I need a place for a couple of days, I said. Ratko looked at me in astonishment for a second and then helped me through the door.

The basement stair was steep.

Each step down was agonizing but I enjoyed the pain. I had made it, I had fucking made it, and every torture now I engraved in memory, another torment notarized and ultimately to be paid for soon in the currency of fear.

9: THE CORNER OF MALCOLM X AND MARTIN LUTHER KING

Those first few days back, it was as if I were an astronaut exploring a city on the planet Mars. The people were not human. They were alien creatures sniffing the cold air and muttering and, in sinister fashion, disappearing down into the earth beneath me to catch clattering, spark-spewing electric cars. Shopping, talking, hauling little versions of themselves to school. I watched from shadows, hoping they wouldn't see that I was a stranger, a being from another world. And I was afraid at any moment that one of them would cry out the usual words: Uitlander, Teague, Jude, Leper. Or no, it would be something that they would understand and I would not, for now even their language puzzled me. Their manner, not hostility exactly, but indifference. The people moving with their long arms and their straight backs, and fast, since for them the outside was merely a place between work and home. These weren't all the populace, of course. There were others who lived there in the parks and streets; you could see them all the way from Mount Morris to Morningside and Riverside, shuffling, aware of me, hiding too, rag people. We would pass and exchange signs in secret; they could see that I also was adrift, apart. We conspired in silence and walked between greens and churches from 125th Street all the way up to the Cathedral of Saint John. Most of the time, I kept it together and I walked, came back to Ratko's, ate and slept.

But some days it was all too much and I expected horrors. I heard weird noises and lights and the trees would be alive; or I'd catch a panorama of wounded birds and jungle animals, or I'd see monsters in parade coming in from Queens and with them giants and the undead and marching bands, elephants, painted floats, and children dressed as rats and crocodiles. Me alone cognizant. Only I could bear witness. Only I was attuned. The other citizens of Harlem were blissfully ignorant of all this noisy caravan coming over the Triborough Bridge. They couldn't see it, but then they couldn't see anything. They were blind, perpetually blind, dazed, like survivors of a great ship intercepted unexpectedly by the shore.

One morning when the sun was out, I took the Queens-bound A train to look at the Atlantic Ocean. Rockaway was cold and the journey by crutch from the subway stop to the beach took me forever. The water was gray and incredible, tangled, bristling. Whitecaps and a howling wind. The sand freezing on my arse. There were half a dozen surfers making attempts on the slow breakers. I watched them for an hour, watched them wait in their black suits for the perfect wave and take it, cutting and gliding and falling in. Maybe I could have done that once, but not now. Fury. I walked farther up the shore where the sea was empty. I sat there and looked and begged the Atlantic to uncover itself. I waited for revelation, for meaning. But the ocean doesn't give you anything, it doesn't contribute, it's a repository, a mirror of yourself, and when I looked I had no reflection at all. I decided to take the train back to Harlem, having learned nothing.

The A train is the airport train and at JFK dozens of people got on, bringing color and difference to the subway car. For them it was the end of a journey; they were tired and relieved. Their talk was excited and loud. It marked them out. And as they got more animated I got less so and dissolved into the plastic of my seat. They were too much, these Homo sapiens, these people. So close, how can they stand to be so bloody close?

The train disgorged them at midtown and by 125th they were all long gone. I was relieved; I'd felt I was having an attack.

It was my stop, so I got up and walked the platform to the exit. Through the turnstile. That walk again, up the subway steps and past the Nation of Islam men in shirts and bow ties. Light rain now, the black Israelites in front of the Record Republic. Normally, they'd yell at the white devil, but there was something about my look. They chose not to see me.

Here's a white man who is going to kill other white men. Yes.

Up the hill. Empty plastic five-dollar crack bags littered everywhere. Men and women gathered around the fake grocery store. The 99 Cents Store. The lamp store. Children wrapped in bear jackets playing with a basketball. PS 125, armor-plated against riot and revolution.

123rd. The street still the same. Danny the Drunk, predictable and living yet. Vinny, drunk with him, both of them sitting on the stoop and leering at the black Catholic schoolgirls. I stood there and looked out at the great city and breathed the autumn air. I was starting to get back my strength for the task in hand. My body had to be strong, but my mind, at least, was already there. I know there are people who triumph over the need for vengeance, who say that loving your enemies hurts them more; that breaking the cycle of violence is the way to happiness. But this was not about being spiritually advanced. This was not about being happy. No.

I spat. The door was broken. I pushed it in and went down.

Ratko's wife was big and white and stuffed food down our mouths to shut us up. She didn't speak any English and was suspicious of what Ratko was telling me. Perhaps he was talking about her, or about a mistress he had in the building next door, or about plans to tip off the INS about her status. One way to get rid of her, send her back to war-torn Yugoslavia.

She fed us sausage so undercooked and bloody that I was sure it was a chastisement. Ratko ate it heartily, though, so it might just have been some Serbian thing. More familiar were overboiled potatoes and slow-baked kidney pies. For pudding she constructed on different days bread puddings and sponges and slab-thick chocolate cake that weakened you and made you drunk before you'd finished it. Ratko fed me vodka and all the time he hinted that tonight would have to be my last and that really, all things considered, I couldn't stay here. I slept in the box room, for the spare room had become the dog's and the dog bullied the family and began howling when I first broached the possibility of sharing space with it. Generally, I have a good relationship with dogs, but your mind needs to be clear and relaxed for it to work, so I let it have the room. The box room was tiny and airless and I slept so well there it was like I was some advanced Zen master in his monastery cell.

When we first talked, Ratko had some good news, some bad news, and some very interesting information. The information was that Sunshine had come by a week after we'd left for Mexico and paid Ratko off and told him that Darkey wouldn't need the flat anymore. Ratko liked me and he was a close old file and so casually he asked Sunshine where I was and Sunshine said that I'd gone back to Ireland, for good. All this only a week after we'd left. One week. The bad news was that Sunshine came with a curly-haired blond guy who departed with my bloody TV and radio and a rucksack full of miscellaneous items. Ratko went in later and sold the rest of my gear for twenty bucks to the tenant across the hall. The good news was that he had saved from the garbage my driving license, social security card, and ATM card in the hope that I might write and claim them one day. The ATM card got me access to about a hundred dollars and I give it to Ratko for board. . . .

We're at breakfast.

Toast, sausage, egg, fried black bread, vodka, and coffee.

Ratko's wife asks Ratko to ask me what happened to my foot, what happened to me, but I give him a look. We talk sports from the paper and about the Kosovars and Tito and why Zagreb is beautiful but Belgrade isn't (the answer, apparently, is because of collaboration).

Yeah, and we talk football. Northern Ireland has no chance of qualifying for the World Cup, but I live a little on the glory days of '82 and '86. What will happen to the Yugoslavian team is anyone's guess.

Once mighty Balkan superpower will split into six, maybe eight teams, Ratko says, sadly. We chew our toast and drink our coffee.

And my friend, Michael, how do you feel? he asks me after a dish of what I take to be a type of black pudding.

In general?

In general.

Well, sometimes I hallucinate about the armies of the dead marching over the Triborough Bridge, but most of the time I'm ok.

He winks at me.

Your sense of humor, he says, and he's inwardly glad his wife has no English.

I finish breakfast, get up, get my stick, go out for a walk, come back . . .

At dinner that night the wife was mumbling loud over the cabbage.

It was getting clear that it was time to go. He broached the subject delicately over vodka, and it was like water off my back.

Really, Michael, I am not kidding. It is perhaps soon that you look for somewhere else to stay. I love you, you stay forever, but Irina, you know.

I know, I said, cheerfully, and continued eating.

For the next few days this theme of my departure was Ratko's relentless leitmotif. But I wasn't taking hints, there was nowhere for me to go. Ratko was being got at from three sides: Slavic hospitality, duty to a friend, and a suspicious caricature of a wife who wanted me out before whatever doom pursued me found me here. And there was doom, the dog had stopped eating and wouldn't let anyone near it, an unheard-of thing until I showed up.

Ben Franklin famously put the limit of fish and houseguests at three days, and his mates were mostly Quakers and gentlemen. I'd been there nearly two weeks. Ratko wouldn't throw me out and he liked having me around but finally the missus was too much: nagging him all night and all day and eventually the poor love cracked, got off his fat ass, packed sandwiches, went hunting, came back blitzed and singing and saying that he'd found me a place.

Ratko knew a Russian guy who happened to be pals with a Jamaican guy who happened to be the super of a building they were doing over on Lenox and 125th. They wanted people in there to keep crack addicts and other miscreants out during the makeover and I could probably live rent-free for a month or two till I got my bearings.

Ratko filled me with food, drove me over at paramedic speed in his Hyundai, talked like mad so I wouldn't notice all the black people, helped me up the stairs, gave me the key, my hundred dollars back, a hearty handshake, and ran away before I could refuse. . . .

I looked around. The place was abominable, but I was only there two or three weeks. That's how long it took for Ramón to find me. But you get the picture: vermin, roaches, and a hole in the bathroom that allowed you to see into two floors beneath you. No electricity, but by some miracle there was cold-water plumbing. The building had six stories, and they had a person in an apartment on each floor. Their job was to keep the homeless out of there while renovations were taking place, and it wasn't too hard a task. The guy prowling the second floor was a huge Jamaican bruiser from some particularly evil part of Kingston who scared the bejesus out of most mortals. He had a shot-gun and he'd plugged someone already and the word had gotten round. Harlem had plenty of derelict buildings, so it made sense to go to an easier place.

Nowadays, Lenox Avenue looks like an ok sort of street and it might be hard to believe it ever was the way I say it was. But back then, I promise you, it was a murder picture. Every other building was a burnt-out graffitied shell. Garbage all over the streets, and people made campfires within the buildings to keep warm. Every floor smelled terrible and, just like in the days of Elizabethan London, you threw your shit out the open hole that should have been a window. The windows weren't boarded up, because people had ripped down the plywood for furniture and the more shortsighted or desperate simply burned it.

I'm sure it wasn't always thus. I might have been living on the same street as the late Langston Hughes or Duke Ellington and for all I bloody knew Ralph Ellison could have been that old, sophisticated-looking guy at the bodega, but it seemed unlikely. The street sanitation was a disgrace, the architecture of the buildings postapocalyptic. It was Belfast, circa 1973, except here there was no civil war as an excuse for the calamity.

There wasn't much to do, either. No safe bars, no movie theaters. In fact, around here the most important landmark was the Apollo The-atre, but you'd be the brave white boy up there on a Saturday night in the autumn of 1992.

And speaking of Apollo, patron of the Muses, true, but also guardian of prophecy and the future, I knew what was going to hap-pen. What was inevitable the minute I stepped off the GWB. I could see it in my mind's eye, I could see it, I could feel it, but I knew I had to bide my time. I had to lie low. Ratko could know that I was back in New York City, but he was to be the only one. Ratko could keep his mouth shut. Did others know I'd escaped from Mexico? I doubted it. The guards saw me fall into the swamp and not come out. So if Sun-shine ever checked, he'd believe the guards, and even if rumors reached him and Darkey that I was somehow alive, why give credence to these paranoid reports? No, they didn't know anything. They were snug, safe in their beds. Eejit safe in their eejit beds.

So I had a place, I was incognito, and I figured if you couldn't speak Serbo-Croat and weren't part of a gossipy little Upper Manhattan Slavic circle, you didn't know I was here. I was getting my shit together, making plans, but before I could do anything big I really had to do something about my leg. I wasn't having nightmares. No phantom limb itches or anything like that, but I was walking too slowly with my crutch, and going up a flight of stairs was like Scott's return from the Pole.

Now, lucky for me I wasn't a million miles away from somewhere I could get help. For if you keep walking on 125th Street you'll eventually get to the Triborough Bridge and the East River, but before that, if you make a right wheel, conveniently enough there's a foot hospital. The New York College of Podiatric Medicine. The hospital will give you an artificial foot to stick over your stump and the physical therapists will show you how to walk with that foot, through weeks, sometimes months, of training. They'll give you drugs, advice, support, and an optimistic glossy brochure with smiling Special Olympians. All this, of course, if you have insurance. If you don't have insurance and your dancer-tragic-accident letter to Gene Kelly got no reply, you are not completely banjaxed, for as I discovered, there is another way:

You show up; you're not an emergency case, so you have to wait. It can be a while, so bring a newspaper. It's a presidential election year, so there's plenty of reading, but you're not an expert and it's hard to tell the difference between the candidates—both would be Tories back home—so instead you read the sports section. There's American football and real football and bizarre things like hockey on ice. The World Series is also coming up, but the New York teams aren't in it. You read and read and you're almost thinking of giving up, but finally a nurse takes your temperature and she's so tired that she falls asleep while doing it. They give you a clipboard to which is attached a pink form. You fill in the details of an imaginary person and give his address and name and social security number. The nurse has already willfully suspended disbelief and leads you along a corridor to another man who might be a doctor. The doctor takes a look at your foot and shakes his head and says things like antibiotics and poor workmanship and where did they stitch you and you make a few things up in reply. The only accurate thing on your form is your blood type and he asks your blood type and you tell him and he asks if you've ever had any of a following list of complaints to which you reply no. He asks you to come back the following week and see some guy, but you hint that by next week you might not be at the address on your form. All this is part of a charade, for soon another man comes (an orderly, a nurse?) and leads you to a room that is brightly lit like a shoe store and packed with shoe boxes that contain feet. The feet are on little hinges and attach to your limb. Feet of every shape and size and skin color, but mostly black. Baby feet, size 15 feet, feet that stink of plastic and grease. He tries on several and gives you the best fit, which is an off-white. He says that really you should learn all about "stump management." He tells you the line about the weeks of physical therapy, knowing full well that neither of you will see the other again. You put the foot in a plastic bag and carry it home. You practice in your apartment for hours until you're chafed, bleeding, crying.

You practice going up and down stairs and you fall a dozen times. You look at your stump and the straps on the artificial foot and you just can't believe it. The horror of it takes your breath away.

But you can't live in that moment and you restrap yourself over the sores and the cuts, the skin-colored plastic of the foot going up over your stump, your hinged foot hanging there alien and ridiculous, until in jeans and socks and shoes it looks ok.

Sometimes, for a brief moment, you can even forget what's happened and think that you're whole again.

It's physical and mental anguish but within the week you're limping on it, but walking nonetheless, and if you didn't know you were an amputee, you wouldn't know, and besides, so many men in Harlem limp already you fit right in.

* * *

When finally I felt strong in mind and body, I hopped an uptown train and went to spy on Bridget. I'd been waiting, I'd been patient. I could wait no more. I had a bushy beard by then and my hair was long and matted under a wool knit hat. I had sea boots and a lengthy black coat, and I could easily have passed for someone who had spent his formative years on a vodka-soaked fishing smack home-ported out of Murmansk or Archangel or some other similarly charming place. Perhaps I had fled the collapse of the Soviet Union and was looking for a ship, though why I thought I could find one in the landlocked part of the Bronx was something I hadn't worked out yet.

I took the IRT and got off a stop early and, before I knew what was going on, I was walking to Shovel's house. By now, Shovel was long out of the old meat shop and up there concocting domestic bliss and sweetness and light with his loving and amenable missus. He didn't know it, but Shovel more than had his revenge on me. I hung around for twenty minutes and then walked north to the Four Provinces.

When I got there, I realized quickly that there were no convenient places to hide up, and the lay of the land was very bad. The whole thing was extremely foolish, and I was pretty sure that if any of a dozen people came by, I would be immediately blown despite my outfit.

Apartment buildings, cars, a few town houses, white people, waste ground about fifty yards up the street, where the kids sometimes played basketball. School was in, so there were no weans, but still it wasn't an ideal observation post at all. The only spot that might remotely work was on the far side of the waste ground, where you could slip into the alley between two apartment blocks. You could maybe sit there in the shadows, looking out across the waste ground towards the street and then farther down to the Four Provinces. I walked over and checked it out, and it was not ideal. If she came out and turned left I'd never see her at all; if she came out and turned right I'd have a chance of spotting her, but it was so far away I'd really have to be looking. And I couldn't squat in the alley indefinitely; sooner or later, someone would lean out his bathroom window and say something or tell someone. Broken bottles, condoms, a smashed TV, a stench from a brown box. Still, as shitty OPs went, it could have been worse and if I could disappear into the shadows it would be ok.

I wasn't exactly an old hand, but I wasn't exactly clueless, either.

In the short time I was in the British Army, I got a whisper from a Jock sergeant, at basic training, that they were grooming me for officer training or the specials, because as the sergeant said: I was a vile, underhanded, sneaky, wee, idle fuck.

I never did make officer selection, because the next week I stole a Land Rover and drove from Aldershot to Cambridge to see a girl. Typical, and like some Mick curse, strong drink was behind most of this little adventure. I returned the vehicle undamaged, but my file had increased in size threefold and I was never to be out of the army's bad books again. I didn't do time for that, which showed how much they liked me, and the Jock sergeant and the captain hurt me more with their disappointment than any punishment. I worked a wee bit harder after that and though I was only in a year they let me take a corporal's course (which I failed), but even being asked showed that I still had some promise. I think they thought if I could get through the first year or two, I might be a useful wee character in and around West Tyrone or the badlands of South Armagh. After twelve months, I was sent to Saint Helena on a recon course and taught to scout and do legwork and OPs, and I enjoyed it and might have made a go of things had I not been woefully immature. I was not seventeen when I joined and far too young to respect authority, never mind the fucking British Army, and a bar fight during the recon course (when I nearly killed a local sheep farmer or fisherman or whatever it is they do out there) was the final straw for Her Majesty and they kicked me out after a spell in the pokey.

But although my experience working for HM Forces had been brief, it had been fruitful. They'd taught me to harden my body, to harden my mind, they'd shown me how to shoot and (more pertinent here) how to do observation layups and how to wait. The corporal's course was to be useful a few weeks later when I was being tailed, but the recon came in useful right now. It was taught by a Geordie SAS staff sergeant who knew his business but could barely speak intelligible English. If you paid attention, though, he came off with some good stuff. He told us how to stay awake, he told us how to kip, he told us that Saint Helena herself was British and that the stories about Napoleon's dick were not true. And among those diverse georgics that he taught us up on the windy cliffs of east Saint H. he told us not to believe in cop shows where you see peelers sitting with mugs of coffee and doughnuts on a stakeout. Never, he said, take diuretics on a layup, especially if you're on your own. If you forget everything else, remember to be careful about peeing. That was it, really, all the rest was about finding a good spot and waiting.

So thanks, Sarge. I had a long pee down the alley, found a good spot, and then waited. I was extremely patient, extremely still. I wasn't smoking anymore and this was better. Easier. All you could do was breathe and look. I squatted in the shadow near a wall for an hour and then I changed my position so that I was sitting cross-legged and then after a time I stood. The movements between each pose were seamless and slow and my eyes never left the street.

I was still quite poised and alert five hours later when Bridget appeared in a camel hair coat, black jeans, black DMs, her hair tied back, a handbag over her right shoulder. She was listening to a Walkman, which would make things simpler. I let her stroll the length of the street and turn right at the corner. I crossed the waste ground; I didn't run, but I walked fast. She was halfway along the road, turning right. She wasn't going to the subway, so I tried to think where she was going. What was down that street? I tried to remember. Another bar, an Irish food store, a butcher's, a paper shop, a bakery, what else? I couldn't remember. Van Cortlandt Park and the IRT were way down the hill but if she was going to the park or the subway she'd have turned left at the Four P. and saved herself the journey of an extra few blocks. A man appeared on the corner in front of me just as I was about to cross from the waste ground. He was a big man in his late fifties or sixties, an old bruiser, black coat, plus fours; he looked like fucking Boris Karloff out for a dander. He was walking at a brisk pace, and if I slipped in behind him and she did look back, she'd notice him only and not me. The big guy turned the corner; I slid over and in behind the bastard.

He made it to the next corner and then I did. Bridget was nowhere to be seen. Unless she'd run she couldn't have gotten to the end of the block and turned again. She'd had to have gone in somewhere. There were a dozen shops on both sides of the street. Maybe the bakery; maybe it was her mum's birthday or something. The big guy went down to the butcher's and stepped inside. I waited at the corner looking nonchalant—which is absolutely the hardest part of tailing someone. It was about five minutes, a lifetime exposed out there in the broad.

She stepped out of the dry cleaner's with a plastic bag over a dress. Small, one of hers, spangly. An event dress, a we'll-fuck-tonight dress. She was heading back the way she'd come. Walking brisk. Swinging her hips. Excited. I eased out of her field of view and slipped down the basement steps of the apartment building on the corner. She'd stay on my side of the street and go past above me about six feet away. I'd see her face, but she wouldn't see mine down here in the shadow. I backed against the wall and waited. All the time there was the possibility that when she went by I'd say something. I'd call her name. Bridget, down here, *ssshhhh*, don't be afraid, Mouse, it's me, my Mouse girl, it's me, I'm alive, don't cry out, pretend you've dropped something.

She'd be astonished, maybe she'd faint, yell, she'd start to cry: They told me you were dead, I thought you were dead. Oh, my God. Jesus, Mary, and Joseph. Sweet Jesus.

I'd whisper instructions to her, we'd meet that night in the park, she'd tell her ma she needed a walk after dinner. That wasn't so unusual; sometimes she went for a walk before starting her shift in the bar. We'd meet in the park and I'd tell her everything. Christ, Bridget, you're not going to believe it. Take a breath. I've been through the mangle a bit, but I am alive. We'll have to be quick. Smart. It isn't safe for me here. If Sunshine found out, if Darkey found out, they'd have to kill me, they'd have to. No choice. They know me. No, no, don't call him, it'll all be lies. Lies. Didn't they say that I was dead? No, Sunshine, too, he's worse, if anything. I promise you it's all true. Don't cry, be tough. They'll notice if you've been crying. Listen, I've it all worked out. We'll go away; you'll book tickets for both of us for this weekend. I can rustle up some documents by then. It'll cost me, but I can do it. I'll get the cash somehow. Don't pack or fucking look at atlases or anything like that. Don't get your hair cut. Change nothing. Saturday morning get up. Say you're going shopping in midtown. Take the train. No extra bags. We'll meet at the 181st Street stop and take the A train to JFK and then fly to: where? anywhere? Australia, there's a second cousin of mine in Queensland. England, I know a couple of people in London, Coventry. Ireland, dozens who could hide us out. A cottage in Donegal. Oh, Bridget, it's so beautiful there: the Blue Mountains, the hills, the loughs, the Atlantic thundering up on empty beaches. You'd love it. I'd get a job in Derry, maybe you, too, we'd raise kids, get a wee fishing boat, a wee rower, teach them to fish, there's surfing there now too, it's not behind the times. We'd use aliases, they'd never find us, never. I know Darkey can pull strings and Mr. Duffy has connections, but we'd be clever. Clever, Bridget, and happy, so happy . . .

I hear her steps on the sidewalk. It's a sharp day. She has a purposeful walk. She gets close.

It was you, Bridget. Please believe me when I tell you that you're the one that kept me going. I thought of you. I was half-mad out there. Christ, the things that happened to us. Only I made it. It wasn't luck, it was all you, Bridget, can't you see that? I'm sure of it. Yeah, I know, I know, I'm a pochle, a liar, there are other girls. I know, you don't have to tell me, but that's behind me. I don't remember them. All that time it was you. I swear it. You.

She's even closer, ten paces till she reaches the corner. She's humming along. Happy. Her boots squeal and she turns the corner. I see her face. Lightly powdered. Radiant. Her hair is darker than I've seen it, tied back. The music on her Walkman is U2, she's singing with it, one of the upbeat ones. She's smiling as she sings. Aye, the dress under the plastic is a fancy cocktail outfit; Darkey must be taking her to some do. Something special, no trip to the pictures this night, it's the Met, or some fund-raiser, or a restaurant in Tribeca or on Central Park South. She's parallel with me for a moment, frozen there, and then she's past. I hear her steps recede down the sidewalk. Fainter and fainter. She turns at the corner. I'm about to come up the steps when, lo and behold, old Boris Karloff appears behind her. Practically skipping now, rushing to keep up, not sure if the whole trip to the dry cleaner's was a blind or not. Well, well, so this is as far as Darkey's trust goes. Even now. God help some boy she meets by accident, what'll happen to him? Maybe he'll win a trip to Cancún through the mail, or is that track too beaten for Sunshine now? Maybe it'll just be a wee hiding behind the bike sheds, a fist punctuating every word: Stay-the-fuck-away-from-her.

Boris turns the corner and I come up the steps. I wait there for a while. In the movie version of the story, I'd pull out a cigarette and smoke it and stand there looking dazed and insensible. But I've given up, I need the extra lung capacity to compensate for other physical concerns. There is no point following her back to the Four Provinces, but it might be interesting to see where Boris goes. I walk to the corner and am just in time to see him get into a blue Ford. I get a read on the number plate and try to compare it with the blue Ford that was on 123rd Street eons ago, but my memory has erased that number and put in its place a series of horrible events. I stare for a while and then pull my hat low and take a long and deserted way back to the subway stop.

*　*　*

I was fucking broke, freezing, living on cold baked beans. The place on Lenox had no gas or heat and, like the people I'd once mocked, I considered burning wood on the bare floor. I'd tried to befriend the Jamaican guy on the second floor, but he was having none of it. I wasn't that welcome at Ratko's place, but sometimes I had to go over to get a square meal.

I wasn't disheartened, though. Quite the reverse. I knew what I was doing. I wasn't just sitting there faffing about. I was mentally steeling myself for what was to come.

One night, to confirm everything, I spent some time in contemplation on the roof of my building. I'd never been able to do the lotus position before, but when you can take your foot off it becomes a bit easier. It was the middle of October and the crisp air was disturbed only by the odd gypsy cab on 125th and a howling crank addict at the subway stop and then, later, gunshots up in the 130s. But you zone it out. My brain was ticking and working fine. It told me things. Patience. Things were going well, but I shouldn't jump just yet. I needed time. I had to be fit. I had to be able to run on a foot I could barely limp upon. I had to be strong and brilliant.

Apollo came up earlier in connection with the future and, you know, a wise thing Apollo urged at Delphi was to Know Yourself, and that's what I had done. Looked within. I wasn't impatient about my plans. However long it took, it would take that long. You're the lucky man whose aim becomes true. Once you are resolved, all other anxieties melt away into nothingness.

The first thing was that I needed money, and I was never much in the thieving line so, obviously, I had to get a job. How? I sat for a while and I considered various options, put my foot on, and went back down into the apartment again.

The next morning I walked to a bar called the Blue Moon near the Metro North stop on 125th. Once a glamorous place, now fallen on hard times, with a large staging area at the back where bands had played and people had danced in the thirties. Like the rest of 125th Street it had seen many changes since then, most for the bad. It didn't have many customers but the ones it did have were older guys and no trouble. Crack cocaine was the vice du jour around here and alcohol a benign and peaceful influence on character in comparison. I'd worked here for one week, nine months ago. It had been called Carl's then. In that period, which is exactly the gestation cycle of a human being, I too had been born again into a different, harder, more venerable person. Carl's also had transformed. It had undergone a change of name and a change of ownership. The Blue Moon had been what it was called about five years ago and was what it had been in its heyday. The record emporium next door to it had become a lottery store. The African craft store had closed. Everything in Harlem is always in a state of flux, but the early 1990s was perhaps the low point in the great neighborhood's fall from grace.

I'd gotten a job at Carl's through Freddie, our mailman, while I was waiting for an interview with the famous Sunshine and Darkey White. Scotchy had found me a place but had let me starve on the street until Sunshine had finally said that I was Darkey White material. Freddie had said that I'd be quite the star at Carl's as the one white busboy within ten blocks.

I went over there at lunchtime hoping that I wouldn't stand out in the bigger crowd.

Crowd. Two guys in separate booths, a barman, and a girl drunk at a stool next to a jukebox. It was a dark place, no width to it at all, just a long bar and a few tables opposite and at the back the closed-down stage, some booths, and a bathroom. No bathroom for women, no decorations except for a few mirrors and a fight poster.

I'd like a beer, I said, and the barman said that if I was a tourist I'd better get out of here and if I wasn't a tourist and I was looking for trouble, he carried, with police approval, a sawed-off shotgun within reach of where he was standing right now.

I said that I wasn't a tourist and I didn't want trouble, just a beer. He took a look at me and poured me a Budweiser, almost all head, and asked for five dollars.

I must have been slightly cut that day because I said to him that I'd give him the five dollars but I wanted a proper beer for my money. We eyed each other. He was an old black guy who looked a lot like Miles Davis, though a little paunchier. After a long minute, he grinned at me and poured me a beer and said that the charge was two bucks. We chatted about American football (of which I know nothing) and when he said would I like another, I came to it.

Listen, Jim, I said (for such was his name), I know times are tough but I need a job. I worked bar many times in New York and I've worked bar in Ireland for years and years. I'm a good worker and honest and I'll take any shift you want. I was here at the beginning of the year when this place was still Carl's.

Jim laughed.

Yeah, man, we need a lot of staff right now to cope with the big rush.

I laughed too. But even though it was almost noon, the daughters of Nyx were still in my corner. I gave him my address and sure enough, as luck would have it, that very day his relief barman quit because he'd just gotten the lucrative understudy job for Macavity the Mystery Cat in a touring version of the show.

Jim came by my place and the Jamaican guy on two nearly shot him, and I ran down and almost brained the Jamaican and but for the fact that he was new in the mainland Americas and still unsure of our ways, he surely would have fucking killed the pair of us. Rather, we solved the situation with rum in his apartment, which was a lot nicer than mine, and Jim gave me the job.

It sure would be a novelty having a white boy keeping bar, and I seemed like I was sincere and trustworthy. He asked if I had any dependency issues and I said that I took too much Tylenol for pains in my leg, and he laughed and said that I might be ok; he did add if I ever tried to rip him off he'd hunt me down and castrate me. The job was Thursday, Friday, and Saturday nights and two dollars an hour, plus tips.

The place didn't exactly fill up at the weekends, but the Apollo crowd brought some business and with tips I was bringing in forty dollars a night, which wasn't bad at all. I took a ribbing and much shite the first night, but by the third I was old news and the abuse was perfunctory and dull. On my very first shift, Jim and I threw out a crack addict who ran in with a bread knife in a pathetic attempt at a holdup.

I was a good barman and Jim liked having me around but, like I say, I wasn't there long since my stint effectively ended when I was offered a more lucrative position in Ramón's organization. It happened like this:

I was in the bar one night when a group of Dominican boys came in. There were six of them. If you were Dominican you only came into this bar in numbers. Definitely a crew: watchful eyes, polo shirts, *Miami Vice* pastel jackets, cashmere coats that dragged on the ground. Mr. T would have envied the gold chains about their necks. They were all packing, and two of them had big muscle jobs that everyone realized could spray havoc and death with gay abandon if that proved necessary, which it wouldn't when you considered that the average age of our clientele was about sixty-five.

They ordered Mexican beers and took a table at the back. They were smart boys and weren't looking for trouble. I wasn't to know then, but Jim had started paying off to them. They were trying to expand their territory from Washington Heights down into Harlem, along Broadway and Amsterdam. Jim had heard bad things about them, but they kept the cost low enough so a dodgy business like Jim's could pay off without too much hurt.

The boss was a little man called Ramón Borges Hernández. Five six, olive skin, handsome, bald, poised, heavy. He looked forty but was younger.

I learned later that Ramón grew up in Santo Domingo and had come to New York about five years earlier. He had many cousins in Washington Heights and within days of his arrival they'd set him up as part of a crew. He was arrested three times and with the third they threw something at him that stuck and he spent some time in Rikers Island. Rikers then wasn't like Rikers now. Even among the Dominican inmates there were daily fights, stabbings, and shit-kicking sessions. And across ethnic and gang lines: rapes, castrations, shank murders. You got an education, and if you survived, you got a reputation and made connections.

Ramón got out of Rikers and was deported to the Dominican Republic under some crazy new get-tough policy, but it didn't take him long to get himself a new passport and a new look, and he was about to head back to America when he got in some unspecified bother and went to prison in, of all places, Haiti. I assume he was smuggling something, but neither Ramón nor anyone else ever spoke about that time. Probably my little portion of Mexican hell was as nothing compared to Ramón's fourteen months in Port-au-Prince.

Still, sometimes, suffering builds character (though not in my case) and when Ramón did come back to Manhattan he was newly invigorated and determined to make the upper city his. He joined a crew working east of St. Nicholas Park and was doing ok for himself until he was arrested and ended up again in Rikers Island. This time, though, he'd been lifted under a lucky star.

If you are the type of person who believes in synchronicity or the power of coincidence or chaos theory or Jungian collective unconscious or other bollocks like that, it might be instructive to learn just how Ramón's luck changed and the small but important role I played in reversing Fortune's wheel. Vanna White wouldn't be in it, I tell you. I didn't realize it then, but Ramón's and my path had crossed inadvertently twice before. Once when Ramón gave encouragement to Dermot Finoukin's foolishness and once with Mr. Peter Berenson, the Eastern European gentleman with Santa trouble. I think I said earlier that all this might be seen as a bit flukey, but if Ramón were still alive I'd have said no, it wasn't a fluke, it was some Ramónian magical cadence that meant he knew me before he knew me. But, actually, poor Ramón was no magician, at least not magician enough to stop Moreno Felipe Cortez from shooting him nineteen times (that means more than one clip) the year after I left New York. Anyway, that was all still to come, and for the moment, it's diverting to see how Ramón made that jump from Triple-A into the Major Leagues.

Ramón was sent to Rikers and he got to know a black Colombian guy from the Bronx called Bill. Blacks and Dominicans didn't pal around much, but Ramón was a charmer and had a knack for spotting talent. Bill, it turned out, was an important middleman meeting mules at JFK and holding the product while deals were done. He had several things going at once, including babying a large quantity of cocaine for a Colombian terror group's drug arm. All he had to do was hold it and keep his mouth shut. Simple. But Bill was also a bit of a fuckup and had somehow punched a cop at (of all heaven's holy fucking places) the Puerto Rican Day Parade. Bill was on a warrant and went to jail and through that he lost his apartment in Riverdale. They wanted Bill out of the building because he was black and Colombian, but heavying him out would look bad at landlord-and-tenant court. Fortunately for them, Bill was now in prison and couldn't (or forgot to) pay his rent (he had a few places), so they kicked him out and put in Mr. Peter Berenson, who had wanted to move from the ground floor to the fourth floor to get a view of Van Cortlandt Park.

I don't know what Bill's troubles were, but clearly he had a lot on his plate and didn't get round to sending someone to look for his stash of coke until December, by which time the apartment was inhabited by someone else—our pal Pete. The Christmas burglar had found nothing, and Bill decided that he would investigate the whole thing when he got out of the clink in the summer.

You might recall that the night Shovel supposedly beat the crap out of Big Andy, as I was coming up the steps from the subway stop Mr. Berenson said that he'd had an intruder break into his place but not take anything. This was Bill out of jail and looking for his cache of cocaine, which was safely embedded in the floorboard. He didn't find it or was too high to get it the first time, which was unlucky for him, because very soon after, Ramón saw him on the street and remembered his tall prison tales and took him to a place where all the pertinent information was extracted. Shortly after that, Ramón or an associate went to Mr. Berenson's apartment, killed Mr. Berenson, and took a sports bag full of cocaine out of the apartment. I sometimes like to beat myself up with the thought that if I'd taken the old Nazi a wee bit more seriously that night perhaps I'd have gone over there myself and camped out and found the cocaine before Ramón did. With a bag full of cocaine to deliver to Darkey, I might have been forgiven all my sins and at the very least there would have been no reason to send all of us down to Mexico. Maybe they'd have gotten to me, but the boys would all still have been alive.

In any case, his little worker bees got going on the stash and with all this free money Ramón transformed himself from a small-time player into a bigger-time player. Ramón flooded his own wee part of the market, undercut the competition, and in no time at all was the cat's pajamas.

It maybe wasn't just chance then that the two areas I'd come across Ramón's baleful influence were in the Bronx and Washington Heights. Both places Dominicans were moving into, Micks moving out of. Places where one could expect that Darkey White's power would be on the wane and that of thoughtful young hoods from Hispaniola would be on the wax. Yes, in this part of town, Ramón and the Dominicans were the future, Darkey White and the Irish were the past. It wouldn't last, but then again, what does?

Ramón was in the group of six that night, and I didn't know it, but he'd come to see me.

You think you can be anonymous in this city, but you can't. Things slip out, people chitter. Everyone's a bigmouth. You can't keep a fucking secret in America. The Irish aren't much good at secrets either, but they're better than Yanks. If a UFO really did crash at Roswell, there'd be a bloody Roswell World there by now.

Someone had blabbed and Ramón had heard about me and sought me out. At that time, I considered this my unluckiest break since coming back to New York. From my position, I was doing ok. I had a job, I had a place, and I was lying low and doing prep work. The last thing I needed was a major player taking an interest in me. But it is possible that nothing at all would have worked out but for my connection with Ramón. Without Ramón, it might have taken me years to find out where anybody lived and without Ramón, Sunshine might have got to me before I got to him.

Ramón was cool and had a lot of bottle. His boys were sitting in the booth drinking Coronas when he came up to the bar alone and sat opposite me.

Ramón's big thing was telling you who the best prospects were in Dominican baseball circles. Largely, he was proved right and I have vague recollections of predictions of greatness for Pedro Martínez, Manny Ramírez, and Sammy Sosa, though doubtless there were others who didn't work out.

Anyway, that's how he started out with me. Baseball, Dominicans. On extremely limited knowledge I kept the chat going, hoping for a fat tip. We talked, and he got another round in. His English was great for having spent so short a time here, but apparently it was because of his uncle, who had gone back to the island after thirty years on 171st Street. He'd been raised by this uncle, who, in his retirement, became a minor and almost famous Dominican poet. After the death of his mother, Ramón was raised by the uncle and a succession of women, none of whom, it seemed, he had much affection for. He told me all this when baseball was exhausted.

Yeah, yeah, very interesting, I kept saying.

Ramón chatted on and on, and it looked like things were going ok, and I was just beginning to wonder if there was any kind of gay vibe here when quite suddenly he stopped talking, blinked, and said:

Listen, enough of this. I'll come to the point, I know you.

You do?

Yes.

Ok, who am I? I said, laughing.

You are Michael Forsythe and you and your crew are the ones who killed Dermot Finoukin in a bar near the Audubon Ballroom in Washington Heights.

I don't know what you're talk—

I was there that day, I recognize you. I want to offer you a job. I'm starting a business in that part of town and I need reliable men who can handle a weapon.

Wrong guy, mate, sorry. Mistaken me for someone else, I said, concealing the fact that I was very close to panic.

Please, don't play games, he said.

Jesus Christ, I was thinking. Ok, be calm. So I was rumbled. Bloody rumbled. Was he a peeler? No, not this side of the Great Divide. What was it that he'd said? Oh yeah, he wanted to offer me a job, because I was such a great fucking marksman.

Ok, pal, your whole crew over there are Dominicans. Now why would you want me? I don't even speak Spanish, I said. *No hablo español.*

He smiled.

Michael, you'll learn Spanish. I need good men, not hangers-on. It pays five hundred a week. Often much more. You do basic protection.

You talk like a cop. How come your English is so good? I asked suspiciously.

Listen to me, Michael, I'm no *puta* gangster smoking the product and blowing profits on cars and whores. My crew are the guys I could get, but I'm looking for quality and from what I've heard about you, you'll fit right in.

What have you heard? From who? How did you know where I was?

Don't worry, it is general information.

This, in fact, worried me a great deal, but my face was studied and blank. I tried to appear relaxed. I grinned and breathed.

Anyway, why would I want to work for you? I asked.

Apart from the money?

Yeah.

I'll help you.

I looked at him. Ramón, a small man, but what presence, like a Dominican Rod Steiger. But even this doesn't do him justice. Ramón took up a great deal of psychic space: he electrified the room and his prison eyes and wary stare brought up everyone else's game, and we became hyperaware just as he was always cognizant of everyone and everything within a pistol shot.

Help me do what? I asked.

I'll help you, he insisted.

I shook my head and tried to figure out what was going on. Was he a fucking mind reader? What did he know? Things didn't seem quite right. Was this a trap of some kind? Had Darkey put him up to this?

Listen, mate, I don't need a job, I already have one. I'm trying to keep a low profile, you know, I said.

I know, he said, and smiled a very irritating smile. I'll help you with that, too.

I began to get a little scared now and measured the paces it would take me to get at the shotgun under the counter. Two steps, and it just pulls out. Neither of us spoke for a while, but I was first to crack:

I need to know how you found out about me, I said, slowly.

He nodded.

I understand, he said.

While he spoke, I tried to figure him out. The half-smile, Rolex watch, gold chain, expensive shirt, and yet it was all low key. This was the bare minimum he needed to impress his subordinates. Ramón wasn't really the type for ostentation.

Two days ago, someone saw you in here, someone who also was there at the bar. And yet I'd heard that you were dead, he said.

From who?

It had been put around that you and your crew had been killed in Mexico, murdered for skimming cream off the top. It had been put around that if that's what happened to friends think what would happen to enemies.

Oh, I said stupidly. If I'd been quicker, I'd have seen right there what the game was, but there was too much information for me to process at once. Something going on, but I couldn't figure out what. If it were me, I would never in a million years hire someone who wasn't a countryman or an old friend. You never go to strangers for this kind of deal. You can never know them well enough. Look at Mrs. Gandhi and her Sikh bodyguards, proof enough right there. The emperor Darius, another example. I had to think pretty quickly. First, was he threatening me? If I didn't take the job, was he going to tell Darkey I was here? Second, what was the hidden agenda? What was it? Ok, thinking. The second part of it I wasn't going to get tonight. Too smart for that. The first I might. I decided the best thing was just to come right out and ask him.

Listen, uh, mister, uh, Ramón.

Yes.

Listen, Ramón, are you threatening me? If I don't take the job are you going to spread it around where I am?

He looked very serious. His lips narrowed, his eyes didn't blink.

I assume you do not mean to be insulting. Please take my card and think it over. We can help each other. That's all.

He handed me a card. It was white and had a phone number on it, nothing else. He turned round and his boys all got up at once. They all walked out without another word.

The door closed behind them, and I knew immediately I didn't have a choice. If I wanted to stay in New York, I'd have to go with him. Even if Ramón wasn't going to say anything, sooner or later it would come out. Darkey had more men and resources. Sunshine would see to it that Mr. Duffy knew there was a problem. Mr. Duffy had dozens of people whom he could call upon to dispose of an irritant like me. In half an hour, my world was somewhere in my fucking whips.

I had no choice. And I knew then. No more spying on Bridget, no more meditating on the roof. The honeymoon was over. I called the number an hour later.

Ramón, I—

He cut me off. He said to say nothing, that he liked to do important things in person and he would come back down. I hung up, both irritated and strangely pleased with this way of doing biz. He came back in just before two. The place was deserted. He came alone. No boys.

He sat opposite.

You've decided, he said.

I stuck out my hand.

Ramón, I said, where thy lodgest, I will lodge, and thy people will be my people and thy god, my god.

He smiled and shook my hand.

And that was that. I went home. Stripped, showered, went to bed. It was all done. Ramón was to be the facilitator. I lay there. Harlem out there in the night, alive and beautiful. I lay and listened.

Ramón is the conduit they've chosen, I said. The last piece.

I closed my eyes and put my hands behind my head. I rested in the long, cold arms of Nemesis and readied myself for the blows to come.

10: A STOLEN CAR TO OYSTER BAY

Ramón turned out to be a brief, enigmatic, but useful presence in my life. He oozed charm and charisma. Gentle, quiet, persuasive, but that's what they sometimes said about the Führer, and you couldn't forget that Ramón's crew was responsible for about a murder a week, although he might say in justification that this was only self-defense. Not that my hands were completely clean on that score (if you counted Dermot) and in any case what was my excuse for the murders yet to be?

They got me a flat on 181st Street on the fifth floor of a building that looked right over the George Washington Bridge and the Hudson. The apartment was amazing, with hardwood floors and long windows and modern appliances, twice the size of the place I'd been in on 123rd Street, and the neighborhood was good. The 180s near the river was a little Jewish section in the middle of Dominican Washington Heights. Mostly older folks, who got on well with the majority community.

My apartment was airy and wonderful. At night, when I wasn't working, I'd sit and look out the big bay living-room windows. There's a bit in *Citizen Kane* when one of Kane's buddies is being interviewed in a nursing home and in the background you can see the GWB, and that's exactly the view I had—except in color.

Nominally, I had become part of Ramón's inner circle: a "lieutenant." He employed me as a bodyguard, and a shifty little man called José gave me an Uzi submachine gun and a Colt .45 semiautomatic. I'd fired a Colt ACP before, a huge, loud, terrifying weapon that was standard issue to U.S. Army officers for seventy years, so the gun must have had some good qualities. I, however, couldn't shoot the thing. I mean, it'd blow the head off anything closer than twenty feet, but for me, at least, it was horribly inaccurate at distance. Also, the magazine would jam, and it made me jump when flames would come out of the barrel. And, of course, I hadn't fired an Uzi. The British Army would never countenance such a silly and vulgar weapon, and I mistrusted it right from the start. I wore a custom jacket that Ramón had a tailor make up for me and carried both guns in shoulder holsters, but the Uzi I kept on the right-hand side without the clip in to make it a bit more comfortable.

Ramón never once revealed his real plans for me and I, for one, simply could not buy his story of needing reliable men. The morning after our meeting, a van showed up for my stuff, such stuff as I had. I didn't see Ramón for the next few days. He told me about the apartment on the phone and hinted that he might meet me there, but I waited for him and he didn't appear. The super saw me in and around and refused a twenty-dollar tip.

The next day, José showed up with a tailor. He gave me five hundred dollars in hundreds and told me to get some shirts and a pair of shoes. A man came and installed premium cable and a phone. Furniture was delivered from Pier 1.

A couple of days after that, a car came for me and took me down to a restaurant near Ramón's place. It was early evening and Ramón introduced me to the lieutenants, who were polite but not particularly friendly. Everyone spoke Spanish all the time. After the introductions I was fitted out with my weapons, and I just sat there sipping Corona.

My whole role in the setup seemed completely false and out of place, but Ramón did his best to make me feel comfortable by having the occasional conversation with me in English about sports and the weather. At eleven o'clock, after what I suppose had been a getting-to-know-you meeting, I rode a cab back to 181st Street.

The next day, I was summoned down again. This time to his loft. The lieutenants were out pounding the beat and I was alone with Ramón, José, and the two bodyguards.

My real job was the unspoken thing between us. He knew that I suspected that it was all a fabrication, and what's more, he knew that I knew that he knew, but he kept his lip shut.

Ramón, if I'm your bodyguard, why don't you want me to live here? I asked him.

You're my bodyguard on important occasions. You have a very special role, Michael, he said. That seemed to end the conversation, and I nodded. Ramón went back to his paper.

I spent the afternoon there. Ramón went into his study and closed the door, and in the evening, the lieutenants came back again with the money.

If you've seen any of the druggy ghetto-fabulous films of the '80s and '90s, you might have the wrong impression of Ramón's lifestyle. It's true that he lived in a nice loft, but there was only one girl (Carmen, a slender, frumpy little thing who lived with her mother at night and only sometimes came to see Ramón in the evenings) and no partying, and no one was allowed to sample the product. Ramón's place contained a white sofa, a dozen white leather lounge chairs, a huge stereo, many CDs, a few coffee tables, but also an enormous mahogany bookcase with books in English, Spanish, and French. The living room must have been the size of a basketball court and the furniture appeared so tiny in this space that it had an ascetic feel to it. Ramón, I think, enjoyed bucking people's expectations of him. He often had people up there, and it was never the way they expected it to be. An old building in the 150s on the river, huge and bare, overlooking a gloomy, leafless park. It sat above three derelict floors of an old middle school. To get up to it, you had to climb the outside fire escape. I suppose that this was for security reasons, although it's conceivable that he could have just been saving his money for the time when he could have the whole building done over in suitable style.

Since most of the boys spoke to one another in fast Dominican Spanish, I was more or less cast as an outsider from the beginning. No one made an effort to get to know me, and I got the impression that they believed that I was one of the boss's whims and would be disposed of when (probably in a few weeks) Ramón tired of me. Since no one made an attempt to engage me in conversation, I took to wandering around the place when Ramón was in the bedroom or in his private study—the only two areas that were out of bounds. I often went out on the balcony for a breath of air, although the air was always a bit dodgy because of the huge sewage plant on 138th Street. I would have enjoyed a smoke, but I'd given it up. Back inside, the boys were chatting and ignoring me. Ramón's bookshelf was interesting: about a thousand books, but fewer than a dozen had their spines broken. Clearly, when Ramón had come into money he'd bought the books all at once to fill out the bookcase, but whether they were a pose or he actually intended to read them I'm not sure.

So there's me reading his books or having a breather outside; Ramón and José are in the study and the other lieutenants are making up baggies. Every day like the first day of school, awkward, unpleasant.

In Ramón's organization, he had about two or sometimes three dozen people working for him on an informal basis. A core of five lieutenants, all Dominican: Sammy, Iago, Pedro, Moreno, and the number-two in the outfit, José. There were two bodyguards, one nineteen-year-old Cuban guy called Devo (like the band), though everybody called him Cuba, and another Dominican guy called Hector. Outside of these seven and me (who became formally the third bodyguard), the rest of the employees were all cannon fodder. At night, the lieutenants would make up the baggies in a lab Ramón had built himself at the back of his apartment—small and white, stinking. It wasn't out of bounds, but the lieutenants saw it as their fiefdom and kept the bodyguards and even José out of there. In the morning, the lieutenants would distribute the baggies to the safety men, who would hold them, and then sellers would hit the streets. Once you'd bought a bag, you'd go to the safety man, who was in an alley or fake store, and if everything was cool, he would give it to you. For every one person selling the five- or ten-dollar baggies, there would be three others keeping an eye on the street and another man who accompanied you to the safety man. Typically, a seller could make about three hundred dollars an hour, up to two or three thousand a day. The seller saw about 5 to 10 percent of what he made, depending upon the caprice of Ramón's lieutenants. I estimated that Ramón was probably taking in sixty thousand a week. I don't know if he had to pay off anyone or what exactly his expenses were, but clearly it was a bloody gold mine.

No one seemed to have any moral qualms about selling crack to addicts who would prostitute themselves or steal or go to the lengths of robbing their own family and pawning their kid's possessions to pay for the stuff. Ramón never seemed to give any lectures about not selling to kids or waifs or madmen, but then I don't speak Spanish, so maybe he did.

Ramón owned a Mercedes, but he drove it himself, and there were very few extraneous expenses.

Ten days had gone by, and every afternoon I had reported for work and hung out doing nothing until evening and then gone home. I'd done bugger-all to earn anything, but I consoled myself with the thought that I had over a thousand dollars now saved, and because of all the plantains and rice and beans, I had gained about ten pounds and was getting stronger.

The time would come when I'd have to say goodbye to this purgatorial existence, when I'd have to do what I'd come to New York to do, but I figured I could build myself up for a wee while yet. Ramón had not revealed why he really wanted me around, and I was beginning to think that he really was just a whimsical eejit who had taken a shine to me.

I made my own routine, and I usually went over there at around one or two in the P.M. The mornings were my own, and sometimes I'd haunt the old places where I used to live in the city. I had a job to do, but I had to wait, not for a sign exactly, or an alignment in the heavens, but I had to know that the moment was right.

My favorite place in the late morning was 125th Street. None of Darkey's boys would ever be down there, and for me it was old and familiar and I felt like a tourist now that I was living on 181st. 125th, badland and desperateland but almost a home. Sometimes I'd walk by Mr. Han's Chinky, but I wouldn't go in, and now and again I paid Jim a visit in the Blue Moon.

When I was feeling particularly good I would set myself projects. I'd try and do five parks in a day, or go from river to river. Or try to find the highest spot in Manhattan. One day I walked the entire length of Fifth Avenue for no reason at all. I was so late I had to call Ramón and tell him I wasn't coming (Ramón, of course, didn't seem the least concerned or interested). Fifth Avenue starts in abject poverty and dislocation in Harlem, but by the time you hit Central Park, you're in the territory of millionaires and that stays with you all the way down to the

Village. I didn't stop in anywhere; I brought a water bottle and a hat and just walked. The canyons opening up and the people getting fancier and more white. Cats and stray dogs and rats disappearing and being replaced by pigeons only. Schoolkids at first in jeans and big jackets and then in blazers and ties. The soundtrack growing steadily all the while: crying radios and jackhammers and people and cars. I'd walked the whole length on a fake foot.

Impressed by this success, I did the walk of Broadway, too, but I had to do it over two days, and I only walked the Broadway that's in Manhattan, for, of course, it goes up into the Bronx (and on to West-chester), but up there is too near the Four P., which was risky. Broad-way isn't so linear an ascent from chaos to civilization. It has its ups and downs, poverty rising and falling like a sine curve. It begins in water, and you can see animals and boats. And then south through park and project, black and Spanish and then black and then Spanish again. A crazy cinema. Bodegas. The Audubon Ballroom. A funeral swelling out from a Mormon church, sorrow seeping through the walls and out the windows. Then, below 120th it gentrifies as Columbia University breathes her love and influence into the surrounding streets, and then there's life for a few blocks and below 99th it becomes the Upper West Side. All the way down Broadway through the theaters, brick stacks, construction sites, porno shows, shops, holes in the ground with the whiff of sulfur.

Yeah, those were three good days, and I was almost happy.

I saw Ramón the night after Broadway and asked him if there was anything he wanted me to do.

Nothing, he said.

I wasn't satisfied with this. I was ready for something. Trouble, heavying, even a minor cutting-out expedition. But Ramón was all patience. Annoyingly so.

Get yourself strong. Relax, I'll tell you when I need you, he said. Walk, move.

I did as I was bid.

I went everywhere. From river to river, from island to mainland and back. The PATH and the subway and the M4 bus.

I went to dour Saint Pat's and I went to Riverside Church and the

great Saint John the Divine, surely the holiest place in the city outside
of Monument Park in Yankee Stadium. (For even a Mick who's never
seen a baseball game in his life has heard of Gehrig and Ruth and
Mantle and DiMaggio.)

I went south, and I had a scare in the Upper East Side when I saw a
boy I knew called Roddy McGee coming out of a bar on Third Avenue,
so after that I avoided the Mick zones and the neutral zones and kept
mostly to greater Harlem. But that was ok. I liked it there. I absorbed
Harlem, I took it in and became part of it. I went all the way from the
West Side Highway to the Triborough Bridge, from Sugar Hill to Manhattanville, from Washington Heights to Inwood Park.

The walking was making me stronger, but Ramón noticed how I
moved and gave me a telephone number. He didn't say anything.

I called the number, and it was a doctor who specialized in the reha-
bilitation of amputees.

I went to see him, and he was an old guy in a nice building off 48th
Street, which I supposed meant that his practice did very well.

He was a Vietnam vet, and although he had not seen combat, he
had worked in navy hospitals in Saigon for two stints, in 1966–67 and
1969–70.

We had a consultation and X rays and he put me on a treadmill.
After it was done, he recommended that I have corrective surgery to
shorten my stump to make it more balanced and comfortable, with a
cleaner tuck at the end.

I absolutely refused. The thought of cutting off more of my fucking
leg was utterly absurd.

But Dr. Havercamp was not to be browbeaten by a civilian patient a
third his age, so he sat me down and explained everything in detail.

A minor operation. One night in the hospital, a week of rehabilita-
tion. Weekly visits for the next few months. I'd be running the New
York marathon this time next year.

He convinced me and bullied me a little, and I saw the sense of it.

I told Ramón I'd need a week, and Ramón said take all the time in
the world, and although I hadn't told him why, the night before my
operation he showed up with a dozen books and magazines and chocolate and a massive jar of vitamin pills from the GNC.

Take these every day, he said, pointing at the pills.

I will, I said.

He asked Cuba to step outside for a moment and when he had, Ramón said confidentially:

Things will be easier now, you'll see.

And as was the case with most things, Ramón, of course, was right.

* * *

Out of the surgery. Morphine dreams. An old trope, the drowned world, New York devoid of people and absorbed like Machu Picchu or Angkor Wat into the jungle. Forest stealing up on buildings, sending seeds here or a root over there or a sapling through there and the whole becoming one organic mass of vines and creepers and glass and concrete. Flamingos in Jamaica Bay, eyries in the Chrysler Building. Seas of orchids on the railway stop at 125th. Dandelions and flowering plants on the fire escapes of tenements. Mahogany and teak and spreading elms. Marshes in the East River and every tunnel a river and every railway a path for animals. The Hudson freezes and over come deer and coyotes and bear. I can see blue-tongued iguanas and lizards, snakes. Piranha and alligators in the reservoir in Central Park. Vultures in Times Square. Jaguars surveying the horizon from the fastness of the roof on PS 125.

Yes, it's an old trope and a common one in New York. A place of escape. Either in the primordial past or apocalyptic future, and you have to be careful about this kind of thinking. Raphael (according to Ramón's copy) in *Paradise Lost* warns Adam about these kinds of thoughts. Think, Raphael says, only what concerns thee and thy being. Dream not of other worlds.

These flights of fancy, though, were helping me cope. An alternative New York was a better place to be, sometimes, than my own head.

A couple of days later, I was on my feet. Visits to the doc. Back up to Ramón. Out again.

I was walking and dreaming and killing time, but I wasn't avoiding the issue. No, I'd seen the future and I was aware that I was in it. Aye. I was dandering and dreaming, but I wasn't mitching my responsibility.

Strong again. A hundred push-ups, a hundred sit-ups, a long walk every morning. I would eat a big breakfast of eggs and plantains, yellow rice, black beans, and then in the second part of the day I would go over to Ramón's and hang out and get my money.

It was ok.

If you could take the vibe, Ramón's was all right. Awkward, dull, Ramón's men always a little afraid of me. Ramón had obviously told them something that had upset them. It didn't help that they already were a superstitious, suspicious, freaky, paranoid bunch. They hadn't bullied me or kidded me; but they were still contemptuous. And they were afeared, jumpy. They kept their distance. Once Moreno tried to stare me down, but he broke first. Cuba was the only one who had much time for me. It was a shame, because from what I'd seen of Dominican culture, it reminded me of Ireland.

Cuba's English was better than the others', and occasionally, while I'd be sitting at the window thumbing through some book, he'd wander across and spend the afternoon with me. He was a kid and didn't know what he wanted in life and spoke frequently of joining the marines. We'd talk about girls and films and sometimes politics. Cuba was a big guy, well over 220 pounds; he hated Castro, and one day, to bait him, I said I'd wear a Che T-shirt, and he gave me a long and impassioned argument about the evils of communism, Castroites and Che. Stuff he'd got from his dad, mostly garbled. He had a thing against Ricky Ricardo from the *Lucy* show, but he never articulated this objection clearly. Cuba had fled the island with his father and brother in 1984, and they'd gone first to Spain and then come to the United States. Apart from Castro, Cuba's other main theme was the stupidity and short-sightedness of Dominicans. Dominicans robbed their children to buy crack, Dominicans had no musical culture, Dominicans had no litera-ture, Dominicans thought they could play baseball, but everybody knew that Cubans were the stars of the baseball world. Dominicans would make nothing of themselves. In whispers he said that even Ramón couldn't escape.

Sometimes we'd drag Hector over, and the three of us would play a retarded version of poker with four cards showing and a fifth blind in your hand. Cuba was very good at this, and though we were only playing for pennies, he would get excited when at the end of a session he'd be a dol-lar or seventy-five cents up over the pair of us. It took me a day or two to realize that the cards were marked, but I played anyway, for the company.

About this time in New York City, there were two hundred murders a month and most of those were drug-related, so occasionally you'd hear gunfire out in the street. Hector, Cuba, Ramón, and I would be around in the afternoon, Ramón in his study doing whatever it was he did and me and the boys playing cards and out there in the street would be the odd gunshot.

It was the lieutenants' job in the daytime to protect their part of the street. Usually the lieutenant and a couple of the watchers would be armed. There were so many independent pushers back then that every once in a while one of them would get uppity and think they were the original Jesus Christ and try to muscle in on Ramón's hard-won turf. The watchers or the lieutenants would shoot them. I'd hear about this, but I saw little of it. Back home, you'd kneecap them, but here they just killed them.

We weren't involved. The bodyguards' job was to protect Ramón, not to patrol the street. Moreno would tell Cuba, and Cuba would tell me—it disconcerted me. These people were out risking their lives, and what was I doing? What was my role in the scheme of things?

He didn't tell me anything, but Ramón had been watching me, waiting for the time he thought I was ready. Whether the incident with Moreno forced his hand, I don't know.

It came a day when Ramón, José, Hector, and Cuba had disappeared in the big yellow Mercedes. I was left completely alone in the house throughout the afternoon, and seeing it as a test of loyalty, I didn't venture into any of the forbidden areas, such as the study or Ramón's bedroom. I hung out on the balcony staring at the Hudson.

By six o'clock, the lieutenants started showing up with their day's profits. Not that their street dealers didn't work at night, but Ramón was always strict about having his accounting at the same time. Tonight, though, Ramón wasn't there, and I was. The lieutenants eyed me suspiciously and got themselves beers from the fridge and sat on the sofa and the white leather chairs to wait.

The boys were drinking and doing an excellent job of not seeing me. After a while, they put the stereo on and started fucking around with Ramón's stuff.

I went over and told them to cut it out.

They asked me who the fuck I thought I was, and Moreno stood up and started cursing me out a few inches from my face. He'd clearly had it with me. A freeloading fucking Yankee who Ramón was fucking in love with or something. He was yelling, and his nose was an inch from mine now and I was thinking, So this is how it ends, the fucking ignominy of it. Me and him grabbing our pieces at the same time. Me getting one off, the lads spraying me so that I'm more hole than cheese.

Moreno was shouting at me and showing me a bullet scar in the shoulder he must have taken in loyal service to Ramón.

Fuck it, Moreno, I said. You boys wanna see a real fucking wound?

They didn't understand, but they stopped while I rolled up my trouser leg, took my foot off.

They didn't know.

Moreno shut up. All of them shut up.

In that silence, standing there with my foot off and feeling utterly ridiculous, Ramón came back.

He slipped in as normal, dressed in a coat too big for him. He looked at us for an embarrassing moment and said nothing. He was with his boys, and he muttered something to José, and José said something in Spanish, and everyone went back to the lab. He called me over, and I sat next to him on the white sofa. I gathered my wits and pulled myself together. He waited until I'd strapped my foot on again.

You're bored, he said.

I shook my head.

Are you strong? he said.

I nodded.

He came straight to the point. His voice was low and in a whisper.

Michael, they stagger things now, they're careful, different places, but we know their meeting is tonight in the old place, and if you want to go we can give you a lift up there.

I didn't need to be told what meeting or who he was talking about. It was time for business.

Ok, I said.

❖   ❖   ❖

Ramón drove me. We didn't talk. He was smoking a cigar and listening to some crazy Dominican music low on his CD system. He left me ten blocks from the Four Provinces and asked if I needed anything. I told him I was ok. I walked to the spot where I'd waited for Bridget, the alley between the buildings that gave me a good view of the front door.

I waited for three hours, until it was after midnight. Come on, Darkey, come on, Darkey, come on, Darkey, I was saying over and over. But no bloody Darkey.

People going in and out, strangers, all of them. Ramón had said something about a change in routine, but I didn't see how that would affect the regulars at the Four P. Eventually, though, at near to bloody closing, I did see a couple of old stagers I recognized, and a wee while after that, Mrs. Callaghan appeared at the side entrance with a box of rubbish. But even so, it was getting late, and I was thinking that Ramón's intelligence wasn't all it was cracked up to be when who should appear in all his Lundy-Quisling-Vichy glory but Big fucking Bob.

I recognized his ugly shadow before I saw him slinking out the side entrance of the Four Provinces, swaying a bit and singing. Cramped, I staggered to my feet and went after him. He was walking down the alley next to the Four P., heading for the empty lot that people used as a car park. I ran across the waste ground and pulled out the Colt. Bob didn't know I was after him even though I was making enough noise to wake the dead and damned, a sort of a half-run, galumphing, and making progress but not exactly doing Warp Factor 8. Bob had stopped at the corner of the lot, and when I got to the street a little up from the bar, he climbed into a red Honda Accord and drove off. I leveled the .45 and took aim, but he was so far away and in the dark and with that gun I'd never get a good shot off. I ran to the main street and flagged down the first car I saw. A cream-colored Cadillac, turning at the corner, probably pulling into the same car park for the Four Provinces. The driver either didn't see me or was ignoring me. I sprinted over and pointed the Colt at the windshield.

Hey, fucker, I yelled.

The driver was a bald man in his forties, dark lawyer suit, somewhat distracted, fiddling with his seat belt, playing around with it, and trying to turn into a space at the same time. He didn't see or hear me and was still driving and almost hit me.

I banged his window and turned the gun on him.

Get out of the fucking car or I'll fucking kill you, I said in pure West Belfast, and that was enough to get his attention.

He stopped the car and looked at me white-faced. He was shitting himself, perhaps literally. I opened the door.

Get the fuck out, I screamed.

He was sweating and nearly crying.

My seat belt's stuck, it's stuck, it's stuck, he was saying in a complete panic.

I leaned over and clicked the release button.

Get out, I said. He still didn't move, so I had to tug the fucker out by his lapels.

He tumbled onto the pavement.

I pointed the gun at his head.

Wait until morning before calling the police, understand, otherwise I fucking kill you and your fucking wife and your fucking dog. Geddit? I said, and got into the car without waiting for a reply. There was a huge box of Huggies blocking the view out the passenger-side window. I chucked them out, stuck the vehicle in drive, and headed off. Bob, of course, was nowhere now to be seen. Jesus.

I drove down the road. Tons of traffic. I turned the corner, heading her up towards Broadway. He'd either have gone left or right. I decided on left and went fast and by pure jammy-dodger luck at the turn across Van Cortlandt I saw him.

Driving cautious, drunk-man speed, but keeping a cool head and not too slow. He was heading east either up the shore or onto Long Island or maybe even doing a turnabout to go down into Manhattan. I tried to think if I'd ever heard anyone speak about where Bob lived, but I didn't recall it ever coming up. He tried to make a traffic light and then aborted the plan and stalled the car, coming to a screechy stop. He was a bit freaked, and he took a couple of tries to get it going again. Someone behind honked him, and I saw Bob undo his seat belt as if he was going to get out of his car and have words.

Bob, stay in the car, don't get yourself arrested, you big shite, I was saying.

He changed his mind about the seat belt and got going again. He took a wrong turn or two and had to double back, and I wondered if he was being especially clever trying to figure out if there was a tail on him. But he wasn't that smart or collected—just half blitzed probably.

He took us on a path through the South Bronx and somehow we ended up in Queens. Bob pulled in at a newsstand and got himself some cigs and a Coke and a copy of *Penthouse*. The newsstand was fairly isolated and I thought about doing it there, but this was no place for business; and besides, I wanted to have a word with the big ganch. So I let him go. He drank the Coke, and it improved his driving.

We went together out past La Guardia and Shea and I became reasonably convinced that Bob lived somewhere on the North Shore of Long Island. It was late and traffic was light and I had a job keeping the big cream-colored Caddy far enough away to avoid getting in Bob's paranoid rearview mirror.

The highway was brightly lit and the cars going too fast, but at least it was an automatic so that my left foot wasn't always on the clutch. It was the first time I'd driven since I'd come back from Mexico and the straps that held the foot onto my leg had almost given way on the run across the waste ground. I wasn't in the mood to do any Long John Silvers, so I was glad they'd stayed on. I made a mental note, though, to go see Dr. Havercamp about those running lessons he was offering before.

Yeah.

The adrenaline was coursing through me. Hours on an OP and suddenly seeing the target will do that for you. And I'd dreamed about Bob, dreamed of this very event, of this very night.

We drove out farther onto the island. The surface of the road went clay-colored and the lines voided themselves into two lanes. I wound the window down, the air cooling my damp skin.

Highway lights, trucks, petrol stations, the city in the rearview, and even in all this light, pollution, stars. Saturn and Venus and a labyrinth of concordances bringing me onward.

Onward to the inevitable. No, it wasn't Darkey's night, but maybe it was Bob's. Aye, and suddenly, there was a cheerlessness within me. And perhaps almost a creeping reluctance. If Bob could only keep driving forever, if only he could keep going. All the way through

Nassau County and Suffolk, all the way to the end of Long Island, where there are potato fields, where Gatsby had his mansion, and on out into the blackness of the Atlantic. Yes, keep driving, over the ocean, and like Alcock and Brown, we'll crash somewhere near Clifden. I know this pub in Galway town, this lovely pub, we'll pull in and have a jar and be on our way. Tell ya, Bob, you think the Guinness in the Four Provinces is good, there they take a year and a half to pull your pint.

A session, and then we'll be off. Sea dogs and rose petals and away from that coast across the Great Bog and up to the mysteries of the Boyne Valley. We'll be in Newgrange for the solstice, where the pagans brought the returning sun. And down at the river. King William was here and James over there. We'll climb Tara and look out over the fifths. And then across another *sheugh*, I don't know, we'll hit Cumbria and the lakes and the Yorkshire Dales. We'll go over oil rigs with their great burning lamps of fire. On east through the Baltic and Russia, and we'll meet the sun again somewhere in the vast wastes of Siberia.

Bob, please understand me, real pain isn't in the body, no, you may think that, but believe one who knows, it isn't in the body or the mind. It's in the spirit.

You'll see. You'll see soon.

Trucks, cars.

The teeming anthills, the moon, kisses of houselight in the shadows. A service station. American girls in jeans and white shirts. Fill your tank, Bob, and be about your way. Don't stop, if you know what's good for you. His black shirt, his little eyes, his hands like the claws of scorpions.

Amigo, despierta, I'm coming. I'm coming.

His fat paw on the lever. He puts in exactly ten dollars and curses when it comes up ten dollars and one cent. You need to lower your blood pressure, Bob. You need relaxation techniques. Yoga, tai chi, meditation. Chant the Om for an hour. *Om mani padme hum.* Maybe it'll help. You're too stressed. Look at ya. He turns and gazes towards the girls. Says something. One laughs, at him or with him? Who can tell? He twists his neck back and rubs it. Stress. Maybe it's a conscience, no? Not bloody Jiminy. But hurry now, Bob, pay. Get your candy bars, you have your smokes already. Pay, go. Back to your car. Hurry. Go.

Amigo, despierta, I'm coming.

Yes . . .

He came out muttering and shaking his head. He got back in and stalled the car again. He tried to talk to a girl in a black Corolla, but she wasn't interested. He drove. I edged out of the shadows next to the car wash. Only another fifteen minutes and his turn signal went on. We cut off the highway somewhere I'd never heard of. People lived here. It was a community. Big houses, streets. Near the water, but actually I had no idea at all where we were. A while ago, there'd been a sign pointing out something to do with Theodore Roosevelt back on the motorway, but this place wasn't it. It wasn't anywhere. Quiet town, nice, pretty, I liked it. He drove away from the shops and the town center and up a tree-lined street that was denuded of leaves, of cover. Bob stopped his car and paralleled it into a spot. He got out and went up a path. His house was a white bungalow with a metal fence around a small garden. There was a shriveled pumpkin on the doorstep. When was Halloween? I'd missed it. I was outside of time, somehow. Had the election taken place? Who won? Who was president? The weeks had blurred. I parked the car slowly. Parking's not my strong suit. Driving's not my strong suit, but parking's worse, and I didn't want to bump anything and have the fucking neighbors coming out and asking me where my fucking parking permit was. Somehow, I squeezed in the big Caddy and crossed the street.

I paused at a tree near Bob's front gate and checked the road for dog walkers and insomniacs and other assorted trouble. Nothing.

Bob was in the living room, and he'd put the TV on. He got up and went into, presumably, the kitchen, got himself a six-pack of beer, came back, and sat there. He opened a cold one and drank and flipped the channels. He wasn't going to shower? No, Bob wanted to calm his nerves after driving drunk all the way home. He would have a few drinks, and then he'd get his shit together. Shower, get out his wankmag, go to bed with a job well done. Another day, another drive home blitzed to fuck and no casualties. No probs for Bob. He drank his beer and tossed the can over his head into a trash can. It didn't go in. I was out there too long. I checked the street again. Yeah, Bob, you're the only victim tonight, mate, sorry. Have a beer and get your head straight, you poor love, it must be shite having to do things all by yourself and with a bunch of new boys, most of whom were green around the gills. Jesus. And what with Ramón piling on the pressure and everything. Poor old Darkey, poor old Sunshine, poor old Bob.

I opened the front gate and went down the path. His garden was dry and unkempt. There was rubbish in it. I stared at the pumpkin, which was carved in far too nice a way for Bob to have done it (unless he had hidden talents). I opened the screen door and stood for a moment in a tiny porch. Letters lay trampled into the floor, a bill, a vote reminder, a yellow envelope from a debt collection agency. I picked them up and looked them over and set them down again. I turned the handle on the front door. It was locked. Fuck. He wasn't so drunk that he hadn't locked the front door. Well, good on you, mate. At least you weren't a total useless shite.

I opened the screen door again and went around the side of the house until I was in the backyard. More garbage, tires, a cement mixer. I tried the back door. It, too, was locked, but there was a top window open in the kitchen. I peered through and checked inside. All seemed to be ok. I put my hand through the top window, flipped the handle on the big side window, and pulled it open all the way. The kitchen door was closed, but under it you could see the flickering light coming from the TV in the front room. I climbed through the window and onto the sink. I was about to go into the living room when I heard Bob get up. I pulled out the Colt and waited there, but he was only swishing the curtains over, and I heard him sit down again. I chambered a round, opened the kitchen door, and went straight into the adjoining living room. The light was on and I adjusted for a moment. Bob's back was to me, and the local news was on the telly.

Bob, I said.

He dropped his beer can and started to get up.

Hands on your head, Bob, it's fucking Banquo, I said.

He puts his hands up, but I think the reference probably eluded him.

Holy fuck, Bob said, and when he turned round to face me, he was white with terror. His hands fell into a pleading gesture.

Hands on your head, Bob, or I'll shoot you.

He put his hands back up, and I motioned for him to sit down in the chair. I turned it around so that he was completely facing me. I sat in a wicker chair opposite. He was smiling weakly at me. Even for Bob, it was stomach-churning.

Christ, Michael, am I glad to see you. Sunshine finally got you boys out, he said he would. But why the gun? Jesus, you don't think I stooled you boys or anything? Ask Darkey. Jesus. Mike. I mean, come on. You know me.

He'd confirmed everything I suspected in one big slabber. The stupid fuck. I nodded.

Listen, Bob, it's important that I know when Sunshine told you about the plan, I asked him quietly, calmly.

What plan?

Bob, just tell me, was it organized a long time, like weeks in advance or was it something that took place in that last couple of days?

No, man, you've got it all wrong. I didn't fuck you guys over. It was a straightforward deal. It just went wrong. You know that. Just fucked up, Bob said, dripping with sweat.

Bob, listen to me. I know nearly everything. Look, have yourself a beer and throw me one. No, roll me one, I said, and we both laughed a little.

Bob picked up a beer and rolled it over, opening a fresh one for himself. I opened mine with my left hand, the right pointing the barrel of the .45 at Bob's chest. The can was Budweiser, but it was so cold you couldn't taste it, so it was ok. Bob was more relaxed now and leaned back in the chair.

Bob was just over six foot and about two hundred and fifty pounds. I've seen heavier men carry it better and I felt bad for him, for a moment.

Ok, Bob, now listen to me. Please don't waste my time denying the fact that Sunshine had you set us up. It's only going to irritate me, and it's a really foolish move to irritate a man who's pointing a .45 at you. Don't you think?

Yes.

Ok, now all I have is a few questions. When did Sunshine tell you about Mexico?

Uhhh, uhh.

Come on, Bob. I'll fucking shoot you right now.

Ok, I was against it. Totally against it. I said so. It was that week, I was as surprised as you guys. I didn't know about it. It may have been in the pipe for longer, but it was sprung on me that week.

I nodded. It was that week. So maybe Bridget's trip to me had been the final straw, or the missing piece of evidence. I wondered why Darkey hadn't just had me shot and dumped me. It puzzled me and I thought for a moment. It was unnecessarily torturing Bob, but the big guy could handle it. The only thing I could come up with was that Darkey did it for the sake of Bridget's feelings. I mean, she's smart. She doesn't look it, but she is. If I just disappeared she'd twig, she'd know he'd murdered me, and Darkey was probably right to think that that might sully the romantic atmosphere. Whereas all of us, all of us, remember, disappear in bloody Mexico, rot there, it seems like an accident. Bridget thinks, Well, gee, Darkey wouldn't sacrifice his whole fucking crew just to kill Michael. No. He wouldn't do that. That's fucking insanity.

I smiled. Aye, sadly, that was it. Sunshine's plan, no doubt. The whole crew would disappear, and she'd be distraught over me. But she'd forget me in time, and maybe she'd just have enough of a wee suspicion of ill will to be more careful with Darkey's affections in the future. Yeah, that was it. I saw it all. The whole thing.

It had been a cascade of events. A horrible escalating fucking disaster. Andy gets the crap beaten out of him, possibly by Shovel. Scotchy thinks it is Shovel, so we get rounded up and I do a Belfast six-pack on him. I'm so shook up, I tell Bridget I need to see her the next day. She comes down and doesn't check her fucking arse. Boris Karloff is on her tail. The evidence gets passed on, it's all confirmed, it's all fucking true, and Sunshine starts organizing things. In the meantime, unfortunately for Sunshine's filthy conscience, I save his bacon at Dermot's, but that doesn't change Darkey's mind. He's cold like that. You make your bed, you lie in it.

The sequence was perfect. The events projected and fixed in reels, and I had no choice about the next act.

How much did you give the Mexicans? What did it cost to get rid of us?

Michael, listen, you've got it all wrong, I—

How much, Bob? I insisted.

He wiped his brow, looked at me.

There was a hundred thousand dollars. I was to take twenty— he began, but he couldn't finish.

Christ, I was worth that much? I ought to be flattered.

Bob's room was bright. He had ferns. I liked ferns. They followed the Fibonacci series, they were orderly. I got up and grabbed the cushion from underneath the wicker seat. I rolled the cushion as tight as I could with one hand. Bob was leaning forward in his seat, a curious but not frightened expression on his face, as if he was watching me attempt origami or something. Things are going a wee toty bit better now, he was probably thinking.

What did Sunshine say had happened to us? I asked him.

He took a sip of his beer.

He didn't say anything, he said to forget about youse, Bob said.

Jesus, weren't you curious? I mean, for fucksake, Bob.

Look, man, you don't ask too many questions, you don't want to know, you know?

I know, I said.

I pushed the cushion against the muzzle of the .45. Bob looked even more confused.

Hey, Michael, you're not doing wha—

I shot him in the chest, and then I got up and moved close and shot him in the head. The first shot had killed him, but it was an old lesson. The noise had been awful, even with the cushion, but probably outside in the street they'd assume it was a car backfiring or a firecracker. Did they celebrate the Fifth of November in this country? Guy Fawkes Night. I wasn't sure.

I went outside, bold as brass, and walked casually back to the Cadillac. The street was deserted, and as far as I could tell, there was no one staring at me from behind net curtains.

Heading out of town, I noticed that the fuel gauge was on empty, so I had to stop for petrol. I pulled in and got five bucks' worth and headed in the direction of the highway.

On the way home I got lost on three separate occasions trying to get back into Manhattan, but finally sometime after four, I made it to the building on 181st. I drove the car ten blocks north and dumped it where I knew someone would take it. I walked to where I could get a clear shot at the water and threw the .45 into the Hudson. I'd ask Ramón to get me a new piece tomorrow.

11: THE 7 TRAIN TO WOODSIDE

The river conjuring me into existence, the sky, the water, the migrating volaries of ducks and geese. The tide heaving the flotsam upstream, against the current—it doesn't look right. Nothing looks right.

I have now killed a man. Killed him as well as can be killed. I look at the swell and the water and try to see if something is pricked. I contain my feelings and dissolve from the world and think. Am I aware of what I did, how does this affect me? I think, cool my brain. Repose. No, on due reflection, it affects me not a whit. I believe not in hell or afterlives. I cannot see how lower forms, bacteria, insects, can be excluded— were we not as they once, long ago? How did we evolve a heaven? No, there is no eternal retribution and I will not haunt myself.

But can I leave? Can I mitch myself away? Yeah. I could. The Hudson is the escape route. I'll go down to the marina at Riverside and steal a boat and head it north. North up into those ice kingdoms. I'm not sure how far I can go. I know there's a canal at Albany, going west. I'll just keep going up until I hit the Saint Lawrence and then I'll make my break for the ocean. Winter, maybe where the Vikings wintered, and then by dead reckoning and short hops, Greenland, Iceland, the Faeroes, the Hebrides, and then on to Rathlin and down the Antrim coast to Belfast Lough. I'll have the Northern Lights and the Pole Star and the sinking moon and I'll make good time on the Gulf Stream. It'll be old and familiar as I cruise up the gray waters of the lough. The great Stalinist power station at Kilroot, the harbor at Bangor, the castle at Carrickfergus. Belfast, brown and flat under the brooding hills. Harland and Wolff, whose cranes will welcome me. The Lagan, the Farset, the Blackwater. *Agua negra*. No.

I turn from the river and walk back to the apartment on 181st. I nod to the super and go up the five flights. The lift works here, but I need the walk. I go to the big living room and sit.

And stare. Still the Hudson and the George Washington Bridge. Dust on the window ledge and on the hardwood floor. Pigeons and assorted flocks following the garbage barge.

The windows are up, and everything is in silence.

I sit there cross-legged on the futon. My mind is emptied of thoughts, and I breathe and exist. Time flows on and around me, pouring people over the bridge into stores and offices. They come over in the early morning and the lights are on in their cars and they leave in the evening and the lights are on again. Time flows, and I sit and breathe and exist without it for an age.

I remember a conversation I had with Scotchy long ago about the ethics of murder. Scotchy was a guy who talked big, and he claimed to have killed a man in South Armagh. The way he bragged about it to Andy and Fergal, I began after a time to believe that he'd really done it. It was a shoot-out, he claimed with shiftiness, but I knew it was something else. Cold-blooded: a capture or an assassination. He'd been part of a cell, maybe not the shooter, but part of it. That night after we left Dermot's, neither of us felt troubled, it was them or us, that was not a problem. That wasn't where the difficulty came from.

Scotchy was not a great reflectivist, but at night when he'd had a few sometimes in the Four P., he set himself to thinking. His argument at the time was existentialist. In the absence of a Supreme Being to set a moral tone and without a future world of punishments, it was up to the individual to seek out his own moral code. Such was his position, though not, it must be stressed, in those precise sentences.

But Scotchy, I said, if you think that the moral center comes only from you, surely that means that other people will be means to your moral ends and not ends in themselves, which is dangerous. This I said, but again not in those words.

Scotchy was ready for me. Ok then, fuckwit, what's the fucking alternative? he asked, and I thought about it, and I didn't have one. I didn't know then and I don't know now. Neither of us had successful relationships with organized religion. We were both troubled. It had become a disturbing conversation, so Scotchy, as he was wont to do, changed the subject to girls and chocolate, much to the relief of both of us.

I sat there and I thought about him and I felt nothing for Bob. Scotchy had me and Fergal swear, and there on the razor wire outside the prison again he had extracted a promise from me. Not in words. He didn't need words. He had made me promise and that bond trumped all other moral sentiments. It wasn't that ethics weren't worthy of thought, but the argument was loaded from the beginning. Bob was dead, and there was one down and two to go and woe to those who would get in the way of sanctioned vengeance.

I stayed in the apartment the next day and ordered up fried eggs over plantains, rice and beans from the Caridad on 180th. It was foggy and dense and rain came and changed the landscape to a better one, erasing the gray Hudson and New Jersey and all but the closest towers of the suspension bridge. With the fog and the ghost bridge, you could be anywhere: Washington Heights bleeding in grays and blues into the moss of deserted places. Lamps from caravans bobbing down the river's edge, the swaying faces of herds of buffalo, recognizable only from their bells, a fort on the far shore, invisible, and down along the ghats pilgrims coming to pay homage to a disappeared sun and bathe themselves and purge their being of present sin. Sadhus washing and children up to their waist and swimming and throwing water and pieces of the moon. And farther down, sandalwood fires casting up smoke and the science of incarnation, the crackling gold of daisies as the funeral pyres and their inky skeletons cloud the sky still more. The burning ghats of the Hudson giving off an aura of incense and tobacco.

On the third day, Cuba came to see me. He came in the morning with coffee and Dominican cakes. He'd also brought real food with him in a pot covered with tinfoil. It was a hot stew his aunt had made up with sausage and ground beef, potatoes, carrots, onion, chilies, and peppers. We heated up the stew and ate it with tortillas. We drank the coffee and ate the cakes.

I asked him how he was, and he said that he was just fine if somewhat disillusioned still by the life of a lower-echelon drug gangbanger. Things were dull and too exciting at the same time. The Dominicans were crazy, and he said again prophetically that for all his smarts Ramón's time on this earth was limited to months or years but not decades, and he feared that he would be brought down with him.

You're a gloomy young man, aren't you? I said, and he responded that I was hardly much older than him, and we compared birth dates and this, in fact, was true. But I said that I was more experienced, having crossed the Atlantic and the equator and having spent time in jail and in the service of my country. He was pleased with that, for only yesterday he'd been down to Times Square to get more info on joining up with the marines. He was heavy, and I didn't see him passing any fitness exam anytime soon, but maybe they'd shape him up. I said that this was an excellent idea, for from what I'd heard, the United States Marine Corps was almost on a par with the Royal Marines and only a notch or three under the Paras, Special Air, five or six Highland regiments I could mention, the Black Watch, the Irish Rangers, the Gurkhas, and several of the better brigades of guards. He couldn't see I was taking the piss, so I let the matter drop.

Cuba had also brought a chess set with him. His father had taught him to play, and he wondered if I'd play with him. I knew that this visit and the chess set could only have been Ramón's idea, but I didn't care. I played him for pennies, and I beat him ten games straight and even when I began without a queen and let him take back any move, I still didn't have much trouble with his game.

He left at dinnertime and said he'd come tomorrow with chicken, and as he was edging out the door he asked if it might be ok for Ramón to come by later that night.

In the army, a big thing you must have is patience. There's so much shit, you have to be the patient boy who plows through it. Cuba had sat with me the whole day and never once mentioned his real reason for coming. You had to admire that.

You know what, Cuba? I think you'll do really well in the marines, I said.

Thanks, man, he said.

We looked at each other awkwardly. He was embarrassed.

So, uh, Michael, is it ok if Ramón comes over tonight? He doesn't want to put you out or anything, he doesn't know how you feel after, uh, you know, killing your friend.

How does he know I killed Bob? I asked.

Ramón, man, he knows a lot. Somebody saw you ditch the gun. Why would you ditch a gun? You know. And then Ramón read it out to us from *Newsday*. He says, he says, uh, anyway . . .

What does he say? I asked.

I don't know if I'm supposed to tell you.

Did Ramón tell you not to say anything?

No, he didn't say nothing, but I don't know if I'm supposed to tell you anyway.

Tell me what he said, I insisted. Cuba was kicking himself for opening his mouth. He was standing in the door and wanted to go. I went over and tugged him back into the apartment. Not violently, but still. I looked at him.

Cuba, sit down a minute, I said.

He sat. He wasn't now putting up any serious resistance. He just wanted to placate his conscience that at least he'd bloody tried.

Well, ok. Ramón said that this proved you were the man he thought you were and you'd take care of Blanco and all the rest. We'd see. Ramón says that's how you'll kill them. One by one. Take them out. He says by New Year we'll have Broadway from North Harlem to Inwood. Blanco will be dead. He didn't say it all like that. Uh. But he did say it. Anyway, I don't know, man. I shouldn't have said anything. I don't know, man. Did you kill that guy?

I nodded.

Cuba nodded too.

Was he your friend? Cuba asked.

He used to be, I said.

Ok, man, I better go. I bring you chicken tomorrow, if you want.

I nodded again, and he left and I went back to the futon and sat there and waited. Only half an hour later, there came a knock at the door. I went over and opened it.

It was Ramón. He was wearing Air Jordans, black cotton trousers, and a blue polo shirt that was really a size too small for him. He had on a gold chain engraved with his name and a black jacket. His hand was out, I shook it, and we retired to the kitchen table. It was dark and the lights were on over New Jersey and the George Washington Bridge. The fog had gone, and I thought that this was a pity.

Ramón had brought a bottle of Bushmills.

Irish whiskey, he said.

Ramón, thanks, but I'm not a big whiskey drinker, I said, smiling, trying not to offend him. It wasn't true, but Irish blended whiskeys weren't my thing at all and on the rare times I took spirits it was only ever the peaty stuff from Jura or Islay. Ramón shrugged and reached in his pocket and gave me a cigar. It was a Cubano and he cut it and lit it for me. I drew it in and it almost knocked me off the stool at the kitchen table.

Fucksake, Ramón, is that spiked? I asked.

It's just good, he said, and then he added: Don't misunderstand, this isn't a celebration. I'm not congratulating you. I'm glad you did what you did, but I know it's your path and nothing to do with me.

Yeah.

But understand me, both our needs are the same, and I know that inadvertently you will be helping me. Please, then, don't be upset if I would wish to help you.

I'm not upset, Ramón.

Ramón nodded and smiled thinly.

Look, pour me a drink anyway. No ice, I said.

Ramón poured us both a couple of full glasses, and we walked them over to the living-room window where we could look out and talk.

I'm not happy with you talking about me to your boys. They're not you, Ramón, I can't trust them, maybe Cuba and José, but not the others. I don't want you talking about me to anyone, I said.

Ramón looked hurt and unhappy.

I'm sorry, Michael, it was a mistake. I had to tell them something, I didn't want them to think that I was stupid to bring you in. They're a jumpy crew all right, but I completely trust them, they're family, cousins, second cousins, and I trust them. Don't worry, none of them will talk.

Make sure they don't, Ramón, I said, looking at him for a full half-minute.

It's ok, he said.

Yeah? I wanted to be anonymous in this city, this wasn't my fucking plan, to have dozens of fucking people . . . I trailed off and drank some of the whiskey.

You did very well, Michael. This isn't the way I thought you'd start, but you did well, Ramón said.

How much do you know? I asked.

I know enough. I know that our paths will intersect here for a while and then you'll go. I know that you'll help me and that you'll want nothing for that help. But I want to help you, Michael. Not for services rendered, for a job done. I want to give support now and I want to give you some money, so that when this is finished you can go anywhere you want.

Thanks.

Times are changing, Michael. You can feel it in the air. You'll have to be smart to survive now. It's all going to be new in the nineties now. You have it, I have it. Bill Clinton is that type of person too.

Who's Bill Clinton?

Shit, Michael, what's your problem? He's the president-elect, Ramón said.

Of the United States?

He gave me a look. He wasn't sure if I was bullshitting him or not.

We sat and drank our whiskeys for a while and looked out at the night. It was cold, and there was a wind making the windows vibrate in and out. For some reason, I was pissed off.

You know, I'm not your fucking lackey and I'm not your boy and it's not fucking right going around telling your fucking Dominican blow-snorting, fucking hoodlum crew that I am your boy, 'cause I'm fucking not, ok?

Michael, I thought I—

Do you under-fucking-stand? I said loudly.

Yes, Ramón said, sadly.

He put his glass down and ran his fingers over his scalp. There was almost no hair there and the gesture must have come from when there was. It made no sense now. He took a breath. He was gearing up for a speech. I leaned back in the chair and relaxed.

Listen, Michael, I don't know your background, but mine is not a cliché of the runaway child who comes to New York and becomes a dealer of *cinco* bags to his own community. My vision isn't a hoodlum one. My uncle raised me, and he was an educated man. True, I did run wild for a while and by the time I was sixteen I knew I could make more money on the black market than I ever could in the legitimate economy. Smuggling, drugs. Drugs are a way in, a means to an end. Venture capital. That's all. When I have enough, I'll diversify: real estate, construction, you'll see, it will be like Blanco.

We called him Darkey, I said, to interrupt his flow. I wasn't in the mood to listen to this.

Why? Ramón asked.

Just a nickname.

Anyway, it will be like him, respected, laundered. I'll have buildings. A landlord. I might run for assemblyman. I want to do good for the community here. I don't know what you think of me, Michael, but I think of myself in good terms. Unselfish terms.

You're selling fucking crack to desperate people.

Ramón winced and leaned back a little.

I'm explaining to you, it's just a means to an end. You know what the Jesuits say, if the ends are just, the means are just.

Don't kid yourself, Ramón.

I'm not kidding myself. I know my plans. I know that sometimes sacrifices have to be—

I knew people like you in the army. Attrition rates, acting all concerned. It's bollocks.

You were in the army? Ramón asked, as if the information had thrown him a little.

Aye.

In Ireland?

No, in England.

They put you in?

I joined up.

Why?

Who the fuck cares? Listen. Don't distract me. People like you, I mean, Jesus, talk the talk but—

Indulge me, Michael, for a minute. Why were you in the army if you didn't have to be?

I don't know. Drop it.

Something happened to you, Michael, Ramón said sadly.

Nothing happened to me.

Something happened to you.

Nothing happened to me. And it's nothing to do with the fucking army.

Ramón smiled at this contradiction and shook his head.

It isn't just that you are from Ireland. I won't ever get to know you, Ramón said, not a question.

I shook my head.

I'll never get to know you either, and to be honest, I don't think I want to know, I replied.

Ramón laughed and went to get the whiskey bottle from the counter. The tension had eased.

Hey, Ramón, do me a favor, tell me about Dermot. He was the trial balloon, wasn't he? It was you, wasn't it? You talked him into crossing Darkey. Didn't you?

Ramón came back and sat down and gave me another full glass. He thought for a second.

A bad business. That wasn't just me. I will say I thought we could protect Dermot, I didn't realize he'd be killed. It was a mistake.

You seen me then, didn't you, Ramón? You've been stalking me. You're like my ghost. I could have had all your coke, too. I mean, Jesus. It's not on, Ramón. You fucking think you own me. You don't own me.

Michael, I want you to think of me as a friend, he said, kindly, but I was spoiling for a fight.

You're a fucking hypocrite, Ramón. You talk and talk but it's all fucking bullshit. You're a callous fucking monster. You think you're so fucking smart, well, you're not.

Ramón didn't say anything. He hadn't touched his glass. He sighed.

You look down, Michael. You're a serious person, but perhaps you should relax more. I could send some girls over, if you want, he said, unhappily.

Girls. Christ, Ramón. Fuck. No . . . Actually, I could do with a girl. Any girl. Jesus. No. Jesus, this whiskey, getting to me. Cigar. Not used to it. It's the time of year, Ramón. It's not me or what's happening. It's the time of the year, do you understand?

Ramón looked a little concerned and shook his head. I was a bit drunk now, rambling.

See, it's November, that's all it is. November's the worst month. January has all the optimism of the new year. February has Valentine's. March is the start of spring. April to May are the pleasant months, you know. June to September is the summer. October has the leaves and Halloween. December has Christmas. But November has nothing. We don't do Thanksgiving. See? We've Remembrance Day. Fucking riot, that is. I used to have to blow taps at it, depressing. Always freezing, bugle would go flat, nightmares. Horrible month. Horrible.

He nodded, but it was clear he didn't know what I was talking about.

Maybe I could get you a glass of water, he said.

Fuck your water. Fuck your water and your fucking whiskey and your fucking cigars, Ramón, I screamed, and let the glass drop onto the floor. It didn't break. I clutched my head and snarled at him.

What the fuck did you come over for? Fucking telling your boys I'm killing all these wankers for you. I'm killing nobody for you. Fucking liar, hypocrite. All your talk. Fucking hypocrite. You're worse than Darkey; at least he doesn't kid himself. Fancy plans, my arse.

Michael, wait—

Don't ever talk about me, Ramón. Is that clear? How fucking dare you? Get the fuck out of here.

Ramón smiled. He wasn't sure if I was pulling his leg or not. If I was being sarcastic or ironic against myself. He seemed uncomfortable.

I stood and yelled at him and told him to get the fuck out and leave me the fuck alone. My head was pounding. I wasn't drunk. It was, as they say at AA, a moment of clarity. I picked up the whiskey bottle from the counter and threw it at the living-room window. The glass was thick and doubled-glazed and the bottle bounced harmlessly off and landed safely on the shag pile rug. My rage boiled over.

That is fucking it, I screamed, and went for him. I tripped, but I got a grip on his arm and bundled him to the ground. All of it came pouring out. Shovel, Dermot, Mexico, Big Bob. All of it. In howls, deflected blows. All of it, like a volcano.

Jesus Christ. Yells, punches, white light thumping between my temples.

So this was it, my breakdown at last. I screamed and spat. I tried to deck him, but he was strong and threw me off. I roared incoherently for a half a minute, grabbing at him, desperate to get purchase on his clothes and throw him through the glass coffee table. Ramón elbowed me in the throat, stood up, and put his hand on the inside of his jacket. He didn't take out the piece, the threat was enough.

Aye, go ahead, do it, do it, I yelled at him, laughing.

Calm down, he said, backing off but keeping his hand there.

I looked at him and thought for a second about trying it on, going for him, but I didn't.

I was exhausted.

We held the pose for half a minute.

Get out of my house. I don't know what you fucking want from me. You're a vampire. That's what you are. And don't send Cuba over either, I said.

Michael, really, I don't know how you got so upset, if I said any—

Are you deaf? Get the fuck out, I said wearily.

Ramón opened the door and went out and closed it gently behind him.

Bastards, I said, and for a while I knelt there, expecting tears, but even when I forced it, none came.

❊   ❊   ❊

I stayed in bed the next day and most of the next. No one came to see me. Cuba didn't bring his chicken. I didn't read. I didn't do anything. I drank brown water from the tap.

Finally I got up and went to a restaurant on Broadway and 189th Street. The menu was entirely in Spanish, and I ordered something that seemed like a stew and when it came it was tripe soup with bits of what looked like embryo in it. I couldn't start on it and left the cash and got up, but the waiter was affronted and wanted to give me something I would like, and since I was the only customer the cook came out, urged me to try the soup. I tried to explain the biblical prohibitions, but he was unfamiliar with them and any form of English I could recognize, so things went badly. The guys were only being nice and wanted to feed me, but I was a wanker and pissed them off and the word *puta* got raised and I left and on the way home picked up some Dominican cakes instead.

That night I got a six-pack of Corona and plugged the TV in and flipped through the channels. There wasn't anything good, really, if you discounted cable access. I saw somewhere that there was trouble in Ireland, but that hardly counted as news.

I went to bed and got up the next morning and decided to go for a walk. I pulled on a pair of jeans and a T-shirt and a sweater and a black raincoat. I walked to the George Washington Bridge and found myself crossing over to the other side. About the middle I stopped and took a look down the Hudson towards the bottom of Manhattan. There was no one else crossing, although traffic was heavy coming over from New Jersey. I wondered what the time was and could only guess at about seven or eight. Had the clocks been put back yet? Did they do that here? They put them forward in the spring, so I suppose they went back in the autumn.

The area on the far side of the GWB was dreary and uninteresting. I explored it for a little while, and at a bakery I got some choux pastry stuffed with custard. It was quite good. They did coffee there too, so I had a cup, but it was so weak and nasty that it wiped out the taste of the good custard thing.

I wandered back in the direction of the bridge and found myself trying to figure out how you got down to the wooded area that I'd looked at so many times from my apartment window. I took a few turns and found a tiny sign pointing to Palisades Park, which seemed to be the spot I was looking for. From my side of the river it seemed an interesting and perhaps beautiful place, with cliffs and trees tumbling down to the water. Of course, now the trees had given up much of their cover, but perhaps it would still be nice. I took a road that was wending its way downward, and before I really knew it, I was in the middle of the forest and deep somewhere under the bridge. It was like that story of the troll and the Billy Goats Gruff.

The men had been tailing me since at least the bakery and probably all the way over from Manhattan. They had been in a blue car but now they'd parked it up the road and were on foot. They were keeping well behind, but I could tell there were two of them, both pretty heavy guys. I imagine they'd picked me up outside the apartment building and followed me onto the bridge, but because of the traffic, they couldn't have gone at walking pace, so they must have made the decision to drive over and wait for me; hoping, I suppose, that I wasn't going to stop halfway and turn back. If I had at rush hour, I would have lost them, but they'd gotten lucky and they were now behind me on the road, a good bit back, so it wasn't life and death just yet.

It puzzled me. If they knew where I lived, why hadn't they just come in the morning and got me? The building had some security, but nothing a professional couldn't get around. My door, too. It would have been easy pickings. They couldn't be following me to see where I was going, because once I'd gone down into the Palisades, the only way back out was the way I'd come. The thing to do would have been to have one man wait back at the car and the other slip down the road after me, to see if I was meeting anyone, or picking up a drop, or whatever. But they weren't doing that. They had parked the car, and both of them were coming down the hill after me. It was an odd thing to do, for if I started walking back up and past them, it would then be pretty fucking obvious if they turned and began following me again. Whereas if there's only one of you tailing the suspect, you just keep walking along if you see him double-back, and then the other guy follows him from the car. But both were coming, and I was pretty sure that the car had had only two occupants. They couldn't have got to a phone, so, unfortunately, the only reason both of them could possibly be coming down this hill at this time was to intercept me and then probably kill me. Nothing else would quite make sense.

This, though, again begged the question as to why they hadn't killed me in the apartment this morning when I was asleep. I thought about it. Perhaps they'd been watching one of a couple of buildings and didn't know which one I was actually in. Maybe they roughly knew where I lived but not exactly. Perhaps they'd just got lucky again, cruising Broadway, knowing that I lived around there somewhere and then spotting me. If they'd reacted fast, they could have got me on the street, but maybe it was too late by then, maybe by then I was up at the George Washington Bridge and up there there'd been half a dozen traffic cops. Even in Washington Heights you couldn't plug somebody in broad daylight in front of six cops and hope to get away with it.

It must have been very exciting for them. There they were chugging along, Sunshine's voice ringing in their ears. He lives in the 180s near Broadway, I've had reports, spies. Just keep driving around and if you see him at all, fucking shoot him first, ask questions later. But don't be stupid. And then suddenly one of them spots me. There he is. There's the bastard over there, look. Look, isn't that him? Tell me if it isn't him. Longer hair, beard, but that's our boy, isn't it? Let me see the picture. Where's that union ID photo? Aye. That's him. Where's he going? Shite, he's crossing the fucking bridge. All right, be cool, don't get crazy, just go over.

Yeah, they'd be all excited. Driving over here, cleaning their pieces, wondering if an opportunity would present itself. And there I was, going down into some park in the middle of nowhere with no one around. Jesus, half the population of New Jersey is going over the bridge above us, but down here it's all quiet, peaceful, no witnesses at all.

I was slightly disgusted with them. I couldn't really believe that both of them would just come plodding down after me, hoping that I wouldn't hear, but then a thought occurred to me. Maybe there was more than one car. Maybe they'd be calling in backup. Four men would be a lot to handle, or perhaps the whole entire bloody crew would show up to give me a once-over before putting one behind my neck.

I'd have to be smart. They, of course, had guns, and I, stupidly, did not.

Use the head. Have to remember. I was lucky, though, because I had experience, I'd been through the mill in Belfast, I'd been through the mill in Mexico, and maybe most important, in the army I'd done those two very useful courses. The recon course on Saint Helena, where I punched the guy and got chucked off and out, and a corporals' course back in Blighty, which I managed to fail, but really there was no shame in that. I mean, you hear a lot about standards these days. They tell you that the Army Rangers is a really hard outfit, except that the pass rate for army basic training is about 95 percent. They don't tell you that the Navy SEALs pass half of their candidates, desperate for manpower. Honestly. So there's tough, and there's tough. Anyway, I did that course in the West of Jock and I redded it, but by way of excuse let me say that the corporals' course of the British Army is one of the hardest bitches in the world. See, the Brits consider corporals the backbone of the whole organization: corporals and sergeants run everything, so you have to be good. You learn exponentially. In four days, you get months, years of distilled experience. It's like the wisdom of the *I Ching*.

Now one of the things I did on the course was a night foot patrol through a forest. There's another foot patrol looking for you and if they find and "kill" you, you lose. In the patrol, it's creepy, and you're approaching a mock village from different parts of the wood, and, believe me, you learn to slow down, to halt your boys, to listen, to hear. People don't know how to listen these days, but anybody can do it.

In that moment on that hill, in New Jersey, after all my slagging off the army, I remembered all of this in an instant and tried finally to do what they told me. Listen, unclog your ears of bog, you Paddy fuck. Try. Listen. Come on.

I stopped, crouched, and cupped my hands behind my ears. Took my hands away, got in a better position. You could barely hear them at all, but if you listened for a minute and sorted the sounds and deciphered them and filtered out birds and traffic and riverboats and ambience, you could tell that first, they weren't running; second, they were walking but their footsteps were not regular, not normal; third, they were walking but they were treading lightly, carefully, they were actually trying not to make too much noise. They were confident, but not cocky. This told me two further things: one, they were dumb enough to think that I hadn't heard them in the first place, which Helen Keller could have done a mile away with a Walkman on; and two, there was probably no backup coming. It was just them, and they, in their half-arsed, crappy way, were trying to be careful. So the two of them and the one of me.

I stood up and started walking again, following the path along the leaf-strewn road, all the way down almost to the river. It was really quite striking. The naked trees with huge branches twisted and gnarled. Underfoot, golden leaves carpeting everything, and in the distance, fleeting glimpses of the Hudson and a mammoth weird city perched precariously on an island.

At the next turning, you approached the water and there was a bit of a grassy meadow and a stony beach. It had to be either at this turning or the previous one. I decided on the previous one because the cover was better. I ran up to the last meander of the road and got in behind a bush just above the path. I hid there and pulled my raincoat close and waited. I was glad I'd been wearing dark colors. The boys were going a wee bit faster now, still careful, but nervous, sensing their big moment was coming up.

If I'd had two functioning feet, the ideal play would have been to let them go past, jump, drop-kick one of them in the back and head (with separate feet), and as he's going down at least try and get a swipe at the other bastard. But with my left foot unreliable, I decided against this. Instead, I'd jump the bigger of the two guys and try and bowl him over into the other and hope somehow that it all worked out.

I waited for the boys, breathed, kept calm, and remembered that I'd actually failed that corporals' course on the very first night. Jesus. Who was I kidding? Distilled experience, my arse. *I-fucking-Ching*. Knowing me, I was almost certainly blitzed that night too. Any U.S. Army week-two reject was probably better than me.

It was in the midst of this period of self-doubt that finally they came. One big and fat, one big and thin. They were both smoking, which was ridiculous. I could have smelled it. I didn't, but I could have. The big and fat one I recognized as Boris Karloff from the tail on Bridget. The other I'd never seen in my life. He was sallow-faced and skinheaded and probably another import from Erin. I wonder if Darkey made him sing bloody "Danny Boy" to see if he was the business. They were both walking fast and neither had his weapon out, which suited me just fine.

The trail was narrow. The Thin Man was on the inside, so I had to go for him first. It would all have to be very quick and very hard. Hesitation would be the death of me. I held my breath, tensed, poised, and then when they were just past, I jumped the bugger. I took off on my good foot and landed on the Thin Man's back. I got my knee into his spine and knocked all the air out of him. My right hand was already under his neck and pulling his head back. He staggered and fell into Boris. The fall helped me, and I twisted his neck hard and tight. By the time all three of us were sprawled in a heap on the ground, the Thin

Man's neck was broken and I'd scrabbled up his gun, a little six-shot revolver of unknown caliber. Boris was fumbling for his weapon somewhere on the ground in front of him. I took a couple of breaths and pointed the revolver at him. I clicked back the firing pin.

Don't, I said.

He stopped what he was doing and put his hands up. He was still lying on the ground with his mate splayed out over his legs.

Car keys, I said.

H-his pocket, Boris said in a sad old man's voice. Boris, I supposed, might even be in his seventies. Why had they sent him on a job like this? His accent had a trace of the Old Country, but it was tempered by years of living here, mostly in Boston, it sounded like. I reached into the Thin Man's trousers and found the car keys and a wallet that I didn't look at. I sat cross-legged beside him, still keeping the gun on his face.

Why didn't you kill me in my apartment? I asked.

We-we didn't know where you lived. We were looking for you. We saw you go up onto the bridge.

You just got lucky?

Yes.

Did you call it in?

We d-don't have a radio or a c-car phone or anything like that.

Sunshine sent you?

He nodded.

Where does he live? Do you have his address?

Boris smiled for some reason and it disconcerted me. He leaned over and said in a whisper (as if there was anybody around to hear):

He always met us at the Four Provinces, always, but I know where he lives. Jackie Mac tailed him one day to see if he was whoring after the weans.

I smiled too. I wonder why I'd never thought of that. I knew he wasn't a pervert, but it might have been good to know where he lived. Could have done the same to Darkey, too. Laziness, I suppose, had been at the bottom of it.

Ok, mate, what's the address?

He told me, but I couldn't find a pencil anywhere in my coat so I had to memorize it. I searched Boris and, finding nothing, I took his Glock

17 semiautomatic pistol, a truly beautiful weapon that became my handgun of choice from then on. I ordered him up and together we lifted his partner off the road, Boris at the feet and me at the shoulders. We dragged him into the woods and I got Boris to cover him with leaves.

When he was done, I shot Boris in the head. I did it quick and without any fuss and covered him as best I could. I checked to see if there were any spatter marks on me, but I was fine.

The car was parked half a mile up the road. It was a blue Ford with a manual transmission, and it took me quite a while before I got it up and running. I'm no driver, and with my injury it was a bloody nightmare trying to get over the bridge and back into the city and state of New York. Everything's relative. A little pain for me, but at least I wasn't in Sunshine's shoes—a man who, with any luck, would not now live to see this day's end.

❖   ❖   ❖

It took me only about ten minutes to realize that the blue Ford was being followed. I noticed the old black Lincoln when I had just about negotiated the hazards of the George Washington Bridge and was making my way through Upper Manhattan towards Queens. There was an Irish neighborhood in Queens, but it wasn't our turf and I'd never been out there. I knew only two bits of Queens: the airport and Rockaway Beach.

The Lincoln was tailing me about five cars back. Two men, both in dark suits and raincoats. I figured they'd been tailing the car and not me, and it was just conceivable that they thought I was one of the two original guys. I wasn't sure where they'd picked me up, but if they'd seen me top Boris and his mate then the game would be up. Of course, they were cops, everything about them said that they were cops. They drove peeler fashion and they gave off that peeler vibe.

Why they were tailing people in Darkey's organization was hardly a mystery either. Darkey had no charmed life and, despite Sunshine's obvious talent, they couldn't avoid the law's attentions forever. Bob's death out on Long Island wouldn't help either. An organized crime unit of the NYPD was finally having to pay a wee bit of attention to Darkey's shenanigans.

How to ditch them was the tricky part. I never drove in Manhattan and I wasn't clear which streets were one-way or where the back alleys were. The one street I knew really well was 125th, and I racked my brain trying to think of where I could ditch a car along there and make a run for it.

Obviously, the first thing was not to let on that I knew a tail was on, so I drove normally and kept cool. I wasn't heading at all for Queens now, just keeping her downtown in heavy morning traffic. I was hitting Broadway and the 130s when a plan occurred to me. The Kentucky Fried Chicken on 125th and Broadway had two entrances, one on 125th and one on Broadway. If I parked the car at the McDonald's on the south side of 125th and then walked over to the 125th Street entrance of KFC (which had no parking lot), it would be the most natural thing in the world for the cops to park near me and wait for me to come out of KFC and go back to my car. They were cops, so they wouldn't think that they'd been spotted and they wouldn't be expecting me to ditch the vehicle.

I drove calmly and slowed down to the McDonald's opposite the KFC and parked the car. I locked her up and waited patiently for the light to change to cross over 125th, which is wide and dangerous at that time of day. With an air of calm I went in the 125th Street entrance of KFC. A homeless guy let me in, expecting change on the way out. I was hungry and I had a few bucks, so I ordered a chicken sandwich and a coffee. I ate the sandwich, but the coffee was too hot and I didn't have the time to wait for it to cool. The windows were so clogged full of posters advertising the latest specials that it was impossible to see through them, and so I couldn't tell if the cops were over there or not, but I guessed they would be.

I went out the Broadway door and looked for the black Lincoln, but of course it was still back in the McDonald's lot. I ran a block up to the subway escalator. At the top of the stairs, I waited for a minute to see if the cops were after me but they weren't at all, they were still waiting for me to finish my breakfast at KFC and come out on 125th. Peelers, always the bloody same.

I checked the subway map and figured the best way to Woodside from there. It would mean a couple of changes at the ugliest part of the morning, but it would be ok.

I bought tokens for the return. I rode the train and lifted a *Daily News* off the seat and, sure enough, the election had been won by the Democrat, Bill Clinton, who was from Arkansas. It was only in that moment that I realized that the state of Arkansas is actually pronounced "Arkansaw," not "Ar-kansas." I'd been hearing *Arkansas* but had no idea where it was. I was quietly delighted with my discovery and wanted to share it with my fellow passengers, but only madmen talk on the subways and I had to keep a low profile.

When I got out in Woodside, the Irish part seemed to be just a few square blocks, surrounded by a much larger Polish neighborhood. It was small, and there were a lot of gossipy-looking witnesses hanging around cafés and Irish bread shops and pubs and the like, but at least I thought that its smallness would make finding Sunshine's place relatively easy. I went in a store, bought a packet of Tayto Cheese & Onion, and munched as I explored.

I'd arrived around eleven o'clock, but in fact it took me until half past twelve to find his address.

Sunshine lived in a wooden house that was painted blue and was three stories high. It didn't look to be a particularly nice house: no garden, the paint scuffed, it was right next to a busy street, the front yard had a few leaves collecting up against the metal fence. Aesthetically challenged, but I supposed that around here it cost a packet. It was close to the subway and the neighborhood was white and reasonably prosperous and safe. There was never a doubt in my mind that maybe Boris had stroked me—he was way too much of a good old boy for that. I had a pang of regret that I'd shot him, but I dismissed it; he would have said that he wouldn't have talked, but he would have. And anyway, it was Boris who'd tailed Bridget that day, Boris who'd passed along the information, Boris who'd set this whole derailing train in motion. Would it have been so difficult to say that Bridget had gone shopping that morning? Give a guy a break.

The way into Sunshine's would have to be the back door. There was no way I could dick around the front in the broad day with people walking by on the sidewalk.

I opened the fence gate and walked around the back. There was a bit of pathetic grass and a paddling pool clogged with leaves and rainwater. A paddling pool. Did Sunshine have kids? No. Maybe he was an uncle? A good uncle, no doubt, smart, generous, creative.

No screen on the back and the door was locked. I'm no lock guy, so the only thing for it would be to break open a window. Sunshine would hear, of course, so I'd have to be ready for him if he was inside. I selected the rear kitchen window, punched a hole through with my elbow, turned the handle, climbed in, pulled out the Glock, and waited for him to show up with his gun. He didn't, and after a quick search of the house, I saw he wasn't home. I'd wait.

I searched the place out of boredom and curiosity, but found little of interest. In a bedroom with lilac bedsheets and matching drapes I discovered a wall safe, but I don't do combinations, either, so who knows what was inside.

There were no books, but I did find an extensive collection of videos. Over a thousand, maybe. It seemed that Sunshine had seen every bloody commercial film that had come out over the last ten years. There was no porn, and most of the films were complete crap. I tried five in a row before getting one that was ok. I put the sound on low and sat close to the box. The flick was about androids, who really are the good guys, and a cop chasing them, who really is the bad guy, in the future Los Angeles. In Los Angeles, it was raining all the time and it reminded me a bit of Belfast in the seventies.

After the movie I just sat. The house gave me the creeps. There were no pictures up and no personal details at all. It occurred to me that this was only his city house and he might have a real place up in Westchester or New Jersey or Long Island. Maybe he never came here at all. Maybe he rented this place out. Maybe he'd bloody sold it. Maybe this was his girl's place. I put in another film. This one was about Vietnam, where it also rained a lot.

I was only about halfway through that when I heard the front gate. I switched off the telly and sat composed in the big leather living-room chair, ready with Boris's nifty wee Glock.

Sunshine came in with a brown bag full of shopping. He was heading for the kitchen, but he saw me from the hall and dropped the bag. I motioned for him to come in. He thought for a moment about making a run for it, but the door behind him was closed and I was pointing the gun straight at him. He was wearing a leather jacket and blue jeans, something I'd never seen him wear before (previously he was always a suit-and-tie man). He was more or less the same, greasy comb-over longer, maybe, but he looked well, tanned, content. Scared shitless at the sight of me, though. He came towards me and started to speak, but I put my finger to my lips. I held the gun against his head while I frisked him. He was clean, and I told him to sit on the floor with his hands on his neck. He began to blubber and explain, but I told him not to speak.

I ripped a page from the notebook beside the phone and gave it to him with a pen.

Write down Darkey's address there for me, I said.

Listen, Michael, please, you don't understand.

One more word, Sunshine, and I'll blow the top of your fucking head off, get me?

He nodded and picked up the paper and pen. He wrote an address. I picked up the paper and looked at it. It was in Peekskill, New York.

I take the commuter rail up there, right? I asked conversationally.

Yeah, Sunshine said, still dry-heaving, though he'd calmed down a bit now.

Look, Sunshine, I'm not going to draw this out longer than necessary. Just tell me, you had a couple of guys on me and—

No, no, I don't know what you're talk—

Sunshine, don't start. Now, how many are there looking for me?

He swallowed and tried to compose himself. He knew I'd seen them. There was no point debating it.

Four.

Do they know where I live?

Roughly.

What do you mean?

We found you, Michael. I found you. Somewhere in the 190s. Jesus, we would have had you tonight or tomorrow or the next day. Soon. A couple of days, that's all we needed. We wouldn't have killed you, though, don't think that. You gotta know I would have had them bring you to me. I like you, Michael. I'm glad you got out. I would have given you money to leave town. That was the plan. Pick you up. Bring you over. Darkey's not here, he would never have to know. I bring you to me and give you cash to leave forever. I like you, I owe you, Michael, I'd never hurt you.

What make were their cars?

What?

Was one of them a black Lincoln?

Er, no, no one I know has a black Lincoln.

What were their cars?

A Ford and a Chevy.

How did you find me, Sunshine?

I'd been hearing rumors, for about a week now.

How, what exactly?

When you killed Big Bob, you woke up a couple of local people. Some old geezer saw a Cadillac pull away. He knows everyone on the street, doesn't know anyone that has a Cadillac. Cream-colored Cadillac. Young guy with a beard. Pretty distinctive.

What else?

Uh, well, you know, if you take the time to go through the police reports, you'll find that a cream-colored Cadillac was stolen not too far from the Four Provinces the night Bob was hit. Someone had followed him from the Four P. See? And that it turned up again in the 190s. Who'd want to hit Big Bob? Like I say, I was hearing rumors. I showed the old geezer your picture. It might be you. Christ, I was so pleased. I figured you were alive. Come back. Hooked up with somebody to get us. Russians, maybe. I don't know. But you were alive. Not hurt, clear from Mexico.

Did you tell Darkey?

I didn't tell him anything. Michael, I wouldn't, and besides, Darkey left with Bridget. They're going to the Bahamas for a few weeks. I'm running the show.

When does he come back?

December, December early, I think. I can check. Jesus. We could clean him out while he's away. Clean him out, Michael. You and me, Sunshine said, licking his lips from nerves, not anticipation.

How exactly did you find me, Sunshine? Who else knows?

It's like I've said, Michael, I'm not lying. Cadillac. Around the 190s. You could have taken the subway from there, but I didn't think so. Who thinks to dump their car and take the subway? You don't, do you?

Not after killing someone. You just want to toss your gun and wash your hands.

Should have had you advising me, Sunshine.

You should have, he said, looking at me, smiling, sweating.

He was keen to talk, talking was his whole life; his quick brains and quicker mouth would save him now.

What was the next move? I asked.

You were around there, but where? Where exactly? If you dump your car, you'll walk at most twenty blocks. I reckoned between the 170s and 200th. I put four men on it from downtown. I was arranging it. Two teams of two. I take it you saw them. Fucking amateurs. Jesus. I was bloody arranging it. You're a goddamn jinx. A bad fucking penny. I mean, Christ, couldn't you just have fucking been cool. I mean, just this once. I mean, Jesus, Michael, please. I would have picked you up, all would have been well. Would have given you cash to go away, no guns.

So it's just two other guys, Darkey doesn't know.

No. Jesus, if you just had waited. I would have had them bring you to me. No guns. It would have worked out for the best.

I guess I'm unlucky.

Luck, nothing to do with it, he said, blinking, wiping the sweat off his lip.

And I had to admit it was nice to talk to Sunshine after all this time. I liked his take on things. He was clever. It relaxed me.

Aye. It's depressing, though, Sunshine, for a guy who's trying to be incog-bloody-nito there's an awful lot of people who know where I am, I said, ruefully.

Sunshine grinned.

Yes. You're trouble. I was always worried a bit about you, Michael. Always.

Why?

Well, your references were good from Belfast and you were in the army and you were no thief. But you were always a bit too smart-mouthed. Too smart for Scotchy. You were the brains and he was the—

Don't talk about him, I said, menacingly.

Sunshine was quick on the uptake and grinned sheepishly and changed tack.

Yeah, but you were too fast and smart, still are.

Is that why Mexico happened? I asked.

No. Not at all. You know why Mexico happened.

Darkey.

Darkey. And I was opposed. You know, I really liked you, Michael. I warned you to stay away from Bridget. Jesus, man, what were you thinking? I trusted you.

I trusted you.

No, I really liked you. You were here three quarters of a year, you were good and reliable, and you weren't a thieving bastard like Scotchy, so Darkey and I were happy.

Mention Scotchy again and I'll fucking plug you, Sunshine, I said.

Yeah, ok. Look, I'm very sorry about what happened. You have no idea. I was against it. You were a great worker.

Until.

Until.

How long did you know?

About what?

About Bridget.

I knew that week. Me, who is normally on top of things.

Aye. Whose plan was Mexico? It must have been yours.

No, not at all. It was Darkey. Darkey, the whole thing. I said no. I said no way. I said send him back to Ireland with a good talking-to, maybe a quiet kicking.

He was much calmer now and I preferred that. He was really thinking he could reason with me. I was cool, I seemed reasonable.

And, Jesus, Sunshine, you sacrificed the whole crew for me. Four good men and a hundred thousand dollars. Incredible. I mean, it was brilliant. Darkey could never have come up with something like that. Brilliant. You must have had contacts with the peelers down there—

Michael, you've got it all wrong, I— Sunshine interrupted.

I cut him off.

Sunshine, please. We both know how it was.

He nodded and sighed. Was he resigning himself? No, not Sunshine, he took an intake of breath and began again:

Michael, you've got to believe me, it was Darkey. Mr. Duffy had contacts with the Mexican police. Cancún police, big tourist area, big drug area. Darkey's plan. The Mexicans get four convictions, and they keep the money. All Darkey, nothing to do with me.

And Bob sets it up, gets out, and we get ten years. Bridget marries Darkey and suspects nothing. Darkey wouldn't sacrifice a whole crew for me. Really, Sunshine, you were very clever.

Michael, I opposed it the whole way. I said to Darkey, We'll send him back to Ireland.

And I suppose if it fucked up and Bob got lifted too, it wouldn't matter, it was only Bob, right?

Michael, why aren't you listening? I knew it was madness. I said to Darkey, This is completely nuts.

Aye.

You're not going to kill me, Michael? Sunshine asked, suddenly serious.

I have to. I'm sorry. Even if I did believe you, it wouldn't matter, I made a promise.

With who?

The jungle.

Cryptic bastard to the last, Sunshine said. He was kneeling on the floor with his hands still on his neck. He leaned forward and started to sob. Gasping with it. Getting hysterical. His hands dropped from his neck, he was getting up, coming over. Hyperventilating.

Do you want to get it over with then, you fucker? he screamed, coming so close I had to step back.

Ok, I said.

He put up his palms and looked at me panic-stricken. He was going to beg, and it would be terrible. He started to cry frantically and dropped back to his knees.

Please, Michael, I have five hundred thousand dollars saved, more in a—

I put my hand up to stop him. He was prostrate before me, his hands together, girning his face off. Breathy, gasping, choking it out. Vomiting with fear. I could smell the fear on him. His bald head, puke on his weak chin and the sleeve of his outstretched arm. His dark eyes filled with tears. No one said this was going to be easy.

Michael, you're a good guy, I know you're a good guy. I'll disappear, you'll never hear from me, for good. Jesus, five hundred thousand, think of it. Darkey has a million, more, we could get it. Millions. Come on, Michael, I know you're a good guy. I know it. I know it. You're a good man.

I shook my head.

Sunshine, I'm not going to draw this out. Tell Scotchy I was asking for him.

What?

You heard, I said, and before he could say anything more, I shot him in the heart.

12: METRO-NORTH

It had rained in the morning and then it had snowed and then it had sleeted and then, as if exhausting all possible combinations of the three, the precipitation petered itself out and stopped. The sky was gray and the sun could only make brief, faded cameo appearances where the clouds thinned. Irish weather, not really like New York at all. Cold, too cold for snow, a weatherman said. It was December.

Last December, I'd come here. It didn't seem like a year ago. It seemed longer.

I thought of Nan. I hadn't thought of her in many months. I'd sent her some money in February and I'd spoken to her a few times, the last occasion in the spring. Nan didn't have a phone, so it was a complicated process of calling the neighbors and then having them go over and getting her and her getting all flustered and coming over and so on. Still, it was no excuse.

In Belfast it would be three o'clock in the afternoon, getting dark. If I called now I'd be admitting that I was alive, but I supposed they all knew that anyway.

I didn't want to call, though. The hassle of it, and every conversation usually degenerated into crossed purposes or farce. Also, I was in no mood to placate Nan's neighbors with lies about my life in America.

I dressed as warmly as I could and exited the building. I scoped about for a Chevy or a Lincoln or any other cars I didn't like the look of. But it was clean. Really, I should have moved to Hoboken or somewhere, but I liked this place, the bridge view, and besides, I was always cautious.

I took the train to Fairway. The one in the seventies. There's one now where we used to take people and give them a hiding, down at the Hudson. A place I thought Darkey and Scotchy were going to take me and shoot me one night a long time ago. A night when Rachel Narkiss was in my life and could have been a major part of a different existence. Such things were not to be.

Fairway was packed full of Christmas shoppers, but I braved it, bought some potato bread, soda bread, black pudding, and sausages. It wasn't the real Irish stuff, but there was no way I could go near any Irish neighborhoods to get the imports. If I needed a fix of the Old Sod, I figured an Ulster fry might help. I took the supplies home and I fired up the old grill and cooked myself one, and it was quite good. Of course, I cooked it in vegetable oil, not dripping or lard, but still.

I exercised in the afternoon for an hour and then did yoga and meditated for another two hours. I slept. I woke and saw the George Washington Bridge light up. I watched the cars move on the decks, and when I was bored and tired, I slept again.

It was another day and gray.

I got up, stretched and meditated for a half hour. I stretched again and did some exercises. I ran on the machine and when I was sweating and exhausted, I showered.

But none of it was any good. Bloody Belfast was still nagging at me.

I opened the fridge. There was still some potato bread left. I wondered if I made another fry, would it cure me. I got out a pan, ripped open the packet of potato bread, and at the smell finally cracked, picked up the phone, and dialed the number.

Mrs. Higgins was in her eighties and slightly scatterbrained and deaf, and it took me a minute or two to explain the nature of my call.

Mrs. Higgins, please, it's Mike Forsythe, you remember Mikey, here calling from America. America. I wonder if you wouldn't mind getting Nan for me, please, if she's around.

Mrs. Higgins said that she was around, explaining that she could see her through the back window hanging out her washing. Mrs. Higgins said that at the moment Nan was talking to Mrs. Martin. I remembered Mrs. Martin: she was a frightening woman who had a soft spot for Nan, but who scared the crap out of me and most of the rest of the parish. Among a number of suspects, it might have been her that grassed me out to the DHSS about working that one bloody time.

She's a bad woman, that Audrey Martin, a bad one, Mrs. Higgins was saying.

Yes, now please, would you mind at all, getting Nan for me, I asked with great patience.

I heard Mrs. Higgins put the phone down and shout across the garden. Mrs. Higgins was also about to do her washing, and before mentioning the long-distance phone call, I could hear her scold the other two for hanging out their washing with the rain about to come on. This was the wrong thing to say, since for the next several minutes they got into a heated discussion and talked with a professional eye about the prospect of foul weather. Mrs. Higgins's and Mrs. Martin's loud voices managed to enter the telephone receiver and carry all the way under the Atlantic to America. This was typical, and I knew the process of getting Nan would take some time. I cursed myself for calling. I put them all on the speakerphone. I put some oil in the frying pan and heated it and waited for Mrs. Higgins to get to the point in hand. Apparently, the Pentlands' dog was barking, which could only mean hail, and the rotted cabbage leaves were still closed, so Nan reckoned the rain wouldn't come until after lunch. Mrs. Martin divined signs in the movement of the birds and concurred with Nan's prediction. Mrs. Higgins, however, had been watching TV. The BBC was claiming that it had been raining all night and, in fact, was raining right now in Belfast on top of all three of them and although the sky was overcast, it was dry, and she had to admit that there wasn't much physical evidence to prove this extraordinary statement.

Mrs. Martin started yelling at children playing on the fence two houses down. Mrs. Martin's voice was booming and loud and might just have carried across the Atlantic without any need for a cable. I shuddered. For reasons that never really came to light at trial, during a jumble sale in the Gospel Hall, Mrs. Martin had brained her husband with a fire iron. She'd gotten a suspended sentence at the district court in Newtonabbey, though it was agreed that had she not been so big and intimidating, and had not the magistrate come from just two streets over, she would have done six months. The weans must have keeked their whips when she yelled at them, and I managed to laugh a wee bit.

There was the sound of panicked squeals and flight and then a brief discussion among the women about the youth of today.

The youth of today must have got the wheels turning, for finally Mrs. Higgins remembered about the phone call and told Nan to hurry because it was coming all the way from America.

I heard Nan come up the path and then come breathlessly on the phone, all excited.

Hello, Nan.

She caught her breath.

Michael, I might have thought you were dead. I'm very angry with you. I haven't heard from you. Your drunken eejit of a da was over and when he asked about you and I said I hadn't heard in months, I could see even he was worried.

I'm sorry, Nan, you know what it's like.

I suppose you're not coming home for Christmas?

No.

Aye. Audrey Martin said that now you wouldn't be.

Mrs. Martin?

Aye.

I don't trust her, Nan. I think she grassed me to the dole about that picture in the *Belfast Telegraph*.

Ach, Audrey Martin wouldn't harm a fly, Nan said.

No, that's true. The lower forms of life are safe from her wrath, but you must admit that the sentient creatures have much to fear, I said, trying to be jokey with her, but it didn't really work. With Nan it never really worked. I started throwing bread and sausages in the frying pan. The conversation with Nan was going as I'd expected—not at all well.

You've a cold, she said. Do you go out without your scarf?

Nan, I lost that scarf ages ago.

See, that's why you've a cold.

Nan, I believe in the germ theory of the transmission of disease.

Aye, you'll see when you catch your death, germ theory up your arse, Nan replied in what for her was uncustomary coarseness. I guessed she was upset about something. Probably me blowing her off for so long.

Look, Nan, I'm sorry I haven't called. Don't be angry with me.

Ach, I'm not angry at all now, Michael. But you can't do this again. Promise me that.

I promise.

Well . . . , she began and stopped.

There was silence now, and I waited for her to say her piece. I waited still as the bacon, egg, soda, and wheaten bread joined the other components of the Ulster fry sizzling in the big pan. I waited as the smell drifted up and filled the apartment and the sausages blackened and the black pudding crystallized. Finally, Nan came to it.

Michael, is everything ok? she asked.

I nodded and remembered to speak.

It's fine. Nan, what is it? What's wrong?

Listen, Michael. Mrs. Martin said you wouldn't be back for Christmas because people are after you.

What?

She saw a couple of policemen come round the other day and they asked all these questions about you. I was out, it was late-night shopping in town, but they asked about you, asked her if she'd seen you. Well, she sent them off with a flea in their ear and no mistake. And for all your talk about her. But Michael, I was wondering if you were in any trouble. They haven't been back, and I've said nothing.

I stopped cooking the Ulster fry and turned off the gas.

Nan, you'll have to go get her. I'll have to ask her about them myself, I said, seriously.

Nan put the phone down and went to get Mrs. Martin, a woman I'd hardly ever spoken to in my life because I'd always been too afeared. I heard them talk in whispers, and then she came on the line.

Hello, young man.

Hello, Mrs. Martin.

How are you in America?

I'm good.

I see. . . .

Listen, uh, Mrs. Martin, I was wondering if you were sure the men who came looking for me were peelers.

I didn't think they were policemen at all, Michael. Your nan said that they must have been, but they didn't look at all like policemen.

They had crew cuts and they were wearing jeans. They might have been your detectives, but I don't think so.

What did they ask?

They asked if I'd seen you, and I said that as far as I knew you were in America, and they started asking all these other questions and I sent them off about their business. I'm sure if they were police they would have showed me a card or something.

Local accents?

I think so, of the most vulgar sort in any case, hardly police.

They weren't police, I said. Listen, thank you. Please put Nan back on. Thank you.

Nan came back on and I told her to tell anyone who came looking for me that she hadn't heard from me in a long time. I told her to tell Mrs. Martin and Mrs. Higgins the same thing, and Nan said she would do it. She didn't ask me why and she must have sensed that I was in some kind of shit. She knew it, but she didn't want to know. I stayed on for a while longer and made up some lies about having a new job and a new girlfriend. I was sure she didn't believe them.

After I'd hung up, I wondered if they would try to get to me through her. I felt weak as fear went through me, and I was terrified for Nan for a moment or two.

No, it was a tough estate and you'd be the brave boy who'd send hooligans down into that one-way street. And an assassin of an old lady in that part of town would never get out of Belfast alive. No, Mr. Duffy and Darkey would come after me, if they came at all.

I suppose they'd just called local people up to check in on Nan to see if she'd heard from me. An interesting thought occurred to me. Maybe Sunshine hadn't passed on the rumors about me. Was it conceivable that they weren't sure if I was alive and out of Mexico? Was that possible at all? Could Sunshine have been telling the truth? Could they really still be in the dark? No. My heart sank. That would be too good to be true. And not after Bob and the boys and Sunshine.

The smart thing, though, would be to keep them guessing. To lie low until it was time. And it's not as if I was doing anything stupid. I was being patient. It was weeks since Sunshine had got topped and yet it still wasn't quite time yet. Not quite yet. Relax them down a wee bit more.

I was still living the life.

I knew no one. I'd seen no one.

The talk with Nan had been the first real conversation in a long time.

Every week Ramón had sent a boy round with money. I was no mad ascetic, so I'd taken it and spent it on things. I'd got myself special sneakers, the running machine. I'd put on weight and got stronger. I rarely left the apartment and then sleekitly, and since it was winter always with my hood all the way up. I spent my time in meditation and exercise. I watched TV and ordered in food and learned Spanish from a book.

When I did go out, it was to distant places on the subway line. Places where I knew they wouldn't find me. I had to go out early in the morning with a crowd. I had to be sly. There was Sunshine's men, and Mr. Duffy's, but there was also the black Lincoln to be considered. The peelers might have got wind of a few things, as peelers are wont to do. They might have got it from any number of sources: a tap on Sunshine's phone, an ID at Bob's place, a slabber among one of Ramón's lieutenants. Still, it couldn't be that exact or they, like Darkey's men, would have come knocking.

I wondered when Darkey was supposed to be back from his hols, but then I realized he would have come back early once they'd found Sunshine. Aye, he'd have to. Yeah, Darkey would be home by now with Bridget. With Sunshine dead, he'd really have his hands full.

He'd be home, and probably he'd be waiting for me. Even scouting up there would be dangerous. If it were me and I was in his position, I'd have a man at the railway station twenty-four hours a day; I'd have a dozen patrolling the grounds and I'd have half a dozen inside the house. I'd also have a dozen looking for me in my last known location, cruising in cars, maybe stopping people in the street and showing them my picture. No, not the latter, Ramón wouldn't allow them to do that, it was his turf. They'd have to be discreet or Ramón's boys would lift them for something, for surely by now Ramón owned the precinct.

I could only guarantee my safety if I stayed in the apartment, but like I say, sometimes I had to move in the outside air.

The day after I called Nan, I woke up freaked and had to get out. I did my usual shifty maneuvers and then rode the bus to the Cloisters and spent a morning freezing up there. A day after that I slipped downtown and took the PATH to some hellhole in Jersey. No tails, no problems.

I was fine, I had outsmarted them. The peelers, Darkey White, that's how you'll beat them, Mikey boy. Your native wit. Your charm. Your Celtic cunning. But don't forget that other legacy of an Irish boyhood. The Paddy curse, not quite American Indian levels, but high enough. Enough to fuck you up. I decided I needed to get drunk, but it would be ok, I could handle it, I could handle anything.

❖   ❖   ❖

I left the next morning after daylight and took a complicated route to a café on 112th Street. It was a Cuban place and I got rice and beans, fried eggs, and toast for breakfast, as well as a big con leche and a juice. It was good and it buoyed me. I was going to go on the piss, but I was still getting paranoid about tails, so I sat in the window seat looking out at the street, memorizing everyone. I walked down to a bar on 79th Street and sat in the blacked-out window, but there was no one I recognized.

The whole week had been depressing. Starting with that call to Nan. I needed this. A release.

The Dublin House, a black hole with Irish bar staff.

Not a good place to start—too chatty. One pint and out.

The Kitchen Bar, the Dive Bar, Cannon's, the West End. A pint in each. I wanted to have lunch, but too many students. South again.

It was freezing. I had my thick navy coat and my knit hat, but I was still cold.

The Abbey Pub, a Brooklyn beer, a nasty lunch of curly fries and ketchup, a cute Dutch waitress who lived in the youth hostel on 103rd and Amsterdam and had not yet been mugged or worse by Les Enfants Brillants, the Haitian street gang that ran Amsterdam above 100th.

We talked, and I told her to move to a Dominican part of Broadway. She asked if I had plans next week and I said I had to kill a guy and she gave me a wide berth after that and I left her a twenty-dollar tip.

I was half tore by now, clearly. I went east towards Central Park and into a library to get out of the cold. Read the last few months of *Time* and *Newsweek*. Things and people I'd never heard of: Hurricane Andrew, Murphy Brown. The security guard said I was singing and asked me to leave. I walked to the subway, stopping outside a liquor store. I stared at the window for a while, and the man gave me an are-you-coming-in-or-not look. I went in. I bought a pint bottle of brandy, and he gave it to me in a brown paper bag. I was thus constitutionally protected against unlawful search if I drank it in the street. It was only encouraging me.

I decided to walk all the way home and drink the brandy as I walked. It was snowing now and I'd lost my hat somewhere. I shivered. I drank the bottle and went into another liquor store and got another one. I drank most of it, too. I'd only walked up to about 106th Street and Broadway when I thought it might be a good idea to take a wee nap in the middle of a snowstorm on a bench in the traffic island.

A cop car came by and some kindly peelers clearly didn't want me dying on their patch, so without further ado they decided to lift me. I think they were only going to move me on or suggest a shelter, but unluckily, as soon as they laid paws on me, I reacted fast, turned, and belted one in the chest.

They were pretty quick with the old pepper spray and it hurt like hell. I went down like a ton of bricks. I couldn't see them at all now and they were right on me. Two of them. Just two. I put it down to the drink. They cuffed me behind my back and walked me without any fuss to a cop car. The cop car already had three dodgy-looking characters inside it, so they radioed in for backup. They searched me and found the driving license that Ratko had rescued for me. That license had never been good for anything and now it apparently was bad for something, because while I leaned against the car and the peeler talked on the radio, I could see his expression change (even through pepper tears). My name was obviously known to someone. I thought of the black Lincoln. The Feds? The other cop was standing beside me. The door was closed. The pepper spray had caught the left side of my face only; if it had been full on, I would have been unable to do anything; as it was, I was pretty fucked, gasping for air and barely able to stand. The snow helped a little, though. Copper number two inside was nodding and getting excited but copper number one was stamping his feet and looking out for the other paddy wagon. My hands were cuffed behind my back, so it would have to be something pretty special, and special isn't easy with a fake foot. Still, it was worth a go.

I shuffled back from the car and made as if to puke. (I'd been crying the whole time, hamming it up as you do if you're still figuring what you're capable of doing and what you're going to do.) The copper turned his head to spit. I tensed, and the copper was looking up and was about to say something, but by then I had jumped straight up and was making my body go horizontal. With my good foot I kicked him in the balls. He was wearing a cup, but I heard it crack. He went down in a sitting position against the door. I landed hard on the ground on my side, got up—try doing that with your hands cuffed behind your back and with a prosthetic foot—and set off running.

The other cop would take a half a minute or so to get his partner away from the door or else he'd have to climb out the driver's side. It would be enough.

I ran up Amsterdam and kept running and cutting streets until I was at Morningside Park. The only people around did that New York thing and completely ignored me. I was handcuffed and crying and running and not a man jack chose to see me. Not even at the Columbia law library, where you'd think they'd be a bit more public-spirited. At the brow of the hill I stopped, took a quick breath or two, sucked in the deep cold air, and ran down into the park, slipping on the big wide steps after a few feet and almost doing a header and breaking my neck. Instead, I righted myself, got my balance together, and skipped on down. I didn't look back once until I was safe in the park at the basketball courts. There were no signs of pursuit. Jesus H. Christ. I'd bloody lost them.

I laughed and jumped about. I'd lost them. I'd lost them. Peeler Pete and his Porky Pals.

Bastards, I yelled, delightedly.

Aye, I'd lost them, but suddenly it put the fear of God in me. It was close. And Jesus, I was on a list somewhere. My name was on a list. My real name. Shit. Drunken Mick stupidity had almost got me lifted. Fucking Paddy Curse.

Farther into the park I found a bloke with a quarter, and he was nice enough to dial the phone for me too. He was a good guy, well into his sixties, skinny, really sweet, and sadly some kind of downer junkie. He didn't like the look of me one little bit, but since I was cuffed, he figured I couldn't be all bad. Ramón came down half an hour later, and I asked Ramón to give the bloke twenty bucks. Ramón did just that.

Ramón and I went back to his place and they cut the cuffs off me in about five minutes.

I haven't seen you for a long time, man, Ramón said later.

We were alone now, the boys gone. I sipped some of Ramón's hot chocolate mixed with cream and brown sugar and wicked Dominican rum.

No.

We're ok, aren't we? he asked.

Yeah.

Good.

He stuck his hand out over the couch, and I shook it. He gave me the gangbanger shake and I went along with it.

You want something for the pepper spray? he asked.

What ya got?

Home remedy.

Ok.

He went off to his kitchen and made a poultice to shove on my bad eye. I thanked him and he said it was no problem. We sat for a while, silent. I had nothing to say and Ramón didn't want to upset me again. I was the first to break the ice:

Listen, I, I probably won't see you again, Ramón. It's going to be this week. I've delayed too long. Darkey's boys are after me and I think the cops now, too. They've forced my hand. It has to be now. After it's done, I'm leaving.

Where to?

I don't know. Australia, Ireland, I don't know.

Ramón looked at me. I couldn't tell what he was thinking. I never could. He was a smart guy in a dumb guy's business, though like I say, all those brains couldn't do a thing to stop the gun of edgy young Moreno F. Cortez, a gun and nineteen fucking bullets (and Moreno a cousin and trusted lieutenant). Moreno, incidentally, got shot in the head about a month later by José Ramírez, who in turn . . . but you know how it goes.

We sat there and talked about trades and signings during the off-season. In Tampa there was some kid from Michigan who was going to be the future shortstop. 1993, Ramón predicted, was going to be the Yankees' year, this year, next year, very soon, he said. He didn't live to see the World Series, or Sosa in the Home Run Derby—it would have pleased him very much.

So, Michael, it will be soon, because of the heat, he said.

Yeah.

You will be careful?

I will.

Do you need any help?

No.

I stood up. We embraced. I didn't say goodbye and afterwards I didn't see him again. His death was just one more stat in the bloody catalog of uptown deaths in the early nineties.

The next day I went down to Gray's Camping and Sport. I looked at camping equipment and sleeping bags. I decided against a tent. I placed an order for a down sleeping bag, which would take two days from the warehouse. That was ok, I said, I'd be back. I bought a big bowl rucksack that was like a Royal Marine Bergen.

I dyed my hair black and shaved everything but a mustache, which I also dyed black. I dressed in jeans and desert boots and a sheepskin coat. I got on the Metro-North at 125th. I took an early morning train to Peekskill, got off, and went to the nearest bar. I found a place to observe the railway platform. I sat there all day. There were no watchers, or if there were, they were very good. I went back to Manhattan and adopted a dog from the ASPCA volunteers on Union Square. They needed my name and address but that was ok too. I took the dog up to 181st Street. I called him Harry. He was a mongrel. A lazy character, who had been housetrained for a house and not an apartment. There is a difference, and I soon discovered what this was. I bought a Peekskill town map and studied it. I found Darkey's place. I lost the mustache and dyed my hair red with blond streaks in it. I dressed in a black coat and brown cords and tasseled brown loafers. I bought myself a pair of clear-lens glasses and a walking stick. I caught the train from Grand Central. I got off at Peekskill. I walked the dog and found the house. From the map it had seemed to be about a thirty-five-minute dander from the Metro-North stop, but when I got up there, the walk ended up taking over an hour. (The map lacked contour lines.) I strolled past the property and checked the initial security. No gatehouse, and I couldn't see anyone in the grounds. A Jeep and a Bronco in the driveway. A Jag in the open door of the garage. I went by, and I let the dog off in the trees. The dog and I found a back area that was thickly wooded and seldom trekked through. There was a boggy wee swamp that you had to wade through, knee-high, to get to a convenient little copse with thorny bushes. If you could make it through the swamp to the bushes, and you had a good pair of binocs, it would make a wonderful place for lying up. Your average private security guard wouldn't think much of it because your average private security guard was a lazy arse and he'd have to wade through the little swamp to get there; and in any case, it seemed far too far from the house. If, however, your average private security guard was a thorough bastard and had a dog sniffing about, well, then you'd be fucked.

I hopped the train back to Grand Central and took a subway to Union Square. I gave the dog back, using the pooping problem as an excuse. I donated fifty bucks to cover my embarrassment.

I washed the dye out of my hair and packed a rucksack with a week's worth of pork and beans and digestive biscuits. Seven cans of beans, seven packets of digestive biscuits. Multivitamins. I bought some Marie biscuits for variety. I bought some water purification tablets and two plastic liter bottles. I bought a funnel with a connecting tube, so I could take a piss without moving. I bought a large bivouac bag and spent a day scraping it from emergency orange to white. I bought the expensive down waterproof sleeping bag and a pair of night-vision binoculars. I bought silk undergloves and thick ski gloves. I bought long johns and sweatpants and fatigues. I bought a stopwatch and binoculars that came with a tripod. I bought a snow camouflage jacket, a snood ski mask, a black wool hat, a black cotton scarf, and a windbreaker. I bought two pairs of wool socks and a pair of cotton ones. I bought a flashlight and boots and, unable to find a knife I liked, I sharpened a long screwdriver and bought a nice new Stanley box cutter. I bought two T-shirts, a sweat top, and a black sweater. I bought a notepad, pens, pencils, and plastic bags. I bought rope, duct tape, and thin leather gloves. On impulse I bought a pneumatic nail gun, but I didn't bring it. I bought matches, a water can, a big bag of Peanut Butter Cups, and a toothbrush. Finally I bought a box of AA batteries, a Walkman, and an audio version of *War and Peace*. Some people think you should get listening gear or infrared body-heat sensors or motion detectors or a device for tapping into cellular phones, but then some people are fucking eejits.

* * *

The house lay on a quiet road, with about two acres around it. A house on each side, all three of them what in Ireland we'd call mansions. The lucky break was that opposite the house was a thick, swampy wood that eventually curved all the way down to the Hudson. I suppose the marsh was why this area hadn't been developed. It was winter and the cover wasn't what it would be like in the summer but still pretty substantial flora nonetheless. There were bushes and big old deciduous trees and some pines and because of the water and the muck it wasn't the place you'd go for an idle walk or take the pet pooch.

Peekskill is up the river, past Sing Sing. It's famous for being the birthplace of Mel Gibson, the scene of an important 1950s race riot and a 1980s sitcom. It's also the home of Governor Pataki and a couple of 1930s socialist utopian communities. Darkey lived quite near one of these communities but in winter almost all of its residents went down to Florida. So really there were very few people around and if you found yourself a convenient little bunker, established yourself in the cover in your bivvy bag, and coated yourself up with snow, you could lie unfound for weeks, months, or maybe even until the spring. Aye, I had to admit that it was a nice wee spot and the only drawback was that it wasn't that near the house and you'd need at least a 12 x 50 pair of binocs or a telescope. I had the binocs only because they were less bulky.

Things had gone smoothly. Napoleon was invading Russia and having a wry old time of it. A couple of the main characters were dead and this was a relief because I'd gotten a bit mixed up anyway. The lying up had been easy. I'd taken the first morning train from 125th and doubled away from the station and back through the woods. I established the OP in darkness and by first light it was snowing lightly and this made things pretty sweet. It snowed all week, and this suited me fine. Peeing was no problem and because of the cover, if I'd chosen, I could have even stood up to go, but I didn't. Water was good too. I used the swamp and the snow. I had water-purifying tablets and with them there was a new development: a pill you put in that made it so that it didn't taste of iodine; this was a terrific invention, and I felt very happy about it. The pork and beans were good too; I ate them cold, but I was warm enough, snug even, and most important of all, I could see a good three quarters of the house through my binocs.

A couple of times, I saw Bridget go in and out. My heart leapt and it was all I could do not to stand up and wave and let her see me. Darkey left and came back every day. He drove the Bronco; Bridget, the Jeep; when they went together they took the Jag. Darkey left early, came back late. He had two personal bodyguards and there were two more who lived on the estate and who came in rotation. There were also two servants: a man in his sixties and a woman about the same age. Four guards, that was all. I was surprised, but not that surprised. Darkey didn't know for certain that it was me. It had been a long time since Sunshine's death. No one knew where he lived and besides, he could look after himself, he was a big boy, hadn't he proved that after twenty years on the street? It took me a full seventy-two hours to be sure of the routine and another three days to check it. I was all ready to go on the 23rd of December, but they'd gone out to a party and they hadn't come back until early in the morning. I was worried about Christmas Eve, too. Wasn't that also a party night? But by one A.M. the cars were still in the driveway and I was fairly sure they weren't going anywhere.

Technically now, it was Christmas Day.

My batteries had finally died. I was three quarters of the way through *War and Peace* and finally getting into the book but if all went well I'd come back and dismantle my OP and sweep it over and take all traces with me to a dump somewhere. I could finish *W&P* on the plane ride to wherever the plane was going.

It still wasn't quite late enough, but there was just enough battery life to listen to the radio. I stuck on classical to calm my nerves. They were doing the nine symphonies and I had enough third-form German to switch off after *Alle Menschen werden Brüder. . . .*

It was time.

I put away the Walkman and listened to the stillness of the woods.

I checked through the binocs again, but there'd been no change. The domestics had been given the day off and aside from Darkey and Bridget, only one guy was walking the grounds, three other guys in the house. The lights were out and you could assume that Darkey and Bridget had gone to bed. If the three men were in shifts, I guessed one other would be awake in the house. That's how you'd do it, split the night into two. One man on the grounds and one man waiting by the radio. The other two would sleep until it was their watch. So hopefully there'd be only two people awake to deal with. That was all. Unless, of course, I'd been a complete idiot. But I didn't think I had. Shifts would be the smart thing to do. Four guys, Darkey, and Bridget. Not one of them had thought to get a dog. Jesus. I mean, did they want to be murdered?

I put on my black sweater, boots, thin black gloves, and combat trousers. I pocketed the duct tape, screwdriver, and Stanley knife. I carried the Glock, too, but I was hoping I wouldn't have to use it just yet. I left the OP and went to a closer spot where I could see the groundsman. There was a small window of opportunity because they did a radio check every fifteen minutes at night, which at least was something you could give them credit for. I spotted the guard. I walked around the hill, following him in his circuit. I'd tail him until I saw him do his check. I knew this character, guard B. His call-ins were irregular. I assumed he was a young guy. The earliest he'd done a check was thirteen minutes and fifteen seconds and the latest he'd left it was seventeen minutes and fifty seconds. He was in darkness, but I knew him and I was well accustomed to the night now. He picked up the radio and called in and said something about it being freezing. He put the radio down and muttered to himself about the cold. I went quickly to the wall. It was eight feet high and topped with glass. Not a problem. I wouldn't even need rope. I went up and over and lowered myself onto the snow on the other side.

At this point, you have to ask yourself, was there no indecision? And no, I can honestly say there was none. If there had been, it would have been before I killed Sunshine. Not here with Darkey. Not now, not tonight.

I stood up, braced to see if he'd heard me. But he wasn't hearing anything. With the radio check done, it would be up to seventeen minutes before anyone would get suspicious. Plenty of time. He was wearing a parka with an enormous hood, so big in fact that it restricted his field of vision to about ninety degrees in front of him. He was walking and muttering and carrying a .38 revolver in a thick woolen-gloved hand. So thick it would make finding the trigger difficult. I mean, I ask you. He turned and the moonlight caught him. I was a bit surprised to see that it was our old chum David Marley from way back when. He'd put on weight. He was humming a Chieftains song and banging the gun rhythmically against his leg. He turned away. I crept up behind him and shoved the screwdriver into his throat at the same time as a knee went into his back and my left hand went over his mouth. I left the screwdriver in and with my right hand I removed the gun from his grip. I had it before he even hit the snow, stone dead. I fell on top of him and we lay for a moment. Blood trickling over the snow. He gurgled for a while, and I removed the screwdriver. I looked at his gun and checked it for cleanliness: in a pinch it would do as an extra. I put it in safety mode and slipped it in my side pocket. I looked at my watch. Fifteen minutes to find and kill the other guard. With luck there wouldn't be a shift change and I could let the other two guards sleep and live. With luck.

I had no glass cutters and I was no alarm guy. I'd searched Marley for keys, but I knew he wouldn't have any. The indoor man let the outdoor man in and out. My plan was to go in the garage door. If the garage door was alarmed I'd have to abort, but I didn't think it was. It wasn't an automatic door, and I'd seen them come in late when the house was alarmed, and when the garage had opened, nothing had gone off; but another time, when they'd opened the house door first: flashing lights, *whoop, whoop, whoop*. But still, that wasn't exactly proof, and if wishes were horses we'd all have a ride, as the Scotch boy used to say. But what else could I do? It was the garage door or nothing. I slipped around the side of the house. I found the garage door and jemmied it up with the screwdriver. It was aluminum and bent easy, and I made just enough space to slide underneath. I was so busy doing stuff I didn't notice that the alarm hadn't gone off until I was in.

The garage was connected to the house by a door that not only was not locked but did not lock. Hubris, if you ask me. I went inside through a room that contained the washer and dryer. Little night lights everywhere, and I saw that I wouldn't need the flashlight. I crouched on the floor and listened, but it was quiet. It was the night before Christmas and all through the house, nothing was stirring, not even Darkey or Mouse.

I walked into a large, airy kitchen with marble counters and many appliances. I looked for a dog bowl or cat bowl or any evidence of annoying pets, but I didn't see anything. I walked into a hall and listened again. The floor was carpeted, the central heating was quietly humming, faint sounds were coming from a room at the end of the hall to the right. I walked down there and listened. Someone was watching TV. The other guard? I spent a minute turning the handle and then I opened the door very slightly. The guard was in front of a small TV set. Jimmy Stewart on the screen. The guard engrossed. His back was to me, turned three quarters away from the door, which made me think that Providence was on my team, for otherwise I would have had to rush him and stab the fucker in the heart or neck, making no end of commotion. I slipped quickly over and put a hand on his mouth and the barrel of the pistol in his ear.

Who? he managed, before I silenced him by pressing in with hand and gun.

Father fucking Christmas. Now hear me. You don't have to die. You don't have to die, but if you make one sound or one move that upsets me, I will blow your brains out. Do you understand? If you do, do not nod your head; I don't want you to move at all, in case I blow your fucking head off by mistake. I'm a jumpy fuck, you see. So instead, indicate that you understand by making a gentle humming sound once.

A frog was in his throat, but he managed a hum. I kept the gun in his ear and went round to take a sideways look at him. A ginger bap, freckly, young. I didn't want to kill him. He was wearing a T-shirt and baggy jeans. There was a duffle coat on a desk beside him. I frisked him and he was clean. I took the duct tape out of my pocket and told him to take his shoes off very slowly using only his left hand. Then I told him to duct-tape his ankles together with both hands, but in slow motion. He was sweating and clumsy, but he did it. His back was to me the whole time, but I didn't particularly care if he saw me or not. On the whole, I suppose I preferred not.

What's your name? Whisper an answer, I said softly.

J-John.

Ok, John, now listen to me. I'm going to wrap your wrists in duct tape, behind your back. I will need both hands to do this for about one minute. Therefore, I will need to put the gun down; however, it will be beside me and if you make any sudden moves at all, instinctively I will grab the gun and shoot you in the head. Do you understand? Hum if you understand.

He hummed. He put out his wrists, and I wrapped them in duct tape behind his back. I picked up the gun again and blindfolded him with the tape. I tilted the chair.

John, I'm going to roll you on the floor; I'm going to do it gently so as not to make any noise. I need you to go limp and cooperate, ok? You can nod now.

He nodded and I laid him on the floor.

Now, John, listen to me carefully. I have business upstairs and there need not be any unnecessary deaths. I will, however, make sure that I fucking kill you if you raise an alarm or make any move at all from this position. Can I trust you not to be stupid? Nod your head if I can. He again nodded.

Good, now first tell me in a whisper when the next shift change is supposed to be.

H-half an-an hour.

Ok, good. You're doing well. Do you wake them?

Yes.

Tell me in whispers where exactly Darkey and Bridget's room is and where exactly the other two guards are sleeping. There are only two other guards in the house, aren't there?

Yes.

He went on and told me where his mates were sleeping and where

Darkey and Bridget were. I gagged him with tape and enjoined him not to move one inch from this cozy spot on the floor. I left the TV on quietly and went outside the room. The stairs were carpeted and curved round in a thirty-degree angle. You could see the whole house from here and it looked quite nice, a bit busy and overdone, but that would be Darkey, not Bridget. I went upstairs and paused at the top. This was the only moment of indecision I had the whole night. Darkey's room was down the landing to the left. The guards' room was the second door on the right. They had bunk beds and slept in the one room, John had said. (Bunk beds indeed, Darkey being a tight bastard, no doubt.) Now the smart thing would have been to go in to the guards' room and cut their throats. But I'd already made a wee promise to myself in the outside that if I could, I'd let them sleep and live. I mean, I thought I didn't care much about finesse, but clearly I did. Even so, just because I said I wouldn't kill them didn't mean I'd jeopardize the whole mission over it. Jesus. What could I do? I couldn't very well have them wandering about the house while I was still in the process of executing their employer. Hmmm. I hesitated. I wondered what would happen if I went into their room and gave them each a hefty blow on the head with the blunt end of the screwdriver. It sounded so plausible, but wouldn't the first blow wake the other guard?

All this went through my brain in a second, and I decided that I would take the bloody chance. It was stupid, but you have to make a decision one way or the other.

I inched up to the guards' room and spent another minute opening the door. There were bunk beds on opposite sides of a small room. The guards were both asleep in the one to my left, one man in the upper bunk and the other in the lower, which again was lucky.

Here goes, I thought, crept over to the lower bunk, and clubbed the guard behind the ear with my screwdriver. I didn't wait to see if it bunned him; instead, I got up immediately and thumped the other guy. I pulled out the Stanley knife to cut their throats, but it wasn't necessary. They were both out of it. I found a lamp, turned it on, and worked fast. I hog-tied both of them with duct tape, blindfolded, gagged them, and stuck them in the recovery position. It was hard because they were unconscious, but it was all done in under ten minutes. I was proud of myself. I hadn't topped them. A regular Mother Teresa, I was. Sparing the innocent.

I walked down the corridor to Darkey's bedroom. I opened the door and made sure there were two persons in the bed. Yes. I felt around for weapons, got one, listened for weird sounds. Nothing. Darkey snoring, Bridget snuffling. It was all as smooth as silk.

I turned the bedside light on.

Bridget, her hair down, beautiful. A rock on her left hand that could have sunk the *QE2*. Darkey, sleeping soundly, tanned, relaxed.

Bridget woke first, looked at me, screamed.

Darkey woke and reached under his pillow. I'd already removed his piece and was pointing it at him. Tight little .38, do the job.

You're alive, Bridget gasped.

I'm alive, I said.

Bridget and Darkey were wearing matching bunny pajamas. For some reason, I'd thought he'd make her sleep in a vulgar low-cut negligee. Instead, this was domestic and cute. Darkey wasn't a bad lad really, I thought.

Bridget seemed to be on the verge of passing out. She threw up in her mouth instead. Darkey was looking at me with no fear whatsoever. Like I say, not a bad lad.

You killed Sunshine, he said. It wasn't a question, just a confirmation of fact.

I nodded.

And Bob, too? he asked. This time, he really didn't know.

Aye, Bob, too, I said.

Jesus, he said, still a ways away from being afeared.

Why? asked Bridget. What's going on? Please. What's going on, honey?

I realized she wasn't talking to me.

Darkey looked at me and looked at her. He read the expression on my face. His number was up.

Sweetie, Michael and I have some business to discuss. I think it would be best if you went into the bathroom for a moment, Darkey said with admirable calm.

What's going on? she demanded, hysterical.

I'd wanted to talk to her, to let her know what kind of a man Darkey was. To let her know about Andy, Fergal, and Scotchy. To tell her what I'd been through. To tell her that he was a fucking monster. Subhuman. That he deserved to die, that she was better off without him. Maybe even better with me. I wanted to make a little speech and tell her everything, to tell her that I was the strong right arm of the Lord's vengeance. But once again, Darkey was correct. She didn't need to see it. It would be better this way.

Darkey's right, Bridget. We have to discuss a few things, just go to the bathroom, there's things you can't hear.

You're not going to kill him? There's four men in the house, all of them armed, you'd never get away with it. They'd kill you, Michael, kill you. My God, you're alive. How? You survived the . . . Oh God, we didn't know, Jesus. Is this about money? Michael, promise me you won't do anything rash. Promise me.

She was looking at me. But she was clinging to him.

Promise me, give me your word, everything can be sorted out, she said. You won't do anything rash. Promise, say it.

I promise, I said.

Darkey hadn't taken his eyes off me.

I'll explain it all later, Bridget, Darkey said. Please, love, do me a favor, just go to the bathroom for a minute. Just for a minute.

But why? she said, sitting up, leaning forward now, almost touching me.

It's business, Darkey said firmly. Now go.

I looked at him with wonder. He looked back at me, his face a study in composure and concentration. What a man. He was old school. He was Darkey fucking White.

Why does he need a gun? We're all friends. Michael, I'm so glad you're alive. Oh my God, Bridget was saying.

Darkey turned and faced her. He could see that I was losing my patience and he wanted to spare her the scene.

Go to the bathroom, for two minutes. Michael and I have to talk business, he said, loudly, forcefully.

She turned to me.

Why do you need the gun, Michael? she asked.

Those eyes. Jesus. How could you lie to her? How could you storm in here, upset her? How could you even think about hurting her or those whom she loved? It was impossible.

I don't trust Darkey, that's all, I said, and gave her a smile. I think it reassured her a little.

And you won't hurt him? she asked.

Me hurt him? I asked.

Yes, she said, soft, anxious.

Her hands folded themselves in front of her, as if in prayer. It unsettled me, rattled me; my weapon hand twitched.

I won't touch him, I said.

She let go her hands and took a knot out of her hair.

Darkey breathed in and out.

I remembered to breathe too.

Ok, she said in a monotone. She believed me. She thought it was a misunderstanding, she wanted it all to go away. Tomorrow was Christmas, this was some kind of bad dream.

She looked at Darkey. Darkey nodded.

Two minutes, he said. The bathroom.

She blinked once, got up, and went to the en suite bathroom, closing the door behind her.

She's gone. You might as well say your piece and get it over, Darkey said in a whisper. I'm ready.

You're a hard man, Darkey, I said, trying to keep the admiration out of my voice.

Yeah, so are you.

Do you want to know why? I asked him, itching to spill the whole fucking story, but realizing now that I couldn't.

I suppose I do, he said, still quite cool. If I could be half as together when my time came, I'd be all right. I sat down on the edge of his bed.

I promised Scotchy, after they shot him, I muttered to no one in particular.

Look, Michael. What if I told you that no one was supposed to die? Darkey said quickly.

Do you think it's the sort of thing you're likely to tell me? I asked.

Would you believe it? he asked.

Honestly, Darkey, now I don't think it matters, I said.

He shook his head. Took a deep breath. His temples throbbed. He smiled at me. I was impressed. Was this the same crazy, impulsive, overacting Darkey White? Maybe, I thought, I was finally seeing the real Darkey White.

Is there anything I can say to make you change your mind? If I offered you a lot of money, or, or anything? he said.

I shook my head. It's a blood feud, Darkey, you know the score. Nothing else will quite do.

He sighed and leaned back in the bed. He looked to one side and then stared at me square in the face.

Ok, Michael, you fuck, do what you've come to do. You realize Duffy will hunt you down and kill you? If it takes fifty fucking years, he'll do it.

Darkey, somehow I never really thought I'd make old bones, I said.

Darkey looked at me and swallowed. He clenched his fists and brought them to his sides.

Get on with it, Darkey said, urgently. I'm ready now.

I raised the pistol, pointing it at his head, but before I could do anything more there was a bang and I was thrown sideways against the closet door. It smashed into the back of my head and I sprawled forward onto the bed and rolled to the floor. I scrambled up but then my foot gave way and I went down again. I looked over. Bridget had shot me in the side. Shot me from the bathroom with a .22 revolver. Silver one.

Fuck, Bridget, I said.

She was walking towards me, shaking all over, eyes wide, face bright. She was determined. Cold. It was an expression I hadn't seen on her before. Jesus, had I ever really known her at all either? Her lips narrowed.

I'm sorry, Michael. I don't know what's between you and Darkey, I don't know what's going on, but I love him and—

I kicked the legs from under her and she tumbled backwards. The gun flew out of her hand and onto the bed. Darkey and I both made a grab for it, but Bridget fell on top of me. The .22 slipped between the bed and the bedside cabinet. I dropped my gun, grabbed a fistful of Bridget's hair, and smacked her skull into the closet door. Her head jarred back sickeningly, and she went limp. I regrabbed my gun and dived for cover at the bottom of the bed just as Darkey managed to find the .22 and began shooting wildly at me. Darkey, full of adrenaline, got off three rounds into the wall before I rolled to one side and shot him in the chest and face and neck. His gun fired another round and then stopped. Blood pumped from him, the left side of his face gone. A bullet had ricocheted off his jawbone, up through his cheek and into his brain. He sat there bleeding and dripping eye jelly onto the pillowcase. His face relaxed and what was left of his mouth drooped into a grimace. He balanced for a moment and then slumped forward. I went over and felt his pulse. It was still beating gently, which afforded me the excuse to lift up his head, take out the Stanley knife, and cut his throat from ear to ear. I checked Bridget and saw that she was ok. Bridget. Jesus.

She loved him. None of this had been necessary. He could have just killed me and told her about it, and she probably would have raged for a while but dealt with it because she fucking loved him. It would have been better that way too. Andy, Fergal, Scotchy, Sunshine, none of them had to die. She loved him, she would have understood. He shouldn't have been so overprotective. Jesus, Darkey. You just didn't have confidence enough in yourself. Darkey White—a lack of confidence in himself? Could have fooled me. Maybe it was that bloody gut he'd got, or his dyed hair. But it hadn't mattered to her. He should have just topped me and been done with it. Scotchy would have done it. But he wasn't sure enough of her and that had killed him.

You fucking idiot, I told him.

And now I remembered that I'd wanted to ask him if he'd ordered Andy's beating way back then. It didn't really matter. It was water under the bridge. I sat on the bed and fixed my foot. Bridget was out for the count. I put her in the recovery position and found Darkey's wallet beside the bed. There was at least five thousand dollars in big bills. That would help. I grabbed the money and found the key to the Jag. I looked at my side and stomach. It seemed quite bad. Vital organs are in your side. I couldn't remember what, but I knew they were pretty important. At least it wasn't hurting yet. I cut off a whack of bedsheet with the Stanley knife and wrapped it around me. I duct-taped it into place. I bent down and hog-tied Bridget with tape. She was still well gone, which was good. I threw a sheet over Darkey so it wouldn't be the first thing she saw when she came to. I grabbed a sweater and a leather jacket from the closet and put them on. I pocketed the .22, so the coppers would have a harder time comparing slugs when the doctors took one out of me.

I went downstairs and checked in on my guard. He hadn't moved a muscle. I regretted killing Marley, it would have been a neater operation without that, but it was too late now. I was dying of thirst, so I drank some water. I went into the garage and turned the light on. I opened the door manually and started up the Jag. I reversed it out of the driveway, closed the garage door, drove to the gate. I had to get out again and open the gate. If I hadn't been wounded, I would have gone to the camp and dismantled it, but there wasn't the time now.

I drove the car down the hill and found a sign pointing to New York. The car handled beautifully. I looked at myself in the mirror. I was pale, losing blood but not too fast. I found the right slip road, drove on, and everything turned into a bit of a blur; I think, but I'm not sure, that I went through a tollbooth and paid a couple of bucks. The drive was all hazed and dreamy, but at one point I stopped at a lay-by and threw the .22 and all the other weapons far into the woods. I got back in the car and drove on again.

In about an hour I was back in the Bronx, and not long after that I reached Manhattan. I left the Jag, doors open, keys in, on 123rd and Amsterdam. Someone would have it within ten minutes, but that's what I'd thought about the Cadillac too, so I left the engine on as well, as extra incentive. I got about a block and took a breather and sort of fell down and then, of all people, Danny the Drunk caught up with me on his way to the twenty-four-hour boozer. Saved my skin, really. He was already wrecked, but I persuaded him to lend me his shoulder at least as far as Columbia U. He did, and went off and started yelling at the guards at the Columbia gates. Somehow by myself I managed to walk up the final bit of hill to St. Luke's Medical Center. I was close to passing out, and I had to stop many times to catch my breath. I found the emergency-room door and went in.

It was the scene you would expect. Packed, noise, fucked-up people, harried doctors and nurses. "Christmas in Hollis" from a tinny stereo.

A nurse gave me a clipboard.

I blacked out for a minute.

A voice, voices. Comforting.

Always the same, Christmas Eve, New Year's Eve.

Yeah.

I don't know. People go crazy.

Yeah.

Well. What happened to you?

I, I don't want to go into it.

Lemme see? What is it?

Uh.

You been shot?

Again, I don't want to talk—

I suppose you know we have to report this to the police?

You do?

Yes.

What about doctor-patient confidentiality?

Doctor-patient, my ass.

Funny.

Here, let me see. . . . Whereabouts you hurt?

Here, side, here.

Ok, let me see now, just lift, oh, oh my goodness. Sylvia, get over here. Quickly, come on.

They put me on a gurney and when they took my jacket off they saw it was actually very serious. Off came my sweater and T-shirt, and I felt a drip go in.

The doctor was black, the other doctor was Indian, all the nurses were black. I was in Harlem, I was back home. There were Christmas decorations, and I realized again it was Christmas Day.

Hey, Merry Christmas, everyone, I said.

You save your strength, son.

I wasn't sure what they were doing now, but it hurt like a mother-fucker.

You know, I don't think your anesthetic's working, I said.

It's working, a nurse said, holding my head, while another began inserting plastic tubes up my nose.

No really, it hurts, a lot.

You're lucky you're not dead, the doctor said, very irritated, and started doing something incredibly painful to my chest. My eyes were heavy. I blinked slow.

Fortune . . . favors . . . fools, I said, and smiled at him before finally contriving a way to lose consciousness.

CODA: ELEVEN YEARS LATER—L.A.

A tap dripping. A car idling. A dog barking. The distant roar of automobiles. The occasional plane. Heat. The hum of the air conditioner. Blue water in the pool. A glass of orange juice undrunk because I think it must be grapefruit by mistake. It's bitter. A leather sofa. A computer, a bookshelf, the blinds half drawn. Dust on them. The dust spiraling up from a faux Aztec-patterned rug. A long hair on my suntanned arm. Hers. A coffee table with *The Economist* and a couple of letters. A painting of a moon and deer. Also hers. A pencil sharpener in the shape of HMS *Victory*. An ashtray. Cigar clipper. Typing paper and soda cans in the wastepaper basket. A coffee cup, the crossword. Sleeping plants. The window. The enormous sky complete with vapor trails. The manicured and watered lawn that will never be quite green.

The room is inert, frozen, still. I look at Granpa's photograph with the sepia faces of the dead. The tap. The dog barking furiously. My stomach growling: it's an hour before she gets home, before I have to make dinner. Depending on traffic, of course. At least I'm not out there. The people running with buckets along the battlements. Fire in the keep. Stress. It's the new millennium and transport is still vehicular and ground-based. How disappointing. In fact, the whole century's been a bit grim so far. I reach out and turn over the cover on *The Economist*. Sometimes it's best not to know. My hand twitches and I close my eyes. Black fields. A faraway place. Observe, see us, see Patrick in the forest rehearsing his prayers, see us walking through it, a wounded arm and cuts on the barbed wire and the bog sucking down our packs.

Cold rain that never gets this cold, not in the temperate brother of the Temperate Island. Aye. Jesus. I blink awake. I stare at the computer, whose background image is the Hubble Deep Field. I stare, and finally the screen saver kicks in, which is the Earth in daylight and nighttime portions. The AC. Reliable, relatively quiet. A rivulet of condensation from off the cooling ducts. Far off, a carnival of pneumatic drills. I get up from the sofa and look in the mini fridge. There is no grapefruit juice. I lie back down again. Think. The tap. The dog. The sound of the engine idling. What foul conspiracy is this? She poured it for me at eleven A.M., just before she left for her afternoon job at the marketing agency. Odd. I lie under the counterfeit mahogany and the multiplications of the ceiling fan. Think. I roll off the sofa and pick up the glass and sniff it.

Footsteps, the gate. Ahh, I see. Consequences. Someone has come to murder me.

In an hour or two, the sun will set and then it will be dusk. The best time to be in this city. Yellow and brown and gold lines will weave the clouds into a picture. The sunsets in Los Angeles. . . . It was not always so. Father Henriques Ordóñez of the Santa Barbara Mission, writing in the 1790s, describes night falling quickly, the sun disappearing like a ghost into the Pacific. Spectacular now because the polluted air scatters the light into its lower frequencies. All this is true. Obvious.

The juice sitting there, sipped, but otherwise untouched. The air conditioner spitting, whining. Another plane. The dog louder now. A picture of the desert. A banana. Oranges. CDs on a shelf: Undertones, Ash, Therapy, U2, Van Morrison, Irish bands all, nostalgia no doubt, pathetic really.

The juice. The dog. A dying lemon tree. I've tried with it. Watering. Starving. Moving from out and back into shade. The tap.

He comes. He has prized the lock on the gate. Prized not picked. This is not going to be about savoir faire. He is medium build, a light gray suit. Pinstripes. Cheap but expensive-looking shoes, slippy soles. White sport socks. He is wearing pilot sunglasses and a brown felt fedora. His face is pockmarked, his nose especially. He is about thirty, but with the skin and the uneasiness he seems older. He is steady on his feet, but clearly he's a drinker. After this job he'll go to a bar and take a shot or two before heading back to report. The weapon is in a

shoulder holster. A longish pistol, perhaps a machine pistol or maybe
the length is a silencer, or maybe it's both. He has another gun around
his ankle. A revolver. His trousers are too short. In fact, the whole suit
looks too small for him. If he were Latino, I'd say that the suit was perhaps his brother's. But he's not, he's Caucasian. He walks up the path
on the left-hand side. A Brit, a Mick. Maybe just a leftie. No, the gun is
over his heart. He's a fucking Paddy, I know it.

He won't be sure about the city. The heat bothers him. He's wearing
a stupid hat. He'll be easy. He's not being particularly cautious, even
though this isn't his town. How have they been briefed? I'm drugged
and asleep? Why hadn't Carolyn been more insistent about me taking
my vitamin C? Nervous, she didn't want to put too much emphasis on
it. Raise suspicion. But the dose was too big. Clumsy, clumsy lass,
never could do anything right.

We've been dating for about half a year. We met at the firm where I
worked briefly as a security consultant. Carolyn's her real name, but
she wants everyone to call her Linnie. That should have been a clue
right there. She's no Bridget, though she is pretty. Pale, thin, blond,
fragile. She's from Athens, Georgia, but likes the B-52's rather than
R.E.M. Another clue.

It was clever that they would come to me through her. She'd be
afraid of them. Wouldn't tell me, wouldn't tell the cops. Must have got
to her yesterday. Was she weird last night? I don't remember. How?
We've got your mother, your brother, we'll get you. . . . I don't know.
They'd question her. What's he like at home? What's his routine? Ok.
Well, we only need you to do one thing. Slip this in his orange juice and
go to work. Don't act weird in any way. Don't do anything different.
She hadn't, nothing I'd picked up on anyway.

Yeah, come through her. They'd be wary of me, the man who killed
Darkey White. You'd think you could just hit me in the street but
somehow it would fuck up, better to get at me from the inside. The
weak spot. Yeah, I'm drugged and asleep and here he comes. . . .

Well, you can't say I haven't been patient. I have. Ten years I've
been waiting. Eleven. Aye, I did the dirty, I had to. The peelers came,
lifted me, and I gave them every goddamn Mick I could. Everyone
who wasn't already dead. Or murdered in a different way: Bridget, me.
It's been so long. So tedious. I've begged them. I've dreamed them

here. I've dreamed me there. Seamus Patrick Duffy, get off your arse. Do your duty.

Oh aye. You're an old man, but that is no excuse. Get to it. Your ancestors were schooled in blood feud, in Ulster, in the wars against the Indians; Christ, for instruction look at the early career of Andrew Jackson. Let not a man stain your honor. Listen to that siren voice. Didn't he break his sacred oath? Only a coward blabs to the police. It's been a long time, but we still have to kill him. Every day that Michael lives we die. . . .

But they didn't come, they didn't find me. Four years ago in Chicago, I was on the elevated train, a man approached me with a gun. Late at night, empty car, one man, one gun. The train jerked and he stumbled forward. I pulled his weapon hand and broke his arm and bolted the train at the next stop. Was it a mugging? I should have checked; I ran instead, but in retrospect I think it was a robbery attempt.

Anyway. I read the papers, I keep up.

Seamus Patrick Duffy died last year. He was seventy-eight and he was in bed. He was the last of the old Irish hoods, the final sad player in a forgotten story. The obituary in *The New York Times* said that in the 1990s the Irish mob was broke, like the Italian mob, like the Russian mob. Now, of course, the unions in New York are incorruptible and no one gambles and no one needs a green card and no one uses drugs. . . .

The Mick assassin takes off his fedora and wipes his face. He's hot and bothered and all he's done is walk from the car.

Oh, the anticipation, watching the calendar and clock. For too long, for far too long. I almost thought you weren't coming. That you'd see that the torture was in the waiting. But really, you're not that smart. You couldn't probe the depth of my psychology.

Who is the boss now? I've heard rumors. They bleed me information. Is it you?

Maybe you've imagined this day. Talked it out, planned it. Well, so have I. It's the distillation of everything that was our world. The apotheosis of our journey together. Time compressed to now. The world has moved on, but we have not. So much is different. But we're locked in together, you and I. I know. And don't worry, I will not disappoint. I've rehearsed this. Again and again. We will all of us play our parts. . . .

I roll off the couch, crawl to the drawer beside the computer, and take out the latest masterpiece from Gaston Glock. I fit the silencer and slip out of the study and into the hall behind the sprawling yucca plant. He's still there. Still coming. I get ready to open the front door, my hand is on the handle, about to apply pressure, and then I almost have a heart attack. There's a creak in the back kitchen. Jesus Christ. I've miscalculated. There is someone already in the house. The idling car. The front gate. And of course, all the time the boys were coming in the bloody back. Up from the gulch and through the neighbors'. The house over on the other side, their Alsatian, Omar, saw the whole thing. That's why he's been barking like mad. Warning me. Jesus, Michael. Getting old. Stupid. Dead.

Fucking hell.

The back kitchen.

It's all been timed. A man in front, a man or men coming in the back. There is no possibility of escape, and Linnie has told them that I'll be on siesta. I sleep in the afternoons anyway, so the draft was just an added kick.

Pretty and with an accent that could straighten out a Jesuit, but Linnie, really, abetting assassins is just not on; if I survive we'll have to rethink our whole relationship.

If I survive this. A big if. These guys aren't bad. They've made a wee plan, got someone on the inside, and they've taken the trouble to come up the gulch, so I suppose they're semiprofessional at least. And they've just sent Paddy here to watch the front. The lowest job available, since, after all, I'm hardly likely to come running out guns blazing. No, I'm sleeping. Somewhere. She tells them I'm a nut about my orange juice, I'll drink it. I'll be in the living room perhaps or maybe if I felt really tired I'd have gone upstairs to lie down. She will have told them I do that. The kitchen boys are talking in a loud whisper. They shouldn't be talking at all, should be pointing. They should have hand signals all worked out. They can't be a regular team or they would. They're a mishmash, assembled from guys who individually are pretty good; perhaps that'll be their downfall: they'll play like England against Norway, individual stars against a team. Except that I'm a team of one.

The top lad's whispering:

Ok, lads. Sweep down the stairs first. When it's secure, we'll all go up together. I'll stay here. He's supposed to be up and out. But you never fucking know. So go careful now, very careful. Watch each other.

Their boss says all this with a bit too much confidence. Too much reliance on Carolyn's abilities; he's an eejit, like me. I can't tell precisely what the accent is, but it's definitely Brit.

Ok, ok, two voices reply.

So, Jesus, there's three of them in the house and one outside. Well, the clip holds seventeen.

I nip from the hall back into the study and look for a place to hide. There's nothing. The sofa is too near the ground and there are no curtains. I'll just have to wait in shadow and pop him as he comes through the door. I get into a crouch and raise the pistol. I'm sweating. God, am I really this out of touch? That's easy living for you. Too many good restaurants in this town. Too much driving. Too much si—

The study door opens. He's young. Pale. T-shirt and very tight white jeans. Sneakers. He has a shotgun. His finger is underneath the trigger. His mouth is open, he's transfixed by the tap dripping from my water cooler. He hasn't even seen me here in the shadow of the corner, and he never will. There is a small spurt of flame and a quiet whoosh and then there is a hole in his forehead that looks like a third eye, blood all over the tiling. I catch him as he falls and ease the shotgun out of his hand. I close the door, turn him over. A wallet, an Irish passport for all love. Sean Glass. Dubliner. Twenty. I rest his head on the fireplace and let the blood drip there. Ok, so there's just two more inside. One skirting about in the snooker or downstairs guest room and the headman most likely in the hall by now commanding the stairs and the doors. That's what I would do. No, actually I wouldn't have spoken at all and I wouldn't have split us up. But getting into his brain for a minute: he'll send a boy left and a boy right and he'll stay in the hall. So he'll see me as soon as I leave the study. And what will I do? Hmmm. I believe I'll just sit here and wait for him to get impatient; sooner or later he'll think: Sean's taking too damn long. I hear him tap the window at the front door, signaling to Pat out there that all's well so far. He walks back down the hall. Nearly at the study door. Is he coming in?

Would you hurry the fuck up, Sean boy, he says from where I thought he'd say it. He's ex-army or I'm the ponce hooring your ma. His accent is all Brummie. Easy.

Aye, I say in me best Dub.

I'm going up, another voice says, and the Brummie lets him go, which I wouldn't do either.

Sean, come on, we're going up, he says.

Ok, I say. Coming.

With the gun ready, I wait for a count of two and crack open the study door. I look down the hall and see that he's all reassured and gazing up the stairs. He has a mustache and chubby blue-white skin. He's short, edgy-looking, and he's wearing an Aston Villa cap. From me to him is fifteen feet of hall. I step out quietly and bring the gun to full extension from my body.

It's me, hi, Death's ambassador.

I put the side of his fat face between the sights and squeeze the trigger on him and of course the fucker moves, having just seen me out of the corner of his eye. The bullet nicks his cheek and smashes into the window beside the front door. He's carrying an Uzi machine gun or some such ignoble wee piece. I shoot again and as his weapon opens up excitedly on the floor, I've hit him in the sternum and the neck and he's going down. The Uzi falls away from him and is silenced, but it was loud enough. I cross the hall and open the front the door and shoot Paddy standing out there gawp-eyed and open-baked. He goes down without protest, and I close the door and wait for the fourth eejit up the stairs to shout "What's going on down there, boss?" or some such nonsense.

Hooorie oop, git down eaaah, I yell up the stairs urgently and put on the Villa hat to confuse him. I hear him run and down he comes, falling the second half of the stairs as the bullet erases all motor control over his legs along with the top part of his head.

Well, it wasn't exactly the Marx Brothers, but it was close, and there was me thinking they were something special because they came up the gulch. I safety the Glock, put it in my trouser pocket, and wipe the sweat from off my hands. An old habit makes me take it out again and hold it. You never put away your weapon until you are absolutely sure. I look at the two bodies in the hall and am absolutely sure. Those boys aren't going anywhere. The alarm on the Brummie's watch starts to beep. I lift up his hand and look at it; it's still on eastern standard time. They must have only just got here. I put it down sadly. Wouldn't it have been smarter to fly in a week ago and acclimatize?

I turn off the watch and take out his wallet and oh my God, his level of incompetence is such that he's brought with him to the hit the cheat sheet with my address and photo and physical description. What if he'd been arrested in situ or on the way?

Jesus Christ.

I paw through it, amused, and then I see something that staggers me. The instructions have been printed out but annotated in a wavy hand that I instantly recognize as hers. Her letters, organizing my death. She's changed how the fee gets paid and where the weapons are to be dumped. So—it is her. She's at the top of the greasy pole, and this is her primary concern. Unfinished business. What Duffy couldn't do, she will.

She had risen, I had heard that, untouched by my indictments and clean. But who ever heard of a woman rising to the very top? I smile a little. Get with the times, son, Ireland's had two woman presidents since last you lived there.

And Christ, it was my fantasy that Bridget would come to kill me, but seeing it here in black-and-white . . . Suddenly I feel nauseated. I need a drink.

But no, business first. Clean up this shit and make the obligatory call.

I open the front door and check the street and am about to start to pull in Paddy before someone sees him and gets upset, when suddenly there's a horrible thumping feeling in my head which translates into a creaky board and that can only mean that young Sean has made a miraculous recovery in the study or there was a fifth member of the team. And wouldn't that just be a son of a bitch, wouldn't that just be pride before a fall and serve me fucking right? Of course, they had a driver, or a safety man, and he's come in to see what's taking so god-damned long.

I drop to a crouch, fire blind behind me a couple of times and dive for the stairs. The hat didn't fool him, for as I dive a bullet hits me in the leg and there are two more big-caliber marks in the front door.

Got ya, ya bastard, he says.

The stairs are up against the wall and make a corner with the front door, so I'm safe here for the moment. To get me, he'll have to come round a blind spot made by the stairs and the wall and I'll have him before he has me. Hopefully. I roll down my jeans. He did get me, the bullet caught me in the plastic foot.

I laugh out loud.

Save your breath, about to die, mate, he says.

I spit and shake my head. Say nothing. Just wait. No sound at all now, except for the tap and the car and the barking dog. I take the Aston Villa cap off and throw it round the corner but that doesn't faze him. He's coming slow. I lift up the Glock and support it in both hands. Just then a black object rolls into my field of vision, and I recognize it as an old GB army-issue white phosphorus grenade. For fucksake. Fuck me and Jesus and the Holy Ghost. A WPG. A corporal killed himself with one of those while instructing us about how dangerous they were in my very first week in the army. I've been a bit phobic about grenades ever since, and high-explosive white phosphorus grenades in particular are very nasty. I think they're banned now.

With my cracked foot I can only get halfway up the stairs before the thing goes off. A boiling white ball of fire. You bury your head, but you don't put your hands over your head. You'll need your hands in a second to shoot people and at this stage you can't have them disabled or worse, burnt off completely. As it is, my back's on fire as I roll onto the landing. I take my T-shirt off before it melts on me. Not badly burnt. I catch my breath. Calm down. Ok, he'll be round after me in a sec, but there's still that blind spot at the bottom of the stairs and he'll be cautious after seeing his mates all curled up there in the hall. He's thinking the grenade got me, but he didn't hear any screaming, so he'll go slow. My trousers are on fire. I pat myself down, and as quick as I can I drag myself to the upstairs bathroom. I open the window, climb out, lower myself down onto the kitchen roof, and then drop from the gutter onto the patio. My leg gives way under me. Somehow I get up. I limp in the back door of the house and through the kitchen and then gently open the kitchen door that leads into the hall. He's there still, slowly making his way to the bottom of the stairs. His gun is one of those nifty Belgian jobs. He's tall, curly-haired, with a denim jacket and black jeans. He's wearing sunglasses. He's inching along. He's assuming I'm dead, but taking no chances. You have to be careful but, you know, sometimes you can be too careful.

Drop it, I say, and he spins wildly around. The Glock smiles and shoots him in the chest four times. He goes down, and I take a breath.

Thank you, Ganesh, Remover of Obstacles, I say to the statue in the hall. It's a joke Ganesh and I share and he grins with his elephant head. For the obstacle is not them, or me, it's the past that cannot be unwoven.

I do a thorough scout, and this time there are no more surprises. They were five of them. But, like eejits, they split themselves up. You've got to hand it to her, after all this time and after all that's been happening on the earth. But don't go cheap, love, get pros. Come on, you're in New York, and I'm in L.A., my dear, isn't that punishment enough? Ha.

Will there be a next time? There will. I know you. I know you now, not then, but now I do.

I hobble to the fridge and crack open a Corona. I take a big gulp. I pick up the phone and dial a number I've memorized these ten years. Ever since they took out that slug and saved my life and came and threatened me and I made a deal to save my sorry ass. I give my code name and then my handler's.

They put me all the way through to his mobile. He's outdoors somewhere near water. It's lapping but it's not breaking; he's on a lake.

How's the fishing? I ask him.

How— he begins, but I have to interrupt him; I'm going to need help quick before the peelers show and there's not much time for idle chatter.

Listen, you were right, my mistake, I want back in the program, I say.

Ok.

Somewhere you get seasons.

Seasons, he says. You get seasons in L.A. It's just that they're all good.

Ok, somewhere with more rain.

More rain? he asks quizzically.

Yeah.

I think that can be arranged, he says.

I'll need to go to a hospital.

Are you hurt?

Just a burn. I'll live.

Lucky us.

Lucky you.

Are there casualties?

Yeah, it's messy.

How many?

Five.

Shit.

Yeah.

Don't worry, we'll keep you safe, he says.

That would be nice, I say. The lie going down as easily as the booze.

I hang up. I pull in Paddy. The smoke alarm goes off and I play around a bit with the fire extinguisher. I make my way to the kitchen and put salve on my burned neck and scalp. I look at the scorch mark in the mirror; it doesn't seem too bad. I grab another Corona. I get a bottle of gin and some aspirin. Shouldn't really be drinking. I limp into the backyard and sit next to the pool.

Omar comes bounding over and barks at me through the gaps in the fence.

Good boy, good boy, I tell him, and he wanders off, pleased.

I finish the Corona and let the bottle drop. I sit up, swallow two aspirin with some gin and water.

I take a long look around. . . .

A south wind is stirring the slender stems of pines. The hawsers bend, and there are murmurs in the clay figurines as the sun dips behind the fence. The evening star waits, beguiled, while airplanes and birds mark boundaries in all that blue abandonment.

The cars sing, the grass creaks in parks and cemeteries. I am calm, erased of all extraneous emotion. Collected. Easy. I feel the pine needles, the warm roads, the scent of butterflies, the sniff of coyotes in those teeming hills.

These are my last days in this town. And when the heat's cooled down and I am safe and far away, I'll disappear. Find you easier than you found me. I can see it. You and I, my honey love. Oh yes, Bridget, I can see your face. You and I in the still of the dark together. And in that moment, and in that place, Death incants a name and, somehow, it doesn't sound like mine.

I close my eyes.

It well may be.

ABOUT THE AUTHOR

Adrian McKinty was born and grew up in Carrickfergus, Northern Ireland, at the height of the Troubles. He studied politics at Oxford University and after a failed legal career he moved to New York City in the early 1990s. He found work as a security guard, mailman, door-to-door salesman, construction worker, bartender, rugby coach, bookstore clerk, and schoolteacher. He lives in Colorado and is working on a new novel.